Tablet of Destinies
An Agency Book
by Lynn Yvonne Moon

ISBN 978-1-953278-02-9 Hard Back
ISBN 978-1-953278-03-6 Soft Back
ISBN 978-1-953278-04-3 EBook

Published by

 INDIGNOR HOUSE™

Chesapeake, Virginia
www.IndignorHouse.com

TABLET
OF
DESTINIES

LYNN YVONNE MOON

This book is dedicated to the missing
who will forever be remembered.

Prologue

The evening commute, tranquil and uneventful, was just the way Jack Lawrence liked it. The powerful engine hummed a rhythmic tune that always seemed to soothe his soul. He glanced at his watch, knowing they'd reach the station on time. The glance was a habit. The sun, now below the horizon, allowed the stars to display their sparkling beauty against a deep, black canvas. A familiar sight for Jack. He loved viewing the heavens this way, and he'd rather be no place else than where he was right now.

The distant mountain terrain was hidden from everyone on board except from Jack's memory. He sensed the tall pine and cedar trees lining the tracks without actually seeing them. Through the darkness, he envisioned the deer and other wild animals snuggling in for the night beneath the low-lying branches.

Jack engineered this route from Butte, Montana to New York for the last forty-some years. A lot changed throughout that time, but the excitement and thrill of controlling such a massive and powerful machine never diminished. Only once during his career did he experience an incident, and the horror of that night still haunted him. A car with a mother and two children had stalled on the tracks. He didn't see the car until after rounding the blind bend at full throttle. Jack pulled on the emergency brake until his fingers bled. The screech of metal on metal had become an unforgiving memory. The train sustained little damage, but the car was demolished.

Sickened and horrified, Jack walked the tracks for what seemed like hours. When he stopped to take a break, he found a tiny red tennis shoe with bloody shoestrings. He picked it up knowing that the little boy who wore it now lay mutilated inside the ambulance where the lights still flashed.

Jack Lawrence kept that shoe hanging from a mirror only inches from his balding head, a silent memorial to that one terrible night over twenty years ago. He sometimes wondered what would have happened to that little boy had he survived, maybe a doctor or a father.

Jack received a new appreciation for the power he controlled with his puny fingers made from a few ounces of blood, bone and flesh. Jack vowed that no one would ever die from his feeble hands again. He memorized every blind curve and every hazardous spot, and when he approached those areas, Jack's train slowed to a manageable speed. Three innocent people died that dreadful night, and Jack swore it would never happen, again.

Chapter One

Devon Arvol walked the perimeter for what seemed like the hundredth time, searching for a clue, any clue. No scuffmarks or footprints in the damp soil, and the ground was still pristine and fresh. He glanced up at the silent but empty train. A simple question seeped through his mind. *What happened to all the passengers?*

"Sir?" A young man approached from behind. "Nothing you asked for is showing up in the databases."

Devon was a large, dark and burly man, half Native American and half Irish. Sometimes his light-brown skin glowed, especially when his nerves were on edge. His long dark hair, pulled back and secured with a band, gave his strong features an authority that frightened most people. So did his history of blowing up when he didn't receive the answers he wanted. Those who worked for Devon once usually didn't work for him a second time. Not wanting the hassle of interviewing new agents for this mission, Devon eased up … a little.

"This is fucking nuts!" Devon's harsh voice echoed through the narrow valley. "Will someone please tell me how three hundred people can simply disappear into thin air? And with no trace."

"The planks are almost in place." The young man shifted from one foot to the other. "To cover the mud?"

"Johnson, yes?"

"Yes, sir."

Devon stared at the young man. For a second, he almost felt sorry for him. He shook his head and his anger boiled as he tried not to vent on the young Johnson. His voice almost inaudible, he whispered, "Make sure everyone's suited. I want nothing disturbed." Devon turned and frowned at the huge engine. "What happened here, ol' girl?" He sighed. "Where are all your passengers, sweetheart?"

"Agent Arvol?" Another voice this time. "Dr. Lewis on the phone."

Devon winked at the silent train. He knew she'd eventually give up her secrets. But would it be soon enough to save the three hundred missing passengers? As he walked to the idling agency car and a call he didn't have time for, Devon glanced over his shoulder. The massive train held his interest as nothing ever had before. He spotted a tiny red shoe dangling from the engineer's window. He studied it for a few seconds. When the agent yelled for him again, he cringed.

"I'm coming," Devon hollered.

"Sir, I have Dr. Lewis on the phone." The agent looked away and blindly shoved the phone toward Devon's face. Devon ducked just in time, avoiding a bruise to the side of his head. Why did everyone act as if Lewis was so important that everything had to stop the moment he called?

"Dr. Lewis," Devon stated, sternly. "How am I supposed to complete my investigation if you keep calling?"

"I have that list you requested," Lewis replied. "There're some interesting passengers on that train of yours."

Devon shook his head. The train wasn't his personal property.

"I'm not sure if you'll recognize anyone," Lewis added. "But we certainly did. Expect Agent Ramsden by morning. She's bringing the list with her. I've assigned her to your case." Lewis paused before adding a few harsh words. "I expect you to be civil."

"Civil? I'm always civil." Devon handed the phone back to the agent. "Don't bother me unless it's really important."

The timid agent nodded.

"Sir?" A younger agent spoke this time. "I believe we found something unusual."

"Unusual?" Devon repeated. "This whole damn case is unusual. What's your name, son?"

"Newberry, sir. Agent Newberry."

"Okay, Agent Newberry. Do we have a first name?"

"Sorry, sir. Steven — Steven at your service, sir."

"Well, Steven at Your Service Sir, how old are you? Twelve?"

Newberry stepped back and glared at Devon.

"Never mind." Devon shook his head and laughed. "Let's see what you found that is so unusual."

Sumner Womack stared at the large and intimidating building that soared high into the bright, blue sky. She was standing so close it hid most of its massiveness from her. The immaculate landscape sent chills down her spine. The landscape was so perfect, so beautiful, that Sumner wondered if The Agency was in competition with the botanical gardens only a few blocks away. As people hurried in and out through the main entrance, Sumner remained still, almost frozen in time. She wished to admire the view for just a few more minutes.

Taking in a deep breath, she steadied her nerves. "Here goes nothing." Her heart pounded as she walked through the large rotating glass doors. Astounded at what she saw, she halted.

The lobby soared up several floors. Shiny metal and sparkling glass sculptures adorned the massive lobby. The place reminded her of a shopping mall.

She read off the name of a large figurine: *Dike, Goddess of Justice*. Next to her stood Dike's sisters, *Eunomia, Goddess of Good Order* and *Eirene,*

Goddess of Peace. Remembering her ancient history, Sumner laughed. These deities were a good pick. The words of the Holy Trinity ran through her mind. *What an odd thing to think about.*

Sumner's eyes followed the water trickling down into the gardens. Each waterfall and fountain were unique. She thought better of reaching down and touching the brightly colored fish that swam along the invisible currents. No, she didn't need to be fired before she even started.

Inside a round reception station from which they could easily observe every person coming and going, five guards dressed handsomely in matching dark suits assisted visitors, questioning everyone. Some visitors used what looked like an optic scanner to gain entrance, while others walked beside an escort. Behind the counter, the room sprawled into a mini shopping mall with restaurants, beauty salons and other fascinating shops. Six giant glass-front elevators shuttled people between the massive upper floors.

As her stomached turned, Sumner approached the enormous, pristine counter. She smiled at the guard, not knowing what to do or say. Everything was so perfect that she was afraid to touch anything. To her amazement, the aroma of the freshly waxed wood calmed her. A little.

"Hi." Sumner lowered her gaze. "Um, today's my first day?"

"Welcome to The Agency," the guard said with his voice monotone and unemotional. "Papers, please."

"Papers?"

"Your new-hire documents? You were instructed to bring them with you."

"Oh, yes." Feeling flushed, Sumner dug through her backpack. "I almost forgot."

"It's all right. Most are a little intimidated on their first day. Not to worry."

Sumner handed him her paperwork and her driver's license.

"Oh, no need for the ID, miss." The guard winked. As he scanned the documents into a computer, she glanced around the lobby. "See that small group over there?" The man pointed.

Sumner turned around. Several people had gathered near a small fountain. "Yes."

"Please join 'em. Someone will be with you shortly. And again, welcome to The Agency, Agent Womack."

Sumner stared at the floor and allowed the words to register — Agent Womack. The Agency was a temporary agency, and she honestly had no idea what she was hired for. Agent? She glanced back at the guard and nodded before joining the others.

Avoiding eye contact with anyone, Sumner found a seat by the fountain. Being called *agent* didn't seem real. Nothing seemed real. She took in a deep breath. A soft mist touched her face and she smiled. Landing a job — any job — just weeks after graduating with a degree in linguistics seemed like a miracle in and of itself. But an agent? What kind of temporary work hired linguistic agents?

Sumner studied the other new employees. Obviously, she was the youngest. At twenty years of age, she felt a little out of place. She was also the shortest at just five feet and a few inches. She was slender with short, choppy brown hair. Her best attributes, at least in her mind, were her dark-green eyes.

Oklahoma City University was just a few miles from her home. Sumner's high school grades were so good she qualified for a scholarship. She continued to live at home and helped her mother with a few bills by working part time at the museum. It took Sumner just three years to earn her degree, graduating magna cum laude. Her professors and friends encouraged her to apply to Ivy League schools for graduate work, but it was time for a change. Graduate school could wait.

Upon graduation, the best she could hope for was a middle-school teaching job or maybe librarian assistant. It was well known around town that The Agency didn't hire just anyone. They were always looking for that *someone special.*

Sumner's friends teased her about joining The Agency because of her interest in obscure languages and symbolism. So, on a dare, she applied as a *semiotician.* Her friends laughed when she told them about her application. "A what?"

"Semiotics," she replied. "The study of symbols."

Sumner was shocked when they called her in for an interview. Now she was just worried about what she had gotten herself into.

A stern voice yanked her from her thoughts. "This way." An older woman stood by a door that blended so perfectly with the wall that everyone looked surprised when it opened. "Don't dawdle."

"Dawdle?" a young man mimicked as they walked through the unusual doorway.

Several desks and chairs, situated in rows as if in a classroom, waited for them. Feeling anxious, Sumner took a seat near the back. Studying the others, she surmised that the four men and three women were closer to her age than she'd initially thought.

The woman who'd ordered them inside now handed out black binders, while a short, older-looking man passed out Agency ink pens. Examining the writing instrument, Sumner gasped when she saw her name inscribed in golden letters. The black leather binder also had her full name in the upper right-hand corner. *How did they know who was who in order to give them out so effortlessly?*

Filling out the paperwork that was handed to her, Sumner's curiosity rose. *What were the others hired for? What's my position?* No one had told her. She just received a letter requesting her to report on this date, at this time, and it was signed by a Dr. Jeffery Lewis.

"Agent Womack?" a voice asked from the front of the room. Sumner jumped as the man's voice bounced off the walls. "Which one of you is Agent Womack?"

"I am." As her hand rose, so did her eyebrows. *Everyone else seems to know who I am, so why doesn't he?*

"Nice to meet you, Agent Womack. I've been asked to process you through."

Puzzled, Sumner gathered up her things.

"Please," the man added not looking at the others who were now staring at them. "Follow me."

Clasping her loose items to her chest, she stumbled through the maze of desks. The older woman opened a door in the back and nodded as they passed.

"Agent Womack, I'm Agent Tarply," the man said once the door closed behind them. "This way."

Entering a smaller office with no windows near the end of the hallway, Agent Tarply instructed her to wait there. Sumner sat in one of the two chairs.

"Agent Womack?" A warm voice at the door startled her. "I'm sorry. I didn't mean to frighten you. Let me introduce myself. Dr. Allen Greghardt." Sumner started to stand, but the older, heavy-set man motioned her to sit back down. "Please do not rise on my account." He sat in the chair across from her. "This place can be a little frightening at times. Once we've talked, I'm sure you'll feel much better."

Devon glared at the technician as the test strip changed color. "Spray paint? Really?"

"Can buy this stuff at any hardware store," the technician replied.

"Are you sure?" Devon asked. "Just everyday spray paint?"

"Yes sir."

As another technician snapped pictures of the golden emblem, Devon scratched his head. "Does anyone know what this symbol means?"

Several agents and technicians searching the train for evidence paused to look. Shaking their heads, they continued with their work. A young woman stood in front of the emblem and smiled. "Fleur-de-lys," she said.

"Which is?" Devon asked, not taking his eyes off the painted wall.

"A flower. It's French for 'flower of the lily.' Gothic, actually. See here." She pointed to the emblem. "Three petals encircled by a band of rope."

Devon wasn't sure whether to thank her or yell at her.

"Because of its three petals, this symbol also represents the Holy Trinity." When Devon frowned, the woman rolled her eyes. "I know you've heard of the Holy Trinity before. The Father, the Son and the Holy Ghost?" She tilted her head to one side.

Devon didn't reply.

"I myself find this symbol quite beautiful."

"This is a lily?" Devon asked, with his anger roaring from somewhere deep inside. "This is a fucking flower? Some idiot spray-painted a golden goddamn flower on the wall?" Devon frowned; his eyes glued to the odd icon. "Why? Why a flower? And why in each of the cars?"

Cursing, Devon hurried out of the train, for this was not the time to explode in front of his agents. Nothing on his case added up, and he didn't like the way things were going. No blood and no sign of forced entry. Just a little over three hundred people simply vanished off the face of the earth.

"Poof … right into thin air," Devon yelled.

"The second coming?" an older agent suggested as he walked by Devon. He stopped and grinned. "You know — the legendary rapture?" The man screeched out a ghostly howl.

"It would at least explain something, wouldn't it?" Devon yelled. "At least it would be something!"

After her meeting with Dr. Greghardt, Sumner felt caught inside a dense fog. Never in a million years would she have thought she'd become an agent for her government. Especially an undercover agent. But that was what she was hired to do.

Now waiting inside the executives' lobby on the top floor, Sumner studied the portraits of those who'd given their lives as undercover agents. No names were listed, just a date of death inscribed on a golden plaque below each frame. Would she someday have her picture posted there too?

"Agent Sumner?" a woman with short, bright-red hair asked.

"Yes?"

"I'm Connie, Dr. Lewis's assistant. Would you follow me, please?"

"Certainly," Sumner replied, tearing her gaze from one of the portraits. A lovely woman with long brown hair had captivated her. She had the most mesmerizing eyes Sumner had ever seen.

"That was Maddie Edwards," Connie said as they left the office. "We all miss her. She was one of our top agents. Unfortunately, she was killed in the line of duty. I hope all that paperwork wasn't too burdensome."

"It was okay," Sumner replied.

Inside the golden elevator, Connie placed her thumb over a small scanner. Sumner flinched as the elevator hummed to life. When the doors opened, Connie smiled. "This way."

The floor seemed way too quiet. The extra-thick carpet muffled their footsteps. Arriving at room 842, Connie held the door open for her.

"This is as far as I go," Connie said. "Welcome aboard and have a great day, Agent Womack."

Sumner nodded. *Agent Womack* — the title seemed foreign but also exciting. Entering with her nerves already frayed, she jumped when a voice boomed.

"Welcome Agent Womack. Have a seat while we go over your assignment." A short older man with dark hair and graying temples stood at one end of the small room, which held a table and a few chairs.

Assignment? I just got here. I'm going on an assignment now?

"I'm Agent Lumer — Mark Lumer. I've been with The Agency a few years now. I know how you must feel. I'm sorry to rush everything, but we need you on a case as soon as possible. You're an expert on ancient symbolism, are you not?"

"I've studied it since I was a child. A hobby, actually."

"Please, have a seat. I'll explain."

Devon stared out the trailer's window, refusing to take his eyes off the large, ominous machine. The sun rising high in the noonday sky cast eerie shadows across the back of the dark train, and this bothered him for some unknown reason. The rumbling from Interstate 90 rubbed his nerves raw. Devon felt a slight twitching in his stomach. For the first time in his career, Devon was afraid.

"How in the hell do three hundred people vanish so close to a busy interstate?" he asked no one, since he was the only one inside the small trailer.

"Easy," a soft voice replied from behind him.

Startled, Devon turned to stare into the crystalline, greenish-pink eyes of an angel, set in the most divine face he'd ever seen. Her hair was a pure white. *Is this the same woman who explained the flowery emblem earlier? No, that agent had red hair, not clear. Can a person have clear hair?* He really needed to pay more attention to who was who on his team. Maybe if he looked at his agents once in a while, he'd remember their names.

"Easy?" he repeated, trying not to stare.

"There's a service road just over there." She pointed toward the trailer door. "From there, they could drive directly onto the interstate. From the interstate, they could send them to just about anywhere they wanted. And no one would see or hear a thing."

"Who are you?" Devon frowned.

"Anais, Anais Ramsden." Anais held out a delicate hand. "I've been assigned to the case by Dr. Lewis. He said he would call."

Trying not to stare too intently, he gently shook her hand. Anais was petite, and her long, colorless hair flowed in waves down her back, almost to her knees. Her eyes were enhanced with thick white eyebrows and long white eyelashes. Aside from the tint of her eyes and a pink rosiness on her cheeks and lips, the woman was basically colorless, resembling a fragile, glass doll.

She studied him. Devon knew when a person was giving him the once-over. It usually happened when he first met them. She glanced around the room. "Why is it so empty in here?"

"French?" he asked absently at the slight hint of an accent. Devon turned and stared out the window. "This is *my* office. I like it empty."

"Oh … um, my parents are French. I was born in Ohio, actually. I guess I picked up their accent a little. Why do you stare at the train so much?"

"Because … it knows something, and it isn't talking."

"I didn't know trains could talk."

"Is there something specific you need, Agent Ramsden?"

"I have the passenger list from Dr. Lewis, and I wish to question the citizens of this town."

"I thought other agents were already doing that."

"Not really," she said. "They're at the local diner. Been there awhile. I stopped for something to eat. Recognized most of 'em. Waitress said they'd been there all morning."

"As usual. By all means, snoop all you want. Don't let me stop you."

"Thank you," Anais said. "Do you want this list, or may I keep it?"

"Keep it. Dr. Lewis said I wouldn't recognize anyone. Besides" — Devon scratched his head — "where in the hell are we?"

"Whitewood, sir. Whitewood, South Dakota."

"I knew the Dakota part." Devon kept his gaze on the train. "Just wasn't sure after that."

"I see." Anais paused for only a few seconds before walking out as quietly as she'd come in.

Devon watched the sun slowly appear over the foothills. The train remained motionless and silent. They were only a short distance from town, and he just could not fathom how three hundred people could disappear without anyone seeing or hearing something. A train stopping in the middle of the night should have aroused suspicion.

Especially on tracks that had not been used in over fifty years.

Holding a fake pistol and a fake knife, with something resembling night vision goggles strapped tightly to her face, Sumner stood in the middle of the empty room feeling silly.

A voice buzzed in her ear. "Agent Womack are you ready?"

Sumner nodded.

"Agent Womack, you must speak into your headset."

"Sorry," Sumner whispered. "I mean, yes, I'm ready."

A loud hum and a vibration tickled her feet. Sumner tightened her grip on her gun. Without warning, a man appeared right next to her wearing a black jumpsuit with *The Agency* embroidered in dark-red letters over the breast pocket. He nodded.

"Are you ready?" he asked. He looked almost cartoonish, so she giggled. "Never experienced a virtual world before?"

"No," she replied.

"This room is big. We've never had anyone run into a wall. You should be fine. Just follow my instructions. I'm not actually here. My body is computer generated. It's safer for you. You cannot run into me, nor can I run into you. I will walk you through your initial training. Once you've passed this course, the next one you will complete on your own. Good luck, Agent Womack."

"Thanks, I think," she said, as buildings and streets appeared around them.

For the next several hours, Sumner learned how to hold her pistol, how to load and reload it, and how to shoot. The training took her through large and small buildings with and without people. She had to discern the bad guys from the good guys. Sumner was killed only once when she forgot to check behind an open door, and she only shot three old ladies who were not supposed to die. At the end of the day, she passed with pretty high marks for a beginner.

"How was it?" a familiar voice asked as she left the locker room.

"Fine," she answered, facing the agent who assisted her earlier in the day.

"I startled you. I'm sorry. Remember me? Agent Tarply? We met briefly this morning."

"Yes, I remember. Thanks for the help."

"Sure, anytime. I must say, it was very nice to meet you." He winked and smiled. "The name's Bill or William. I prefer Bill. I work in registration."

"Nice to meet you, Bill." He was close to her age, and although he seemed a little unsure of himself, she liked him. He wasn't tall, maybe five-seven or eight. Bill had the reddest hair she'd ever seen, and his eyes were a deep, dark brown. Freckles splattered across his face gave him a simple, childish quality. A quality that attracted her.

"I guess I'll see you around?"

"I guess," Sumner replied, a little sorry to watch him go.

After a full day's work, she was tired and wanted nothing else but a hot tub of water. Tomorrow would be no different than today — report by six for more harsh and rigorous training. In fact, her schedule was nothing but training for the next several days, and she was already feeling the exhaustion.

After a deep sigh, Sumner slung her new Agency gym bag over her shoulder and headed for the elevators. All she needed was a good night's sleep, and to be left alone. Well, alone for just a little while.

Chapter Two

It'd been almost a week, and nothing new was reported from his field agents. The case was running cold. Anais Ramsden stared at her notes from the previous evening. She'd already talked to every person living within twenty miles, and not one saw or heard a thing. Even those who lived just down the road didn't remember anything unusual; no vibrations or noise that would normally come from such a large train. How odd. It was as if the whole town simply fell asleep early that night and slept soundly. Before she forgot, she sent an email requesting that the town's water supply be tested for drugs.

"Morning," Devon mumbled, plopping down behind his desk.

"Good morning." Anais kept her eyes glued on her paperwork.

"Anything wrong?" Devon slurped coffee from his extra-large mug.

"Just a lot of oddness." She looked at him and frowned. "It's hard to believe that not even one person saw or heard something." She dropped her eyes back to her notes.

Devon took another long drink. He glanced out the window at the quiet, menacing train and frowned. "What do you know, ol' girl, that you're not telling?"

"Excuse me?" Anais asked.

"Nothing." Devon grabbed a package from his in-box and tossed it onto Anais's small desk.

"What's this?" she asked.

"More information on the passengers. Arrived late last night."

Anais ripped open the envelope. After a few seconds, she grabbed her purse. "I'm gone. I'll call in."

"Later," Devon mumbled. For all he knew Anais could be on her way to Alaska, and he honestly didn't give a damn. He was at a dead end anyway, and any enthusiasm from an agent was golden right now.

A few minutes after she left, he decided to walk the train's perimeter again. There had to be something he missed — some little detail he hadn't noticed before.

He refilled his mug with hot black coffee — the thicker and stronger, the better. As he left the trailer, he almost tripped over a young woman anxious to get in. His arm bumped directly into her chest and hot coffee jumped from his mug, splashing and burning his arm.

"Damn." He shook off the steaming liquid.

"Sorry."

"Who the hell are you anyway?" He headed back into the trailer for paper towels.

"Agent Sumner Womack, sir. I've been assigned to the case. Are you Agent Devon Arvol?"

"Unfortunately." Knowing his wet arm would freeze in the cold air, he grabbed his jacket.

"Agent Arvol, sir?" Sumner ran after him. "What do you want me to do?"

"Your job, whatever the hell that is."

Anais sat in a rental car watching the traffic. It was seven in the morning and she was anxious to start the day. She thought about Devon. In a way, she felt sorry for him. Such a proud man. For him to sit back and know there was nothing he could do had to be pure torture. Instead of thinking about where the missing people were, Anais decided to concentrate on who they were, where they lived, and where they worked. Most important was *why* they were on *that* particular train on *that* particular night. Anais believed that if she could answer those simple questions, the rest would fall into place — hopefully.

The missing passengers had come from all over the United States. To visit each one would be cumbersome, maybe even impossible. She'd already plotted a few locations on an old-fashioned paper map. It would take months for her to go through the whole list, but at least she was working on something real instead of an empty train filled with graffiti.

A knock on her window startled her. Almost dropping her orange juice, she rolled down the window. It was the old man from the convenience store.

"You left this on the counter." With a trembling hand, he held out a receipt. "Not sure if it's important or not."

"Thank you."

"Uh-huh," the old man replied before walking away. He stopped and glanced at her one last time. She grinned and shook her head.

Her fair skin and hair non-color always attracted attention. She wasn't fully afflicted with albinism, just partially. Her mother was full blown — no pigmentation. Her father, an Italian, gave her what little color she had. She radiated a true innocence that was naturally appealing, giving the illusion that she was a fragile, ethereal spirit and the very essence of femininity.

Anais was anything but. She had always been active in sports and preferred jeans to a dress any day. Although frequently outside, her skin never darkened. Sunscreen was her makeup no matter the weather.

Having the albinism gene sometimes made life difficult, but at an early age, Anais promised herself she would live her life to the fullest.

Glancing at the dashboard clock, she flinched. It was getting late; time to get a move on. Punching the first address into her GPS, Anais sipped the rest of her juice. At least the weather was cooperating — it would be cool with no chance of snow.

Sumner studied the color and texture of the paint. Each car had the same exact symbol. What interested her was not so much the emblem itself, but the size of it. It wasn't small by any means. Each emblem was at least four feet in height and almost the same in width. The emblems barely fit on the train's walls.

She noted that whoever sprayed them did so with precision. No runs or streaks. It definitely had not been applied with a brush or there'd be bristle marks. No, someone used a sprayer, which meant the person had a natural talent.

The pattern was created with the utmost attention. Each strand binding the lilies resembled a real rope with all the groves and lines. Almost three dimensional — truly amazing. Sumner had never seen anything like it.

"What do you think?" A growling voice reverberated through the small space. Devon stood in the aisle, smiling. He was almost too tall to fit comfortably on the train. Holding back a giggle, she grinned before turning her attention back to the golden emblem.

"Well," Sumner replied, "this is an amazing piece of art. I mean, it was definitely spray-painted. Maybe to the point of almost … well … like silk screening or something similar. Someone definitely took their time. If you believe these were created in a hurry, there had to be more than one artist. And the train would have had to be parked to spray with such detail. Impossible if moving. I mean, there are no mistakes."

"What about the emblem itself? What's so special about it?" Devon stuffed himself into a small seat.

"The fleur-de-lys is an ancient emblem that predates Christ. Many Christians associate it with the Holy Trinity, but it also predates that. It was first discovered in France, or the land we now call France. We're not sure how old it really is. Some scholars compare it to a fertility thing. Pure blood stuff."

"Explain … please."

"See the flower petals, here and here?" Sumner pointed. "They represent the woman's, you know … private parts." Sumner blushed.

Devon grinned.

"And this center part here — to some it represents the lily, but to others it represents the man's, well, you know, male genitalia."

"Interesting. I can almost see that." Devon glanced out the window.

"The rope symbolizes the bind that happens between a man and a woman — the bond or love." Sumner smiled. Devon sat stoic. "The stalks here at the bottom, they represent the harvest or child that's produced from that bond."

"Hmmm, and this is associated with the French?"

"The monarchs, yes. The ancient writings state it represented purity to King Clovis the First. All the French kings declared their right to rule came directly from the gods."

"Gods? You mean there were more than one?"

"To the French monarchs and other ancient cultures, yes."

"Really? Right to rule directly from a god. Hmmm, did they get that in writing I wonder?" He winked at her.

"Of course not." She giggled. "They actually believed that God ruled through this symbol. Not sure how he did that, exactly. And what's even weirder is that King Clovis's people believed him when he declared it."

"Was this symbol used only in France?" Devon asked.

"No. There was a monarch in Florence who used it in his coat of arms, if I remember correctly, and then there was a pope that used it once. It's found all over the world, but it's mostly famous in France. But the scholars don't believe it originated there."

"Really?"

"Yes. The Boy Scouts use it as their symbol with the three petals. Stands for faith, wisdom and chivalry."

"You know, you're right. I knew I saw that thing somewhere before. I'll bet that's where I remember it from. My scouting days."

"Probably. Some countries use it on their flags, such as Quebec. This emblem isn't anything new. But the question is, what's it doing here on this train?"

"Good question," Devon said.

"You just found this train parked here, like this?" she asked. "Abandoned?

"Unfortunately, yes. Not a soul on board."

"Missing people?" Sumner asked with concern. "How many?"

"I take it you've not been briefed?"

"I just started with The Agency. This is my first assignment. I was told to come here and analyze these symbols. That was all."

"I know you're a little green, but this is ridiculous. Let's get something to eat and I'll fill you in." Devon frowned. "I don't like it when my agents are not fully informed. The Agency seems to like it that way. I don't. I believe in sharing all the details. I'm hoping that one of my agents will see or discover something that another missed. And that one little thing just might break the case."

Sumner followed Devon off the train, praying that he wasn't relying on her to solve the riddle of the missing passengers. She was a linguistics major — not a detective.

As she drove down the two-lane road, the small homes made Anais think of her parents. It'd been years since she lived with them. Stopping in front of the modest home, Anais watched as several young children ran past to catch a school bus. It reminded her of being young and carefree. The woman standing at the front door gave Anais a strange look but waited for her, nonetheless.

"Hi." Anais walked toward the woman.

"What can I do for you today?" the woman asked.

"I'm not selling magazines or vacuums," Anais said as she pulled out her badge. "I'm Agent Ramsden from the FBI."

The Agency's agents were cross-referenced through the FBI. Although they did not work directly for that agency, they were given FBI badges just in case someone checked up on them. The Agency was the most covert and classified of all the federal law enforcement divisions.

"How may I help you, Agent?" the woman asked, narrowing her eyes.

"Does a Dr. Samuel Worthington live here?"

"That's my father-in-law. Is something wrong?"

"May we go inside where we can talk?" Anais glanced around.

"Certainly." The home was impressive but not large. Fine furnishings decorated the room they entered. "Please have a seat." The woman sat in a chair across from Anais. "Now, what about Sam? Has something happened to him?"

"We're not sure. When was the last time you saw or spoke to Dr. Worthington?" Anais asked, pulling out her notepad.

"I'm not quite sure." The woman stuttered; obviously, she cared about the man. "A couple of weekends ago, I believe. Why?"

"Do you know where he is now?"

"On a business trip somewhere up north. Would you please tell me what's happened?"

Anais realized that no one from The Agency had contacted her — and probably none of the relatives of the other missing passengers, either.

"Answer my questions and I'll be happy to explain why I'm here. What type of business is Dr. Worthington in?"

"He works for Helios Corporation as a research facilitator. What's happened to him? I'm frightened. Perhaps I should call my husband, Arnold."

"Please, just a few more. Is he still married?"

"No, his wife died some years ago. Please let me call my husband," she begged.

"Go for it." Anais jotted down some notes.

"My husband is coming right home," the woman said after she hung up, sounding relieved.

"I'm sorry. I didn't get your name."

"Lidia. Lidia Worthington. That's Sam there." She pointed to a small frame sitting on the mantle. It was a picture of a man holding two young girls.

"Are these the two who ran after the bus this morning?"

"Yes, they're our daughters. Sam just worships them. Has anything happened to him?"

"We're not sure." Anais frowned.

As they waited for Lidia's husband to return, Anais explained the best she could about the missing passengers, and Lidia told Anais what she knew about Sam's work, which wasn't much.

"What's going on?" a man asked from the other room.

"Thank goodness." Lidia ran to her husband.

"I'm Arnold Worthington. You have news about my father?"

"Not exactly." Anais held out her badge. "I'm Agent Ramsden with the FBI. Your father's name is on a passenger list we're investigating. We need to know if he was actually on that train."

"Yes, he is … I mean, was. I mean …" The man's hands shook. "I spoke to him just before he boarded."

"Cell phone?" Anais asked.

"Yes, he has one," Arnold replied. Then he must have realized what Anais wanted. Pulling out his phone, he tried to call his father. After several attempts, he dropped his phone on a table.

"No answer?" Anais asked as the man shook his head. "May I have that number, please? And by any chance, do you know what your father was working on?"

The man took out a pad and wrote on it as he answered her. "At Helios? No, we make it a rule not to talk about business when we're together."

"What do you do, Mr. Worthington?" Anais asked, finding it odd that a father and son wouldn't share stories about their workdays.

"I'm an attorney for the state," he answered as he handed Sam's number to Anais.

"Thank you. Do you have an address for your father's work? I'll also need his home address, and can you tell me why you're listed in the directories but not your father?"

Arnold's eyes darkened. *Fear?* "He didn't feel it necessary. My mother died a few years back. He prefers to be left alone. He doesn't live far from here. He finally seems happy again. It took him a long time to get over losing my mother."

"Here." Lidia handed a card to Anais. "It's Sam's business card, and I put his address and home number on the back. I had a few of his cards in the kitchen. You never know when they might come in handy. Do you have any?"

"Any what?" Anais asked.

"Business cards," Arnold replied for his wife. "She collects them."

"Oh, certainly." As she dug through her case, Anais's heart broke for these people. It was obvious they cared deeply for the missing man. "I believe I have what I need. Either me or someone from the agency will call if we hear anything." Anais gave her FBI card to Lidia and shook Arnold's hand.

"Please, find him," Arnold begged.

"That is what I'm trying to do," Anais replied. "I'm sorry to be the bearer of such news. I truly am."

As she drove away, Anais called in to report that the passengers' next of kin needed to be contacted, immediately. It was strange that they had not been already. It just wasn't like The Agency to ignore such a detail. Then it dawned on her that perhaps there was a reason they didn't want them to know. *But what could that possibly be?*

As they drove through the small town with only one stop sign, Sumner concentrated on the old buildings. The quaint town had somewhat of a Western feel about it. Devon stopped at a small diner. As they waited for their food, Devon told her everything about the case that he knew.

"Now that I've filled you in, tell me about this emblem. If a crazy person decided to hijack this train and kidnap the passengers, what would this emblem have to do with it?" Devon nodded as the waitress sat their food in front of them. "Thank you."

"Interesting question." Sumner took a bite of a sour pickle. "Not sure. As I said, the fleur-de-lys is associated with France, and French is the language of love. Not abduction."

"And that corresponds to the man-woman thing you mentioned before?" Devon smiled.

"Yes. Exactly. There are several dialects that are included in the romance languages, and they're all descended from the Romans and their Vulgar Latin."

"Vulgar? You mean crude?" Devon had a weird look on his face.

"No." Sumner laughed. "Vulgar in Latin means common. It was the common language of the middle ages. Eventually, it became part of the Romance languages, or so we call them today. The scholars of the middle ages used a more cultivated language that was not used by the regular citizens. We call it Medieval Latin. It was a more scholarly form of speaking. Separated the scholars from the common folk."

"Segregation of the classes?" Devon suggested.

"You could look at it that way. Remember, ideals and life were much different back then. Instead of money to separate people, it was education. The more educated a person, the higher standing he had in society. Today, you can have all the education in the world, but still be the poorest on your block."

Devon laughed and nodded. "I can't help but feel that this is somehow all connected. How do you know so much about this stuff, anyway?"

"It's a hobby. I started it when I was young. I studied linguistics in college and took some art history classes, but I couldn't seem to get enough of symbolism. They don't really teach it in school, at least not the schools I went to. So, I researched it on my own."

"I understand from The Agency that you have a photographic memory. Is that correct?"

"I'm not sure I'd call it photographic. Everything I read about symbols or anything new I find I seem to retain. It's hard to explain. I have tons of information about different symbols in my head, in my computer and boxes, and plastered all over my bedroom. I drive my mom crazy with the stuff."

"I guess what's hard for me to understand is all the aspects. You've mentioned love, war, heads of states, types of governments and religion. And all of that surrounds just one little symbol. Hard to grasp."

"That's what makes it so exciting." Sumner couldn't explain fast enough. As she tripped over her words, Devon chuckled. "Just think about it. How can so much be centered around one little emblem of a flower? And the power thing."

"What power thing?"

"All through history, people have been hungry for power. In my opinion, the desire for power and money comes from us mimicking the gods. How else could we learn such a terrible trait?"

"Interesting ... the flower. Is there anything special about that particular flower?"

"The lily? Well, it's always been associated with the Madonna or Virgin Mary." Sumner took a sip of her soda.

"The Gilded Lady," Devon mumbled.

"Gilded Lady?" Sumner repeated softly. "As in, covered in gold?"

"Or made from gold or enlightened as if from gold." Devon frowned. "Or to be pure."

"Hmm, interesting concept. The only gilded ladies I know of are a few statues here and there. Nothing that has to do with the fleur-de-lys, directly."

"For some reason that just popped into my mind. Maybe it's the golden color of the emblems in the train. I don't know." Devon threw his napkin onto his plate. "Time to go."

Sumner stared at the napkin. "I'll do some research on it. The original gods were obsessed with gold. Collecting it was their life's work."

Chapter Three

Anais swung by Dr. Worthington's office instead of visiting the next person on her list. She knew better than to ignore her urges. She stood in front of the impressive building. At over twenty stories high, it seemed to touch the heavens. With an immaculate barren landscape, the place gave her a sense of sterilization, among other things, that upheld her rigid perception of the corporate environment. The huge building housed only one company — Helios Corporation — that was dedicated to researching world history. Their main products were scholarly papers and teaching aids such as training materials, movies, and textbooks. *How could researching history bring in enough money to finance such a large place as this?*

"May I help you?" the receptionist asked with an extraordinarily forced smile as Anais entered.

Anais held out her badge and tried to smile back. But she wasn't sure how convincing her face looked. The woman was so translucent and fake, it took all Anais's strength not to laugh and say something sarcastically evil. "Hi." Anais used her hand to hide a growing grin. "I'm Agent Ramsden. I need to speak with someone from your HR department."

"I see," the woman replied with another fake smile.

Anais took a seat. It wasn't long before a short, heavy-set woman with graying hair exited the elevator and headed straight for her. Anais stood to greet her.

"Agent Ramsden, I'm Hester Palance, HR manager. What can Helios do for you today?"

"I need information on one of your employees, a Dr. Samuel Worthington."

"Oh?" Hester widened her eyes and frowned. "Is there a problem?"

"We're not sure. Is there some place we can talk, privately?" Anais glanced around the empty lobby.

"I hate to be presumptive ..." The woman paused as if the conversation had become a little sticky. "But do you have a search warrant for the information you seek?"

"Oh, why of course." Anais, dripping with pleasantness, handed the woman an order with the local court's jurisdiction printed at the top.

It was one of the benefits that made working for The Agency so enjoyable. They prepared their agents for anything. Anais had search warrants for each name on her list that was signed by a local administrative judge just in case it was needed.

The woman looked puzzled. "This way."

Stepping inside the elevator, the woman pushed the button for the fifteenth floor. Music played from small speakers near the top. They reached Dr. Worthington's floor, and his office was directly across from the elevators. Hester swiped her badge on the electronic lock and pushed on the door. Stepping inside, Anais gasped. Bookshelves lined each wall from floor to ceiling. They even framed the doorway. His ceiling had to be over fourteen feet above her head, and thousands of books were stacked just as high. From what she could tell, they were mostly about ancient civilizations.

"What is Dr. Worthington working on now?" Anais asked as she rummaged through some papers on his desk.

"It's classified," Hester replied.

"Classified?" Anais glanced up at the woman, who now looked concerned. "World history, classified? Since when?"

"Since now," Hester said harshly.

As her anger heated, Anais glanced away and counted. This was one aspect of her job that she could do without. *Why can't people just answer my questions? Why is it that some just have to argue or be stubborn about it?*

"Not a problem." Anais continued to count silently in her head. "I'll have a need-to-know paper sent right over. Email address? I don't recall reading that Helios Corporation housed classified contracts for our government. When were they awarded?" Anais glanced up at the woman and winked.

Frowning, Hester said, "What I mean is … it's *company* classified — not government."

"Glad you clarified that, Ms. Palance. Now, if you don't mind, I have a job to do, and I must know what Dr. Worthington was working on."

"What do you mean by *was*?"

Before Anais could answer, the door flung open and banged against the doorstop. An angry-looking man stood rigidly in the archway with his hands on his hips.

"What's this all about?" He was about as tall as he was wide. A receding hairline and graying temples suggested fiftyish. Dark-rimmed glasses and large bushy eyebrows framed his clownish face.

"I'm Agent Ramsden. FBI." Anais held out her badge. "I need information on one of your employees, Dr. Samuel Worthington. It seems he's missing."

"What do you mean missing?" he asked.

"And you are?" Anais asked, now in more control of herself.

"John Stipleton, senior vice president here at Helios Corporation. If one of my employees is in trouble, I need to know about it. Ms. Palance, why didn't you notify me right away?"

"Well …" Hester paused as if contemplating something. Without answering, she turned and stared out the large window.

Not taking her eyes off the woman, Anais said, "We are not sure if Dr. Worthington is or is not in any trouble. That is why I am here. I'm conducting a full investigation into the matter. Now where was Dr. Worthington headed on this business trip — exactly?"

"Chicago," Stipleton stated very matter-of-factly, "to a symposium." He also turned and stared out the window.

Anais walked over and glanced out. Aside from a dimming afternoon sun, not much could be seen. Shrugging and shaking her head, Anais cleared her throat before speaking. "Am I missing something?"

"What do you mean, Agent Ramsden?" Hester asked, nervously rubbing her hands together.

"It's getting a little bizarre in here if you ask me," Anais stated.

"No one asked you," Stipleton replied.

Anais stepped back and folded her arms across her chest. She was losing her patience with these two. "I have a court order, and I will search this room for as long as needed. And you will answer my questions. If not, well, you can tell it to a judge." Anais waited for one of them to snap back, but neither did. She then added, "You're hiding something."

"Excuse me?" Stipleton glared at Anais.

Anais ignored the pig-headed individuals that were now watching her intently. As she rummaged through the bookshelves looking for clues, they sighed loudly. What clues she was looking for exactly, she had no idea. But she searched, nonetheless. Nothing looked out of the ordinary. Books on ancient cultures and relics seemed to be the most prevalent.

"Dr. Worthington must love old things," Anais said to no one in particular.

"What do you mean?" Hester asked.

Before Anais could answer, Stipleton jumped in. "I don't see how any of this is relevant. I highly —"

"I highly recommend you cooperate, Mr. Stipleton. I have a job to do, and if you waste any more of my valuable time, I'll have you both locked up before you'd have time to call out for help."

Mr. Stipleton straightened, adjusted his tie and coughed.

"What is this?" Anais asked, now pulled from her anger. A framed plaque balanced precariously on one of the larger shelves.

"What's what?" Stipleton asked. Hester remained silent, probably too afraid to talk.

"What's in this frame? Looks like a stone carving," Anais surmised.

"Well, whatever it is, it's personal property that belongs to Dr. Worthington," Stipleton said.

"A doctor? A doctor of what?" Anais stared at the strange carving. "Help me take it from the shelf. It looks heavy."

"That is not ours to play with, Agent Ramsden," Stipleton said. "I insist that you cease immediately."

"And if you do not help me, I will find someone who will, and they may not be as gentle." Anais glared at Mr. Stipleton, who pulled out a handkerchief and wiped his forehead. "Do I make you nervous, Mr. Stipleton?"

"Very." He positioned himself to help remove the heavy object. "Geography. Dr. Worthington has several PhDs in geography and ancient history."

Once the object was safely on the floor, Anais examined the frame more closely. Only a few screws held the back to the glass case. Scrambling through her bag, she located her small pocketknife that housed a screwdriver. With the glass cover removed, she found that the stone was not permanently attached to the backing. Only a foam encasing held the stone in place. Putting on a pair of thin rubber gloves, she smiled and carefully pulled the stone from its secure holder. "Someone took great care in having this mounted."

"Evidently, Dr. Worthington cared about this little trinket and wished to have it protected," Stipleton stated. "And not messed with."

"I'm aware of that." Anais examined the stone. "Seems to be an original. But that would be impossible." Holding the ancient relic in her hands gave her the most uneasy feeling. *How could Dr. Worthington possess such a thing?* "This almost looks — no, it's not Egyptian. Maybe Sumerian?" Anais glared at the two nervous Helios employees.

"Dr. Worthington has traveled the world many times over. Perhaps he found it on one of his trips," Stipleton suggested.

As Anais examined the stone, Stipleton and Hester edged closer to get a better look. The stone was obviously from an ancient wall, but where? The edges were not jagged but smooth. Maybe from being touched by human hands throughout the centuries. The odd carving had a metallic glaze.

"What is it?" Hester asked.

"I don't know. I've never seen anything like it. I mean, look at this. Definitely two individuals standing in front of a hovering object. I believe there's three or four beings sitting inside the object itself. Then there's a door here, with what looks like a light bulb. Or something that's surrounding a door or portal. I mean, this is definitely a cord that's plugged into this box here. I hardly think they had electricity back then. Look at this flower-looking spiral thing. I have no idea what it is. It's amazing. Right here is an animal I don't recognize." She allowed her gloved finger to trace along the carved lines. "The carvings resemble Sumerian in style, but I can't guarantee that without further analysis."

"Further analysis?" Stipleton huffed.

"I will not take this item with me, but I will have an agent pick it up. We need to examine it." Anais used her phone to snap several pictures of the stone.

"We'll just see about that!" Stipleton almost growled.

"Yes, of course." Anais carefully set the stone back into its foam casing. "That was fun, wasn't it?"

As Stipleton continued to state his objections, Anais snapped photos of the many books lining the massive shelves. Once satisfied she had enough pictures, she sent all the photos to The Agency with a message to have someone officially confiscate the stone. With nothing else to investigate in Dr. Worthington's office, she excused herself from the two very angry and confused individuals still fuming in the middle of the room.

Once back in her car, Anais glanced at the clock and then at the map with all her red circles on it. It was late. *Time to call it quits.* She would drive to her next destination, find a hotel room and end her hectic day. As she pulled out of the parking lot, an Agency car with the letters *FBI* on each side drove in. Anais giggled.

Devon was back in his office scanning the list of the missing passengers. Not one name jumped out as remotely familiar. The engineer, a Jack Lawrence, meant nothing to him. Then again, why would it? Devon didn't ride trains. The trailer door flung open and startled him. Grabbing his coffee mug before it fell, he glared at the intruder. The passengers list swirled to the floor.

"Sorry, sir." Agent Newberry glanced down at the papers and frowned.

Shaking his head, Devon gathered the list that had scattered across the small trailer. "What's up?"

"Well, sir, we found a strange carving."

"Carving?" Devon glanced up and narrowed his eyes.

"Yes sir. This one is actually carved into the wood. Found it in one of the cargo bays. We didn't see it until we unloaded the freight."

"Where's Agent Womack?" Devon tossed the papers into a nearby tray and ran out the door, leaving Agent Newberry alone by the blazing heater.

Devon tried not to cast a shadow as Sumner studied the carving. "What is it?"

"Well …" Sumner considered her words carefully. "Have you ever heard of the tree of life?"

"A tree of life?" Devon tossed up his hands. "This is just wonderful. Not only do we have a fucking flower, but now a goddamn tree. What in the hell is going on around here?"

"I'm not sure how this relates to the fleur-de-lys," Sumner said. "It's just that this carving reminds me of the tree of life."

"Okay, I'll play." Devon knelt. "What is the tree of life?"

"I take it you've never danced around a maypole." Sumner smiled.

Devon sighed as he glanced at his agents who snickered.

"Out!" Devon yelled, standing back up. "Everybody out, right now. Except for you." He pointed to Sumner who had started to rise.

"Oops." Sumner sat back down on the train's floor.

Devon knelt in front of her and glanced at the colorful carving. "Okay. Talk to me, Agent Womack."

Sumner wasn't sure how to start, or if she could even get him to understand. But she'd try.

"Trees have symbolic meanings in religion, sex and cultural. For example, the Garden of Eden had a tree where Eve picked an apple. We use trees for Christmas. Trees are used to draw ancestral lineage. In China, there's a tree that represents immortality. It produces one peach every three thousand years. If you eat it, you live forever."

Devon snorted and Sumner paused. He nodded for her to continue.

"In Egyptian history, life and death are encased in a tree. The tree of life is in almost every culture including Norse, Hebraic and Japanese. Trees are even found in the Epic of Gilgamesh and the myth behind the philosopher's stone. The tree of life represents not only life, but the continuation of life — immortality. Good against evil, dark against light, things like that."

"Almost fits with our lily, doesn't it?" Devon glanced down at his hands.

"What do you mean?"

"The woman-man thing, about bearing a child." Devon pointed directly at the tree carving. "A tree that depicts ancestry and Eve. As I said before, it's all linked somehow. We just have to connect the dots to see the bigger picture. That's what we do as agents. Connect the dots."

"Some dots." Sumner bent in closer to re-examine the carving. "See the roots? They're supposed to represent hell or the underworld. Here in the middle, where the trunk breaks through the ground, is earth. And of course, the branches represent heaven or reaching into heaven."

Devon stared at the carving. "I've seen and heard of such things before, the symbolic etchings."

"Where?" Sumner asked. "In a museum?"

"No. Tribal stories. I'm of the Lakota of the Great Sioux Nation," Devon explained. "From my mother's side. We have our legends about Mother Earth and the gods, such as the spirit rooted in the wise old tree of the forest. The leaves represent the wings of an eagle that sees evil approaching and warns our people. It makes sense. If birds flock from a tree, there has to be a reason. As a little boy, I loved hearing my grandmother speak of such things. Now that I'm older, I spend most of my time fighting bad guys instead of listening to bedtime stories."

Sumner smiled. She understood where Devon was coming from. As a child, she too enjoyed listening to stories, but as she aged, she started questioning her surroundings, and instead of wonderment, she was filled with bewilderment.

"Don't get me wrong," Devon added as he studied her. "I'm proud of my heritage and all. It's just that —"

"I understand," Sumner said. "Honest, it's not easy being green, as Kermit the Frog would say."

They both laughed.

Chapter Four

Jack Lawrence coughed several times and rubbed his runny nose. He was lying on a chilly and damp concrete floor. He had no idea where he was. Every joint in his body ached — cold and stiff. A sharp pain shot from his head and flew down to his freezing toes. At sixty-seven, his thin, frail body required heat and a dry room. Grit dug into his back as he wiggled his hips to ease the pressure. A musky odor smothered him as he gasped for air.

Through blurred vision, Jack made out a faint haze hovering just above his head. As hard as he tried to sit up, Jack's arms refused to hold his weight. It took all his strength just to breathe. His eyes teared as they fought against the dim light. *Does hell have a cold floor?* He heard a weak cough. He was not alone.

"Who's there?" a frail voice yelled. Jack heard another cough. Again, the frail voice spoke. "Is somebody here?"

"Yes," a high-pitched and much softer voice replied from somewhere closer to Jack. "I'm hurt."

"Me too," Jack said. "Is there anyone here who can help us?"

A woman shouted from farther away. "I don't think so. There are two dead lying next to me. I think my leg is broken."

"Stay still," Jack yelled as he again tried to take in a deep breath. *Damn that hurts.* "I think there's something wrong with the air."

"I think this place is just really dirty," a man shouted. "There's dirt everywhere."

Jack rolled over onto his stomach, and his face slapped against the cold concrete floor. Stars sparkled across his vision, and he fought back the darkness overtaking him. He could hardly control his neck muscles. He brushed off his face the best he could. Dust flew everywhere, making him sneeze. With eyes shut, Jack pushed himself onto his elbow.

The stench of rotting flesh made him gag. Bile rose from deep within, and he struggled against the desire to be sick. "Does anyone know where we are?" Jack asked.

No one answered. Jack rose to his knees and moaned.

"Don't move if you're hurt," a woman shouted.

"It's just old age and the cold," Jack replied.

Having endured long hours of training when in the Army, Jack knew he needed air and lots of it to regain his strength and clarity. He panted to bring up his oxygen level. After a few seconds of heavy breathing, his dizziness seemed worse instead of better. He simply had no strength. If only he had a wall to lean on, but only empty space greeted him as far as he could see.

"Someone please say something," he begged.

A man hollered from Jack's left as a woman yelled from his right. The man sounded closer.

"I hear a man's voice. Say something again," Jack called out.

The man recited a poem — 'The Raven.' Jack crawled toward the sound. "*Once upon a midnight dreary,*" the man recited.

"How appropriate," Jack stated as his hand glided atop the dirt and filth. When his fingers hit something hard, he jerked back. "Is that you?"

"No," the man replied before continuing with the poem. *"While I pondered weak and weary, over many a quaint and curious volume of forgotten lore ..."*

Jack couldn't focus. The dust was just too thick to see anything.

"While I nodded, nearly napping, suddenly at my chamber door ..."

As he tried to move, Jack realized it was a body blocking his way. He shook and shook the person, but there was no response. He found the neck and searched for a pulse. Nothing.

"Jesus," Jack whispered.

"... there came a tapping, as of someone gently rapping ..."

Again, Jack followed the ghostly voice reciting the poem. When it seemed he was close, his head bumped into a hard mesh. Reaching out, he realized what it was — chicken wire.

"This may be as far as I can go," Jack yelled.

"Why?" the man asked.

"There's a fence here."

"A what?" the man yelled.

"Chicken wire," Jack hollered. "I think we're caged in."

"My god!" The woman screeched from across the room. "Where are we?"

Jack tensed as he listened to the woman crying from an unreachable point. He had no idea where they were or for what reason they were there, but he knew their time on this planet would probably be short, and that their deaths would not come easy.

"How many are still alive down there?" Scott Lansing asked as he paced the room.

"I have no idea," the woman answered, staring at him. "Besides, why should we care?"

Scott stared back at the woman he married over twenty years ago and accepted the fact that he didn't know who she was anymore. This whole situation made him sick to his stomach. He now wished he had never gotten involved. Military or no military, government or no government, money or no money, Scott wished he were anywhere else but there.

"We only have to wait a little longer and then we can leave," the woman said. "We just have to make sure no one goes down there. Now, that's not difficult, is it?"

"You're sick, Melissa," Scott snapped. "Where did the others go?"

"I have no idea," she answered, taking a long sip of her rum and coke. "They came, dropped off their bundles and left. They did their job, now we do ours. Then we get paid. Okay?"

"You never told me that some would be dead," Scott yelled.

"I didn't know," Melissa huffed.

Scott stared out the window. The beautiful blue sky sparkled with freshness and serenity. The airplanes landing or taking off just a short distance away made everything seem so normal ... so every dayish. Denver was beautiful this time of year.

"I'm going to go see if I can help any of 'em." He turned away from the window.

"Are you crazy?" she yelled. "We're not allowed to do that. We were told to make sure no one goes down there."

"I don't give a fuck. I can't take this anymore. It's wrong, Melissa."

Scott darted from the room and ran down the hall to the heavy metal door. He felt a tinge of apprehension. Placing his hand on the cold handle, he heaved the door open and gagged at the stench.

"Melissa!" he screamed out, coughing. "My God, get over here."

"What now?" Melissa peeked around the door and down the hallway. "Damn, what is that awful smell?"

"Some of them have really died," he cried out, "and now they're probably rotting."

"Who gives a shit? Close the damn door before you stink up the whole building."

Scott shook his head as he gazed through tear-soaked eyes at the living hell at the bottom of the stairs. The room was about the size of a small aircraft hangar and held a maze built from chicken wire. Inside the cages were men and women of different ages and ethnicities. No blood, just a filthy, stinking mess of skin and bones and clothing. Scott recognized the lingering odor. It was a gas. A gas he was very familiar with.

"My God, is anyone alive in here?"

People screamed out for help. Some begged to know where they were and why. Scott couldn't answer them — not because he didn't want to, but because he didn't have all the answers.

He spotted an older-looking man pushing himself off the floor. Scott ran down the stairs and climbed on top of the wire cages. For some odd reason, it was important for him to get to the old man. The cages were about four feet high and six feet square. Just large enough for two or three people to lie down in. After cutting his hands on the wire and banging his knees a couple of times against the metal rods, Scott finally reached the older man.

"What's going on in here?" Scott yelled.

"That's what I want to know," the old man replied.

"What's your name?" Scott asked.

"Jack Lawrence. What's yours?"

"Scott …" *Shit! I shouldn't have said my name.*

"Well, Scott, do you know what this place is?" Jack grabbed the wire with his fingers to help steady him on his knees.

Scott flipped the answers through his mind. Should he tell them where they were? *Crap, what do I have to lose? Everyone's just about dead — including me.* Once law enforcement got involved, his life was over anyway.

"The Denver airport," Scott said. "How many of you are in here?"

"I have no idea. Why are we here?"

"I don't know," Scott answered. "I've got to get you some help."

"From whom? The authorities?"

"Yes, 911 or something," Scott almost screamed as he tried to count the bodies.

"What day is it today?"

"Wednesday," Scott said.

"Wednesday? Damn, it was Saturday when I was on that train. That means it's been almost a week. How can that be? No wonder I've soiled myself."

"I've got to get you out of here," Scott said. "Let me find something to cut this wire."

As Scott searched the huge room for something, anything to release these people from their cages, screams and cries for help echoed through his ears. Tears streamed from his eyes, and his body shook with fear. As he crawled over the wire cages, he spotted two small children lying side by side in a barren cage; whether they were alive or dead, he did not know. How or why someone would do this to another human was beyond his comprehension. The captives were either lying still, crying or shaking uncontrollably. Glancing back at the stairs, the room seemed to have gotten larger. With no strength left, Scott collapsed on the cage he was crawling over, gasping for air. The gas hovering just above the cages was now burning his lungs. He knew it was a matter of time before he, too, succumbed. But death would be better than living with the memory of this horror.

Sumner scanned the pages on her computer, looking desperately for the information she knew was there somewhere. Thrown about the small bedroom were pages and pages of paper and books she had collected since childhood. Her once neat and tidy room now resembled a tornado-destroyed house.

"Oh my," her mother declared from Sumner's doorway.

"I know, I know," Sumner mumbled. "I've just got to find this one thing and then I'll clean up."

"What are you looking for, sweetheart?"

"I have this old Sumerian text that had pictures of clay tablets and writings. The English translation was down one side. I don't remember if it was in a book, magazine, on paper or electronic. I know I have it somewhere."

"Does this have something to do with your new job?"

"Yep and I've got to get back as soon as I find it." Sumner spoke without taking her eyes from her computer screen. "There's a plane waiting for me. I've got to find it."

"A plane? Well, you did land yourself an interesting position, didn't you?"

"Yeah, I guess." Sumner pulled two books out of a box and tossed them across the room. "Not it."

"Sweetheart, you still have stuff in the attic. Want me to get it?"

"That's right! I forgot ..." Sumner yelled out as she ran from her room.

Her mother shook her head and smiled as she picked up the pages to reorganize the mess. Sumner loved ancient history, and her mother always believed Sumner would attend graduate school and become a college professor. She was surprised when Sumner pranced home and announced that she'd found a job at a temporary agency just down the street. "I think I'll work a few years and make some money. I'm kind of tired of classrooms," Sumner had said.

"I found it!" Sumner yelled from the attic.

"I'm glad," her mother hollered back.

After a while, Sumner entered her room carrying a large box full of papers and magazines. Her room was almost back to normal — neat and tidy.

"Mom!" Sumner called down to her mother who was now in the kitchen. "You didn't have to do this."

"I know," she answered. "Just trying to help."

Sumner sat on her bed, flipping through the pages. Colored pictures of ancient scrolls and their translations greeted her. She shoved what she needed into a smaller box. With her purse hanging over her shoulder and the box safely in the trunk of her car, Sumner said her goodbyes to her mother and headed back to her strange and mysterious case.

Feeling more frustrated than successful, Anais stared at her list, struggling to connect the dots. It had been two days, and she'd only investigated five out of three hundred. The most interesting was Dr. Samuel Worthington and his stone tablet. The other four included a teacher, a banker, a social worker and a gas station attendant. How a gas station attendant fit into the puzzle was a piece she didn't have time to solve right now. She sat in front of a Gerry Miller's house, pondering the possibilities. Who this Gerry person was she had no idea. But the only way to find out was to go inside and ask questions.

She stared at the front door of the small home. It couldn't have many bedrooms — maybe two at most. From where she sat, the yard was also tiny. She took a deep breath and knocked on the bright-yellow door. An elderly woman answered with a big smile.

"Hi," Anais said. "I'm Agent Ramsden. I'm looking for Mr. Gerry Miller. Does he live here?"

"Nice badge, Agent Ramsden." The old woman grinned. "But *Ms.* Miller isn't here right now. Is there something I can help you with?"

"It's imperative that I reach Mr., um, Ms. Miller. Do you know where she is?"

"On travel, I'm afraid. I don't expect her back for several months," the old woman replied. "She's my daughter, you see."

"May we sit and talk?" Anais asked.

"Certainly." The woman opened the front door all the way.

Inside, the house seemed much larger than it did from the outside; with space for two or three bedrooms, a small living room and a kitchen. The house was clean and modestly furnished.

"Now, what is this all about?" the woman asked.

"Name ma'am?" Anais asked. She wasn't going to make the same mistake as she did at Dr. Worthington's house.

"Karen Miller."

"And Gerry is your daughter?" Anais asked.

"Geraldine. Yes."

"And what does your daughter do, Karen?"

"She's an archeologist for the university. What's going on?"

Anais explained about the train and the missing people. How Gerry's name was on the passenger list, and how it was Anais's job to search for her. Karen sat quietly.

"Perhaps I should show you something," Karen said in a serious tone.

"Excuse me?"

"Agent Ramsden, my daughter's been all over this world. She's a professor of ancient civilizations at the university here in town. Her area of specialty is Sumerian culture. How much do you know about the Sumerians?"

"Not much," Anais replied.

"Gerry knows a lot. Perhaps too much. She's been studying them for the last fifteen years or so. She has information that many will never know about."

"What would this have to do with the train and missing people?" Anais asked as she followed the woman outside and toward a detached garage.

"You see, my daughter warned me about this day. Said there were people trying to cover up the truth."

"Truth?" Anais asked. "What truth?"

"Truth about who we are and where we came from."

"I'm confused." Anais held the screen door so Karen could use her key to enter.

As the door opened, the alarm system beeped. Karen walked to the control panel and punched in a code. She smiled as the beeping stopped.

"You can't be too careful these days." Karen pulled out her keys again. "This way."

They climbed a flight of stairs to the second floor. Once the locked door was opened, Anais walked into a finished room over the garage. It was a huge office, and it was obvious that Karen's daughter was, in fact, an archeologist. Findings from around the world hugged the walls. A huge rock, taller than Anais and with unusual carvings, sat proudly in one corner.

"Wow," Anais declared as she entered.

"Impressive." Karen's eyes widened. "I know."

"Hey," Anais stated with surprise. "See this picture? I think I had the real thing in my hands the other day."

"Really?"

"Okay, what's going on?" Anais asked.

"Sit down, Agent, and get comfortable. I need to tell you a story."

"It's about time you got back to work, Agent Womack," Devon said into his cell phone. Although half joking and half serious, he needed her with him to unravel this bizarre and eerie case.

"It was worth the trip. I should be back by nightfall. I can't wait to show you what I have."

"Terrific," Devon said his voice gruff as usual. "Just get back, soon."

"Will do." Sumner placed her phone into the cupholder between the seats. Although The Agency flew her home and back, it was still a long drive to the abandoned train site.

As she drove throughout the afternoon, Sumner's mind went to work. *Why would a train be left abandoned like that?* Then it hit her. If someone wanted those people for a reason, it would be important to keep those searching busy. Keep them looking somewhere else, like on a stupid train. *Then why the emblems, why the carving?* To keep them even busier?

As the afternoon progressed into night, Sumner's mind rolled through the possibilities from fiction to reality and the possibilities were endless.

It was getting dark when Anais realized she'd been with Karen for hours. But what the woman was telling her was so interesting and intriguing, she didn't want her to stop talking.

"You see, Agent, my daughter knew that what she'd discovered, what she'd found, the real rulers of the world wouldn't want anyone to know about."

"But why?" Anais asked. "I mean, it explains so much."

"That is just it; it explains too much. You see, Anais — may I call you Anais? It's such a pretty name."

Anais nodded.

"If you want to control people, you have to ensure they are afraid of something. And if you take away their fear, you also take away your control."

"I don't understand." Anais frowned.

"Many have known about this for a very long time. Over thousands of years, history and religion have changed. It's only recently that people started opening their minds to accept such possibilities."

"It isn't crazier than saying the rapture would happen, or that a god would judge us someday including the dead. It isn't any crazier than any of those theories."

"Perhaps, but could you imagine what would happen if every person on earth had absolute proof that everything they'd been taught in school, that which was supposed to be the truth, was actually a lie? A cover-up?"

"Kind of cool and exciting to me," Anais said.

"Perhaps for you, but not for the millions who're sitting around just waiting for Jesus or their messiah to come rescue them. It would be a total shock and not everyone would buy into it. Then there are those who'd go off the deep end — riots, lootings, or worse — wars."

Listening to the woman, fear flew through Anais. It wasn't until she'd left the woman standing at her front doorway that Anais realized things went much deeper than just an abandoned train and missing passengers. She needed to report back to Devon — immediately.

Chapter Five

Devon watched, fascinated, as the two women shared their stories. *They're so young,* he thought, *but so smart. They remind me of Carrie.* Devon's heart ached for Carrie, and he wanted to call her. He needed to tell her how much he loved and missed her. But he couldn't — not now. She would call him when she was ready. "Okay, let's get down to business."

"Sure." Sumner stepped closer to Devon.

"Of course," Anais said.

"Here's the report on that stone of yours." Devon handed Anais a sealed envelope. "Let's hear what it is — or is not."

Anais anxiously ripped open the packet and glanced through the papers. "Wow! It's real. The stone is over six hundred thousand years old."

"May I see the pictures?" Sumner asked.

"Oh, sorry." Anais handed the photos of the stone to Sumner. "I forgot you don't know about the stone yet. I was going to visit every passenger's home and workplace to see if I could find anything that would give us a lead. I only got to a few. There were just too many. But two of the passengers were amazing. A man, Arnold Worthington —"

"You're not talking about Dr. Worthington the famous historian, are you?" Sumner gushed.

"Yes, I believe I am, why?"

"He's one of missing? He wrote a book on the Sumerian culture and how they're connected to us, and the giants, and other strange creatures." Sumner studied the pictures of the stone. "Do you know what this is?"

"I thought it might be part of an ancient wall or something."

"Well, perhaps, but it's very ancient writing. Very old — could predate the Sumerian culture."

"What era was the Sumerian civilization?" Anais asked.

"Historians say about three thousand years ago. Dr. Worthington was working on a theory that the culture was much older. More like hundreds of thousands of years. Maybe even millions. They had the first written language. Dr. Worthington could read their language as easily as we read English. A tablet, similar to the Rosetta stone, allowed him to decipher their writings. So many interesting stories are on their tablets. This tablet, it talks about —"

"Wait! You read Sumerian?" Anais asked.

"A little." Sumner kept her eyes on the photos. "Not as good as Worthington. This stone's talking about 'those who from Heaven came.' It was a popular statement for the Sumerians. All of their writings speak of the gods who came to Earth to create us."

Anais's eyes widened. "Does this have anything to do with that Planet X stuff? I heard about Nibiru and the Anunnaki."

"Why, yes it does." Sumner stared at Anais. "Website research?"

"No. A woman told me about it just yesterday. Her daughter is missing, a Gerry Miller."

"Not Dr. Geraldine Miller, the famous archeologist?" Sumner's voice cracked as she realized that some of the missing people might have been involved in the same thing.

"Okay, what's going on?" Devon interrupted.

"Not sure yet." Anais glanced back at Sumner.

"Can someone explain some things to me, please?" Devon said.

Sumner glanced down at the picture, then over at Anais and back up to Devon. It was quiet for a few seconds before she spoke. "Devon, in your culture, what does it say about where we came from?"

"You mean the Great Sioux Nation's beliefs?" Devon asked.

Sumner nodded.

"Um, well, the nation now has Christianity mixed into it. All the missionaries and such. But the original teachings — is that what you're interested in?"

"Yes," Sumner replied.

"As I was told by my grandmother, in the beginning, *Gichi Manidoo* made the *Mide Manidoog.*"

"The what?" Sumner asked.

"The *Mide Manidoog*, it means spirits, so to speak. Think of it as the interconnection and balance of nature and life. My people do not think of earth as being separate from us. We believe we are one with nature."

"Okay, go on," Anais said.

"Well, *Gichi Manidoo* — or God, as you probably know him by — first created two men and two women, not just one and one. These four couldn't think or reason for themselves. So *Gichi Manidoo*, God, destroyed them and created new beings. More rational and able to think. In other words, he scrapped the first four and started over. He wanted people who could think for themselves. Then *Gichi Manidoo*, God, told them to multiply, and he paired them off, thus creating the *Anishinaabe,* or the First People — the Original People. When *Gichi Manidoo* discovered that his people would get sick and die, he provided them with the sacred medicine so they could live and prosper. Otherwise his people would all become extinct."

"So far you're right on with the Sumerians' stories," Anais said.

"Yes, that's correct." Sumner laughed. "Please, continue."

"I was taught that between God and the earth there were four lesser *Manidoog*, or mini gods."

"Enki and Enlil from Sumerian!" Anais jumped into the conversation. "They were the sons of the great god, or great leader of the people. There is a huge resemblance here."

Devon paused for a moment to restructure his thoughts. "Doesn't match Christianity."

"Not supposed to," Anais said. "I'll explain later. Continue, Devon."

"According to legend, *Gichi Manidoo* wanted people, or the *Anishinaabeg*, taught about his sacred medicine. He used the lesser gods to do the teachings. Anyway, as the story goes, *Gichi Manidoo* sent a boy to live with a family on Earth. They already had a child that same age but adopted the boy anyway. Their child died. The adopted child said he pitied them for being so sad. Therefore, he decided to bring the child back to life. Make them happy again. With the help of some tree bark and a bear, they brought the child back."

"Cloning?" Anais asked.

"Cloning?" Devon repeated.

"Yes, that could work," Sumner said, excitedly. "The only problem with our cloning is that we have no way of incorporating the memories of the deceased into the new body. But if we were more technologically advanced, we probably could. After all, memories are just electrical impulses that are stored in the brain. Just like a computer stores data, our brain stores data."

"Of course and wow." Anais shook her head. "What a concept."

"What are you two getting at?" Devon asked.

"Go on; what else?" Sumner urged.

"Well," Devon explained, "a bear entered the tent and walked around the boy four times, and the boy came back to life. Then the father had to listen to a verse from the bear."

"Do you remember the verse?" Sumner asked.

"No, but I could find out. Why?"

"Just curious. Go on," she coached.

"As the story goes, the adopted child taught the family all the secrets of life and medicine. When he was done teaching them everything he knew, he went back to *Gichi Manidoo*, with the knowledge that the people would survive. Oh, the story was called *Gwiiwizens Wedizhichigewinid,* or 'Deeds of a Little-Boy.'"

"Did the gods or boy ever return?" Sumner asked.

"Not that I'm aware of. My people still gaze to the heavens awaiting their return."

"And your people passed down this teaching, correct?" Anais asked.

"Yes, that's correct. So how does all this fit into the Sumerian stuff?" Devon asked.

"Well," Sumner began, "the Sumerians have their own teachings, which were quite similar. They wrote on cylinders and when rolled onto wet clay created a tablet that they then baked. These hardened tablets have lasted for centuries and tell great stories, many of which mimic the modern Bible. Most frightening was the *Anunnaki,* who were 'the Watchers.' They came from the skies in huge floating cities. From reading the tablets, this is what I've concluded, as did Dr. Worthington and Dr. Miller.

"Many years ago, perhaps as many as two hundred thousand or more, a race of beings came to our planet to mine for gold. They needed the gold to purify the air on their dying planet. I've researched this subject and there are chemists from Queensland University who discovered that the air in medieval churches were cleaned by gold nanoparticles. They painted their stained-glass windows with gold, which somehow purified the air."

"Nano-what?" Devon asked.

"Nanoparticles. It's called nanotechnology. It basically refers to a field of science where we control matter on a subatomic and molecular scale. The pharaohs and Renaissance potters also were early nanotechnologists. I can get you the articles later to read on your own. Anyway, when gold nanoparticles are energized by the sun, they destroy airborne pollutants. You know, volatile organic chemicals or what scientists call VOCs. It's a cool study. So, when I read that article and applied it to the Anunnaki stories, I was amazed. What was written in those ancient tablets could actually work."

"What worked?" Devon asked.

Sumner shook her head and sighed. "Using gold to purify their air, silly. Are you even listening?"

"Okay, so we have people coming to Earth, from where? Another planet?"

Sumner nodded.

"And they dug up our gold. Then what did they do?" Devon asked.

"Some of the Anunnaki were tired of all the mining," Sumner replied. "They felt they were doing all the hard work. When they rebelled, the rulers realized they needed a new group of workers before there was a huge riot. Since there were people-like creatures on Earth at that time, maybe the Neanderthals or something similar, they started with them. They couldn't communicate or teach them anything as they were. So, someone from their civilization started experimenting. They mixed their DNA with early human DNA, and after several failed attempts, well, eventually they created us, modern humans."

"Okay, I see some similarities between their history and my people's. Go on."

"After they created us and enslaved us for mining and other purposes, the Anunnaki ruler came down and said that since we had their DNA inside us and the ability to think for ourselves, and had emotions and such, that it was against their laws to enslave us. Therefore, we had to be set free. But, since they created us, it was only right for them to teach us their ways and give us their knowledge, which they did, sort of. The Watchers eventually left Earth or died off. Left us here alone to grow and prosper. When they returned years and years later, the Anunnaki liked what they saw in the human women, so they inter-married and had children. But there was a problem. They discovered that if they directly mated with an Earth human, the children born to them were mutants."

"Mutants?" Devon asked. "How exactly?"

"There's quite a difference between genetic splicing and the combination of a sperm and egg," Sumner explained.

"Terrible mutants," Anais added. "So terrible they had to be destroyed."

"Let's not get ahead of ourselves." Sumner held up her hand. "But yes, when the head ruler returned thousands of years later, he wasn't happy. In fact, he was terrified by what he saw."

"How long did these Anunnaki live?" Devon asked.

"Thousands and thousands of Earth years," Anais replied.

"Yes, and not only had they created these terrible mutated giants, but they had also experimented with animals. Horrible experiments that went terribly wrong. You've heard the old stories about half horse, half man, or half bird, half lion. All those creatures from ancient mythology actually lived at one time. So, the space-ruler demanded that all life on this planet had to be destroyed."

"But we're still here." Devon squinted.

"Yes, we are," Sumner said. "Somehow, the ruler knew that the polar caps would melt. That the water would flood the Earth. Great way to solve his problem. All life should have been destroyed, thus righting a wrong. But the Anunnaki scientists who created us were terrified at the thought. They loved us as their children and demanded that our human population be spared. They were related to us, genetically."

"That's where the Noah Ark story comes into it!" Anais seemed excited that she heard this story only yesterday.

"All of this information is in the Sumerian clay tablets?" Devon asked. "Honestly? You wouldn't shit me now, would you?"

"Honestly," Sumner repeated. "We wouldn't shit you."

"So, why hasn't anyone officially told us this?" Devon asked. "Why not teach it in school?"

"They cannot," Sumner said.

"Why not?" Devon asked.

"Control," Anais replied.

"Control?" Devon repeated. "You're not making any sense."

"If you want to control people," Sumner explained, "you have to make them afraid of you. You have to bring down their self-image."

"It'd never work," Devon said.

"Why do you think Constantine did what he did back in 306 AD?" Sumner asked.

"The old Roman ruler?" Devon said. "What did he do, exactly?"

"He was the one who combined the Christian religion with the Pagan religion. He was the one who commissioned the Bible, and it was his council that decided which books to add and which books to take out. Remember the Dead Sea scrolls? They helped to fill in the gaps of the Christian religion that Constantine tossed out. The Christian religion talks about a savior, the son of God that comes and rescues us from our sins. Think about it, Devon. Why did the Anunnaki ruler want to destroy us?"

Devon shook his head and sighed. "Because of the mutants?"

"Because of the atrocities created by *his* people. In the story of Sodom and Gomorrah, God destroyed those cities in what can only be described as a nuclear explosion. He felt the need to purify the earth. The Anunnaki easily destroyed those cities where the mutants lived that were not affected by the floods. Think about it. The tablets also tell of how angry the ruler was the last time he was here, and that he demanded all of the Anunnaki to return with him. He was so angry that he had all the spaceports destroyed, so that no evidence of them ever being here remained behind. That is how mad that ruler was, this supreme ruler, this God."

Devon sighed. He looked around and remembered he was in the trailer next to the deserted train, where all the people had vanished. "I need coffee." He stood.

"Every religion has the same stories. Purification from a God for our sins," Sumner said. "It all makes sense if you stand back and take a good long look. Something happened a long time ago and we were created. The Anunnaki needed a slave race to mine their gold. Expendable people."

"This is the same story the old woman told me. But she went even further." Anais walked over to Devon and patted him on the shoulder. "Said the real rulers of the world know about this. They want to hide the truth from us. Keep us in the dark."

"Why?" Devon asked, trying to tie this all to the mysterious and evil train sitting only a few feet away.

"Supposedly, the god's DNA still resides within some of us," Anais said. "Remember the rumors about the holy bloodline? There was a blook and a movie about it a few years ago. How Joseph supposedly took the pregnant Mary away and hid her in France to protect the holy bloodline. That she was supposedly pregnant with Jesus's child."

"Yes, of course. Who's not heard of that story?" Devon replied. "I saw the DaVinci Code."

"Look at it as if that story were true. What if the holy bloodlines, the purebloods, were individuals with mutated DNA? Would that mean that some of the mutants actually survived the destruction; lived through the great flood?"

"So what? Who'd care?" Devon argued. "What would any of that have to do with any of this — the train or the missing passengers?"

"Two of those missing passengers were very prestigious doctors in the area of Sumerian culture and civilization," Sumner said. "They were conducting extensive research into the theories of the Anunnaki, and whether we were or were not their descendants. If man's six hundred thousand years old, or older, then evolution goes down the drain. All religion could be destroyed overnight. Lots of lost income for many religious leaders. Good reason to kidnap a lot of people. Prove that the ancient gods were real."

"It would also mean that humans did in fact walk with the dinosaurs and with the giants," Anais added.

"About those giants …" Devon said.

"There's proof," Anais added.

"There's proof?" Devon asked.

"In bones, in graves and in pictures," Sumner said. "Throughout history, there have been very tall people. The Bible talks about the Anunnaki and the giants. The book of Genesis: *there were giants in those days.*' Seems Constantine didn't take everything out after all. Left behind little hints everywhere if one only *reads* the words. Most people just get all crazy and dream about being saved and floating into the clouds with the invisible man who lives there."

"We have bones from these giants?" Devon asked.

"Yes," Sumner said. "It was Dr. Miller's life to study them. In fact, I remember reading a paper she wrote where she — wait." Sumner ran to her box of material and rummaged through it until she found what she was looking for. "Here." She handed Devon a magazine article. As Devon read, she continued to talk. "Dr. Miller found enough bone marrow for a DNA analysis. What she discovered was amazing. We have similar DNA, but the giants have certain DNA particulars we do not. All giants had six fingers and six toes. They also had a second row of teeth."

Devon stared out at the train and frowned. If a very unstable individual wanted to ruin the world's financial system, then bringing down the world's religions would work. However, that would mean that the missing passengers were being used as guinea pigs. It would mean that their DNA was being tested and compared to the rest of the world for abnormalities. Devon shook his head. His fear grew and his mind whirled. The more the girls talked, the more he was starting to understand. Their rantings were staring to connect a few of his dots.

"Tell me more." Devon placed the article back into the box.

"According to Sumerian mythology, the Anunnaki are the fifty great gods." Sumner closed the box and sat it on the floor next to Anais desk. "Each city had its own god or ruler, or however you want to look at it."

"Like a governor or mayor," Anais added. "And they were not like us — not human."

"What was most interesting to me was that many of these city gods resemble the patron human saints of orthodox Christianity," Sumner said. "Almost as though Constantine took the pagan gods and made them into Christian saints. You see, the reality is there; it's just that the basics have been changed or skewed over time."

"Interesting," Devon said. "We're comparing ancient Sumerians to Christianity because?"

"Because," Sumner explained, "it makes perfect sense. Someone is searching for the ancient gene. The God-gene."

"And we have a God-gene because of Christianity," Anais replied. "It all fits."

"To you," Devon said, still staring at the train. "Anything else I should know about?"

"Yes." Sumner replied. "The Anunnaki or the *Igigi*, the minor gods, had various phrases such as *dan-una, da-nuna-ke-ne* or *da-nun-na*. It means something like 'those of royal blood.'"

"That royal bloodline again," Devon interjected. "Royal blood. And much of the royal linage are intermixed inside regular society?"

"Correct," Anais said. "It's easier to grab regular people than it is to grab royalty. Buckenham Palace would take a stance against it."

"But not the commoners," Devon whispered.

"To me, it's interesting," Sumner said. "In Sumerian times, the person in charge of the heavens was *An* or *Anu*, the sky god, and the other members were his offspring, his children, or lesser gods. The story says that his two sons, Enlil and Enki, were in charge when the inter-marrying was going on. When An left Earth, all the strange crap started happening. Mutations in both humans and animals started popping up, and at that same time, the brothers also started fighting. Both wanted to rule Earth — alone. Enki was said to have been the one to create humankind because he was in charge of the gold mines. He was probably the one that came up with the idea of mixing us with animals."

Devon refilled his coffee cup and whispered, "Pretty heavy stuff. But not a bad theory. Better than nothing. Weird, but better than nothing."

"Here." Sumner had rummaged through her box again, pulling out another sheet of paper. "Here are some of the original gods when all of this genetic testing was going on."

Devon read the names aloud. "Ashnan, cereal grain goddess. Enkimdu, god in charge of canals and ditches. Enbilulu, god in charge of the Euphrates and Tigris rivers. Ereshkigal, queen of the Underworld, hmmm. The list just goes on and on. Ninkasi, lady who fills the mouth. What's that supposed to mean?"

"Oh, the art of brewing medicines, to heal the sick," Sumner explained. "A doctor, so to speak."

Devon shook his head, adding, "Uttu, goddess of weaving and clothes. This is way too much info for me. All these titles of the various professions are similar to what we have today. I get it. However, you honestly want me to tie all of this history to the missing passengers because of a DNA search?"

The girls nodded.

"And if we tie it all back, how does it help us to find 'em?" Devon asked with a serious look plastered across his face.

"I want to see the reports from the agents who're visiting the homes and workplaces of the missing," Anais said. "I think it will tell us something, perhaps give us a clue."

"Give us a clue," Devon said. "Maybe, but I wouldn't hold your breath."

Chapter Six

It was late. Devon stood in front of the dark and silent train thinking, again, about what happened to the three hundred passengers. He prayed silently that they were still alive. The small tennis shoe hanging from the mirror caught his eye, and he couldn't resist a closer look. Climbing up the side of the massive iron car, the machine felt cold to the touch. An agent collecting fingerprints stopped to stare at him.

Devon studied the small red shoe. Reaching up, he carefully unhooked it from the mirror. "There's blood on the shoestrings."

"It was tested, sir. The blood is old. Records indicate that a Jack Lawrence was the engineer on this train. He was involved in a fatality about twenty years ago. A mother and two young boys. That may be one of the boy's shoes."

"Why would he hang a dead child's shoe on his mirror?" Devon asked.

"As a memorial?" The agent shrugged. "To remind him."

"Who'd want to be reminded of something like that?"

"Someone who'd want to ensure it didn't happen again," the agent said with surprising insight.

"Okay. Makes sense in a macabre sort of way."

Devon left with the small shoe in his hand. When he reached his office, he hung the keepsake on his desk lamp. Leaning back, he studied it; then he glanced back out at the silent train.

This train could not have been the same one involved in the accident. It wasn't old enough. The engineer, Jack Lawrence, must have kept the shoe with him. The more he thought about the shoe and the dead child, the more Devon's respect grew for the missing engineer.

"Jack Lawrence," he said, not expecting a reply.

"Jack Lawrence what?" a voice asked from the dark shadows.

Devon startled. "Would you stop doing that?"

"Stop what?" Anais asked.

"Stop popping out of thin air like you do. That's what. What are you working on that's so important you're here so late?"

"I'm bothered."

"About?"

"Out of the three hundred missing passengers, two hundred were in the field of ancient history, religion or archeology. Everyone was working on *something* that had to do with the Sumerian civilization."

"Must have received the final report?"

Anais nodded.

"Why do you consider that to be so bothersome?" Devon asked.

"Because the Sumerian culture is not that high on anyone's list, or so I thought. I checked. Would you believe that almost every government in our little world is hiring experts in this particular field right now? And all of these experts were headed to a special historical symposium in Chicago that centered on none other than the Sumerian culture. I find that troubling." Anais picked up some papers. "Agent Lumer worked up the results from the information gathered about the passengers. I'm glad I turned the work over to him. I'd still be out there if I hadn't. Anyway, I think we should concentrate on who took them and why."

"I agree." Devon stood and clicked off his desk lamp. "But there are no answers in this trailer. Agent Ramsden, let's call it a night."

Anais glanced at her watch. "I didn't realize it was almost midnight. Very well. Night, Devon. See you in the morning."

"Uh-huh." Devon locked the door behind them. The crisp night chilled him. After one last glance at the silent train, he headed for the hotel and a warm bed.

Jack Lawrence opened his eyes. *I must have dozed off. How many died while I slept?* Shaking his head, he tried to clear his mind. The floor felt colder than before. Maybe his old body was finally giving out after all.

"Anyone else awake?" he called out.

Silence.

"Shit." Jack pushed himself onto his hands and knees. "Someone, anyone?"

After several minutes, a faint voice finally replied. "I'm here. It's me, Scott. I must have passed out."

Jack coughed. "My cellphone is missing."

"Try not to talk," Scott said. "This air's nasty. You're under the airport."

The sound of metal grating against metal told Jack that Scott was moving across the top of the cages.

"What airport?"

"There's gas in here." Scott coughed. "If you breathe in too much, you'll pass out again."

Jack was dehydrated, hungry and his hands shook uncontrollably, which meant his sugar level was too low. He wasn't sure how much longer he could hold on before he passed out for good. Again, a loud scraping sound of metal on metal grabbed his attention.

"I made it back to the stairs," Scott said. "I'm going to find help. Stay as close to the floor as you can. I promise I'll be back."

A loud bang echoed. Jack understood that they were again alone. The man named Scott was gone. Not wanting to waste energy, Jack rested on the hard, cold floor. For the first time in over forty years, he prayed to a god he never met. He didn't pray so much for himself, but for all the others in that large room who were in worse shape than he was.

More snow had fallen during the night. Devon stared out his hotel window wondering why a new blanket of whiteness always made everything look so fresh and clean. Taking another large gulp of coffee, he thought about his wife, Carrie. He still had not heard from her, and now he was worried. Pulling out his cell, Devon sent her a short message. Within a few seconds, her reply beeped in.

I'm fine. Case is crazy. Miss and love you, too. Will call soon — Carrie.

At least she was alive and healthy. The two had worked cases together, grown close and married. All was good until Carrie lost their first child. Now, Devon waited for her to come back to him.

A rap at the door pulled him from his thoughts. Peeping through the small hole, he smiled and opened the door. "Good morning, Agent Womack."

"I need you in the train." Her face flushed, she looked as if she'd just run a marathon.

"What's up?"

"We found another carving. It's an owl, and …" She glanced away. "We have a dead body."

"No identification." Anais stood as Devon and Sumner entered the small train car.

"Why didn't we find her earlier?" Devon asked.

"Hidden behind these crates," Sumner replied. "I noticed an odd odor late last night. When we moved these crates, I saw her foot. That's when I called in the forensic team. I didn't want to wake you."

"Good catch, Womack." Devon knelt next to the body. Glancing up at Sumner, he frowned. "I take it you've never seen anyone dead before."

"Only on TV." Sumner averted her eyes.

"Nothing to be afraid of," he said. "They can't hurt you. But they *can* communicate."

The female victim looked to be in her early twenties with long, golden hair pulled into a ponytail. If released, it probably would have fallen halfway down her back. Devon estimated her height to be about five and a half feet, and her weight at about one hundred and twenty pounds. A large gash on the side of her head meant she had died from a blunt-force blow. It would have been quick and maybe painless. He doubted she even realized she'd been hit.

"Manicured fingernails," Devon said. "Jeans and a white sweatshirt. Do we know who she is?"

"No. Nothing. No ID," Anais said. "Just her hand."

"What's wrong with her hand?" Devon asked.

"Nothing; she's pointing." Anais stepped over the woman. "To this crate over here."

"What crate?" Devon glanced around.

"Oh, we already moved it." Anais shined her flashlight toward the back of the car.

As the darkness faded, Devon gasped. Carved into the train's side was a large owl. "A bird?"

"Yes," Sumner said, "but there's more to it."

"Owls are not good symbols," Anais said.

"Not if everything points to the Sumerians," Sumner added.

"Alright, ladies," Devon said. "Explain."

"The owl represents evil omens," Sumner replied. "Or the devil."

"In other words," Anais added, "death and destruction."

"Death?" Devon repeated. "And destruction?"

"Death," Sumner said.

"And destruction." Anais frowned.

Gasping for air, Scott leaned against a metal pole. As the planes roared from the other side of the chain-link fence, he couldn't stop thinking of the dying people. *How could my wife get us involved in such a horrific scheme?* Coughing for the last twenty minutes didn't stop the pain rolling across his chest.

"What are you doing out here?" Melissa glared at him from the metal doorway.

"Breathing," he replied.

"We're not supposed to be out here."

"Ask me if I give a shit." Scott glared through the fence and wheezed as a plane took off.

"Get in here, you dumb shit!" As Melissa's voice echoed through the hangars, he cringed. "It's five in the morning. Are you nuts?"

Turning, he stared at the large metal building. His wife looked like a tiny doll standing next to it. One small light near the top cast an eerie gloom throughout the parking lot.

The sound of a truck engine froze Scott. *Are they coming for their prisoners now?* As the truck turned the corner, Scott closed his eyes and prayed. Expecting a bullet through his forehead, he relaxed as the sound faded. He took a little peek and sighed as the taillights disappeared into the darkness.

Walking up to her, he wondered what he ever saw in the woman he married. Her beauty used to come from somewhere inside. Over the last several years, however, she painted her attractiveness on her face each morning. The curves that once excited him now repulsed him. No longer was she his sweet and innocent girl. No ... Melissa had become something darker, something more sinister.

"I'm going to save 'em." Scott glared at her.

"No, you are not. They'll kill us for sure."

"Again, ask me if I care." He turned away from her.

Scott pulled out his phone and then stumbled, falling to his knees. He reached up to rub the back of his head and then stared at the blood covering his fingers. Glancing back at his wife, he sighed at the sight of a large metal rod that aimed straight for his face. With a loud *ping*, his world darkened around him.

Walking to his trailer, Devon wondered what destruction he'd be facing. As for the death part of the omen, that had to refer to the three hundred missing passengers. Without a break in the case, those people were as good as dead.

He noticed a small group congregating near his trailer door.

"Agent Arvol?" A man about Devon's height but much skinnier cuddled a black briefcase in his arms, looking like he was about to cry.

"Yes," Devon replied. "And you are?"

"I do not know who these gentlemen are," the man answered, "but I'm from Northern Central Railways. I'm here to discuss the sudden appearance of our train, here in this town, and the missing passengers."

"Name?" Devon asked, unlocking the trailer door and stepping up.

"Gauge Nithercott," the tall, skinny man replied. "I'm the railroad's head investigator."

Shaking his head, Devon grabbed the man's card before climbing the last few steps. He ignored the other three who stared as if they idolized him or something.

"If I could just have a few minutes of your time." Gauge Nithercott followed Devon into the trailer.

"No, you may not have a few minutes of my time. If you're an investigator, then go investigate. And then …" Devon winked at the skinny Gauge Nithercott. "You tell *me* what *you* find."

"But sir —" Gauge Nithercott lowered his eyes.

"Just go investigate the sudden appearance of your train."

Nithercott maneuvered around the other three struggling to get through the small trailer door. Shaking his head again, Devon aimed for his desk.

"Sir, we found this man hiding in a basement."

"Ah yes, you're two of my agents," Devon said. "Didn't recognize you out there. You're Agent Steven Newberry at Your Service Sir if I remember correctly."

The agent smiled. "Just Agent Newberry will work."

"Okay, Agent Newberry. Hiding in a basement, you say?"

"Yes sir."

"And you're Agent Johnson, right?" Devon asked the other man.

"Yes sir." Johnson held on tightly to the old man they had found.

"Hmmm," Devon said. "Is it a crime in this town to hide in one's basement?"

"Not really, sir." Newberry frowned. "This man didn't sleep through the night like everyone else did. Said he saw the whole thing from behind the store."

"He says, does he?" Devon stood.

The man appeared to be in his seventies or eighties. Sprigs of dirty-blonde hair framed a large balding spot that dominated his head. The strong sour odor filling the room suggested that the man needed a good scrubbing. Perhaps his clothing could be burned.

"How can we trust what he says?" Devon asked, backing away to open a window.

"I'm not sure," Agent Johnson stuttered.

"Agents, you're dismissed. As for you, I don't know your name, take a seat."

"Dismissed?" Newberry asked. "But *we* found him."

"And your point is?" Devon replied.

The agents lingered for only a few seconds before shutting the door behind them. With the room now silent and chilled from the open window, Devon started the coffee maker.

"Would you like a cup?" he asked the man who kept glancing around the room.

"No," he replied. "Am I under arrest?"

"Not arrest." Devon chuckled. "I'd rather call it 'detained for questioning.'"

"What do you want from me?"

"To know what you know," Devon replied. "Full name?"

"Don," the old man answered. "Donald Gruber."

"Don, it's nice to meet you. I'm Devon Arvol. May I ask how old you are, sir?"

"I'm ninety-four."

"I was off by a few years." Devon smiled.

"Excuse me?"

"Nothing." Devon changed the subject. "Would you mind sharing with me what happened that night?" Devon held his empty coffee cup close to his chest.

"I can do better than that," Don said.

Devon stared at Donald Gruber and cocked his head to one side. *What game is this man about to play?*

"I can show you," Don said.

"How much will it cost me?"

Don's eyes widened. "Nothing."

"I don't get it." Devon sat his cup on the table.

"At first I thought you all were a part of it," Don said.

"A part of what?"

"Part of what happened here. That's why I hid from your people, your agents. But when you stayed longer than a few days, I figured you might be from our government. Are you from our government?"

Devon nodded.

"So, it's safe to talk to you, right?" Don leaned forward. "I mean, you won't shoot me or lock me up?"

Devon shook his head.

"Okay then, here." Don pulled out his cell phone. After playing with it for a few seconds, he handed it to Devon.

Devon watched several men wearing black overalls transport what looked like sleeping passengers from the train into several idling diesel trucks. A few were hand carried, while others were moved on stretchers. Devon estimated about twelve different people working the transport — all different body types.

"I was in my barn when I heard the train come into town. Northern runs these tracks from time to time. Maintenance and all. Just in case. Not sure in case of what, exactly. At first, I thought maintenance workers, but when I heard the brakes, I knew something else was up. Too big of a machine for maintenance, you see. I'd been busy all day with one of my mares that's been in labor. Once I knew she'd be okay, I headed to town to get a better look." The man shivered.

"I'll close the window." Devon stood.

"Sorry for the smell," Don said. "Been in hiding a few days."

"Not a problem. Please continue."

"It was late, real late, maybe about three in the morning or so." Don rubbed his forehead. "I was on foot, you see, so it took me a while to get into town. And when I came over the small ridge back there, I noticed that the air smelled really funny. A strange, sweet smell. Not right for around here."

Devon glanced back at the small video and noticed that the workers had something covering their faces. *Gas masks?*

"Once you've smelled it, you never forget." Don sighed. "War. Once you've experienced that stuff, you know right away to run the other way."

"Gas?" Devon asked. "They used a gas to silence the town? Do you know the name of the chemical?"

"No." Don shook his head. "The Army never told us no name. But I remembered that smell. Ran straight to my basement and sealed off the windows. Used a wet cloth to breathe through. Got a little dizzy but didn't fall asleep."

"I see."

"Remember, gas goes up, not down." The old man pointed toward the heavens. "Doesn't stay around long either."

Devon nodded.

"I waited. When the lights didn't look as hazy outside, I went back out. Hid behind the store's dumpsters and filmed. Sorry I couldn't get closer. They had this whole place lit up as if it was noontime."

"That's why they didn't see you," Devon said.

"Yep, as long as I stayed in the shadows, I was invisible to them. War strategy."

"May I keep a copy of this video?"

"Yes sir. There are several on there — maybe three?"

Devon plugged Don's phone into his computer. After downloading the three files, he emailed them to Dr. Loomsbury, the head analyst for The Agency. Maybe Dr. Loomsbury could enhance the recordings and zoom in on the trucks' license plates. Without more detail, it was just men, dressed in black, moving bodies from point A to point B.

After handing the phone back to Don Gruber, Devon excused the man, telling him an agent would be escorting him and buying him something to eat. Perhaps after the man had a long, hot shower.

Scott moaned as he tried to clear his head. The first thought that flew through his mind was that he was being held prisoner, just like Jack Lawrence. They were holding him until they had time to kill him. Peeking through his semi-opened eyes, he couldn't see much but the room smelled of alcohol and antiseptics. Opening his eyes a little more, he realized he was in a brightly lit room. *A hospital?*

"How are we feeling, Mr. Lansing?"

A woman. A nurse? "Where am I?"

"Mercy Hospital," she replied. "Couple of deliverymen found you in the airport's parking lot. Head bleeding. Someone got you good last night. Cracked your cheekbone a little, too."

"Yeah," Scott said, "real good. My head's killing me."

"Nothing broken. Just a little bruising and one small crack. You'll be released tomorrow," she said. "The police wish to speak with you. If you're up to it."

With the word *police*, Scott's stomach twisted into knots. Now his stomach hurt more than his head. "What about?"

"Well ..." She checked his IV. "Weren't you robbed?"

"Oh." Scott relaxed a little. "I don't know."

"I'll get your things for you," she said. "Then you can check."

The nurse rummaged through a small closet before handing him an envelope. Scott dumped the contents onto the bed. Between his legs rested his wallet, car keys and a receipt. He already knew he hadn't been robbed. Because Melissa had been the one to clobber him. *Wait until I get my hands on her, the bitch.*

"Mr. Lansing? I'm Officer Smith. May I ask what happened last night?"

Scott stared at the woman officer. All he could think about were the people trapped in the cages. He had to get out of the hospital and back to that warehouse. *Their lives may depend on it.*

"I just checked my wallet," Scott said. "Nothing taken."

"What happened?" she asked again.

"Don't know. Was coming out of the warehouse and wham. Someone hit me. Don't know why."

"I see," she said. "And you were there because?"

"I was watching the warehouse."

"You don't look like a night watchman," she said.

"More of a babysitter. Friends. Doing 'em a favor."

"May I ask who your friends are?"

"Am I under arrest for being knocked out or something?"

"Just filling out my report," she replied.

"Then put in your report that nothing was stolen. Maybe my rescuers found me before they could get to my wallet."

"Maybe." She jotted something on her notepad. "Just seems odd that you were, how did you say it, babysitting an empty warehouse."

"Empty?" Scott repeated. Not wanting to give anything away, he submerged the fear that was rapidly consuming him. "Yeah, yeah, empty."

"Well, if you think of anything, give us a call." The officer handed Scott her card with her report number on it, then left.

Pushing the card into his wallet, Scott rang for the nurse.

"May I help you?" a woman asked through the intercom.

"I'd like to be released," Scott said.

Chapter Seven

Devon summoned Sumner and Anais to his computer. "Ladies, take a look at this."

"Can't tell much from this video." Sumner's eyes were glued to the screen.

"I can tell it was dark outside," Anais said.

"Why didn't you ask more questions?" Sumner glared at Devon.

"What was I supposed to ask? I believe he told me everything. He hid, took videos, then went home and slept in his basement. Was he supposed to invite them to dinner or something?"

"No," Sumner said. "But how did the paintings and carvings get into the train?"

"I doubt if he got close enough to see that." Devon shook his head.

"He got close enough to know they gassed everyone," she said.

Agent Newberry entered the office with a cold breeze following him.

"I hate March." Sumner shivered.

"Only a few more weeks and it should warm up." Anais held her hands over a small room heater.

"Sir," Agent Newberry said. "I have the coroner's report. I waited for it as you instructed."

"Appreciate it." Devon accepted the report from the trembling agent. "Stand over there and warm yourself."

Newberry walked over and stood near the small heater. He couldn't take his eyes off Anais's majestic face.

"What's wrong, Agent?" Devon asked, glaring at the man.

"Nothing, sir." Newberry looked at the small window.

"Didn't your mother teach you that staring was rude?" Devon frowned. "She's pretty, I know. But that doesn't give you the right to stare at her." Devon paused as he read over the report. "Sumner, pull up the name Kelly McGruffin, will yah?"

"McGruffin?" Sumer repeated.

"Yes," Devon replied. "Anything?"

"Um, actually yes," Sumner said. "She's an artist. Known for her ability to paint in perfect 3-D. Wow, check out her website."

"Her portraits look more like photos than paintings," Anais said, watching from over Sumner's shoulder. "How do you know her name?"

"Dental records." Devon shook the report in the air.

"She's a three-time winner of the DA Society Challenge." Sumner read from off the screen.

"What's a DA Society Challenge?" Newberry asked.

"Digital artistry," Sumner replied. "Every year they have a challenge. Each year the subject matter is different. Last year it was to paint something and have it look real. Kelly painted bathroom doors, and everyone tried to use them."

"Restroom doors?" Devon asked now glancing over at Sumner's computer screen. "Must have been a big canvas."

"Actually, she used the museum's wall." Sumner laughed. "People were running into the thing. They thought they only had to push on the door or walk into the room. Too funny."

"Oh yes," Devon said, "a broken nose is always something to laugh about."

"I doubt if anyone broke their nose," Anais said. "Wish I could have seen that exhibit. So, our dead lady was an artist."

"I told you that whoever painted those emblems was good," Sumner said. "Now we know. And her bathroom doors are still on the museum's wall. I've got to go see this."

"Alright, ladies. We have some work to do," Devon said. "Sumner, I want you to visit Miss Kelly's home and office, or studio. Anais, I want you to visit this DA Society. Find out who Kelly was working for."

"You mean commissioned," Sumner added.

"Oh okay, whatever," Devon said. "Find out everything there is to know about her. Now go." With his *go*, they ran out of the trailer and were soon on their way.

Agent Newberry frowned at Devon. "What about me, sir?"

"As for you, I want you to find out what type of gas was used on this town."

"And how do I do that, exactly?" Newberry asked.

"How long have you worked for us?" Devon wasn't impressed. Was this agent actually that stupid?

"Never mind," Newberry said. "I'll contact Loomsbury. I'm sure he'll send me something to collect the samples in."

Devon shook his head as the agent left the trailer. After the door closed, he again thought of his wife, Carrie. Now, she was someone who was fun to work with — always several steps ahead of everyone else.

Scott stood in front of the warehouse staring at the rusting metal door. *If Melissa were still here, would I have the courage to confront her? Just who does she think she is, hitting me over the head like that?* Something about her always did frighten him. Exactly what that was, he wasn't sure, until now.

No good standing out in the cold. Might as well jump right in. Pulling on the door, Scott's heart stopped. The room, dark and empty, sent panic through his veins. Feeling weak and chilled, he needed to lie down. His head still pounded as if it would explode. The doctors told him to drink plenty of liquids, but the thought of putting anything into his stomach made him gag. Ignoring the spinning room, Scott ran down the darkened hallway to the large metal door. He prayed that the people were still there.

As soon as he entered, his worst fears were confirmed. The huge concrete dungeon was empty. No cages, no dirt, no human waste. No evidence that anyone was ever there.

"Jack Lawrence!" Scott's words echoed through the empty room. "I'll find you, Jack. I promise. I will find you."

Agent Newberry stood in the middle of town holding a small portable vacuum. As the tube filled, he sighed. Throughout his short six-month career with The Agency, he always got the stupid jobs, the dumb jobs, the no-frill jobs. Now, he was in charge of walking through town collecting air samples. Next, he would enter each house, rub down the walls with a small wet sponge, and then, after packaging everything up, send it all back to headquarters. Loomsbury would assign someone else to take the townsfolks' blood samples. No, he just got the stupid jobs. The meaningless jobs.

"Whatcha doing?" a young boy asked, staring up him.

"Taking air samples."

"Why?" the young boy asked.

"Gotta find out what put you all to sleep that night."

"You mean the fairies?" the young boy asked.

Newberry stared down at the boy. One thing The Agency insisted on was that their agents listened to everyone and took everyone seriously. *Why would this boy mention fairies if he didn't see or hear something?*

Kneeling to meet the boy eye to eye, Newberry asked, "What do you know about the fairies?"

Gasping for air, Jack wondered why his clothes felt so wet. He pushed himself into a sitting position and groaned. The room, hot and stuffy, was even darker than before. Reaching up, he felt nothing. *What happened to the wire cages?* As his eyes adjusted, he could just make out the shadows of people around him — many people. *Ah, that's why the room feels so humid.* Blinking several times, he tried to make out what else was in the distance. But he couldn't see a thing.

"Hello?" Jack yelled out, hoping someone would answer. All remained quiet. "Please. Anybody?"

"I'm here." It was that man's voice again.

"Where are you?" Jack moaned.

"Not sure. Sounds as if you're to my left."

To his left. Like that was going to help. "What's your name?"

"Sam, Samuel Worthington," the voice said. "What's yours?"

"Jack." Jack inched his way toward the voice. "Jack Lawrence. I'm the engineer. I mean, I was."

"Do you know what happened to us?" Worthington asked.

"No. Were you the one reciting the poem earlier?"

"That was me," Worthington replied.

"Can you recite another so I can find you?"

"Certainly." Worthington coughed a few times. "How about a De La Mare story — *Is there anybody there, said the Traveler …*"

"Again, appropriate," Jack whispered.

"*… knocking on the moonlit door. And his horse in the silence champed …*"

"Sam?" Jack hollered.

"You sound close," Worthington replied.

"Reach out your hand."

"Just a sec. Let me sit up."

Jack leaned back and rested against his legs. "We've gotta be close."

"I don't feel any — oops, sorry."

Jack felt a slap across the back of his head.

"Not a problem." Jack grabbed hold of the arm that belonged to the hand.

Pushing a body aside with his knee, Jack used his other arm to crawl closer to the voice. When he felt the man's leg, Jack almost leaped into his arms. They hugged and cried. Not wanting to let go, they grasped each other as if their lives depended on their one lone hug.

Jack took in a deep breath. "Are you hurt?"

"Not real sure. Maybe just hungry."

"Well, I'm a mess," Jack said.

"I can smell."

"I do apologize," Jack added, scooting back a little. "My age doesn't help matters much."

"Please don't apologize. I too have wetted myself. At least we're still alive."

"The question is, for how long?" Jack said.

"Is there somebody there?" The sound of a female voice boosted Jack's spirit a little.

"Yes, who's talking?" Jack looked around, but it was too dark to see anything.

"I'm Gerry," she said. "I'm hurt."

"Hold on," Jack said. "Keep talking; we'll find you."

"Who else is there?" Gerry asked.

"It's me, Sam."

"Sam, is that you?" Gerry was crying.

The two men crawled toward the sound of her tears until they found her. Gerry smelled like vomit.

"Try to ignore the odors," Jack whispered.

"Who's there?" It was another voice, a much younger voice.

"We're over here," Jack yelled out. "Now who's talking?"

"I'm Elizabeth," she said. "I can't find my mom or dad. Can you help me?"

"How old are you, Elizabeth?"

"Eleven," she said.

Reaching out, Jack cringed as her head brushed along his fingertips. "Take hold of my arm, Elizabeth."

Her small hand grazed his fingers. He grabbed her arm and pulled her in close. Crying, she trembled in his tight embrace.

"We need to know how many others are here," Jack said.

"We need to be able to see," Worthington replied.

"My cell phone's missing." Gerry held on to Jack's arm.

"A phone would give us a little light," Elizabeth said.

"Does anyone have a cell phone?" Jack called out.

"I have one. No reception though." A far corner of the room brightened. The light cast an eerie hue around the man who had spoken, giving Jack the impression of someone from the spirit world. The room looked much larger than before. At least he couldn't see any cages or smell any chemical fumes. "Haven't had any service since the train."

"Most of our phones are missing," Sam said.

"Are the people near you alive or dead?" Jack yelled out.

"Both," the man replied. "My name's David, David Reinhoist. I'm with the University of California."

"I remember meeting you on the train. I'm Samuel Worthington. Remember? I'm the one that works for Helios Corporation."

"Sam? It's great to hear your voice. Does anyone know what's going on?"

"Not yet," Jack yelled.

"I'll come to you," David said. "Keep talking so I can find you."

The light floated toward them maneuvering around bodies.

"Where are we?" Gerry asked.

"I heard someone say Iraq," Jack replied. "I hope I wasn't dreaming because I tried to etch it into the floor with my pocketknife … when we were in the cages. Not that it'll do any good."

Gerry sighed. "I'm sure you were just hallucinating. Who'd let you keep a knife?"

Jack felt his pockets, empty. "I hope you're wrong," Jack said. If he imagined it, then there was nothing for anyone to go on to rescue them.

"Hey." David knelt beside them. "Got light. Just can't make a call. Damn phone."

As the light hit the floor, the reflection revealed their faces. Worthington, heavily bruised along the right side of his head, looked forlorn and defeated. Dried blood covered Gerry's face and neck. When she moved, she grimaced in pain. Examining her closer, Jack cringed. A large gash along the left side of her head needed several stitches. Jack hoped it wouldn't get infected. Maybe it was a good thing it was still bleeding. David looked dirty, but otherwise unscathed. And little Elizabeth's cheek and upper lip swelled to where her right eye remained closed. Tears stained her face.

"It's nice to finally see you," Jack said.

"Yes, it is," Worthington added.

"Now what do we do?" David asked.

"We take inventory." Jack glanced around the room. "We need to know who else is alive."

"They're black with green stripes," the young boy said. "And mean looking."

"What's your name, son?"

"Everest," the child replied. "Like the mountain."

"Well, Everest, like the mountain. Can you show me where you saw these fairies?"

"Sure," Everest replied. "And there's one still sleeping there."

Newberry followed the boy through the town. As they approached an older looking home, the boy darted into the backyard. Near several trees, the boy stood tall and proud. Newberry followed his gaze down to where the creature was partly covered by pine needles. Agent Newberry examined the little creature, wondering if the kid had just pulled him into an embarrassing hoax or something worse. He dropped to his knees to get a closer look. Using the back end of a writing pen, Newberry cautiously moved the thin spines off the little guy.

"This is one of your fairies?" he asked.

"They're not mine." Everest laughed.

"You actually saw this thing fly?"

"Lots of 'em," Everest explained. "They were all over my bedroom window. My mom said they were just moths. I didn't believe her. I hid in my closet."

"Smart boy." Newberry couldn't take his eyes off the dead creature. After snapping several photos with his cell phone, he called Devon. "I need you to see something, sir."

Sumner read over her notes again before walking up to the building. Correct address, she just couldn't believe it. A warehouse made from corrugated steel and rusting along the seams didn't look like a place where someone would live. The large windows, grungy from age, wouldn't need curtains. No one could see through them anyway. Behind her, the dock had long since rotted and fallen victim to the pounding waves. One lone car that probably hadn't started in years sat motionless in the empty parking lot. Weeds living among the concrete cracks had withered under the now thawing snow.

"Could she really live here?" Sumner asked as a chilling breeze swirled around her. Pulling her collar closer to her neck, she shivered. After rubbing her hand against her nose, Sumner shoved her notes into her jacket pocket. Time to find the entrance. Taking a couple of steps toward the tin door, floodlights blasted her from every side.

"Someone is here, somewhere," she whispered. "Hello?"

No answer. The parking lot remained silent. Taking another few steps, no new lights attacked her.

"Here goes nothing," she said.

"Do you often talk to yourself?" a gentle voice asked from behind.

Darn. This was exactly what killed her during the simulations. Sumner wanted to slap herself. Why she kept forgetting to check behind her, she had no idea. Turning around, she smiled.

"You must be looking for Kelly." Standing in the dimming afternoon light, the young man of about twenty resembled a saint. The water reflecting what was left of the sun engulfed him in an aura of innocence. It was as if Kelly's guardian angel had suddenly appeared from out of nowhere.

"Good afternoon." Sumner pulled out her FBI badge. "Do you know Kelly? Is she a relative or a friend?"

"We share an apartment," he said. "I'm Michael. Her boyfriend."

Sumner froze. *How can I break such horrible news to this precious, angelic guardian?*

"Kelly isn't home right now. She's on consignment and won't be back for another week or two."

"I see." Sumner couldn't remove her eyes from his stunning face.

"Is something wrong?" he asked.

Sumner nodded as her tears welled. She wanted to reach out to this man and comfort him somehow.

"Would you like to come in and sit? Maybe talk?"

Sumner nodded. She followed him through the old tin door, which squeaked loudly. Ancient hinges barely clung to the frame. After the door banged behind them, a dull yellow light cast an ominous glow throughout the empty warehouse. Aside from a few stacks of metal here or there, the place was otherwise vacant.

"We're on the third floor." He glanced over his shoulder. "Lift is over here."

Michael grunted as he pushed up on a metal grate. Once it clicked into place, he stepped onto the cracked, wooden platform, motioning her to follow. The floor sank a little from her added weight. She wondered if the old thing would fall apart, plunging her to a painful death. Michael tugged on the grate a few times before it fell into place. Moving a large lever on the wall to the number three, the elevator slowly moved. Loud grinding gears ricocheted off the concrete floor, rebounding between the metal walls. Michael scrunched up his shoulders and grinned as if to say *sorry*. Sumner nodded. She wasn't sure if she could have subjected herself to such a painful sound every time she needed to leave her home.

80

"We moved in about a year ago," Michael said over the noise. "Took us a while to get used to this."

Sumner glanced away. The thought of having to tell him about Kelly raked through her.

"This way," he said. As the grate clicked again, locking into place above their heads, they stepped directly into the loft. Most of the light came in through the skylights high above their heads. Now that the sun had settled in for the night, the room's dark shadows gave her the creeps. She shuddered.

Michael walked around turning on different lamps. Sumner knew right away which corner of the loft belonged to Kelly. Rows upon rows of canvas leaning against one another were her first clue. Sumner aimed straight for them. Picking up one of the smaller paintings, she sighed. The cup looked real enough to grab. As she moved the canvas in front of her, the cup moved with her. Kelly was a remarkable artist.

"She's amazing, isn't she?" Michael asked. "This one here's my favorite."

He held up a painting that gave Sumner the feeling of looking out a window and stealing a glimpse into a mystical world. As he moved the canvas, the waterfall in the distance bristled to life. A bird sitting on the windowsill looked real enough to fly away if spooked.

"Beautiful," Sumner said.

After he sat the canvas on the floor, Michael's gaze made her feel as if his essence had somehow penetrated her soul.

"I see your badge. This is about Kelly, isn't it?"

Sumner nodded as a tear ran down Michael's face. "I'm sorry," she whispered.

Chapter Eight

Devon glared at the dead creature encased in a clear plastic bag. When Agent Newberry handed the *thing* to him, he thought it was a joke. But the more he stared at it, the more it reminded him of something dark, something evil. Something his people had warned him about many years ago.

"Where did you find this?" Devon asked.

"My new friend found it." Newberry glanced over at Everest. "He showed it to me."

"And you knew where it was because?" Devon asked the child.

The boy had to be about seven or eight years old. Just a little taller than Devon's desk. Black curly hair dominated his small head. Large freckles splattered across his dark nose and cheeks asserted his innocence, giving only a hint of stubbornness.

"They tried to get into my bedroom," Everest answered.

"What's your name, boy?" Devon held the plastic bag next to his desk lamp to get a better view.

The creature was no longer than Devon's hand. Two arms and two legs attached to a small body that almost looked human, although way too skinny. Florescent green with sprinkles of red adorned the body and wings. The wings were translucent. Its head reminded Devon of a mouse or maybe a mole with long jagged antennae. The extra-long stinger didn't look like anything he'd want to have to fight off.

"I'm Everest," the child said. "Do you know what that is?"

"No." Devon reached for his reading glasses. "Do you?"

"Yeah." Everest smiled. "It's a fairy."

"Doesn't look like any fairy I ever saw," Devon said.

"You've seen a fairy before?" Newberry asked. Devon glared at Newberry from over the top of his reading glasses. Newberry coughed before glancing away.

Devon shook the bag a few times. The thing was definitely dead.

Another cold blast of air swirled around the room, and a tall, thin man walked through the door. The dirty white jacket that fell past the man's knees, along with the oily unkempt hair, was a dead giveaway as to the intruder's identity.

"Loomsbury," Devon said, holding up the bag with the dead creature. "Any idea what this could be?"

Loomsbury tilted his head. "Interesting. Never seen one this big."

"What is it?" Devon asked.

"*Mantispidae*." Loomsbury accepted the bag and studied the large insect. "Sometimes they're mislabeled as lacewings."

"A what?" Devon asked.

"Similar to a praying mantis," Loomsbury replied.

"It's a praying mantis?" Devon asked. "An insect?"

"Kind of," Loomsbury said. "But this one's the largest I've ever seen. Some people see these flying around a window and confuse them with fairies."

"It *is* a fairy." Everest slapped his hands on his hips.

"Close, but not quite." Loomsbury smiled down at the boy. "Cute kid. Yours?"

"Not quite," Devon replied. "How many of these did you say you saw, Everest?"

"Lots," Everest said. "They covered my window. And they carried flashlights."

"Luminescence?" Loomsbury took a closer look. "Now that is interesting. Could very well be. I can see little hairs on the abdomen. Perhaps that's what they're for."

"How can hair light up?" Everest asked.

"Chemicals," Loomsbury said. "The insect releases a chemical that runs through the follicles. When it reaches the ends, the hair lights up."

"That's cool!" Everest said. "Can I have my fairy back now?"

"I'd like to keep it," Loomsbury said. "If you don't mind."

"Could that thing sting a person?" Devon asked.

"Don't see why not," Loomsbury replied. "It has a pretty big stinger."

"Venom?" Devon asked.

"Possibly." Loomsbury kept studying the extra-large insect.

"Take it with you and let me know exactly what it is." Devon handed the boy a twenty-dollar bill. "Is this enough to cover the cost of your fairy?"

"Yeah." Everest grabbed the money. "Thanks, mister."

"You're welcome." Devon smiled. "Are there more of these things out there?"

"No," Everest answered. "All the others flew away."

"Did you see where they went?" Loomsbury asked.

"No," Everest replied. "Too dark. I think the train scared 'em."

"Loomsbury." Devon smiled. "May I ask a simple question?"

Loomsbury nodded.

"Since when do insects have fingers and toes?"

Scott's feet throbbed in his shoes from pacing the cold parking lot. "What's taking them so long?" He breathed loudly, his anger swelling from deep within. Tugging on his parka's collar several times, he trembled. A gust of cold air churned around him, slapping his legs with wet leaves. "I hate winter."

He watched a plane soar into the clouds. Grabbing hold of the chain-link fence, he pressed his face against the cool metal.

"Fucking bitch," he whispered between clenched teeth. "Where in the hell are you, Melissa?"

Taking in another deep breath, he lowered his head to use the links as a scratching post for his forehead. He woke up in the hospital with a headache, and it still plagued him. A plane's loud roar reminded him of his wife's nagging mouth. Rubbing his fingers lightly across the stitches that closed the six-inch gap on the back of his head, he sighed again.

The bitch actually hit me with a metal pipe. Has she totally lost her fucking mind this time? I guess money's more important to her than me.

The sounds of an approaching car grabbed his attention. Just a plain, black SUV. He watched as an older man stepped out, closed the driver's side door, and waved. After glancing around the parking lot, the man straightened his tie, tugged at his pants and headed straight for him.

"Are you Scott Lansing?"

Scott nodded.

"I'm Agent Mark Lumer." He held out a badge. "FBI."

Scott wasn't sure what to say.

"Confused?" Mark asked. "That happens sometimes. You reported you have information on some people you believe were kidnapped?"

"Um, yes."

"And you were mugged … out here?" Mark asked. "By your wife?"

Scott nodded and touched his stitches again. He winced as a sharp pain caused his eyes to water. *How could he know about Melissa?*

"Come, sit with me inside my car. It's cold out here. I won't bite. I promise. I'm a little too old for that."

Mark opened the passenger door. Either an invitation to defrost or to die. As more wind slapped his neck, Scott hoped his decision meant defrosting. *But then again, at this point what difference does it make?* His wife had already tried to kill him. Sitting inside the warm vehicle, he did feel a little better.

"How did you know it was my wife?" Scott asked once Mark closed the driver's side door.

"You just confirmed it for me. We know you're married." Mark smiled. "And we watched your wife move out of your apartment earlier today."

"You what —?" Scott wasn't sure if he should cry or jump for joy.

"Your landlord is a very talkative individual." Mark chuckled. "Most people are, actually, if given the chance."

"My landlord?" Scott repeated.

"We check everything," Mark said. "Now, tell me about the kidnapped people you believe you saw."

Anais stood in front of the brown-bricked Bradbury Building on South Broadway. Though she never liked Los Angeles, she still welcomed the warmer weather. No rain in the forecast and the air was a comfortable sixty-seven degrees. She wore only a light sweater over her silk blouse. Her bulky winter coat remained behind inside her hotel closet.

Her destination was suite 402, the corporate home of the Digital Artistic Society. Walking through the narrow building's entrance, the low ceilings reminded her of the alleyways of Paris. Her eyes fell across the filigree ironwork in the central atrium. As she admired the building from the inside, a small tour group strolled past. The place was mostly iron, wood or brick. *Absolutely amazing.*

"May I help you?" The guide must have just finished her tour.

Anais smiled. Again, most people could not ignore the pure-white woman in their presence.

"I'm Agent Ramsden." Anais held out her badge. "I have an appointment with the Digital Artistic Society."

"Certainly," the guide said. "Suite 402. If you'd follow me."

Entering the caged elevator, Anais remembered playing in one as a child. Paris was loaded with beautiful, quaint old buildings that were full of history and art. Her parents immigrated to the US before she was born. But annual trips to visit her grandparents meant precious time spent overseas. As the wheels clanked, Anais smiled, feeling as if she'd somehow come home.

"Here we go." The guide pushed open the gate. "It's just down the hall on your right."

"Thank you." Glancing up, Anais was astounded by the glassed-domed ceiling opening the place up to the morning sunlight. "Beautiful."

"Yes." The guide closed the elevator gate. "It is."

Anais walked slowly, immersing herself in the overwhelming beauty. When she reached the suite, she glanced over the railing for one last look before opening the door.

"May I help you?" the receptionist asked.

"Yes," Anais replied. "I have an appointment with Dr. Berrystein."

"You must be Agent Ramsden. Please, have a seat."

The small lobby comprised of a desk for the receptionist and two overstuffed chairs. There wasn't much room for anything else. Waiting, she checked her phone messages. All quiet, just the way she liked it.

"Agent Ramsden?" A woman, maybe in her fifties or early sixties, smiled at her from the small doorway.

"Yes." Anais jumped to her feet. "Dr. Berrystein?"

The woman nodded. "Follow me." Dr. Berrystein's office was just as small as the reception area. Enough room for a desk, a filing cabinet, and one bookcase. Anais sat in the only other chair. "How may we help you today?"

"I need to know where you assigned Kelly McGruffin. Who was paying for her service?"

Dr. Berrystein glared at Anais. "We do not give out that information." Dr. Berrystein tilted her head to one side, adding, "Client confidentality."

Anais studied the woman's face. Light age lines creased her eyes at odd angles, giving away the fact that she wasn't young anymore. Gray hair streaked with white also dated her. Makeup applied just right and a scarf of violet and yellow draped over one shoulder gave her a fresh and open appearance. Anais wondered how much effort it would take before Dr. Berrystein cooperated. *Or will I have to hand her a court order?*

"Dr. Berrystein," Anais said in a low voice. "May I show you a photo that I took of Kelly just yesterday?"

Dr. Berrystein nodded.

Anais pulled out a large color photo of Kelly lying on the train floor — covered in blood, the back of her head smashed to pieces, her brain, already liquified, pooled under her right shoulder. Anais looked at the photo for only a second before handing it to the woman.

Slapping her hand over her mouth, Dr. Berrystein gasped. "This is Kelly?"

Anais nodded.

"Who did this to her? Why?" Tears pooled in the doctor's eyes.

"That's what I've been assigned to figure out."

Shaking her head, Dr. Berrystein flicked her gaze between the photo and Anais.

"Let's start over," Anais whispered. "Who was Kelly working for?"

With her hand still covering her mouth, Dr. Berrystein nodded. "Of course. Of course."

"I counted forty-two dead just coming to you." David sat down next to Jack. "Some so close to it I almost added 'em in. But thought better of it. Best not to play god. We're in trouble here, aren't we?"

Jack nodded. "I believe so."

"I tried the door," Elizabeth said from the other side of Jack. "It's locked."

"I wish I could help," Worthington whispered.

"I think your ankle is broken." David patted Worthington on his good leg. "You just rest."

"Just sprained," Worthington said. "I can crawl."

"We need food and water." Elizabeth rubbed her one good eye. "Everyone's in bad shape, aren't they?"

"No windows and the doors are locked," David said. "I'd say things are pretty dire for us right now. And yes, young lady, I think many of us are in very bad shape."

"I agree," Gerry whispered.

"What if we banged on the door?" Worthington asked.

"I doubt if it'd do any good," Jack said.

"Let me give it a try." David stood.

It took him a while to get over to the stairs using just his cell phone for guidance. After climbing the concrete stairs, he banged on the metal door several times. When no one answered, he yelled out. Still, the door remained closed and locked.

"Well," Worthington said to the others. "I guess that answers that question."

Sumner waited patiently as Michael spoke to Kelly's parents on the phone. Although she gave him all the information she had or could give, the majority of their questions would have to wait. Sumner remembered when her mother told her that her father had died. The pain was unbearable. She must have cried for months. In many ways, delivering such news to another felt just as painful.

Placing the cell phone on the desk, Michael stared out the dirty window. "She's never coming home, is she?"

"I'm afraid not."

"How do I go on without her?" he asked between sobs.

"I don't know."

"What can I do to help?" he asked. "To find those responsible."

"Give me everything you have about her recent assignment. No matter how insignificant you may think it is."

"Certainly." He walked over to Kelly's little corner of the loft. "I'll log onto her computer. There might be something there."

Sitting in front of Kelly's computer felt weird, as if she were walking on sacred ground. Remembering her training, Sumner pulled up the internet and logged into The Agency's mainframe. She glanced up at Michael.

"Okay," Sumner warned. "Once I hit the *Enter* key, everything on this computer will be uploaded to my agency's server. Is there *anything* you'd prefer not be shared?"

Michael shook his head and looked away.

When she hit *Enter*, the screen blanked and the keyboard froze. After a couple of seconds, the screen flashed, *Agency Download in Progress — Please Wait*. As she waited, Sumner searched for the right words to soothe Michael, but she could think of nothing to say that would ease the pain of losing the woman he loved. Several minutes later, the screen blinked a few times before flipping back to normal.

"All done," Sumner whispered.

"There's something over here that might help." Michael opened a drawer in a small cabinet and pulled out a file. "Here."

Flipping to the first sheet, Sumner gasped. A list of the Sumerian gods stared back at her. *Anu, Enlil, Enki, Ereshigal* — they were all there. But why? Skipping past the list, a color photo of the ancient ruins of the city of Ur with the ziggurat visible in the background fascinated her. *Why would Kelly have a photo of the ziggurat?* Flipping to the next page, Sumner gasped at the photo. A carving of Pazuzu, the Sumerian king of demons, stared back at her. His evil face, a cross between a human and an animal, made her skin crawl. His body, with a lion's mane and feet like a bird, always gave her the creeps. Supposedly, Pazuzu's father was Satan. His brother was the archangel Michael.

A carving of the tree of life, similar to the one found on the train, appeared on another sheet. But this picture had more to it. Two figures sat next to the tree with a large snake off to one side. Not wanting to think about demons anymore, she closed the file.

"Where did this come from?"

"The company that commissioned her," Michael said. "The pictures in there made me nervous for Kelly's safety."

"I can see why. May I take this with me?"

Michael nodded.

"Anything else?" she asked.

"You may want these sketches, too." Michael pulled out three canvases.

"The fleur-de-lys," Sumner said. "Three different versions? How odd. This is the one that she used on the train."

"Kelly painted this inside a train? Why?"

"Have no idea. Do you know how much Kelly was paid?"

"Lots." Michael closed the drawer and pulled open another. "Here."

Sumner stared at the deposit slip — $500,000. "The check cleared? Didn't bounce?"

"It cleared," he replied. "Didn't bounce."

"They paid her in advance and then killed her?"

Michael nodded again.

"Did you ever meet any of 'em?"

"No. Wish I had though."

Sumner wrote down the bank account number in her notebook. She'd have the check traced tomorrow. "Follow the money," they told her in training. "You'll always find the answers if you follow the money."

With several canvases under one arm, the file tucked inside her briefcase and with a heavy heart, Sumner said her goodbyes to Michael. Leaving him alone at the empty warehouse just didn't feel right. As waves splashed onto the dock, she allowed her tears to fall. A full moon lit up the parking lot as if it were early morning. Looking into the night sky she wondered if any of this was real. *And where is God when you need him?*

As she slid into the driver's seat, her phone rang. "Agent Womack."

"Sumner? It's Mark Lumer. I have someone you need to meet."

Standing inside the empty warehouse, Mark wondered where and how anyone could move so many people so quickly. Maybe being close to the airport was a contributing factor. If that were the case, the missing passengers could be just about anywhere right now.

"How could they get rid of the cages so fast?" Scott asked as he paced the floor. "I mean, just a day ago, I was on top of 'em talking to Jack. We were right here."

Mark glanced over at the man and shook his head. Obviously, Scott was close to losing it.

"Hey," Scott yelled out. "You, agent person. Over here." Mark watched at Scott fell to his knees. *Is he going to kiss the concrete or something?* "Hey, man, get your ass over here!"

Mark hurried to the kneeling man. "Yes? You rang?"

"Look here. Jack left me a message."

Mark, now on his knees, stared at the etchings. "There's definitely something here. It's a scratch of some kind. I can hardly make out what it says."

"I see a capital *I* and an *r.*" Scott ran his finger over the scrapes.

Mark pulled out a small flashlight. As the light spread across the floor, the word popped out as if written in ink. "Iraq?" Mark stared at Scott.

"They took them to Iraq?" Scott asked.

"What's that drawing?"

"Looks like a pyramid or something." Scott said.

"There are no pyramids in Iraq." After reading something on his phone, Mark tilted his head to one side. "Believe it or not, five transport planes left for Iraq just this morning. How convenient." Tapping on his phone again, he waited a few seconds before saying, "Dr. Lewis, I have a lead ... yes sir. Five private transport planes left early this morning for Iraq. We also found the word *Iraq* scratched into the floor of this warehouse ... coincidental? I'd say so ... Yes sir. I'll be in touch." Mark sat back on his heels and rubbed his forehead. "Making plans to search overseas."

"I'm going too!" Scott demanded.

"Ah, no?" Mark said.

A grinding sound jarred Jack and David awake from a deep sleep. They covered their eyes and squinted. The blinding light was painful. Nudging Worthington and Gerry, Jack wondered if this was the end.

"Someone's coming," David whispered.

"Lie back down," Jack said. "Pretend you're sleeping."

"*Aistayqaz!*" It was a man's voice. "Wake up. Wake up! *Aistayqaz!*"

Not wishing to die today, Jack sat up. Pulling in all his courage, he yelled out. "We don't understand. What do you want us to do?"

"*Aistayqaz!*" the man ordered again.

"*Taeam,*" another voice said. "*Waqt alttaeam.*"

"What?" Jack shouted. "We do not understand."

"Get up!" another person yelled, stepping down the stairs. The men all carried automatic rifles. "Time to eat."

"We're hurt," David yelled out. "Some of us need medical attention."

"*Hadi!*" the first man said. "*Akl.*"

"They're saying it's time to eat." Gerry crawled over to Jack. "*Happy eating* is what they're saying. I don't see any food."

"I guess we'll have to wait," Jack said.

Several women entered carrying large plastic containers. They nodded as they sat the containers on the floor near the stairs. Wearing colorful clothing and what looked like scarves over their heads and covering their faces, the women nodded and waved their hands over the containers. It looked like they were urging them to come and see what they brought.

"Food?" Jack glanced over at David.

David stood. "Since I'm not hurt, I'll go see."

One of the women left behind a small lamp, which illuminated part of the large, cold room. David maneuvered around the sick or injured.

He bent down to see what was in the plastic containers, then reached in and pulled something out. Holding it to his face, he took a small bite.

"They've brought something to eat," David yelled. "And water!"

There was a stampede of those able to move.

"What about those who are hurt?" Jack hollered. "David, stop them!"

"He's right." David held out his hands. "Slow down, please. We need to share this. Can someone help me distribute the food?"

Several people raised their hands to volunteer.

"Great," David said. "We need to make sure that everyone eats something."

"We need to know who's still alive," Jack said.

Chapter Nine

Lewis read over Devon's report. Looking closely at the photo of the strange creature inside a plastic baggie, he scratched his head. "Connie?"

"Yes?"

"I need Loomsbury to come to my office."

"Will do." Connie's voice trailed off.

Lewis walked to the large floor-to-ceiling windows. Outside, all looked as it was supposed to. Trees swayed in the wind. A light snow covered the grass and shrubs. Blue skies, with just a few puffy clouds here or there, made for a perfect picture. Everything appeared tranquil and peaceful. The problem? Lewis held the photo of a very strange creature that looked eerily human.

A couple of knocks sounded before the door flew open. "You asked for me?"

"What is this creature? The one from the town where the train was abandoned."

"Not sure," Loomsbury said. "DNA results are not back yet."

"Could we be looking at DNA tampering ... again?"

"Perhaps," Loomsbury said.

"These creatures were flying around the night the town was asleep?"

Loomsbury nodded.

"Anything on the air quality?"

"No," Loomsbury replied. "Whatever it was dissipated by the time we took our samples."

"As soon as the DNA results are in, I want to know about it."

"Yes sir," Loomsbury said.

"Did the creature really have fingers and toes?"

Loomsbury nodded again.

"This is not good." Lewis turned back toward the windows. "Dismissed."

Loomsbury closed the door behind him.

"Connie," Dr. Lewis said into the air. "Get me Dr. Greghardt."

"Yes sir," she replied.

"I'll never get used to just talking into the air," Lewis said to no one but himself.

Connie's voice floated through his office. "Dr. Lewis, I have Dr. Greghardt for you."

"Allen, I'm concerned." Lewis said. "I just had a conversation with Dr. Loomsbury, and we may have another case of DNA tampering."

"This is not good," the deep voice replied. "If this is more tampering, we have a huge problem."

"I knew this issue wouldn't go away easy," Lewis said. "Tampering with human DNA seems to be the thing to do these days."

"I'll pull in a special task force if I have to." Greghardt coughed. "Should I brief the president?"

"Dr. Lewis?" Connie's voice interrupted the conversation.

"Yes, Connie."

"Mark Lumer's on a line. Says it urgent. Should I patch him through?"

"Yes, please," Lewis replied.

His new phone system was going to drive him crazy. Glancing over at his empty desk, he wondered if they'd ever use a real phone again. Now all calls were patched directly into his office through various speakers and microphones. All he had to do was talk, and the other party could hear him loud and clear.

Mark's voice filled the room. "Dr. Lewis, as directed, I've confirmed that at 1:45 this morning, five private transport planes left for Iraq."

"Dr. Lewis?" Connie interrupted the conversation, again. "I have Devon on the line now. He says it's critical that he speak to you."

"Great," Lewis yelled. "Patch him in. Let's just have a party in here."

"A little touchy, Jeff?" Greghardt asked.

"Dr. Lewis, Devon here. We may have a break as to where the missing passengers were taken."

"A break?" Lewis chuckled. "Mark, you go first. Where do you believe the missing passengers were taken?"

"Iraq," Mark replied.

"And, Devon, where do you believe they are?"

"In the ruins of Ur," Devon said. "Which just happens to be in Iraq."

"In my opinion," Greghardt said, "one plus one always equals two. And anytime two of our agents agree on something, I recommend we follow through."

"Devon," Lewis said running the different scenarios through his mind, "pack up but leave a small crew behind. Get yourself and your agents to the city of Ur. Mark, you go too."

"Iraq?" Mark asked.

"Is there a problem?" Lewis said.

"I had hoped my days in the desert were over," Mark replied. "Not a problem. See you soon, Devon."

"Who's left on the line?" Lewis asked the air.

"I am," Greghardt said. "I'll be in your office tomorrow. We can talk more then."

"Very well." Lewis sighed. "Connie?"

"Travel arrangements already made," Connie said.

Mark couldn't take his eyes of the beautiful, crystal-like woman. Every so often, Anais would glance at Mark who kept staring at her. Sumner flipped through a file she refused to share, and Devon didn't know if bringing a stranger to the train site was such a good idea.

"What's your name again?" Devon asked the confused-looking man.

"Scott Lansing."

"And you're here because?" Devon asked.

"Because this is all bullshit!" Scott huffed, agitated. "There were hundreds of them down there. All suffering. Hungry, dirty, hurt. I can't just sit here and do nothing."

"What do you want to do?" Devon asked.

"I don't know." Scott stood and walked to the window of the trailer. The train gazed back at him through the morning sunlight. It looked like it was thinking about something. "That's a nasty-looking train."

"She's hiding her secrets," Devon said.

Scott turned around and sneered at Devon. "I don't know who you are, nor do I care. But I'm going to find Jack Lawrence. I promised I would help him. I refuse to let that man down."

"You met Jack Lawrence?" Devon asked. "Personally?"

"Well, he was under me inside a cage at the time," Scott said.

"And what was he like?"

"What do you mean?" Scott asked.

"I don't know. There's something about the man that impressed me."

"He's tough," Scott said. "Here he was lying in a cage, hurt and dirty, and only cared about everyone else."

Devon shook his head. "I can't just take you with us." He had been searching an empty train, finding nothing, when this Scott Lansing stranger essentially appeared from out of nowhere and claimed to have met all of them. *Why is my luck so terrible and others' so great?*

"Why not?"

"Training for one," Devon replied. "Protocol for two. And —"

"And nothing, shit!" Scott scowled. "If it hadn't been for *my* phone call, you'd never have known about 'em. Give me some credit. I'm the one who passed out from the gas and —"

"Gas?" Sumner jumped into the conversation. "What gas?"

"There was a cloud of gas floating just above the cages. When I crawled over to Jack, I breathed it in."

"We could test your blood," Sumner said. "Get an idea of what they used?"

"Not a bad idea." Devon tapped on his phone. "Karl, can you take a blood sample for me? Thanks." He ended the call. "He'll be right over."

"What good will tests do?" Scott asked.

"It might give us an idea who we're up against," Mark said. "Let us know if it's military, or what?"

"So?" Scott asked. "Am I in or not?"

"Let me make a call. I'll see what I can do," Devon said. "I'll regret this, I'm sure. Alright team, we leave in the morning. Get some food and rest. We'll compare notes on the plane."

"Commercial?" Sumner asked.

"No," Devon replied. "Military. Better if we fly in directly."

The food didn't go very far and soon stomachs were growling again. Everyone was hungry. It took a while but working together they moved the dead to one side. Without something to cover them, the odor was almost unbearable.

"I can't just sit here and do nothing." David jumped to his feet.

"I'll go with you," Elizabeth said. "I don't want to just sit here either."

Jack tapped the back of David's leg. "Where are you going? What are you looking for?"

"Anywhere for anything," David replied.

As the two made their way toward the stairs, Elizabeth glanced back at Jack. "Jack's hurt and he's old."

"I know," David said.

"Do you think he'll survive this?"

"Don't know." David pulled out his cell phone and clicked on the light. "My battery won't last much longer. So, let's make the most of it while we can."

From the stairs they scanned the room. It seemed that the place was made from sand and mud. Very old looking.

"Let's follow this wall and see where it takes us." Elizabeth walked back down the stairs.

"Why not."

After a few minutes, the others were far behind, hidden within the darkness.

"This wall is very long." Elizabeth glanced at David.

"I didn't think it went this far back. I honestly thought we were in a smaller room."

She ran her hand along the wall and sand fell through her fingers. "We're underground."

"You mean like in a cave?"

"Maybe," she replied. "Your light's dying."

"Won't last much longer."

"We'll get lost in the dark." She kept her hand on the wall.

"Hope not. But what difference would it make? No matter what we do, we're dead ... eventually."

"Stop!" Elizabeth ordered, halting.

David bumped into her. "What is it?"

"There's something here."

"Something? Like what?"

She grabbed the phone from David's hand and shined the dim light toward the wall. They both gasped and stared at something very odd and evil that was carved into it — a figure of a human with large wings that reached over its head and fell past its feet. Feet that looked more like talons than toes.

"I've seen this before." Elizabeth traced her finger along a wing. The carving was larger than she was — six feet or more.

"Yes, I have too. This is the demon Pazuzu."

"Yeah, here's his scorpion tail."

"Look over here." David walked around her. "This looks like Lamashtu."

"The demon who ate babies for a snack?"

"See here? A lion's head with donkey teeth," he whispered and lowered his eyes. "It has to be her."

"Next to Pazuzu? I thought the Sumerians used Pazuzu to keep Lamashtu away."

"They did," David chuckled. "He was stronger than her. Him being male and she being female."

"Anything else around here?" Elizabeth asked.

"No, I don't believe so. Let's keep walking and hope my phone doesn't die."

Wearing an Army camouflage uniform, Scott strolled down the ramp of the large military transport plane. The airstrip seemed to roll out forever and looked larger than a ten-lane highway. Most of what he could see beyond the Ali Air Base didn't look promising. Just sand and more sand.

"Not as hot here as I thought it would be," Scott said to Sumner. He glanced at the Great Ziggurat dominating the horizon.

"No, it's not," she said absently. "Hey, Anais? The missing can't be here. The ziggurat is actually inside this base. How would they get them in here? How could they get past the guards?"

"This place will tell us more once we start snooping." Anais stared into the desert as she walked down the long ramp. "Don't forget that there were four sister cities at one time. All interrelated, Ur, Eridu, Uruk, and Nippur. The other three are just ruins now. Ur would be their best bet to get to where they want to be."

"Where do they want to be?" Sumner asked. Staring at the ziggurat, she shook her head and frowned. "Oh my. You want to search for the ancient forbidden room, don't you?"

"Forbidden room?" Scott asked.

"This way, please." A uniformed military man waved for them to follow.

Walking toward the Jeeps, Scott repeated his question. "What forbidden room?"

Sumner laughed at his curiosity, patting him on the back. "The ziggurats aren't supposed to be hollow. But none have been fully excavated. The Sumerians used bricks made from a mud clay. After many years of heavy rain, they eventually melted into a big heap of dirt and rock. That's why the structures have eroded away so badly."

"Then what room do you want to find?" Scott asked.

"It's supposed to be under the ziggurats," Anais replied. "Underground, not inside."

"Take a seat." The military driver pointed to the Jeeps as the group reached the vehicles.

Anais climbed into the front vehicle's back seat. Scott climbed in beside her.

"You see," Sumner said from the front seat, "each ziggurat is supposed to have many hidden rooms under them. In the ground."

"None have been discovered yet," Anais added. "That we know of."

"Then how can you say that they're there?" Scott asked.

"The Sumerians left behind stone tablets and cylinders full of their teachings. They tell of great rooms under each ziggurat where the gods would congregate. In other words, where the gods met and talked to the humans."

Scott chuckled, shaking his head. "Mythological stuff." He grabbed the roll bar as the Jeep jerked forward. "Bullshit stuff."

"No bullshit stuff," Anais yelled, trying to be heard above the engine's roar. "Real stuff."

As the Jeeps rumbled through the base, dust swirled in huge brown clouds behind them. Warm wind pelted their faces, stinging with sharp, cutting sand. Sumner slapped her hands over her eyes. Anais leaned forward and hugged her legs. Scott kept his eyes closed. Dust churned as the Jeep skidded to a stop in front of several large trailers. Coughing and sneezing, the small group climbed out.

"Where are we?" Sumner asked.

"Our home for the next several days," Devon replied. "Grab your things."

Their new home consisted of several small, white trailers. Climbing the few steps to one, Sumner opened the door and walked inside. Anais followed.

"Dusty." Sumner ran her fingers across a table.

"I guess we bunk here," Anais said. "We can clean up later."

Dropping their bags, they stared at each other, both obviously thinking the same things.

"There's a store on this base, girls," Mark said from the door. "It's not as bad as you may think. Let us get settled in and we'll go grocery shopping. Just watch out for camel spiders."

"Spiders?" Anais asked. "What spiders?"

"Who are you bunking with, Mark?" Sumner asked.

"Scott," Mark said. "Who else?"

"Devon bunks alone?" Anais asked.

"Yep," Mark answered. "Just the way he likes it."

For the rest of the day, the small group shopped and cleaned. Settling in took a little longer than expected. By nightfall, they were eating pizza at a very small restaurant on the base.

"The beds are hard." Sumner sipped her soda.

"Yes, they are." Mark pulled another slice of pizza from the platter.

"You've been here before?" Sumner asked.

"Many times," Mark said. "When I worked for the Space and Missile Defense Command in Huntsville. Almost got blown up a couple of times while in Iraq. You'll get used to it here."

"Will we get blown up?" Anais asked.

"I doubt it," Mark said. "We should be safe as long as we stay on the base."

"Good," Scott said.

"So, what's the plan for tomorrow?" Devon asked.

"We visit the ziggurat," Anais said. "Search where we can."

"And what are we looking for?" Mark asked.

"Anything with writing on it," Sumner replied.

"Okay," Devon said. "Let's get some sleep and we'll reconvene tomorrow morning at five."

Loomsbury stared at the odd creature. The body and wings sparkled in the light. Laying it on a glass slide, Loomsbury carried it to the electron microscope. He placed the slide on the platform, nudged it into place and closed the door. He stood back and sighed, pulled off his gloves and wondered if all the bad stuff was starting up again. Genetic splicing of the human genome was not only dangerous but also, in his mind, a crime against nature. As he sat at his computer, the image of the creature came into focus. Twice he blinked before he believed what he was seeing.

No hair, but the forehead reminded him of a concave shield. Up close, Loomsbury noticed two human-looking eyes. Unfortunately, they were shut, so he could not see the pupils. Maybe after dissection he'd get a better view. The nose resembled a dog but with the skin more pronounced. No cheekbones that he could see. The lips were definitely human. Between the lips, Loomsbury counted four sharp teeth.

Moving down to the neck, he noticed it was proportionately a little longer than a human's. The taut skin allowed him to examine the muscle tone. The human features amazed him; he traced an arm to the hand and counted six fingers and a thumb, each with nails. Looking at his own hand, he counted three knuckles. On the creature he counted four.

"How odd," he whispered.

The legs, like the neck, were much longer, perhaps twice as long relative to human measurements. A knee, ankle and foot. Similar to the hand, the foot had six fingers and a large toe. Otherwise, it was shaped as he expected. Between the legs were what looked like male genitalia.

"Definitely a penis and scrotum," he whispered to the screen. "This little guy is a guy."

Chapter Ten

Sumner slapped her hands on her hips. "It's five in the morning. And, we're standing on the top of this ziggurat. For what? I'm cold and I want more hot coffee."

"I don't have any to give you." Mark picked up an old stone and examined it. "You want us to look for words?"

"Yes," Sumner replied. "On walls or ceilings or floors."

"Floor is full of sand," Scott said. "Where's Devon?"

"He said he'd catch up," Anais replied. "Something to do with Dr. Lewis or something."

"There's not much up here," Mark said.

"That's why you have a shovel," Sumner sighed. "You honestly believe we have shovels just to lean on?"

"Funny," Scott answered. "Where do we dig?"

"Wherever the man says we can." Anais pointed to a man wearing a white shirt and khaki pants.

"Hello," the man said. "My name Dief Mohssein Naiif al-Gizzy. I curator here. My father curator here before me. His father before him." Dief was a little over five feet tall and wore his dark hair short. A neatly trimmed beard and mustache gave his suntanned face a shield against the sun's demanding rays.

"Nice to meet you, Dief." Sumner held out her hand. "I'm Agent Womack. But you can call me Sumner."

Dief clasped her hand and kissed it. "Nice to meet you, Sumner."

"I'm Agent Ramsden or Anais."

Dief took Anais's hand and stared into her angelic face. "You a goddess."

Anais smiled. "No, I'm no goddess. Just don't have any pigment."

"And you are?" Dief asked, glancing at the two men.

"Agent Mark Lumer and Scott Lansing," Anais said.

Dief shook their hands. "You look for Sumerian text on walls?"

"The older the better," Anais replied.

"All old, but I show you." Dief waved his hand for them to follow.

Walking through the rubble wasn't easy. Crushed brick sprawled out in all directions.

"American military help restore our ziggurat," Dief said as he walked. "Very good people."

"It's a beautiful place," Sumner said. "We *should* help restore it. After all, this place is our heritage, too."

"Yes, it is world's heritage," Dief said. "Okay, here some writing."

Sumner knelt before the brick. Examining it closely, she murmured, "Anais, hand me a flashlight."

"Sure," Anais said.

Shinning the light at the wall, Sumner frowned. "It's a date. The Sumerians used the moon to count the months. Twelve lunar months was a year to them. They had to insert an extra month about every four years or so to keep the seasons accurate."

"What does it say?" Mark asked.

"You read Sumerian?" Dief asked.

"I've studied the Sumerians ... so yes," Sumner replied. "It says it was built — or completed — in the season of *Emesh*, which means summer, on the day of one hundred and sixty-six. That would be during June or close to it."

"Anything else?" Dief asked.

"Yes, it says it was built to ... *accompany* — yes, the word means 'accompany' or 'to help' or 'be in addition to' — *our Anu, our Father from the heavens.* The word *an* mean 'sky' or 'heavens.' Everything the Sumerians did had something to do with heavenly bodies."

"If what you say is correct," Dief said, "then this place much older than we thought. Anything else?"

"No." Sumner stood. "Anymore?"

"Yes. Follow me." Def led them to the back of the ziggurat. "This is part of ancient wall. We have not worked much here yet."

"How high up are we?" Scott asked.

Anais glanced over the side. "Have no idea. Hundred feet?"

"Wouldn't want to fall off this thing." Scott rubbed his forehead.

"Tell yah what," Mark said. "You don't push me and I won't push you."

"You've got a deal," Scott replied.

Sumner knelt near the crumbling wall. "There's more here. I need a ..." Sumner dug into her small pack, pulling out a soft-wire brush. Sweeping it along the brick, years of caked-on sand fell. She gasped. "What is this?"

"What is what?" Dief knelt next to Sumner.

"This." She swept away more sand. "Wow."

The more Sumner used her brush, the more the artwork came to life. Two odd creatures with extra-large leg muscles faced each other. One looked more human than the other and held a tall staff. The other creature had the head of a bird, but a human body. The creature held something in its hand that resembled a pinecone. Each wore something similar to a wristwatch. The bird creature had a double set of wings and long, curly hair. The human creature wore a woven beard that almost reached his stomach, a headdress and, again, a double set of wings. Sumner's stomach tightened as she brushed away more sand.

"So, what do we have along here?" Sumner whispered. "Ah-ha. Another tree of life. Almost like the one carved on the train."

"It's different," replied Anais, dropping to her knees to get a better look.

"And look here. We have Ahura Mazda in his flying machine above the tree," Sumner said.

"Who's A-her Mazda?" Scott asked.

"Ahura Mazda," Sumner repeated. "He was 'the wise one.' Or the one true god of the universe. He was the center of the Zoroastrian religion."

"Never heard of Zoroastrianism," Scott replied.

"You probably wouldn't," Sumner said. "Zoroastrianism is almost extinct, but in many respects, its basic teachings are the foundation for today's religions."

"What's Ahura Mazda doing on Ur's ziggurat?" Dief asked.

"Good question," Sumner replied.

"Was he a god or a man?" Mark asked.

"He was both," Sumner answered. "During ancient times, rulers were often considered both a king and a god."

"So why the wings?" Mark asked. "Was he part bird or something?"

"No," Anais replied. "Scholars do not believe so. The bird wings are supposed to represent a craft of some kind."

"Like a spaceship?" Scott asked.

Anais nodded.

"Can you read this?" Dief asked.

Sumner concentrated. "'Only those pure as Ahura Mazda may enter through these walls.'"

"Enter where?" Scott asked. "I don't see any doors."

"I'm not sure." Sumner swept away a little more sand. "There's more. It says — No, wait! It's a warning of some kind."

"A warning?" Mark repeated. "I don't like warnings."

"Something about not entering the sacred …" Sumner sighed. "We don't have a word that matches this. The closest word would be something like *sky-space* or *airspace*."

"Airspace?" Scott repeated.

"Yes. Do not enter the airspace of Enlil without *ebebu*." Sumner sat back and tapped her head. "Ebebu … umm, purity … pureness … filtered."

"Like cleansed?" Scott stepped back and looked around.

"Maybe," Sumner said. "Let me rephrase to match our way of thinking."

"Our way?" Scott asked.

"Yes, we think differently than people thought a long time ago," Sumner explained. "Everything changes over time. Even the way we think changes as our culture changes."

"This is getting complicated," Scott said. "I just want to find Jack."

"'Do not enter the space of Enlil without pureness of heart,'" Sumner read. "There, that does it."

"Not for me," Scott said.

"We need to be clean," Anais added. "Are we clean?"

"Clean?" Scott asked. "You mean, as in taking a bath?"

"Maybe," Anais replied. "Or clean as in being a good person. Don't know."

"What about the Maza guy?" Scott asked.

"Enlil was a god," Anais added. "Seeing Enlil referenced is more common than Ahura Mazda. In some respects, they're interchangeable. Almost like a last name."

"It also says —" Sumner wiped away more sand. "— that the opening, the *bit*, um, the house? Yes, *bit* means house. Opening Enlil house — Wait. The word's *abatu*. Umm, 'destruction.' Ah, I see it now. Okay, are you ready?"

"No," Scott whispered.

"I think we're going to die," Mark stated.

Sumner laughed. "So negative, Mark. Okay, it says, 'Through Enlil's door to house, unclean is forbidden.'"

"Okay," Mark replied. "We won't track in any mud."

"You're Jewish?" Scott asked Mark. Mark nodded. "Aren't Jews hung up on being clean and eating only kosher foods?"

Mark smiled. "I guess you could say that."

"Then it fits," Scott said. "Judaism's been around a very long time. Maybe it started with the Sumerians. So being clean would fit."

"Interesting theory," Mark said.

"It's much more than that." Sumner raised her hand. "It's hard to translate because Sumerian words mean more than ours do. It's more of a warning, actually. Something like 'Danger, bringing in dirt will destroy you.' But not dirt such as disgusting or nasty."

"How could bringing in dirt destroy anyone?" Scott asked.

"When I worked for the Army, we had clean rooms," Mark said. "Especially when working on the space station. A little dust on a control board could destroy everything, everybody."

"True," Anais said. "I can think of many places where dirt would be dangerous. An operating room, circuit board factory, a wind tunnel."

"Okay then." Scott scratched his head. "We have to make sure we are clean."

"Where's the room?" Mark asked.

"I'm getting there." Sumner swept away more sand. "Why haven't you found this before, Dief?"

"I do not know," Dief replied. "I guess we have been busy in other places."

As the sand fell away, another carving grabbed her attention. Several humans with odd heads or headdresses stood near a door where it looked like a smaller man was being electrocuted.

"Are they zapping the guy?" Scott knelt behind Sumner and Dief. "Didn't know they had electric chairs back then. Sorry, I mean electric doors."

"They're not executing him," Sumner replied. "They're transporting him."

"Transporting?" Scott repeated. "You mean like 'Beam me up, Scottie?'"

"The Sumerian gods used portals," Sumner said.

"Portals?" Scott chuckled. "Hey, I think I like these guys."

"So where are these portals now?" Mark asked. "And will the portals lead us to the missing passengers?

"We dig," Anais said.

"Dig where?" Mark asked.

Standing up and brushing off his pants, Dief looked like he'd just seen a ghost.

"What is it?" Sumner stood and patted Dief on the back.

"I think I know where to look for this portal," Dief replied.

Devon stared out the window into the vast desert. After the conference call with Loomsbury and the others earlier, he wondered who was involved in what appeared to be a broad and diabolical attempt to alter human biology. Loomsbury believed the creature he examined to be real, which meant that someone was not only playing with genetics, they were actually creating new forms of life. And the three hundred missing people all hailed from the same scientific field. That was no coincidence.

Devon rubbed his eyes, wishing Carrie were there to help with the puzzle. He needed her more than ever, emotionally and professionally. At the sound of his phone ringing, his heart pounded. It was Carrie's ring.

"Hi, baby." Carrie's voice flooded a void he'd been harboring for a long time.

"Hi, sweetheart."

"What's wrong?" she asked.

"It's this case." Devon wiped his eyes. "I could use your help."

"Really?" Now she sounded excited. "How?"

Devon explained everything he knew. He wondered how crazy he sounded.

"Well," she said. "You always did seem to get the interesting ones."

"Can you help?"

"I don't see why not."

With tears filling his eyes, he rubbed his forehead and sighed. "Thank you."

"I'll call Lewis and make arrangements. Maybe I can be there as early as tomorrow. Would you like that?"

"Definitely," he said, not wanting to sound too excited.

"You're not sharing a room with anyone are you?"

"Nope. I'm all yours."

"You've always been *all* mine." She giggled. "Love you, Devon."

"I love you, too."

Staring at his now quiet phone, he chuckled. Why didn't he have more faith in their relationship? Why did he always doubt things when it came to Carrie?

As darkness closed in on them, David and Elizabeth hit a dead end.

"Now we know how far this wall goes." David felt the bricks in front of him and sighed.

"Maybe," she said. "But let's keep going anyway."

"Go where? We're at a dead end." Fearing that his phone battery would die completely, David clicked off the light. Now they'd have to use the wall to guide them.

"Just keep following the wall," she said. "If we get back to Jack and the others, then we'll know we're just in a big room."

"Fine." As he walked with his hand along the wall, the roughness of the bricks was suddenly replaced with a cold, metallic smoothness that gave him pause.

"What is it?" Elizabeth asked.

"There's a corner here. And the wall feels different."

"Yes, much smoother."

"Something's not right." David flipped on his light.

The sudden brightness almost blinded them. They were encased in a brilliant, yellow hue. From the floor up, the room — not a cave — was covered in what looked like pure gold.

"Cool." Elizabeth moved away from David.

"How big *is* this place?"

"Big," she replied. "Over here." Near a tall green pedestal sat several torches. "Do you have a lighter?"

"I don't smoke." He picked up a torch and smelled it. "Sulfur?"

"All adults smoke. Why don't you smoke?" Elizabeth shook her head. "Lighters are useful."

"Cancer of the lungs is not," he said.

"There has to be a way to light these. Help me look around."

Although his phone now gave off little light, it lit the golden room as if it were daylight. Knowing they had little time left, they frantically searched for anything that would bring a torch to life.

"What are these?" she asked, picking up several stones from a golden bowl.

"Maybe flint?" David grabbed two rocks. "Hold this." He handed his torch to Elizabeth.

Striking the two stones together, a spark flew into the air and circled before dying off. The next strike he held next to the torch. As the spark hit the material, the torch bloomed to life.

"Fire!" Elizabeth yelled. "Now I know how a caveman feels."

Using Elizabeth's torch, David lit his. "Let's explore this place."

"How did we end up in here?"

"I'm not sure." He studied the amazing artwork surrounding them. "It didn't seem like we went around that many corners."

High in the ceiling, carved archways covered in gold and inlayed with various jewels displayed an amazing kaleidoscope of color and brilliance. David had never witnessed anything like it. All along the walls, remarkable paintings and sculptures depicted everyday Sumerian life. Rows upon rows of jade columns filled the room. A crystal-clear pool reflected the beauty from the center.

"Are all the colors jewels?" Elizabeth asked.

"I believe so. These columns are definitely jade. I've never seen one this big. The red must be rubies and the purple are probably amethyst."

"It's beautiful in here," Elizabeth whispered. "What is this place?"

"There's a second floor above us." David pointed to a golden railing.

"How do you get up there?"

"Must be stairs around here somewhere," he said. "What's down here?"

Walking between the huge columns, an odd feeling of being home passed through David. But his home was simple walls with common paint. He'd never been in such a place before. *So why do I feel so comfortable?* It was as if he'd lived his whole life here.

"Another room?"

"Holy moly," David whispered.

Inside the second room, rows upon rows of sculptures towered above them, as if daring them to enter. Each was made from or covered in gold.

"Hey, aren't these lamassu?" Elizabeth asked. "Yes, they are. See their wings. They have a bull's body and a human head. Supposed to guard against evil. Why so many of 'em?"

David couldn't answer her. He was shocked beyond words.

"I'm going to count."

David watched Elizabeth's torch dim as she ran through the statues. The beauty of these magnificent creatures captivated him, placing him in a hypnotic trance that he couldn't or didn't want to escape from.

"There are too many to count," Elizabeth yelled out from somewhere in the room.

"I believe you'll find three hundred and sixty."

"Why that number?" she asked, running back to him.

"It's the number of the unknowable."

With forceps in his left hand and a scalpel in his right, Loomsbury cautiously cut the creature's body from its neck to just below its bellybutton. The skin, although tough looking, surrendered easily to his blade, as if he were cutting through water. Insects, having an exoskeleton, were usually hard. But this creature had soft skin and internal bones. Loosening the skin from the organs, he couldn't believe what he was seeing. He needed a closer look. He placed the creature back under the microscope, hoping he could make out more on his computer screen.

"Leonora?" Loomsbury yelled out.

"I'm right here," she said from across the room. Leonora Priddleton was young, only a few months past her thirteenth birthday. Always wearing her dark black hair in braided ponytails, she looked even younger than her actual age. But her maturity was closer to a forty-year-old woman. Dark ebony skin accented with dark-rimmed glasses enlarged her pure-black eyes. Standing at just a little over four and a half feet, her lab coat brushed along the floor as she walked over to him. Light-pink tennis shoes with green shoestrings poked out from under her white lab coat. Loomsbury chuckled. She never ceased to amaze him, and he admired her for her wisdom and great mind.

"This is impossible!" he said.

"What is impossible?"

"This thing has both human and insect organs. The heart and lungs are definitely human. However, I see a gut and a midgut. How could this thing even exist?"

"Impossible." She waved her hand in the air. "It could not have been alive."

"But it was." Loomsbury cocked his head to one side.

"Then someone is messing around with genetics again."

"I think this is the venom sac, here." Loomsbury zoomed in closer. "I've got to know what's in it."

He placed the little creature back on the table and carefully dissected out the small organ. Sitting it inside a petri dish, he sealed his little treasure with a lid.

"Would you like to run the tests?" he asked, handing her the dish.

"If you wish." Leonora took the small container and raised it to her eyes.

He could almost feel her fear and knew she didn't want to have anything to do with it. However, she was the best technician in The Agency, and if he wanted answers he could trust, she was the person to assign.

"I wish."

Standing under an elaborate archway near the base of the ziggurat, Sumner couldn't believe what she was seeing. Two protective deity statues guarded an entrance. *But an entrance to where?* These mythological creatures with human heads, the bodies of bulls and bird wings had to be over twenty feet tall.

"What are these things?" Scott asked.

"Lamassu," Dief replied.

"They're the illuminators of the constellations," Anais said from behind. "They open the gateways to the stars."

"They have too many legs," Scott said. "Why five?"

"No, only four," Sumner replied. "You see, the two front legs are for looking at them from the front. But if you stand on the side, you will only see four."

Scott walked over to Sumner and chuckled. "I see it now. Very ingenious. So, from the side view, the things are walking, and from the front view they're standing still."

"Exactly." Sumner patted him on the back. "Hang with us — you'll get it."

"A tetramorph," Anais said, "symbolizes the combining of four elements into one."

"What elements?" Scott asked.

"Elements of the zodiac," Sumner replied. "The ox or bull, the lion, an eagle and a human."

"Taurus, Leo, Scorpio and Aquarius," Anais said.

"Matthew, Mark, Luke and John," Mark added, walking past them into a small chamber. "The four gospels."

"Confusing," Scott replied.

The chamber behind the two statues had just enough room to fit everyone. The low ceiling allowed even Anais, who barely reached five foot four, to touch it. Standing arm to arm and back to back, they stared at the brick walls.

"Why are we all just standing in this tiny room?" Mark asked.

"Good question." Dief squirmed as the others pressed into him.

Staring at the wall mere inches from her face, Anais whispered, "I smell water."

"I do too," Sumner said, from near the entrance.

"How does one smell water?" Mark asked.

"Musty, damp," Anais replied. "It feels wet in here."

"I don't feel very stable," Mark said.

"Claustrophobic?" Anais hit Mark's shoulder with the side of her head. No one could raise their arms. Not enough room.

"No," Mark said. "The floor feels, I don't know, brittle?"

"Brittle?" Sumner asked.

"It's as if the floor's not strong enough to hold us," Mark said.

"Now that you've said it," Sumner replied, "it doesn't feel right."

"I recommend we leave." With Scott's one step, the floor vibrated slightly before disintegrating, leaving only empty space between them and what waited far below.

Chapter Eleven

"**U**nknowable?" Elizabeth asked. "What's unknowable? I never heard that concept before."

"I believe we have stumbled into the house of Anu," David replied.

"*Anu*?" she repeated. "You mean — *the* Anu?"

David nodded.

"Impossible. He's only a myth."

"So you say," he said. "Is our god real?"

"Of course."

"Have you seen him?" he asked.

"Of course not."

"Then how do you know he is real?" David approached a wall and stared at it for a moment before raising his torch high above his head and touching it to the smooth surface. Flames shot up from along the walls, instantly lighting the chamber. From where they stood, hundreds of doorways and stairways popped out of the darkness in all directions.

"How did you know to do that?" Elizabeth asked.

"I didn't. I had a hunch. In the ancient text, Anu's house was lit by oil that ran through channels along the wall — just above his head. I figured if this were Anu's place, it would work. And it did."

"We need to tell the others." She pulled her hair behind her ears.

"I believe *out* is this way," he said, trying to retrace their steps.

"So why is Anu *unknowable*, and how does three hundred and sixty fit into it?"

"What did your parents study?"

"Sumerian burial rituals," Elizabeth said. "Why?"

"If they had studied the Sumerian gods, then you would have heard of the unknowable."

"Teach me." She followed him as he searched for their entry point.

"The Sumerian gods relied heavily on the cycles of the sun and moon. Which, by the way, is twenty and thirty days, respectively. Or the number three."

"Three?" she repeated. "Okay and how do you get three from two-thirds?"

"Ratio. The difference is a third or three. Now multiply the sun by the moon and you end up with six hundred."

"Six hundred ... one-third ... I don't get it." Elizabeth stepped out of the golden light and into the darkness of their original path

Holding the torch in front of him, David stayed near the wall so they wouldn't get lost. "What numbers do we have? We have a three, a six and a two. The ancients divided the day into time-miles or a Babylonian mile. Since a day is one revolution of the earth, the ancients divided that one revolution into twelve parts."

"Twelve parts?"

"Twelve hours," he said

Elizabeth nodded.

"If we subdivide a time-mile into thirty parts, we get three hundred and sixty subdivisions. Or the degrees of a circle."

"What's so unknowable about that?" she asked. "That's just ... a circle."

"First, where did the three hundred and sixty degrees come from? Someone didn't just pull it out of thin air. It meant something. Something that related to the moon and sun."

"I still don't get it."

David stopped walking. "Turn around." He tugged on her arm.

"We're going back?"

"No." Using his free hand, David helped her turn around in a circle.

"Okay, now what?"

"This is the unknown."

"I don't get it," she said.

"The area of a circle will forever be unknown. The nature of Pi keeps us in the dark. Wherever there is a cross, there is also an invisible circle." David knelt and traced a large cross on the floor. Then, where the two lines intersected, he drew a smaller circle.

"I've seen that symbol on churches." She studied the lines. "Wait, I think I understand."

"The Sumerians always asked whether there was substance to our universe. If yes, where does the spirit or god-thing dwell? How can one prove that the spirit exists when there is also matter all around us? The two cannot coexist unless one is a veil of the other. If there is matter, then there is a god-veil. And vice versa. Unfortunately, there's no way to prove it."

"I thought I had it," she said. "But I just lost it."

"You were born?"

"Yes," she replied.

"And you've grown and learned?"

"Yes."

"Eventually, you will marry and have your own children."

"Maybe, someday."

"Then your child will grow and learn. Am I right?"

"Probably."

"The circle of life, Elizabeth. Three hundred and sixty degrees of an unknowable. Where will it end? Where did it start? In other words, which came first, the chicken or the egg?"

"Whoa. The Sumerians thought that deep all those years ago?"

"Deeper, actually. According to the Sumerians, we invited the gods into our lives by allowing ourselves to live in the unknowable."

"The mysteries of life," she said. "Reminds me of Adam and Eve. Living their life of innocence. Once they ate from the fruit of knowledge, they were forbidden to remain in the garden."

"Exactly."

Almost tripping over someone, she whispered, "I'm so sorry."

"So, we're back where we started from," David said.

"In more ways than we know," Elizabeth added.

"David? Elizabeth?" Jack hollered. "Is that you?"

"Yes," David replied. "Wait until you see what we've found."

"Some of us were taken," Jack yelled out. "They came and took some of us away."

"How do you know who was taken?" David asked.

"For one, the dead bodies are gone." Jack wiped his forehead with the back of his hand. "And several folks are asking. People are missing, David."

"Not good." David said as Elizabeth peeped around him. "Let's take roll. We know how many we started with. Let's see how many are here now."

"The venom is from a wasp?" Loomsbury read over Leonora's findings a second time. Shaking his head, he added, "Impossible."

"That thing" — Leonora pointed to the dead creature — "is unnatural and just plain evil. If a person were to get stung by it, they probably would die. The venom's over a million times stronger than a regular wasp. On most insects, the stinger is also for laying eggs but there's no evidence of that here. No peptides or enzymes. There are several tubes or veins present, and I have a nasty suspicion what one of them is for."

"And what would that be?" he asked.

"Extracting blood."

"Excuse me?"

"See here, on the film." Leonora handed him the negative. "There are several tubes and one goes directly into that little pouch. When we tested the substance, it was human blood."

"So, these creatures would sting a person, maybe kill a person, and then steal their blood?"

"Something like that," she said. "I'm not sure of the exact order."

"We need to find out where these creatures came from." Loomsbury glanced down at the papers again. "The boy said there were several of them flying around that night."

"Do we know for certain if they stung anyone?" Leonora asked.

"Not that I am aware."

"Probably a good thing," she said. "Anything else I can test for you before I leave for the night?"

"Yes, check it for reproductive organs."

"The thing has a scrotum and penis." She giggled. "What else do you want to know?"

"Are they working?"

She laughed. "Not anymore."

"I meant, when it was alive."

"Fine." She shook her head. "I'll check." Leonora giggled again before adding, "Can you find me a female to test it out?"

"I can't find my agents," Devon reported to the base commander. "I'm worried."

"Our curator is also missing," the base commander replied. "I'll dispatch a search party in the morning. It's too dark and dangerous now."

"Useless piece of shit," Devon hissed once the man walked away.

Standing in water that just topped her shoulders, Sumner coughed as she wiped her eyes. "Is everybody okay?"

"I am," Mark replied.

"I'm all right," Anais said.

"Scott? Dief?" Sumner yelled. "Scott? Answer me."

"I have Scott with me," Mark said. "He's hurt, but he's breathing."

"Where's Dief?" Sumner splashed through the dark water. "Help me find Dief."

As the water-world lit up, Sumner glanced over at Anais. "Thanks."

"You're welcome." Flashing her light around the room, Anais yelped. "Over there!"

Dief, leaning against one side, didn't look so good. As Sumner scooped him up in her arms, his body almost slipped from her grip. "Dief?"

"Let me see him." Anais splashed over to them. "He has a pulse."

"Thank God." Sumner held back her tears.

"Where are we?" Scott asked.

"Are you okay?" Sumner asked.

"I think I hit my head," Scott said. "What the hell happened?"

"The floor gave out," Mark replied.

Anais flashed her light toward the ceiling. About two hundred feet above their heads, a small rectangular hole remained threateningly dark.

"Well, we're definitely not going to get out the same way we came in," Scott said.

Angling her light around the small enclosure, Anais sighed. With no way out, they could end up sitting in their watery grave forever.

"Will they come looking for us?" Sumner asked.

"Of course," Mark replied. "Unfortunately, they don't know exactly where we are. Remember, Dief hadn't told anyone about this place yet."

"Great." Sumner studied the small area. The water room was much larger than the opening high above. A small brick ledge just above her head wouldn't be wide enough for them to climb on. The walls, made of brick and rock, looked sealed. No hand or foot holds. Their future didn't look too bright at the moment.

"Then, we wait," Anais whispered.

With the morning light came more frustration for Devon. Standing next to the base commander, he wasn't sure if he should yell at him or just cuss him out. The man was an incompetent jackass. Wanting to be somewhere else, Devon went inside and paced around the small office in the command center. Before his anger reached its boiling point, his phone rang.

"Arvol here."

"Devon?" It was Carrie.

"Where are you?"

"Just landed," she replied. "Where are you?"

"In the command center."

"Good, I'm heading your way now."

Running through the tiny building, Devon almost tripped out the door. The bright sun blinded him for a few seconds before he focused on a Jeep bouncing in his direction. To his relief, a woman with long blonde hair waved at him from the passenger seat.

"Carrie!"

She jumped from the rolling vehicle, and Devon grabbed her in his arms just before she hit the ground. Swinging her around in circles, the feel of her body filled him with renewed hope. "Thank you, God," he whispered to the heavens. "Thank you."

"Hi," she said as they stared into each other's eyes.

"Hi," Devon whispered, bending down to kiss her. "Thank you for coming."

Her warm kiss was invigorating. As his heart bloomed with love, a large smile covered his face. He never could hide his true feelings from her.

"I missed my husband." She pulled away from him. Her eyes, emanating a deep concern, bothered him. Devon could tell she was hiding something. "Let's get my things."

With her bags stacked in the base commander's office, Carrie held Devon's hand as the Jeep bounced them toward the ziggurat. The enormous structure grew as they got closer. So did Devon's heart. Maybe she was finally over losing their baby. Maybe she finally realized it wasn't her fault. It just wasn't the right time.

After jumping from the vehicle, she frowned at Devon. "So, you've lost your agents?"

"I didn't lose them," he said. "They just never came back last night."

Carrie shook her head. "How do you know they're here?"

"This is where they said they'd be."

"Since when does that matter?"

Together they climbed to the top of the ziggurat. Carrie walked around, looking for clues. Devon called in to touch base with the useless commander.

"I found footprints around back," she said. "They lead back here. Obviously, they were looking for something. Wait a minute." Yanking out her cell phone, she picked out Agent Mark Lumer's number first. When she received a voice recording, she glanced over at Devon. "Who else is on your team?"

"Sumner Womack and Anais Ramsden. You already know about Mark. But none of them are answering their phones."

"I'll still try the others." Since her Agency phone housed all Agency numbers, she tried Agent Womack. No answer. When she tried Agent Ramsden, static hit her ears. "Got 'em. Anais's phone must be on. I can trace 'em."

"How do you do these things?" Devon asked.

"Unlike you," she laughed, "I hang around with Loomsbury." Carrie tapped on her phone, then waited. "Hey, they're almost directly under us."

"Under us?" Devon repeated.

"There's no way to get under this thing," one of the men in uniform said. "It's solid."

"Well," Carrie said, heading for the stairs and the long walk down, "obviously, there *is* something under here that isn't as solid."

At the base of the ziggurat, Devon glanced around. "What's your idea?"

"What's that building over there?" Carrie pointed to a group of small ruins. "My signal seems stronger in that direction." She took off at a jog. Once she reached the ancient structure, she waited until Devon caught up with her.

"Will you quit running off?"

"I'm not running off. I'm rescuing your agents, the ones you lost. This place looks like an old temple." Carrie stared at the decaying structure. "These were once columns. Before they crumbled halfway to the ground."

She circled the small building and entered through an opening on the side. Using her cell phone as a guide, she followed the signal. When she reached an old archway with two huge lion–human statues, she paused.

"Hmmm." She smiled. "Wonder what we have down here?" Stepping into a smaller area behind the statue, she flipped on her flashlight. "Hey, there's been a cave-in."

"A what?" Devon asked, running up to her.

"Whoa there, cowboy." Carrie pulled him back. "I don't need you falling in, too." Dropping to her knees, she flashed the light into the hole. "Hello? Anybody down there? Any lost agents perhaps?"

Several loud cries echoed back.

"Get me some rope!" Devon ordered their escort. He knelt next to Carrie. She smiled and he shook his head. "You have a knack for this stuff."

"And you don't," she said. "You just like to go after the bad guys."

"There's something odd about the venom." Leonora held the results in her hand.

"Oh?" Loomsbury walked over to her.

"Very odd. For one, LD95."

"A 95 percent lethal rating?" he whispered. "We need to find out where these creatures came from." Loomsbury glanced down at the glass box. He didn't like where this case was leading.

The hot water running down Sumner's face felt heavenly. As steam filled the room, she filled her lungs with the damp, clean moisture.

"Are you alive in there?" Anais yelled through the door.

"Out in a minute," Sumner yelled back, turning off the water.

Examining herself in the mirror, she counted sixteen cuts and scratches. Although given a clean bill of health, she was relieved when the doctors also gave them antibiotics. Two pills a day for the next ten days. The last thing she needed was to suffer through a strange exotic disease.

"Feeling better?" Anais asked as Sumner opened the bathroom door.

"Much." As Sumner dressed, a light knock echoed through their small trailer.

"I'll get it." Anais jumped up. "Hi Carrie."

Carrie smiled as she stepped through the door. "I wanted to talk to you about that water-room we found you in. I think it was an elevator at one time."

"An elevator?" Sumner repeated.

Carrie nodded.

"How could it be an elevator?" Anais asked. "They didn't have electricity back then."

"Maybe," Carrie replied. "They did have ropes and pulleys."

"Jack, you're right. Someone took the dead."

Elizabeth frowned and sat down next to Jack and Worthington. She stared up at the golden ceilings. "Everyone else is here now. But fifty are missing, and I still don't know where my parents are."

"What's the last thing you remember?" Worthington asked.

"Falling asleep next to my mom," Elizabeth replied. "How about you?"

"Reading a magazine," Worthington answered. "What about you, Jack?"

"Just finished dinner. Received a call from my fireman …" He trailed off.

"What is it?" Worthington leaned forward, gripping Jack's arm.

"My crew," Jack replied. "I had two brakemen, a junior engineer and a fireman. I haven't seen them since I woke up in that damn cage."

"There're a lot of people here," Worthington said. "We started off with almost three hundred. They could be anywhere."

"No." Jack shook his head. "They would have found me by now."

"What else do you remember?" Elizabeth asked.

"As I was saying, just finished my dinner. Mac called over the radio and said something about a disturbance of some kind. Then nothing, except waking up in that damn cage. I want to explore these golden rooms."

"Everyone does." Elizabeth giggled. "David said we'll be safer here."

"We've accounted for everyone who's left." David took a seat next to Jack. "We have no food. But at least there's water. Although we don't know how safe it is to drink."

"We're going to die without food anyway," Jack said. "So what difference does it make now? Let them drink and be a little satisfied."

"Many are exploring the halls and stairs." David rubbed the back of his neck. "Gives them something to live for. Renewed energy."

"Good," Jack said. "I wonder if our captors will come looking for us once they discover we're gone."

"I'm sure they will." David sighed. "Yah know, discovering this place would have made all the difference in my life once. But now ..."

"I know," Worthington said. "Just think. All of us here except for you, Jack, would have given our lives to discover such a place. Knowing that we'll die soon takes all the fun out of it."

"Not for me." Elizabeth jumped to her feet. "I'm going exploring."

"The swelling on your face has gone down a lot," Jack said. "Your lips are almost normal again. Has anyone seen Gerry?"

"She ran off with a couple of her friends down one of the hallways," Elizabeth said. "I have my own torch. I'm going to see what I can find."

"Don't go too far." Jack winked at her.

Chapter Twelve

Standing on boards just inches above the water, Sumner and Anais examined the bricks.

"They're old," Anais said. "I wonder how old."

"Thousands of years." Dief stepped off the rope ladder and onto a wooden platform.

With lights mounted from above, the room looked smaller than when they were trapped inside.

"I wonder if the divers found anything." Sumner glanced into the water.

"We'll find out shortly I'm sure," Anais said.

"There are some strange markings on the walls." Sumner rubbed her hands over a rough section. "See here. These grooves. I'll bet there were boards here once."

"I agree," Dief said.

"Afternoon." A man's voice echoed from above.

"Hello?" Sumner glanced up as a man climbed down.

"I'm Dr. Woolley. I'm here to assist you."

"And what exactly are you a doctor of?" Anais asked.

Stepping off the rope ladder, Dr. Woolley held out his hand. He was of average height with dark hair and eyes, and he was wearing an officer's uniform. Anais thought he was handsome. When he saw Anais, he froze.

"I know." She smirked and shook her head. "I look like a goddess. Now what are you a doctor of? And why are you here?"

"Mechanical engineering, but my minor is ancient civilizations. I study ancient structures. I'm here to assist you."

"Great," Anais said. "Then start assisting."

"Name's Aaron, Aaron Woolley."

"Officer?" Sumner asked, shaking his hand.

"Lieutenant Colonel." He stared at Anais.

"Well, I'm Sumner and this is Anais, and this here is Dief." Sumner smiled as the men shook hands. "We're studying these grooves in the wall."

"I'm sorry," Aaron said to Anais. "I do not mean to stare at you."

"Yes you do. I'm an albino. Not full blown, just partial."

"She almost glows in the dark." Sumner giggled. "Now, can we get to work?" As Sumner ran her hand over the wall, bubbles erupted around them. A diver poked his head out of the water, and Anais bent to assist.

"We found old boards and some chains. Maybe a drain, but we're not sure."

"All hooked up," one of the men yelled.

Dief glanced around. "Normally, this isn't how we work."

"I know," Sumner said. "But this is a special case."

"What can it hurt?" Anais asked.

"Depends," Dief said.

"Depends on what?" Scott asked.

"On whether or not it's a trap." Looking defeated, Dief added, "Give the order to go."

Aaron nodded. "It's a go," he said into his radio.

The two lines of men outside the hole gripped the chains attached to the boards at the bottom of the well and heaved. As the chains tightened, the small group took several nervous steps away from the old temple. The men holding the chains jerked on them twice, and then something gave way, and the chains dropped to the ground.

"Now what?" Aaron asked Sumner. "Halt!" he said into his radio.

"That wasn't very exciting," Anais said.

Carrie ran to the two large statues and glanced into the small room. Everything looked fine. The men pulled the chains from the hole, and she laughed when they hauled out a round metal handle still connected to several planks. A gurgling sound, as if a plug had just been pulled, echoed from the hole.

"Can we have the lights back on?" she yelled. Staring into the darkness, she shrieked with excitement as the lights blared to life. "The water's gone. Bring a longer ladder."

Walking through the golden hallway alone felt a little odd but also exciting. Elizabeth kept glancing over her shoulder. *Good, no one is following.* The mythological creatures carved into the walls were intriguing, but it was obvious that she was walking in circles. She'd passed the same faun fighting with a human twice. Pulling off a chip of wood from her torch, she laid it on the floor. If she passed this way again, she'd know for sure she had retraced her steps.

Passageways led off in all directions, but not wanting to get lost, she stayed in the main hallway. At the end she made a left turn. She studied the hybrid creatures — half snake and half human. Several more steps and she made another left. Down this hallway, creatures that were half fish and half human adorned the golden walls. Soon she was passing the harpies — half human and half bird. After making another turn, she found the centaurs. Then she was back with the fauns, and there was her little chip of wood. Right where she'd left it.

"So," she said to no one. "This hallway is a complete square. I think I'll try this doorway. It should lead me to the center of this maze."

Glancing through the large entryway, she couldn't believe what she saw. The walls were no longer gold but pure white. Another hallway. With her torch lit, the smooth and shiny walls were as bright as a noonday sun.

"White gold," said a voice behind her.

Almost dropping her fire, Elizabeth faced a smiling David. Sighing with relief, she then snarled. "Don't do that!"

"Sorry. Didn't mean to frighten you."

"Well, you did."

"What did you find?"

"That the hallway has lots of great carvings, but it's just a big square. Wanted to see what's in the middle."

"Mind if I join you?"

"Did Jack send you to spy on me?"

"Kind of," he said.

"Great." Elizabeth stepped into the pure-white hallway. "So, what do you think this place is?"

"Have no idea. This whole complex is way beyond my knowledge. I study languages, not art."

"I bet we're in another square maze." Elizabeth smiled. "Sumerians built lots of these. Let's go through that door there. Maybe we'll find the middle."

"Sounds good to me. After you, my lady."

Stepping through the next doorway, Elizabeth froze. This time, the walls and floor and ceiling were a sparkling, crystalline red.

"Rubies?"

"A mosaic of rubies." Elizabeth stared at the pearly-white four-legged creatures, stacked one on top of the other, that stood out in stark relief on the blood-red walls.

"Amazing," David whispered. "Unicorns? Made from what?"

Elizabeth stepped closer. "The white isn't a stone. Bone maybe? Hope it's not human. That'd be gross. This thing over here has to be a bull, but what's that thing?"

"A very skinny something." David laughed. "Look, another doorway."

"Let's go." Elizabeth walked toward it. Allowing her torch to take the lead, she gasped when they entered the pure-blue room. "I know what this stuff is."

"What?"

"Lapis lazuli," she replied. "It's a blue stone. My mom and dad were studying it. They believed it was used to allow the kings into heaven. There's so much of it here. This is a very rare stone."

"We're also not in a hallway anymore." David walked into the center. "We're in a chamber. What's this stuff?"

Elizabeth stared at the heap of junk in the middle of the room. After a while, she laughed. "I don't know."

David examined the remains more closely.

"A large beautiful room full of rotten wood," she said.

"I wonder what this was … originally?"

Elizabeth suggested, "Maybe a table and chair? But for what?"

"Any idea about this place?" David asked.

"Ur-Nammu maybe? Do you see any writings anywhere?"

"No," he replied.

"Then let's keep searching."

Climbing out of the square hole, the man in uniform didn't look happy. "That rope ladder is only a hundred feet. We're nowhere near the bottom."

"Let's get more rope over here," Aaron ordered.

"Yes, sir," the young man replied.

"I think we're going about this all wrong," Sumner said.

"What do you mean?" Aaron asked.

"I doubt if he examined the walls as he climbed down," she replied. "If you didn't want someone finding what you were hiding, you wouldn't put it at the bottom of a pit. That's like an *X* marking the spot. Someone went to a lot of trouble to plug it up and add water. I'll bet there's a hidden passage on one of the walls."

Aaron stared at Sumner, then nodded. He ordered several harnesses and ropes using his radio. "We'll go down together. All four of us. Each will have a wall to examine. Anais, you and Sumner and Dief will join me."

"Sounds like a plan," Devon agreed.

"Found 'em," Leonora stated. "The turkeys couldn't hide from me."

Loomsbury glanced at her as he filled the coffee pot with fresh grounds. "And?"

"You're aware that human DNA cannot be patented. Right?"

Loomsbury nodded.

"Supreme Court ruling back in 2013 or so," she said. "However, they did allow for cDNA to be patented."

Loomsbury cocked his head to one side as he filled the small machine with water.

"Synthetic DNA?" she hinted.

Loomsbury shook his head. "I wonder when we'll get one of those coffee-by-the-cup machines."

"You've been sleeping under a rock or something? It's where a second strand is added to an RNA single strand, thus creating a synthetic DNA strand."

"Oh?"

Leonora picked up her cup from the dish rack and placed it on the counter. "I'll get you some info on it. Anyway, I cross-referenced the little guy's cDNA with the patent office and voila."

"Sounds like you got a hit." Loomsbury pulled off his reading glasses and stared at her.

"Yep, got a hit. Ever heard of Inter Diagnostics Incorporated?"
Loomsbury shook his head.

"Well, that little fellow belongs to them," she said. "They're headquartered in Cherry Hill, New Jersey. I pulled a report, and as of today, they have over forty laboratories in over forty countries around the world."

"Where should we start?" he asked.

"Since Raja Ampat is off limits for manufacturing, I found it rather interesting that they have a huge laboratory on one of the islands."

"Raja what?" he asked.

"West Papua, Indonesia. They're located on Misool Island," she said. "Their website states that they specialize in human genetics. And I have two tickets to get us there. That is, if your passport's up to date."

After dangling from the ropes for over an hour, Sumner sighed. "I have to pee."

"Sorry," Anais said. "I believe you're stuck for a while."

"That's right," Aaron added. "They're not pulling us back up for another hour or so."

"Fine," Sumner said. "There's nothing here. Have them drop us another six feet."

"Another six," Aaron said into his radio.

As the ropes shuddered, the four descended deeper into the square hole. The lower they went, the higher the temperature rose.

"I'm sweating." Sumner wiped her forehead with the back of her hand.

"You're complaining, again," Anais said. "But you're right. It's hotter down here."

"Hold on," Aaron said. "Why *is* it so hot down here? Dief?"

Dief touched his wall, then jerked away his hand. "We get out of here. Something wrong."

"Up, now," Aaron ordered.

As the ropes slowly moved, Sumner's leg brushed against the hot bricks. "My God!" Sumner screamed. "Get us out of here. I just got burnt."

"Your leg," Anais yelled, kicking herself away from the heated bricks.

"Get us out, Aaron," Dief shouted. "Now!"

"Up, now!" Aaron yelled into his radio.

Their feet dangled in the hot air while the men above hurriedly pulled them up. As the hanging passengers banged against the walls, an explosion blasted just a few feet below. Hot lava splattered the bricks where just moments ago Sumner had burnt her leg.

"Get us out of here!" Aaron screamed into his radio.

They flew upward, kicking and pushing against the scorching bricks. Hot steam melted the bottoms of their boots, and the girls screamed. Strong hands yanked them from the steaming hole.

A medic tended to Sumner's leg as the others were doused with cold water.

"What happened down there?" Scott asked.

"We hit one of those traps Dief told us about." Aaron chuckled. "My God, that was too close."

"I'd say," Anais said. "How's Sumner's burn?"

"I'll live," she replied. "Just going to be limping for a few days."

Dust flew as a Jeep skidded to a stop. Carrie jumped out and ran over to them.

"Are you okay?" she asked with concern filling her eyes. "I heard everything on the radio."

"Just a little scorched." Sumner stood. "See, all better."

"What happened?" Carrie asked.

"Don't know," Anais replied.

"Cave-in," Dief answered. "We set off trap."

"Wonderful …" Carrie walked over to the steaming pit. "Too hot to look in. Can we send down a camera or something?"

"Pit has no bottom," Dief said. "Maybe ancient lava flow. Stopped up to make trap."

"Means something important is down there," Anais said.

"Who are you?" Devon asked.

"Although I do not have to tell you" — the man glared at him through narrowed eyes — "I'm Colonel Oliver Rose."

"You're the base commander now?"

"Correct," Colonel Rose replied.

"What happened to the other guy?"

"Transferred," Colonel Rose said. "And since I'm in charge, I want *your* people off *my* base."

Devon stared at the huge man. Colonel Rose stood over six-six and probably weighed a ton. He wasn't fat, just big. His arm muscles alone probably weighed as much as Carrie did — each. As he glared at Devon, his bald head burned a bright red. Understanding more than he wanted to, Devon nodded.

"Tonight!" Colonel Rose barked as Devon shut the door behind him.

"We've been ordered off the case?" Carrie asked.

"No, not off the case," Devon replied. "Off the base."

"Who in the hell does he think he is?" Aaron asked.

"The base commander," Devon replied.

"There wasn't a change in command ceremony," Aaron stated.

"Ceremony or no ceremony, the man's in charge," Devon said.

"Now what do we do?" Sumner asked.

"We leave," Devon answered.

"But —" Anais said as a burst of hot air filled the room.

Mark stood in the trailer doorway and frowned. "Seems we have a worm on this base."

"Oh?" Carrie asked.

Allowing Dief in first, Mark closed the door. Staring at the small group, he shook his head.

"Spoke to Lewis and Greghardt. We have to leave at once. A special transport will be here within the hour."

"But our missing —" Anais started to say.

Mark held up his hand. "We're not off the case. Seems that Colonel Rose was transferred here this morning. Unexpectedly."

"Just this morning?" Carrie asked.

"Yes." Mark looked at her. "By a John Hershawl. Ever heard of him? Director for military affairs at the CIA."

"CIA?" Anais repeated.

"Central Intelligence Agency," Mark explained.

"I know that," Anais said. "But why the CIA?"

"Ever heard of Inter Diagnostics Incorporated?" Mark asked.

Everyone shook their head.

"It's a bio-research firm out of New Jersey," Mark explained. "Specializes in human-DNA sequencing."

"What do they have to do with any of this?" Scott asked.

"According to Loomsbury's assistant, Leonora," Mark explained, "they created that odd flying creature."

"What odd flying creature?" Scott asked.

"A small human-looking thing about so high." Mark used his hands to show three inches. "Found dead near the abandoned train. According to a local child, many of the things were flying around the night the passengers were kidnapped."

"Sounds like Bible prophecy," Scott added.

"A little," Sumner said.

Mark continued his story. "John Hershawl has strong connections to that company. It's a major contributor to his Hershawl Foundation — millions."

"Hershawl Foundation? Since when does an associate director of the CIA have enough monies to have a foundation of his own?" Carrie asked.

"Exactly," Mark said. "Loomsbury and Leonora are on their way to one of the labs in Indonesia. We're going to Dur-Kurigalzu."

"I've been ordered off the base too," Dief whispered.

"What?" Sumner asked. "They can't do that."

"Seems that they can," Mark said. "So Dief will be coming with us as our guide."

"I've just been reassigned too." Aaron held out his cell phone.

"Where to?" Sumner asked.

"Camp Lemonnier," Aaron replied. "It's in Djibouti, Africa."

"Africa?" Anais repeated.

Aaron nodded.

"Would you like to come with us?" Mark asked.

"Would I?" Aaron replied.

"That was what I was asking you." Mark chuckled. "Get your things together. All of you. Aaron, I'll take care of your transfer. We could use your help and expertise."

Chapter Thirteen

Colonel Oliver Rose frowned as he spoke into his phone. "Rose here."

"I need them detained," the deep and scratchy voice demanded.

"Sorry, but they just took off." Colonel Rose wiped the sweat threatening to sting his eyes.

"Call them back." The deep voice turned into a high-pitched screech that hurt Rose's ears.

"I don't have that authority," Colonel Rose explained. "It's not a military transport."

"Then shoot the fucker down," the voice ordered.

"Shoot?" Colonel Rose repeated. "You're ordering me to shoot down a civilian transport?"

"Now!"

Colonel Rose stared at the phone not believing what he just heard. Rubbing his forehead again, he dialed another number.

"Sir," the voice replied.

"The transport that just left, where is it now?"

"Circling over Batha," the voice replied.

"Do you know where it's headed?"

"Baghdad," the voice answered. "It's on the manifest."

"Baghdad? Just great."

Colonel Rose rubbed the back of his bald head as if it would bring The Agency group back. A habit he never could break. Not one to accept orders just because they were orders, he thought for a moment. Unless there were real good reasons to kill someone, he usually avoided it. He'd rather not have to explain to his maker after his death why he did what he did. Better to contemplate such things while a person was still breathing.

"Sir?" the voice on the other end of the phone asked. "You still there?"

Slamming down the receiver, Oliver sighed. *Now what should I do?* Grabbing a private cell phone, he dialed the number he was told to memorize. After a couple of rings, he spoke softly. "Patch me through to Dr. Lewis."

"I guess we'll never know whose room that was." Elizabeth's voice echoed as they walked down the empty hall.

"I guess not," David said.

After several false turns, Elizabeth stopped. "I think we're lost."

"I believe you are correct."

"None of this looks familiar." She stepped around another turn. A huge blue archway startled her. "I definitely do not remember this thing."

"Wow!"

"Wow is right." The arch towered high above their heads. From floor to ceiling, shiny blue and red gems glittered against the light from his phone. "How tall do you think this is?"

"Tall," David said.

Elizabeth shook her head and sighed.

"Maybe twenty feet?" he added, probably noticing her aggravation with him.

"Maybe." Elizabeth stepped under the archway. Before she could get too excited, she spotted several lights floating toward them. Her stomach tightened.

"Maybe we found a way back." David stared at the approaching people.

"I don't like this," she whispered.

"Now that you've said it, neither do I." As the lights floated closer, David hollered out. "Hello?"

Fear ran through Elizabeth. "*Shhh*!" Elizabeth grabbed David by the arm. "We don't know who they are. What if they're the jerks that kidnapped us?"

David held his breath.

They turned to run, but three men wearing red robes adorned with golden fringe blocked their path. Elizabeth whirled in the opposite direction, but that escape was blocked now too.

"David, we're surrounded." Tears filled her eyes.

Five robed men stood gawking at them.

"If they were going to kill us, they would have already. These are not our bad guys. *En* …" David stuttered and cleared his throat. "*Ensi?*"

One of the men smiled and nodded. He pointed into the darkness. David stood frozen. The robed man nodded again, and again pointed into the darkness.

"I think they want us to follow 'em," David whispered.

"We're outnumbered," Elizabeth said. "What do we have to lose?"

"Just our lives."

"We might lose those anyway," Elizabeth said. "We have no food, remember?"

"Let's go." Mark grabbed his bags and exited the aircraft. He turned and said, "We have rides waiting for us."

Stepping off the ramp, Anais glanced around. It seemed odd that the vehicles idled so close to the plane. Hurrying, she almost tripped. Aaron grabbed her by the arm.

"You okay?" he asked.

She nodded and jumped into the nearest black SUV. Aaron, Sumner and Scott climbed in behind Anais. As soon as the others were safely inside the other vehicle, she watched the outside world blur past. Although they were exiting the airport at almost full speed, people ignored them, as if two hurried black SUVs were nothing unusual. Clicking her safety belt around her waist, Sumner screamed as the SUV bounced several times, swerving to avoid civilians. Flames shot up as a blast boomed outside.

"Hold on," their driver yelled.

"What's happening?" Sumner asked.

"Someone must want you dead," the driver yelled. "Hang on!"

Another explosion and the SUV bounced again, barely missing a young child. Outside, civilians dropped to the ground.

"I hope they're not hurt," Anais said.

Sumner nodded. Scott and Aaron stared out the window, their eyes as large as golf balls.

Just ahead, several old military-style trucks screeched around the corner, their machine guns aiming straight for the SUVs. Before they could release their load, a black chopper zoomed over the SUVs toward the trucks. What sounded like a missile buzzed past before hitting one of them. Tires, metal and people flew out in all directions. As the second truck aimed its guns at the SUVs, another missile slammed into its side, flipping it over several times before it exploded into the side of a building.

"Roger AK173," the driver said into his headpiece. "Thanks for the help."

"Now what?" Sumner asked from the back seat.

"Those are our guys up there," the driver yelled, pointing his finger toward the heavens. "They'll stay with us for a while."

Anais glanced back at Sumner who smiled tensely before raising one eyebrow.

Elizabeth wondered if her death would be quick and painless. At the end of the long, dark hallway, they stepped into a sparsely furnished room. The walls, draped in colorful cloths, felt warm and inviting. Not exactly a place to execute someone. More of a place to invite a person to tea. In the middle, she counted three large, round tables with several chairs. Reminded her of a conference room. One of the men motioned for them to sit. With nothing else to do or say, they sat. Smokeless lamps blazed from the corners. One of the men confiscated their torches. He nodded and smiled while dipping them into a reflective liquid. The flames died without smoldering.

"I hope we get our torches back," David whispered.

As they waited, Elizabeth played with the ends of her hair. David scratched his head. One robed man waited with them. Before long, the other men returned with trays of food. Several women dressed in similar robes carried pitchers. The women were adorned with golden jewelry.

"They're going to feed us?" Elizabeth asked, a huge smile decorating her face.

The men filled two plates and placed them on the table. A short man who couldn't stop giggling handed them a wooden spoon. Elizabeth admired the odd utensil shaped like a leaf. Another man motioned for them to eat.

Shrugging, Elizabeth took a small bite. "Mmmm, good."

"Yes, it is," David said.

Accepting a bowl filled with a clear liquid, Elizabeth took a sip. "Water!" After she emptied the contents, one of the women refilled it for her. Nothing ever tasted so good. With her tummy almost full, Elizabeth sighed.

"If this stuff's poisoned," David whispered, "then what a way to go."

"How many?" A woman's voice surprised them.

Holding her breath, Elizabeth turned to stare into the face of a beautiful woman wearing a golden headdress. "Who are you?"

"I could easily ask you the same," the woman replied.

"I'm sorry. I'm Elizabeth Ferguson."

"I'm Dr. David Reinhoist." David reached out his hand as Elizabeth stood. "I'm with the University of California."

The woman stared at his hand before taking it into hers. "Again," the woman said, a little softer this time, "how many are there?"

"Of us? About two hundred or so," David replied.

"We started off with over three hundred," Elizabeth said. "But they took some of us away. If they weren't dead already, they probably killed 'em."

"Took?" the woman repeated. "Killed?"

"Kidnapped," Elizabeth said.

"Kidnapped, by whom?" the woman asked.

"We don't know," David answered.

The woman studied the two and nodded. "I am known as Ningal."

"Nice to meet you, Ningal." David nodded. "May I ask … where are we?"

"You stumbled into our home," Ningal replied.

"Home?" Elizabeth repeated. "Down here?"

"This is what's left of the city of Ekurmah." Ningal smiled as if revealing a long-lost secret. "Some used to call our city Nippur."

Elizabeth froze. As her heart pounded, she placed her hand over it. "Nippur?" Elizabeth whispered. "Ekurmah? *Ekur* is Sumerian for 'Mountain House.'"

"I am impressed with your knowledge little one," Ningal said. "This is the House of the Exalted One."

"Ur-Nammu?" Elizabeth asked.

"No, my child." Ningal laughed. "You are with the family of Bur-ra-Bu-ri-ia-aš."

"Lineage of Enlil?" Elizabeth said. "One of the original gods?"

Ningal nodded.

"Are they still alive?" Elizabeth asked, glancing around. "The original gods? Are they here? They were supposed to live for thousands of years."

Ningal laughed again. "No, my child." She shook her head. "They have not been with us for a very long time. King Nazi-Enlil is our ruler.

We must gather your friends," Ningal whispered. "They require food and water and rest."

"Why here?" Sumner asked. "Why Dur-Kurigalzu?"

"Why not?" Mark replied. "It's the closest ziggurat I could think of. Sorry, I was in a hurry, and I don't do well under pressure."

"You do realize there are seven ancient cities between here and Ur?" Sumner asked.

"Uh, no." Mark glanced around as if not wanting to admit he didn't know the area.

The huge rock-like structure jutted up toward the clouds, four times higher than the brick walls that surrounded it. It reminded Mark of a pile of dried clay.

"Yes." Sumner counted on her fingers. "There is Sippar … um, and Babylon, Kish, Nippur … Isin, Girsu, and … oh, we cannot forget Uruk." Sumner smiled.

"Oh, please, never forgot Uruk." Mark stuck out his tongue. "Show-off. What is that thing?"

"What thing?" Sumner asked.

Mark pointed to the huge rock.

"That is what's left of this ziggurat. All ziggurats were made from brick and dirt. The insides mostly solid. Held the weight of the structure."

"Isn't that cheating?" Mark asked.

"Maybe," Sumner replied. "They've lasted this long. If it weren't for the recent wars, these ziggurats would be in better condition."

"Who did this damage?" Mark asked. "Us?"

"Mostly terrorists," Sumner replied. "Humans tend to destroy a lot of historic sites. Sometimes by accident, other times on purpose."

"What a waste." Mark glanced around as if searching for something.

"Do you think that new base commander tried to kill us?" Anais asked.

Nodding, Sumner sighed. "I'd bet on it."

"Most definitely," Devon said. "I could see it in his eyes the moment I met him. Seven other cities, huh? We're that far away?"

Ignoring his question, Carrie frowned. "Corruption? You could see corruption in his eyes?"

"See it, smell it," Devon said. "There was something else too. Something that frightened me."

"How can you smell corruption?" Aaron asked.

"Believe me, you can smell, taste and *feel* corruption," Scott said. He rubbed the back of his head remembering the iron pipe and how it felt when it made contact with his skull.

"This place is in worse shape than Ur." Anais stared at the rock.

"If there was a way in at Ur," Mark said, "then there'll be a way in here."

From the back of the room, Elizabeth watched as her friends ate. A few, looking around apprehensively, didn't eat much but others gorged themselves. She scanned the room for Ningal.

"Elizabeth?" Jack waved at her from a nearby table.

"Hey!" She smiled and patted him on the shoulder.

"You're an angel, yah know. If it weren't for you, we'd have surely starved to death."

"I wouldn't get your hopes too high just yet," she said. "We still don't know what's going on. Or who these people are."

"Well ..." Jack sipped on his water. "They all seem pretty friendly to me."

"Excuse me." Slipping away, Elizabeth ran up to Ningal. "May we talk?"

Ningal smiled. "Of course little one. Follow me."

Ningal pulled aside one of the drapes, exposing a hidden hallway. As they walked down the passage, their footsteps echoed off the bare, white walls. Near the end, Ningal pushed open an old wooden door. They entered a small room. Several chairs stacked with pillows and throws gave the place an inviting feel.

"Please sit." Ningal pointed to a chair.

"Ningal." Elizabeth sat in front of her. "How did you learn English?"

"I attended college in America," she nonchalantly replied, as if everyone attended college in America. Then she added, "I understand how confusing this must be. Unfortunately, I can only share so much with you."

"Why?" Elizabeth stared at the woman. How could someone hide in a cave be so educated, so proper?

"We're all that's left of our civilization. Once, our people were counted in the tens of millions. We covered the lands above and below. Our cities were vast and large. We cared for and protected our crops. At one time, we were known as the Sumerians. Now, what is left remains here. In these caves. We are safe from the outside world. Away from the hatred and deceit. Only a few of us ever leave this place. And when we do, it is only to educate ourselves."

"You didn't originate down here, did you?"

"Oh no." Ningal walked around the room, adjusting a few of the pillows. "We migrated here many generations ago. War is never a good thing little one. Especially when your enemy comes from above."

"Where did you come from?"

"I was born here. But my people once lived where the Nile River no longer flows. In the land you call Africa. It was not a desert back then, but a fertile land filled with many exotic trees and animals. Then the evil ones came and changed the direction of our river. Our land died. Became the hot, dry sands of today."

"Wait a minute." Elizabeth held up her hand. "Enemies from above? What are you talking about?"

"Many years ago," Ningal explained, "when our people lived on top of the land, a large war destroyed not only our cities but many others. There was once a huge city far off to the west. The powerful weapons pushed that land farther south. Many people died."

Elizabeth shook her head. "Pushed the land … war from above … who *was* your enemy?"

"We do not know," Ningal said. "They arrived in huge flying ships. Their ships traveled swiftly through the clouds. After the great air war, our enemy destroyed the domed cities in our clouds, and on our moons, and on our sister planets."

"What sister planets?"

"Venus and Mars."

Elizabeth shook her head. "Domed cities on our *moons*? What moons? We only have one."

"The moon you see today is named Luna. The other moon was named Selene."

"How big was this other moon?" Elizabeth asked.

"Just a little smaller than Luna."

"And what happened to this other moon?"

"It was destroyed in the great air war. For years, rocks fell from the skies, causing mass fires and great earthquakes. Those were the terrible days. The fearful nights. Many of us moved underground."

"Are you joking?"

"No, my little one." Ningal smiled. "Have you never heard of the underground city in the Derinkuyu district in Nevşehir Province, Turkey? Or what about the one in the Cappadocia region of Turkey? There are others, but the largest are in Turkey."

"I heard of the first one, but not the second. There are others?"

Ningal nodded.

"Did you travel between the cities? Before the great war?"

"Oh yes. We had sea ships and the tubes. The tubes were everywhere."

"Tubes?"

"I believe your scientists found remnants on Mars," Ningal said. "They do not understand what they are seeing. At one time, the tubes carried our people all over our worlds. The ones on Earth are deep and not yet discovered."

"All over? And these bad enemies destroyed everything? Every great city?"

"Living on the land was no longer viable. They poisoned the air. Just walking to the surface, one would die from the great sickness."

"How terrible. Who'd do something like that?"

"That no longer matters," Ningal replied. "It was a very long time ago. What happened back then we no longer talk about. We simply learned from our past transgressions and hide."

"When the land died, you … I mean, your ancestors moved down here? Into these caves?"

"Making a very long story very short, yes." Ningal smiled.

"What about money?"

"We do not use money here," she said. "However, we have access to it, if and when, there is a need. Our home" — Ningal waved her arms through the air — "must be protected at all costs. If outsiders were ever to come, they could destroy everything we've worked so hard to protect. We would no longer be us. We would die or become one of them. That can never happen."

"I understand," Elizabeth said. "We have bad people after us. Maybe it's not safe for us to be here. Maybe we should leave."

"We know all about the bad people. We have taken precautions. There are others looking for you. We will guide them here, so they will find you. We will protect you while you are here. The bad people will not be permitted to enter."

"How will you keep 'em out?"

"We have our ways," Ningal said. "Allow me to escort you to your *ginsuga*. Your bedchamber. You must rest now."

"Dr. Lewis?" Connie's voice echoed off the walls.

"Yes, Connie?"

"Dr. Greghardt's here to see you."

"Send him in."

Lewis stood and stretched out his back. He'd been with The Agency for many years now — more than he wished to count. Every case was different, and this one worried him. It reminded him of the case with the twins, Dakota and Nevada. He wondered how their mother, Early, was doing. Dakota and Nevada would be about ten now. Early had been put through hell. She didn't deserve what happened to her. But she was a fighter. She did what was necessary to stay alive for her children. Now in government protective custody, he wondered just how much of a normal life they'd ever have. Those beautiful little girls had the ability to stay underwater for about thirty minutes. Spliced with dolphin DNA, their lungs were twice as strong as a human's.

Then there was little Lizzie. The memory of her left him teary-eyed. Unfortunately, things didn't go quite as smoothly for her as it did with Dakota and Nevada. Lizzie was more horse than human, with a deformed chin and nose. Instead of feet, small hoofs adorned the ends of her slender but muscular legs. The light-golden hue she had at birth finally disappeared when she was about two. Her long blonde hair was just as coarse and thick as a horse's mane. Dakota and Nevada would eventually be able to join everyday society. But not little Lizzie. She would forever be hidden away from the rest of the world. Forever be alone.

"Jeff," Allen Greghardt said as the door shut behind him. "You're thinking about something. Talk to me old friend."

"Just thinking about the DNA case. I'm wondering how Lizzie is doing these days."

"She's fine." He dropped ice into a glass. "She's about five now, talking and everything. An absolutely beautiful little girl. The plastic surgery shortened her jawline. Her nose they'll work on when she's a little older. I think when she's an adult no one will be the wiser."

"You honestly believe that?"

Greghardt nodded as he poured a golden liquid over the ice. "Jeff … brandy?"

Lewis shook his head.

"I'm here because I'm concerned."

"I am too." Lewis sat on one of the sofas.

"More than likely, we're not concerned about the same things." Holding his glass and wearing a large frown, Greghardt sat across from Lewis. "Ever heard of a John Hershawl?"

Lewis thought for a moment. "Isn't he that strange guy from the CIA? The one who acts like he's a god or something?"

"That's the one." Greghardt took a sip.

"He's still there, huh?"

Greghardt nodded.

"What's he up to now?"

"A lot of *no good*," Greghardt replied. "He's ordered a hit on our small group in Iraq."

"Did he now?"

Greghardt nodded again as he took another sip. "Mark's aware of the issue. He'll handle it. Keep 'em safe. It seems that our strange coworker has a close friend. A Colonel Oliver Rose. Ever heard of him?"

"Actually, yes." Lewis smiled, nodding. "Connie?" Staring at the ceiling, Lewis spoke into the air. "Bring in Oliver Rose's file, please."

"He's one of ours?"

Lewis nodded. "Small world, Allen. Rose called a little while ago … Thank you, Connie. Here." Lewis passed the file to Greghardt. "Said he'd been ordered to kill Devon's group. Wouldn't say who ordered it."

"Probably a good thing." Greghardt flipped through the file. "Good man?"

"Very good. I trust him."

"Then why didn't he expose Hershawl?"

"Not sure yet."

"Do you know who Hershawl's connected with other than the colonel?" Greghardt tossed the file onto the small table.

"Maybe it's time to find out." Lewis stood and stretched. Maybe it was time for a drink after all.

Chapter Fourteen

"This complex is only excavated on the southwest side." Dief shaded his eyes from the bright afternoon sun.

With her eyes on Mark, Sumner patted Dief on the back.

Dief smiled. "This place was basically abandoned after the Iraq war."

Although several of the ancient buildings around the ziggurat had been reconstructed, they had still sustained heavy damage. Some walls and archways remained intact, but the place looked almost demolished.

"Obviously," Mark said.

"We have no shovels." Scott walked up to them. "We can't dig."

"We also have no weapons," Devon said. "And no water. Basically, no anything."

"We have our credit cards and phones," Anais offered.

"I just spoke to Dr. Lewis." Carrie stuffed her phone into her back pocket. "Supplies are on their way." Carrie spread a map out on the sand. "I was wondering. Maybe we should go to Uruk. It's closer to Ur. See?"

Aaron glanced at Carrie's map. "Or Girsu. It looks even closer."

"The problem is," Sumner said, "not much is left of those places."

"Correct," Dief said.

"Not much here," Anais added.

"Where do you recommend?" Devon asked Dief.

"Uruk," Dief replied.

Devon shook his head. "Then we go to Girsu. Carrie, call Dr. Lewis and schedule a pickup."

"Wait." Scott held up his hand. "Dief just recommended Uruk. But you asked for a ride to Girsu. Why?"

Dialing her phone, Carrie said, "Because that Rose guy will be expecting us to go to Uruk."

Samuel Worthington rocked back and forth on the balls of his feet. "Not sure what they did," he said, smiling. "But, whatever it was, it fixed me right up."

"Me too," Gerry added. "They didn't look much like doctors. But they sure knew what they were doing."

Jack rubbed his stomach. "That drink they gave me makes me feel like a kid again. I have more energy than I know what to do with."

"May I show you to your rooms?" Ningal asked from behind, startling them. "You must rest now."

"Don't feel much like resting," Worthington said.

Ningal nodded. "I understand. But you will tire soon. It would be wise if you were lying down."

David grinned as he joined them. "No one wants to sleep. We all want to explore. But Ningal's right. We must rest first."

"Excuse me?" Carrie almost screamed into her phone. "You can't what?"

"What's up?" Devon asked.

"Seems that our new friend, Rose, has a surprise waiting for us at both of those sites," Carrie explained to Devon. Holding up her finger, she shook her head. "Fine." Clicking off her phone, she sighed. "They can't come for us right now."

"Then we wait," Devon replied.

"We can't wait too long," Mark added. "We have no supplies. No food or water."

"Where is everybody?" Carrie asked, glancing around.

"Exploring," Mark said.

"Hey," Sumner yelled from behind an old brick wall. "I think we found something."

Jogging over to her, Devon ran the last few days through his mind. He was traipsing through a desert in Iraq looking for three hundred train passengers that went missing in South Dakota, a whole world away, because of a damn flower, a colorful tree and an owl. Absurd.

"What did you find?" Carrie asked as sweat ran down her face.

"Not sure," Sumner replied. "Over here."

"Where are we going?" Devon asked.

"You'll see." Sumner descended the stone steps.

Leaning against a wall and looking anything but pleased, Mark gave Devon the eye. It took everything Devon had not to laugh.

"What's wrong, Mark?" Devon asked.

"The last time I followed these two ladies into the dark unknown, I fell into a bottomless pit. Thank goodness someone plugged it up, so we only hit water."

Devon chuckled. "Then why do you keep following 'em?"

"Nice place," Loomsbury said as they stood in the dark in front of the Swiss-Belhotel in Sorong.

"Be nice." Leonora slapped Loomsbury on the arm.

"Looks like a third-world country." Loomsbury frowned. "Smells like a third-world country."

Leonora smiled.

Loomsbury sighed. "Now that you've dragged me out here at four in the morning, what now?"

"The hotel was nice." Leonora glanced over her shoulder. "And it's warm here. Back home you'd be cold right now."

"Back home, I'd still be asleep." Loomsbury also glanced over his shoulder. The four-story building, decorated with balconies and extra-large windows, *was* rather comfortable. He had to give her credit for that. Nevertheless, the surrounding buildings and community didn't look safe or sanitary. "Okay, the hotel *was* nice. But —"

"But what?"

Before he could finish his thought, a rickety-looking taxi skidded to a stop in front of them.

"This must be our ride," Leonora said.

"Our ride? Will it hold together? Where's he riding us to?" Loomsbury asked, climbing in after her and closing the car door.

"To the islands, please," Leonora said to the driver.

"He's driving us to the islands?"

"No, silly." Leonora giggled. "He's taking us to the docks where we'll board a boat, and then go to the islands. Here." She handed Loomsbury a map.

Loomsbury lit up the back seat with his cell phone. "Which island are we going to?"

"That one there." She pointed to a large land mass surround by smaller islands. "Here are the recon photos taken from the air. You can just make out the laboratory between all the greenery."

"How many islands are out there?"

"Hundreds," Leonora said. "Didn't you study world geography in school?"

"We never studied this place."

"Maybe you should have."

As the taxi soared down the streets of the small town, Loomsbury studied the beautiful photos of the lush green islands and the deep-blue waters. The place resembled an enchanted land harboring many enchanted secrets.

"I can almost see the water." Leonora pointed out the window.

"It's too dark to see anything out there."

"The sun's just starting to rise."

The car slowed to a stop. Leonora paid the driver and thanked him for his time. Standing on a broken slat from the pier, Loomsbury stared down at the water slapping against the pilings just below his feet.

Leonora giggled. "Are you going to be okay?" She patted his back. "I mean, I know they never let you out much and all, but ..."

"I'll survive. Where's this boat of yours?"

"This way." Swinging her pack over her shoulder, Leonora took the lead.

The dock creaked beneath their feet as they stepped over the large gaps. Loomsbury wondered if the planks were even connected to the dock. Boats of different sizes and shapes lined both sides, with not an inch available for another vessel. A large white boat with bright-blue sails waited for them at the end of the pier.

As they approached, a man waved. "You must be Dr. Loomsbury and Dr. Priddleton; who's who?" The man of about fifty or so, with dark hair and eyes, smiled.

"I'm Leonora Priddleton and this is Dr. Loomsbury. Don't even know if he has a first name. Do you have a first name, Dr. Loo?"

Frowning, Loomsbury held out his hand. The man shook it.

"I'm Bob, by the way," the captain said.

"Bob?" Leonora repeated.

"Not really my name. Everyone just calls me that. So, I kept it. Welcome aboard."

"Nice boat." Loomsbury took a seat. "This thing is huge."

"Medium. She's a Lagoon 52, like the old catamarans. I can take her places others only dream of."

Loomsbury nodded.

"Latrine's below. Make yourselves comfortable," Bob said as he climbed the stairs leading to the top. "And if it makes you feel any better, Dr. Lewis asked me to go easy on you two."

"Dr. Lewis?" Leonora repeated, following Bob up the steep steps.

"I'm employed by the same firm you are." Staring down at her, Bob winked.

"Then, is this your boat? Or The Agency's?"

"It's mine," he replied. "Happily bought and paid for by our employer."

"Then, you're ours for the whole day?"

"I'm yours for the duration," Bob said. "We have enough provisions to last a week or two if necessary."

"Do you live here?"

"Not on this boat. I was born on these islands."

As Bob guided the boat into open waters, the sun broke across the horizon as if lighting the way. Loomsbury stood on the deck, not taking his eyes off the beautiful sunrise. Across the waters, he admired the mountaintops glittering as if covered in gold. Birds flew overhead as if welcoming them to this mystical wonderland.

"Hi." It was a female voice. "Name's Amy."

Loomsbury turned. With her hands resting on her hips, a dark-skinned girl smiled. She was probably early twenties. Long, straight-black hair fell past her waist, and a yellow bikini barely covered her curvy young body.

"Hello." It was all he could think of to say.

"I guess you could call me the first mate on this ship. I cook and clean, among other things," she said. "What would you like for breakfast? Did Bob show you around?"

"No." Leonora climbed down the stairs. "Just said the bathrooms were below and to make ourselves comfortable."

"Then please, allow me." As Leonora stepped off the last step, Amy waved her hand. "Here is our sitting area. We eat here, too. Unless it's raining. The kitchen is over there — my space. Please, take whatever you want if you're hungry or thirsty. I try to keep it stocked with munchies.

Just dig through the cabinets. Down here is a full refrigerator. Soda and beer in the smaller fridge over there." Amy pointed to the other side of the kitchen. "The cabins are below." They followed her down another flight of stairs. "Dr. Loomsbury, you're in here. Dr. Priddleton, you're over there. Bob and I are at the end."

"We have cabins?" Leonora asked.

"Fully stocked cabins," Amy replied. "Jeff thought of everything."

Loomsbury walked into Leonora's room. Amazingly, her window opened up to create a small deck. The berth had a queen-sized bed and a full bath. When he opened a closet, Leonora gasped.

"Something wrong?" Loomsbury asked.

"No, just that it's full," Leonora said.

"Should be your size," Amy added.

Loomsbury laughed. It was amazing what The Agency did for their agents.

When Amy left them alone to explore their cabins, they found laptop computers and flat-screen TVs. Leonora checked out every drawer and cubby. Loomsbury checked out his shower and bed. Before long, the two surrendered to their hunger. Bob must have dropped anchor because he was at the table shoveling eggs into his mouth, along with several strips of bacon.

"Here yah go." Amy sat plates of food in front of them.

"Smells wonderful," Leonora said. She took a bite. "Wow. It's great."

"Thank you," Amy said.

"I think we'll be happy here," Loomsbury added.

"We've been with The Agency for about five years now." Bob grabbed another piece of toast. "I get a new boat every two years or so. Take people wherever they need to go. Been almost all over the world."

"All over the world?" Amy repeated. "I don't think so. We stay mostly in this area. We've traveled as far as New Zealand to the south and Japan to the north. And we dropped off an agent on the island of Samoa once. Other than that, we stay here."

"To me," Bob said, "that's all over the world."

"So, where are we headed today?" Loomsbury asked, placing his dishes in the sink and staring out at the bright-blue waters.

"Misool Island," Bob replied. "It's one of the larger ones."

"Ever dropped anyone off on Misool before?" Loomsbury asked.

"Nope. Parts of that island are off limits to most. Very protected. There's a resort or two that's been there awhile along the eastern coast. However, if you try to drop anchor on the wrong side, you'd be surrounded by armed boats before you know it."

"So, what's your cover?" Amy asked, placing a plate into the dishwasher. "We're husband and wife. We're husband and wife in real life too, so it fits."

"I see." Leonora giggled. "Loomsbury's my dad."

"That works." Amy laughed as she cleared the table. "He almost looks like your dad. Just a little lighter in color."

"He looks funny without his lab coat," Leonora quipped.

"I think we can raise sail now." Bob climbed the stairs to the bridge. "Would you like to help, Dr. Loomsbury?"

Loomsbury pointed to himself. "Me?"

"Yes you," Bob said.

"Certainly."

Leonora watched as Loomsbury shakily climbed the stairs, following Bob. *He can hardly tie his shoes by himself. This should be interesting.*

"What are these?" Devon asked.

"Stairs," Sumner replied.

"I can see that. Where do they go?"

"How am I supposed to know?" Sumner stepped down into the dark hole.

"Whoa." Devon pulled on her arm. "We don't know what's down there."

"Anais, Aaron and Scott already went down. I came back for you two."

"See what I mean," Mark said from behind.

"I'm beginning to." Devon followed Sumner down the steps, even though he didn't want to.

Without a railing, Mark's nerves were close to fraying. If he tripped now, he'd take all three of them out at once. "I need a flashlight."

"Here." Sumner squeezed around Devon. "Take the lead. I'm staying with Mark." Sumner grabbed Mark's arm. "I won't let you fall."

"Oh, this definitely gives me great comfort," Mark replied.

The carved stairs were steep. Almost a forty-five-degree angle. The deeper they traversed, the cooler the air.

After several minutes, Mark whispered, "I need my sweatshirt."

"I wondered when you'd say something," Sumner said. "You've been shaking for quite some time now." Helping him with his backpack, Sumner pulled out a light-gray sweatshirt and handed it to Mark.

"Let's sit for a few," Devon said.

"I could use a drink," Mark grumbled.

"Actually ..." Sumner held out a water bottle. "I just happen to have some. Would you like to share?"

"Yes," Mark replied. "I would."

The group rested before tackling the stairs again. After what seemed like an eternity, a dim light lit the tunnel below.

"We must be almost there." Sumner squeezed Mark's hand.

"Thank God," Devon said. "This was getting monotonous."

"Hey, about time you showed," Anais said once the small group reunited.

"It's amazing down here," Scott said. "There are hallways leading in all directions."

"How do we not get lost?" Devon asked.

"Good question," Aaron said.

"Should we split up?" Anais asked.

"No!" Mark stated before anyone else could reply.

"I agree," Devon said. "I'd feel better if we stayed as a group."

"Fine." Sumner walked over to Anais and rested her head on her shoulder. "Pick a tunnel."

Mark glanced around. To him, all the passages looked the same. Dark.

"You may go in now." The young assistant waved toward the Oval Office. "The president is expecting you."

Lewis nodded before entering the impressive office.

"Dr. Lewis," Cadel McKinley held out his hand. "It is so good to see you again."

"Yes, it is." Lewis shook the president's hand.

"And to what do I owe this pleasure? Please sit." President McKinley waved his arm.

"I'm here to discuss a small issue." Lewis walked to the white sofa and sat with a sigh. "John Hershawl."

President McKinley nodded. "You mean my director for military affairs?"

"Correct."

"And what has Mr. Hershawl done now?"

Lewis shifted his weight to his other hip. Clasping his hands together, he coughed.

"I see," President McKinley said. "That bad?"

"It isn't good." Lewis smiled.

The president stood and straightened his jacket. "Any suggestions? Jeff, you know how I feel about corruption."

Lewis nodded.

Sitting across from Lewis, President McKinley whispered, "My ancestor, President William McKinley, had a saying: 'All a man can hope for during his lifetime is to set an example.' Perhaps it's time to set an example for Mr. Hershawl."

"Maybe," Lewis replied.

"Okay, Jeff. Tell me everything you know."

"Certainly, but remember, your ancestor was shot when he walked in your shoes."

President McKinley chuckled.

"Either she's totally loony or there's something to her stories," Elizabeth whispered to David.

"Why don't we just ask her?" David said.

"Ask her what?" Worthington asked.

"It's time to eat," Gerry said. "Not time to complain."

"I'm not complaining," Elizabeth replied. "I'm just saying."

"Saying what?" Worthington asked.

David wiped his mouth. Sitting down the cloth napkin, he frowned. "Ningal told Elizabeth some of their history last night and it frightened her."

"It didn't frighten me," Elizabeth said in a low voice. "What she told me was strange. That's all."

"Then let's ask her about it," Worthington said. "What harm would it do?"

"*Silim.*" Ningal walked up to their table.

"May all be well with you too." Elizabeth stood.

"My little one." Ningal placed her hand on Elizabeth's shoulder.

Elizabeth looked up at her. "Ningal, before I fell asleep, you told me some interesting things about your history."

Ningal nodded.

"Is any of it written down?" David asked. "Recorded somewhere?"

"Why yes," Ningal replied. "Would you like to see our library?"

The others jumped from their chairs at the same time and replied, "Yes!"

Lewis glanced around the parking lot. A flock of birds swooped down between the cars. *Must be something good to eat over there. Wonder what they found.* He entered the memorized number into his cell.

"Davenport."

"Karl, Dr. Lewis here."

"Yes, sir?"

"Alpha ... Epsilon ... Phi ... Gamma."

"Confirmed."

Staring at his now silent phone, Lewis chuckled. Damn if he didn't love his job.

"Colonel Rose, here."

"Alpha ... Epsilon ... Phi ... Gamma," the deep voice recited.

"Confirmed." Rose nodded.

After hanging up, he stood and stretched out his back. Taking in a deep breath he wiped his forehead with his hand.

"I need a drink."

Chapter Fifteen

"**I** believe we chose the darkest tunnel," Mark said after walking for what seemed like hours.

"It is quite dark down here," Devon said.

"Would you two quit complaining?" Sumner snapped. "You've done nothing but since we got here."

"I'm tired," Mark said.

"My feet hurt," Devon said.

Sumner sighed. "Honestly?"

"There's something ahead," Scott whispered.

"I see it too," Aaron said.

Anais scooted past Dief as the small group headed toward the light. Listening to the echo from their steps, Anais wondered if they'd survive this little excursion or end up dead — their bodies discovered years later by a wandering archaeologist.

"I wonder what these caves were made for?" Sumner held on to Mark's arm.

"That's a great question," Aaron said. "I see no reason for such long tunnels."

"Ah man," Scott yelled from up ahead. "I think we're in trouble, guys."

Aaron hurried to catch up with Scott. Sumner and Anais froze in place. Devon squinted, trying to see through the darkness. With nothing else to do, the small group inched forward. Anais thought about her mother and father. *Will I ever see them again?*

It took a few seconds for their eyes to adjust. Only a few feet away, several men wearing red robes with golden trim surrounded Scott and Aaron.

Letting go of Mark's arm, Sumner stepped toward the robed men and nodded before falling to one knee. With her palms up and hands together, she raised them above her head while staring at the floor.

"*Silim*," she said, still not looking up.

The robed men turned toward her. One of them stepped forward, reached down and pulled her to her feet. "*Alka*," the robed man said.

Turning to Devon, Sumner grinned. "He wants us to follow them."

"Are you okay?" Leonora grabbed another towel. Rubbing it over Loomsbury's head, she held back the urge to laugh.

"I'm fine," Loomsbury said.

"Are you sure you didn't hit anything?" Bob asked, kneeling next to him.

"Of course I hit something." Loomsbury dried his forehead. "The water."

"He's fine." Amy yanked on Bob's arm and whispered, "Leave the man alone."

"Damn Amy," Bob said. "The man fell over twenty feet. He could have broken something."

"He did." Leonora wrapped another towel around Loomsbury's shoulders. "His pride."

"You two go up top." Amy shook her head, pushing Bob toward the stairs. "I'll make sure Dr. Loo gets washed up."

Leonora knelt in front of her friend. "Are you *sure* you're okay, Dr. Loo?"

"I'm sure." He patted her shoulder and winked. "I'll get changed and be right up."

Nodding, she grinned. "Don't you ever do that again. You scared me."

"I scared me too," he replied. "Now get. I'm fine, honest."

Leonora nodded at Amy. When Amy nodded back, Leonora kissed Dr. Loo on the cheek before climbing the steep stairs.

"I guess your friend isn't good around boats?" Bob asked.

"He's a scientist," Leonora said. "Not a deckhand. What happened?"

Bob turned the wheel as he talked. "Not sure. One moment he was standing there and the next he was in the water."

"Typical," she said.

"You care for that man, don't you?"

Leonora nodded. "He's the closest thing I have to a father. Mine left before I was born."

Bob said, "From now on, I'll keep a closer eye on your friend ... um, dad."

"I'd appreciate that."

"Hey!" Bob pointed over the wheel. "Take a look."

"Dolphins?" Leonora whispered. Climbing down the steps, she leaned over the metal railing and laughed as several dolphins surfaced, blowing water into her face. Gliding over the crisp blue surface, white ripples surrounded their boat as several dolphins jumped and swam beside them.

"Hey, Leonora," Bob yelled.

Turning, she saw him point to the front of the boat. "What?"

"Lay down on the nets," he ordered.

Leonora dropped to her knees and crawled onto the netting. On her stomach, she scooted to the front. As the boat slowed, the ripples eased. A gentle rocking moved her from side to side. Reaching over, her arms were not quite long enough to touch the water. The dolphins circled around a few times before surfacing in front of her.

"Get your suit on," Bob said, standing behind her. "I've already dropped anchor. We can rest for a while."

"But the dolphins?"

Bob smiled. "You haven't lived until you've swam with the dolphins."

Elizabeth followed Ningal down the long corridor. David, Jack, Gerry and Worthington hurried only a few steps behind, and several other scientists trailed along eager to see what Ningal had to share. The corridor, brightly lit by lights hidden along ridges near the ceiling, fascinated Elizabeth. She couldn't tell if they were powered by electricity or something else.

The corridor ended near a landing. The many steps leading down looked not only ominous but dangerous. With nothing else to lose other than her life, Elizabeth scrunched up her shoulders and descended the stairs. About halfway down, vibrations tickled the bottoms of her feet.

"What's that?" Elizabeth asked.

"You are indeed being honored today," Ningal replied. "King Nazi-Enlil shall preside. Please keep your heads lowered as the king passes, I beg of you. Once he is no longer in front of us, you may raise your eyes and admire him from behind. No mortal may gaze directly into the king's eyes without permission."

The group stared at her.

"Please, if you cannot, then we must wait up here."

"I agree," Elizabeth whispered, skipping down the remaining stairs.

At the bottom, the group stood quietly together and stared onto what looked like a huge highway. However, this road was deep underground.

The enormous cave stretched out in all directions. Elizabeth could not see the ceiling or distant walls. As she watched, several rows of men wearing dark red-and-green robes walked toward them. Each stared up at the heavens while pounding on their drums. With every step, their synchronized beating pulled Elizabeth into a mystical dream-state. Behind the drummers, four rows of men wearing only baggy green pants played something that sounded like a trumpet. Next, women wearing the same red-and-green robes stared straight ahead as they played an instrument with little bells. Their long black hair adorned in metallic gold and silver ribbons swayed as they walked. Next, several men playing stringed instruments strolled past. Violins? Behind them, extremely large elephants decorated in gold and precious gems carried women with harps. They wore green robes and the same golden headdresses as the dancers.

The strong bass from the drums echoed through the large cave, vibrating the floor and walls. Elizabeth felt as if she had suddenly landed in the middle of a symphony orchestra. The natural acoustics were amazing. The music, beautiful and enticing, enthralled her.

Several feet after the elephants, white tigers walked calmly next to men carrying very long sticks. Elizabeth was amazed by how tranquil the animals were acting. About twenty women dancers followed. They wore something like white bikinis with long silk skirts. Elizabeth's eyes were glued to their unusual movements. Their long, wavy hair swept across the floor like waves crashing along a shoreline.

After they passed, Ningal held out her arms. As several men carrying a huge golden chair approached, she lowered her hands. Perhaps the signal to lower their heads? Elizabeth glanced at David. With his head bowed, eyes closed and his hands shaking, he looked terrified.

The trumpets sounded louder, as if they were playing right next to her. Growls from the white tigers filled her with fear. Wanting to watch but knowing better, Elizabeth balanced on the balls of her feet inside a sacred place she never knew existed. A place she never wanted to leave. Keeping her head bowed low, only the bottoms of red robes filled her vision.

After a short pause, Ningal tapped her shoulder. Elizabeth glanced up and watched the back of the procession walk away. Touching David's arm, she smiled as he opened his eyes. David passed the signal on down the line.

As the others opened their eyes, Elizabeth held her breath. Behind the king, guards walked slowly, carrying long, sharp staffs. Different weapons clung to the various straps hugging their strong, muscular bodies. Although she didn't see guns, the men looked like a massive force no sane person would want to provoke.

As the procession left the small, speechless group, Ningal smiled. "This way."

John Hershawl stood on the steps of the Capitol Building and stared at the reflecting pool. The cherry trees should bloom within the next several weeks. How long had it been since he accepted the position at the CIA? Twelve years? Fifteen? Did it even matter anymore? Maybe retirement would be a better choice. How he found himself in the predicaments that gave him such heartburn was way beyond him.

Knowing that his driver would wait patiently at Garfield Circle, John decided to take a short walk to calm his nerves. He glanced into the sky and nodded at the bright morning sun. Although it was a cool fifty-eight degrees, the sun hinted at warmer days to come. The soft sound of his feet against the cold concrete sent chills up his spin. *Am I doing the right thing?* Maybe he should just tell his superior to bite him. No, he didn't have the strength or courage for that.

Stepping onto Southwest Drive, he waited for several cars to pass before jogging to the other side. John shivered and pulled his collar in tight. *Where is this cold air coming from? The trees won't bloom until next month if this keeps up.*

Standing in front of the Botanical Gardens, John sighed. He walked up to the entrance and paused as two elderly women approached. Pulling open the door, he waved them through. One lady smiled and the other nodded.

"Morning ladies," John said.

"Thank you, kind sir," the smiling one replied.

As the door closed behind him, another chill ran up his back. It felt as if someone was watching him. Shaking his head, he ignored the odd sensation.

He flashed his membership card at the attendant, and she smiled as he walked past. Maybe the tropic section would feel good about now. Entering the huge display, he listened to the flowing water. His nerves relaxed a little. Again, he came face-to-face with those two old ladies. They again smiled and nodded as they passed.

Pulling out his phone, he checked the time. The scheduled call should come in a few minutes. He had to calm down; otherwise his thoughts would be too scrambled. This was not the time for scrambled thoughts.

Taking in a deep breath, he studied one of the tall and exotic trees and paused at the sensation of cool, humid air. The sound of fluttering wings made him jump. Glancing around, he almost tripped over one of the old ladies who was following the trail of a butterfly with her finger.

"I'm sorry." He stepped aside.

"What's the matter sonny?" the elder woman asked. "Did you see a fairy or something?"

John stared into her serious face. She couldn't possibly know about those abominable creatures. As her evil grin spread, his heart jumped into his throat. Before he could reply, the old woman grabbed her friend by the arm. She glanced over her shoulder and winked as they walked away.

"What the fuck?" he whispered.

"Excuse me?" an attendant said.

Shaken and confused, John wasn't sure what to do. "Um, nothing. I'm sorry."

"Please watch your language in here, sir," the botanical garden attendant replied.

She heard me? Damn, she must have good ears. He glanced at his cell; only a few moments to spare. He needed to find a private place where he could talk freely. The area for medicinal plants seemed like a good place. Who in their right mind would walk through there?

Opening the door, John gasped. *These are medicinal? I should probably get some of these for my bedroom. Maybe I'd feel better.* As he walked, the garden pulled him into a calmness he hadn't felt in months. Just as his world settled down, his phone chirped. Grabbing the thing before it jumped out of his shirt pocket, he sighed. It was the familiar number that always terrorized him.

"Hershawl here."

"John," the frantic voice replied. "We have a problem."

"We have lots of problems. Can you give me a hint?"

"Did you hit the target?"

"No," John said.

"Why not?"

"Colonel Rose said they'd already left the base. He sent a couple of trucks after 'em, but they had backup."

"Backup? From where?" The voice sounded even more frantic.

"Have no idea. Is this what you wanted me for?"

"No. New arrivals were added to the schedule. The blood didn't match from the last batch."

"How many this time?" John asked.

"About four hundred."

"Where are they coming from?"

"New Zealand."

"Jesus, New Zealand?" John sighed and his shoulders slumped. "Are you sure they're really out there? Are you sure you'll find it?"

"We'll find it," the voice replied.

"Then what?"

"Then we take what we need so we'll survive. It was all explained by the ancients. Don't you remember? If we do not have the DNA signature in *our* blood when the gods arrive, we'll be euthanized."

"Yes, yes," John whispered. "The gods will only want their *own* living on this planet. So, tell me. If the gods made their *own*, and we're not a part of that group, then where did *we* come from?"

The phone fell quiet.

"Hello?"

"I don't need any of your bullshit philosophical questions. I'm sending the information your way. Make sure the group makes it past the Canadian border. I want them shipped directly to the New Jersey lab. You're their escort. No hired help this time."

"Fine." John shook his head.

"Just do your job and they'll be no problems."

"Isn't that what you said about the train passengers? Just get those scientists and geologists and there'd be no problem. Isn't that what you said?"

"How in the hell was I supposed to know that one of the guardians would crack?" the voice said.

"You should do better background checks on your employees."

"I just sent a message to your secured account. John, I'm warning you. Don't fuck this up."

Taking in a deep breath, John again shook his head. The man on the other end was a complete idiot. A moron. *How did I ever get myself hooked up with this crazy religious group anyway?*

The entrance to the Orchid Room was just ahead. As he approached, he frowned. The two old ladies were standing there. *Are they waiting for me?* One held the door open.

"Thank you." He walked past.

The older woman nodded. "No, thank you, young man. Thank you very much."

As the door shut behind him, he chuckled. *What was that all about?*

"Elsie," the older woman said, staring at her cell phone. "We must sit while I make my call."

Elsie sat on a nearby bench. "This is a nice place to rest."

"Yes, it is." Dorothy tapped on her phone while watching the door to the Orchid Room. *No need for any surprises.*

"Colonel Rose here," boomed the stern voice.

175

"Alpha … Epsilon … Phi … Gamma," Dorothy whispered into her phone. "Mission complete. Full conversation and data sent to headquarters."

"Thank you," Colonel Rose replied. "Good, would —"

Dorothy clicked off her phone before Rose could complete his sentence. Cramming the phone into her purse, she rested her hands in her lap. "It's been a long day, Elsie."

"Yes, it has," Elsie replied. "Perhaps it is time to go back to the hotel."

"Yes, perhaps."

"We need to call Dr. Lewis and check in," Elsie said. "It'd be easier if we call him from our hotel. I don't really like these little telephones."

"Let's get some lunch, sister." Dorothy stood. "I'm hungry."

"Did you see that beautiful orchid back there?" Elsie wrapped her arm through her sister's and leaned against her shoulder. "I love you."

"Ditto kiddo," Dorothy whispered.

Leonora screamed with delight as the dolphin pulled her through the warm water. Holding onto the dorsal fin, she felt like she was floating on air. As the dolphin slowed, another came up beside her. She switched to her other hand, and the new dolphin took off. The warm water rushed around her legs, sending ripples of exhilaration all through her. Never in a million years could she have imagined something so wonderful, so pure, so innocent.

Glancing up, she saw the boat. The dolphin was taking her back. As they came to a stop, Leonora rested her head against the slender animal's back. "Thank you."

The dolphin chirped several times as if saying, "You're welcome."

She reached up and Bob grabbed her arm, pulling her from the water.

"That was so much fun!" she yelled. "Wow!"

"I told you. Nothing compares."

Leonora glanced into Bob's caring eyes. "Thank you for that."

Laughing, he replied, "You are quite welcome."

Sitting next to Loomsbury, she laughed, the pleasing sensation of freely soaring through the water still with her.

"You enjoyed that?" Loomsbury asked.

"It was amazing," Leonora replied. "Imagine if we lived out here. I think that's how I'd want to go to work every day."

"Your lunch would get wet."

"Who'd care," she said, towel-drying her hair.

"I believe I'll stay on this boat or whatever it's called."

Leonora smiled at her dear friend. "I understand." After wrapping the towel around her waist, she climbed the stairs. Bob winked at her. "What other secrets does this place have?"

"I know a great cove where the fish are amazing," he said. "We'll stop there for lunch one day."

"What's the plan?" Loomsbury asked.

"I thought we'd drop anchor just off the island near the resorts. People will think we're tourists. Tomorrow you two can explore the land."

"Cool." Leonora stared out at the setting sun. Several dolphins jumped from the water, spinning as they landed. As her heart soared with excitement, she wished she were out there with them.

"Looks like they're saying good-bye," Bob said.

Leonora waved at the jumping dolphins.

Chapter Sixteen

"**D**r. Lewis?" Connie's voice echoed through the office. "Agent Tarply is here to see you."

Lewis sighed. "Send him in Connie."

After entering Lewis's office, Agent Tarply remained near the door. Glancing at the frightened man, Lewis chuckled.

"Bill, come in and sit. I won't bite ... much." Lewis waved at him to sit down.

"Yes sir." Agent Tarply sat at the far end of the long white couch.

Lewis smiled. "Would you like something to drink? Coffee? Soda? Water?"

"I'm fine, sir."

Lewis sat across from the shaking agent. "You have a report for me?"

"Yes sir." Tarply pulled out a couple sheets of paper and handed one to Lewis. "The bank didn't want to cooperate. Had to use a persuasive argument."

"Oh?"

"Just a few broken fingers, sir."

"Broken fingers?"

Tarply chuckled. "Kelly McGruffin was not paid by the Digital Artistic Society. She found the consignment through the organization, but they did not hire or pay her."

"Who did?" Lewis asked, knowing the answer would probably be Inter Diagnostics Incorporated.

"Helios Corporation."

"Helios? Interesting." Lewis stood and walked toward the large glass windows. "Connie?"

"Yes sir."

"Connect me with Agent Ramsden."

"Yes sir."

"I don't like our new phone system," Tarply said as he reviewed his notes.

"Neither do I. What else did you find?"

"The check was cut from Bank Rakyat Indonesia. It's one of the largest banks in that country."

"Who owns it?"

"Interestingly, it's seventy percent government owned."

"Who holds the other thirty percent?"

"IPO, that stands for Initial Public Offering. The stocks are sold to the public. I guess you could say that it's owned by the government and its citizens."

"Interesting."

"Helios holds several bank accounts around the world. The funds of interest just happened to go through that account."

"Didn't hide it very well, did they?"

"Probably didn't feel a need to do so, sir," Tarply said.

"Anything else?"

"The account is described as research and development. Current balance is a little over forty million."

"Forty, you say?"

"Yes, sir," Tarply replied.

Connie's voice intruded again. "Dr. Lewis?"

"Yes, Connie."

"We cannot reach Agent Ramsden. I also tried Agent Lumer and Agent Womack."

Agent Tarply's head jerked up when Sumner's name was mentioned. Lewis noticed right away.

"Devon?"

"No answer, sir."

"Contact Colonel Rose," Lewis said. "Find out what's going on over there."

"Already have," Connie replied. "Awaiting a return call."

"Sir?" Tarply stood. "If Sumner's involved, I'd like to volunteer my help."

Lewis nodded. *Why do my agents always have to get involved with each other? Staying at arm's length is always the best. Less emotion, less pain.* "Of course. I'll make the arrangements."

"I've completed all the required training," Tarply said.

"Never been on assignment before?"

"No sir," Tarply replied. "I work for Administration."

"Administration?"

Tarply nodded.

Lewis rubbed his forehead.

"I can do it," Tarply said.

"Perhaps, but you'll need help."

"Help, sir?"

Lewis held up his hand. "Connie?"

"Sir?"

"I need Agent Nathaniel Edwards, please."

"Nate? Maddie's husband?"

"Yes, Connie, please."

"I believe he retired, sir."

"He did. Your point is?"

"Yes sir."

"You'll need help." Lewis winked at Tarply. "This man is good. Very good."

A fresh but familiar voice came through the intercom. "Jeff?"

"How is everything, Nate?"

"Let me see. Charlie's working for the police force here in town. Tiffany and Sydney are fine. How about you?"

"I'm about ready to call it quits," Lewis said. "Getting too old for this crazy stuff."

"I know you didn't call to see how everyone was doing. What's up?"

"Nate, I need your help."

"I'm listening."

Jack wasn't sure what to think as they followed Ningal down the huge, underground highway. After watching the king's flamboyant display, he wasn't sure if they were safe or not. "Sam? What do you think?"

"Interesting," Worthington replied.

"Is it normal for a king to not want to be looked at?"

They kept walking. "You have to understand a few things," Worthington said.

"Such as?" Jack frowned.

"Kings of today are not the same as the kings of yesterday. We know very little about our ancient rulers. All we have are statues, paintings and wall writings. The exact culture that surrounded these ancient people remains vague to us."

"But to not look him in the face?"

"In our Bible, does it not say that if we look directly into God's eyes we would perish?"

"Something like that." Jack tried to remember his Sunday school classes. All he could remember was that Jesus loved him.

"The king that just walked past is a real king. This civilization has continued with their ancient culture as if it were only yesterday. What we are watching, experiencing, is the real deal. Inside this king flows the ancient royal blood."

"I've heard about royal blood in Christianity. Wasn't there a movie about it?"

"Yes, but only speculation," Worthington said. "Jack, what if Jesus was one of these people? What if Jesus was born from their royal blood?"

Ahead of them, Ningal walked up to a huge wooden door. "This way."

The tall, wide hallway beyond the door reflected their images as if made from mirrors. The light brightened as they walked and dimmed automatically behind them.

"Do you have electricity here?" Jack asked from near the back of the group.

"Electricity?" Ningal repeated. "Something similar."

"Similar in what way?" David asked.

"Similar in that it brightens our rooms," Ningal replied.

Jack wondered what they were missing as they passed several closed doors. Glancing up, he stared into his own face. Looking down, he saw himself again. The whole place was nothing but mirrors. "It's weird in here," Jack whispered.

"I agree," Worthington replied.

"The walk is to ensure you have a transparent heart," Ningal explained. "Only those with a clean mind and spirit may enter the house of Enlil."

"We're going to Enlil's home?" Elizabeth asked.

Ningal laughed. "No, my little one. You already walked Enlil's golden halls. We allowed you entry to save you from your enemy. The room I will take you to now safeguards many of Enlil's things. Think of it as a storage room. I believe you can relate to that."

"A storage room of the gods," Gerry whispered. "What an odd comparison."

"Your god is mythical, Dr. Miller," Ningal said. "Our gods are real. Therefore, our gods have mortal things. A bed. A chair. A chamber pot."

Elizabeth giggled.

"Interesting," Worthington said.

Near the end of the hallway, Ningal stopped at another huge wooden door, which looked old but well maintained. Covered in gold, the light it reflected almost blinded them.

"Now I see why a person cannot look directly at a god." Jack covered his eyes. "They wear so much gold; it hurts the eyes."

"I believe you are catching on," Ningal said.

"Why so much gold?" Gerry asked. "Is it to show off their wealth?"

Ningal shook her head. "Not at all, Dr. Miller. Wealth is nothing to a god. The gold is a purifier. Gold sprinkled in the air removes nanoparticles. Gold released in the upper atmosphere shields us from radiation. Processed gold taken as a supplement improves health. Jack and Dr. Worthington were treated with etherium gold. It helps to rejuvenate the body. I believe they are still adding it to your water in the mornings. Feeling good today, Dr. Worthington?" Ningal asked. "Jack?"

Jack and Worthington glanced at each other and nodded.

"Wearing gold that touches the skin will have the same healing effects," Ningal said.

"You mean, gold was never fought over because it's worth money?" Gerry asked.

"What is important to you, Dr. Miller?" Ningal smiled. "Your health? Or wealth? Without health, how could you enjoy wealth?"

"The words are only different by one letter," Elizabeth said. "Maybe they mean the same thing."

"You are very wise little one," Ningal said. She pushed on the golden door. As it swung open, the small group froze in place, scanning the large chamber. Again, they were greeted by two huge lion-human statues both over thirty feet tall.

Jack tapped Worthington on the shoulder. "The other ones were not this big."

"Never seen anything like this," Worthington said.

Ningal walked between the statues and knelt. Lowering her head, she whispered something that sounded like a prayer. Standing, she turned to the group.

"You may enter, but do not touch. Only the caretakers may handle the sacred items."

"I agree," Elizabeth said. "Can I go look now?"

Ningal walked past the two statues and stood aside. Elizabeth ran into the room that was filled with items from different eras, taking in everything. The others took their time entering the gigantic cave. Jack stared at the enormous, ancient Egyptian furniture that looked almost new. He easily passed under a four-legged stool with a seat made from animal skin.

"Gods sit in chairs," Ningal said from behind. "Common folk sit on pillows. These are Enlil's furnishings. You must understand that our gods lived many thousands of years."

"If I live to be a hundred," Worthington said, "I'll be happy just to have been here."

Jack's eyes fixated on a golden box. "What's this? Why so huge?"

"A chest," Ningal replied. "A place to store blankets or books."

"Your god had books?" Jack asked.

"Yes," Ningal replied. "Our *gods* could read."

"Jack," Elizabeth hollered from across the room. "Come see what I just found."

"At least it wasn't a bottomless pit this time," Devon whispered to Mark as they followed the robed men.

"I'm telling yah," Mark said. "Women are nothing but trouble."

"I heard that," Anais yelled from up front.

"I did too," Sumner added.

The men wearing robes ignored them. Walking quietly with three in the front and three in the back, they didn't seem to care whether the small group spoke to each other or not.

"Excuse me?" Devon said to one of the men. "Do you speak English?"

The man cocked his head to one side and smiled.

"I don't think they speak anything," Mark said.

"They probably speak Arabic," Dief added. "Let me try." Dief turned around and walked backward. "*Marhabaan.*"

Again, the robed man cocked his head to one side and smiled.

"That definitely worked." Devon shook his head. "Great job, Dief."

"I know some Spanish," Scott said.

Devon laughed. "I doubt very much if they speak Spanish."

Sumner turned around and said, "*Hadu.*"

The robed man smiled. "*Silim.*"

"What did you say to him?" Devon asked.

"Rejoice," Sumner replied. "He said, 'May all be well with you.' It's a Sumerian greeting. There's no word for *hello* in their language."

"Sumerian is very different from the languages of today," Dief said.

"Ask where they're taking us," Mark said.

"*Tabalu itti?*" Sumner said to one of the robed men.

"*E sharra,*" the man replied. Then he pointed toward the front of the small group.

"What'd he say?" Scott asked, now walking backward with Sumner.

"In laymen terms … to their ruler." Sumner's eyes widened as she walked.

"They're taking us to their leader?" Mark repeated. "Great, just great. Doesn't that mean they're going to eat us or something?"

"Eat us?" Sumner repeated, turning back around. "I sure hope not."

John Hershawl snapped the seatbelt into place. Looking around, he wondered how long before liftoff. He opened his magazine and glanced through the list of articles. Maybe he'd read about how Hollywood was taking over the world through the use of Adrenochrome. Should help pass the time.

"Excuse me kind sir," an elderly woman said from the aisle. "Would you be so nice as to lift our carry-ons into the overhead?"

John glanced up and smiled. Then he frowned. The two old women from the Botanical Gardens in DC smiled down at him. Standing, he grabbed the first carry-on. It was so heavy he could barely lift it.

"What's in here?" he asked. "A dead body or something?"

One old lady giggled. "Or something."

After pushing the second bag into the upper compartment, he sighed. "There yah go."

"Thank you, Mr. Hershawl," the second lady said.

His heart almost stopped beating. After winking at him, she sat in the seat across the aisle. *How in the world did she know my name?* As more passengers scooted down the aisle, he tried to get her attention. "Ma'am?" John reached out. "Ma'am?"

"Excuse me." A heavyset man pushed against John's extended arm.

"Ow!" John cried out. "You almost broke my damn arm."

The man laughed. "Shouldn't have it out where others are trying to walk."

"Shhh!" The old woman placed her finger over her mouth. "They'll kick you off the plane, Mr. Hershawl, and we must get to the border on time. We have friends flying in from New Zealand."

His heart pounded. He had to know. "Ma'am, how do you know my name? How do you know about the arrivals?"

The old woman grinned. Holding up her iPad, she turned it toward him. "You're on social media as being in charge of Washington," she replied. "You're an important person. Wait until I tell my grandchildren that I actually sat next to the president. They'll never believe me."

As he stared at her, a bright light hit his face twice. *The damn bitch took a picture of me!*

Laughing, the old woman showed him his photo. With his mouth hanging open, his eyes wide and his skin pale, he looked like he was about to puke.

"Look, Dorothy," the old woman said to her partner. "I got a picture of the president of the United States."

"That man's not the president, Elsie," Dorothy said. "He's just a government employee."

186

"Oh no." Elsie argued. "Look here. It says so on social media. Right here …"

John sighed as he slapped his head back against his seat. *Fucking old biddies. Almost broke my damn arm and just got the shit scared out of me. I've gotta retire!*

"Good afternoon," the captain announced, "and welcome to Delta Flight 479, non-stop to Montreal …"

"Sir?" The stewardess tapped John on the shoulder. "You must fasten your safety belt."

John glanced down and sighed. After struggling with the bitches's bags, he'd forgotten about his belt. "Certainly."

"A little forgetful these days, are we, Mr. Hershawl?" the old lady said from across the aisle. "Hey, Dorothy, look. These are such beautiful fairies. I think I'll order some to hang in my window. What do you think, Mr. Hershawl?" The old woman turned her iPad toward him again, showing images of several fairy figurines. Their wings, a florescent green, glittered on the screen.

"Lovely." John cleared his throat.

"Do you believe in fairies, Mr. Hershawl?" the old woman asked.

"I don't believe in a damn thing anymore." John closed his eyes.

As the steaks sizzled, Leonora's stomach growled. Amy stood ready holding a large plate. When the meat was ready to eat, Amy placed the steaks in the middle of the table. The meat was still sizzling.

"Wonderful." Leonora sat next to Loomsbury.

"We have steaks, baked potatoes, a garden salad and fresh fruit." Amy shoved a large spoon into the creamy fruit.

"Well, it looks delicious." Loomsbury placed a steak on his plate.

"Steak sauce?" Amy sat two bottles on the table.

Bob sighed and scooted his chair closer. "Let's eat. I'm starved."

"I saw you swimming with the dolphins today," Amy said.

Leonora smiled. "That was amazing." Leonora slapped butter onto her baked potato. "I'll never forget it."

"You'll need to come back and visit so you can swim with them again," Amy said.

"I will."

"What's up for tonight?" Loomsbury asked.

"We'll eat and rest. The fireflies should be out later," Bob said. "They're not like your southern flies back in the states. These things are huge. Wouldn't recommend provoking 'em."

"Big flies?" Loomsbury repeated. "How big, exactly?"

"Larger than my hand." Bob held out his hand. "And these hands are not small."

Leonora's eyes widened as she stared at Bob. The dead creature she examined was about that size. And that creature was capable of making light just like a firefly.

"Dr. Loo?" Leonora glanced over at Loomsbury.

As if reading her mind, he said, "Are the large flies found only around here? Near this island?"

Bob nodded as he chewed.

Chapter Seventeen

"What did you find?" Jack stood behind Elizabeth.

"Look at this." Elizabeth pointed to what looked like regular dishes and utensils. However, these were way too big.

"Is that a shovel?" Jack chuckled.

"No." Ningal laughed. "Those are Enlil's fork and spoon."

Jack shook his head, amazed. "How big was this Enlil guy?"

"Follow me," Ningal said. "We have a life-size statue of him."

Walking through the stacks of goods and large furniture, Jack raked his memory for anything about giants. All that came to mind was the *Jolly Green Giant*.

"Here he is." Ningal pointed to a statue of a huge man sitting in a chair similar to the one Jack saw earlier.

The man, if standing, would have easily topped sixteen feet or more. His knees reached higher than Jack's head. With a long bushy beard and eyebrows, he wore a robe similar to the ones the men here wore.

"Enlil?" Gerry asked, standing next to Jack.

"Was he really that tall?" Jack asked.

"According to the ancient writings," Gerry replied, "yes."

"And this person was a god, not a king?" Jack took a step closer to the statue.

"Both actually," Gerry replied.

"What's he carrying?"

"The Tablet of Destinies," Ningal answered.

"What's the Tablet of Destinies?" Jack asked.

"The laws handed down by the all mighty, Anu," Ningal said.

"Do you still have these tablets?" Gerry asked.

"Yes," Ningal said. "They are on the far table near the library. Follow me."

"Tell me more about Enlil," Gerry added as they walked. "Please."

"Enlil was a great and fair god," Ningal said. "He only loved one woman, Ninlil. Together they bore four children who were eventually assigned as watchers. Nanna, their eldest son, monitored the phases of our moons. At one time, this world had two. Nergal controlled the burials of humans. He monitored the gravesites. Ninazu healed the sick. She specialized in the care of humans. Their fourth child, Enbilulu, worked with canals and the movement of water. Very important position. Many parts of this world would not sustain life if the water did not reach it."

"What about religion? What were Enlil's belief as to where his people came from?" Gerry asked.

"Enlil followed the father's teachings. That they were molded from the primeval void of space. Their souls shape the cosmic waters and bend time. Time encircles us, causing our reality to repeat itself."

"It's all part of the numbers from the unknowable," Elizabeth said. "The circle of life."

"Very good, my little one." Ningal stroked the top of Elizabeth's head.

"Unknowable?" Jack asked.

"Life goes on," Elizabeth said. "David explained it to me."

The little boy's red tennis shoe flashed through Jack's mind. "Then why do babies have to die?" Tears clouded his vision. "It's not fair."

"What's wrong, Jack?" Elizabeth asked. "Are you thinking about our kidnappers?"

"No." Jack shook his head. "I was responsible for the death of two little boys. It was a long time ago. I couldn't stop my train."

"An accident?" Gerry asked.

"A bad one," Jack replied. "A car stalled on the tracks. It was a nasty curve. I was young and traveling too fast. We were late. Extra-large shipment took longer than expected to load. Being stupid, I wanted to make up time. By the time I saw the car, it was too late. I braked, but there wasn't enough room. Plowed right through 'em. Killed a mother and her two boys." Jack cried into his hands.

"Come with me, Jack." Ningal touched his arm. "I wish to show you something."

Tearfully, Jack walked behind Ningal as Elizabeth held his hand. Gerry and David and Worthington followed. At a far wall, Ningal pointed. Carved by hand, a sky map filled the wall.

"What is this?" David asked.

"It is our home," Ningal replied. "Mother Earth is here." She pointed to a small blue ball circling a large yellow sun. "Enlil's world is here." Now she pointed to a larger planet just outside the system.

"This is our solar system?" Worthington asked.

"You do not recognize it?" Ningal replied.

"There are too many planets," Worthington said.

"Not when this map was created. Tiamat" — Ningal pointed to a world that was just past where Mars should have been — "is now the asteroid belt. Its moon was called Mars, which as you know is now our fourth planet from the sun. Here is the planet Paititi. Over here was —"

"What happened to these worlds?" Worthington ran his finger along the path of Tiamat.

"When Enlil's home world, Nibiru, returns and circles in close to our sun, it disturbs the other worlds. Sometimes with tragic results. Many generations ago, Tiamat was destroyed when one of Nibiru's moons collided with it. The gas giant Neptune was split in half by another pass-by. That was when Saturn was born."

"Will the planet Nibiru come back?" Elizabeth asked.

"Eventually," Ningal replied. "However, it takes many Earth years. Over thirty-six thousand."

"Will it destroy Earth?" Elizabeth asked.

"No, my little one." Ningal hugged Elizabeth. "The path is now set between Mars and Jupiter. We are safe here."

"When is it expected to return?" Gerry asked.

"Not for another ten thousand years," Ningal said. "At that time, we also expect the return of our gods."

"You mean Enlil and Enki?" Elizabeth asked.

"Enlil is no longer with us. He died many Earth years ago. Enki will return," Ningal said. "You are a very smart girl. You know of our gods."

"Thank you," Elizabeth said. "My parents were archeologists."

"Were?" Ningal asked.

"I do not know what happened to 'em," Elizabeth replied.

Jack stared at Ningal. "What does all of this have to do with the little boys my train murdered?"

"Life is just a circle, Jack," Ningal said. "The planets revolve around the sun in a circle. Our galaxy flows in a circle. Therefore, our lives move in a circle. Once we leave this body, we are elevated to the next density. The little boys you believe you killed are now living in another dimension."

"I don't believe that," Jack said. "I won't believe that."

Ningal glanced back at the statue of Enlil and nodded. "Then I shall show you, Jack Lawrence."

Taking him by the hand, Ningal pulled Jack toward a door no one had questioned. It was just as large as the one they used to enter this grand cavern, but without all the gold trimmings. When she opened the door, a wave of heat slapped Jack in the face.

"I will show you where your boys are now living," Ningal said. "You will not be hurt, but we cannot remain long."

As the door closed behind them, Jack's heart raced. *Did I just doom myself to an early death?* If so, perhaps it was just punishment for killing that family. The darkness surrounded him. Reaching out, Jack couldn't even see his own hand.

"Why no light?" Jack squeezed Ningal's fingers.

"Do you know of ascension, Jack?"

"No."

"We live in a domain of densities. On the first level, awareness is at the point of physical matter. It is where the Provider combines matter and energy — the creation of atoms and molecules. First density allows our frequency to convert into a genetic code. It is when life begins within the mother's womb."

"Kinda makes sense."

"In second density, life does not possess awareness. It is where biological matter is created. Ego must have a strong frequency in order to exist."

"Like the stuff we see in a microscope," Jack said. "Sounds logical."

Ningal laughed. "Not exactly, Jack, but that understanding will serve for now. We live in the third density. Here, Earth humans develop individuality. They are able to remember their past and understand that they have a future. They are also aware of the present. Vibration is high enough that the illusion of a *one* in connection to the *whole* can emerge. Some animals live in this density with us."

"You mean like a dog?" Jack's mind swirled.

"No, my friend." Ningal laughed again. "More like a dolphin or whale. Some animals reside in the fourth density."

"How many densities are there?"

"We are aware of seven. Humans are slowly transitioning into the fourth. They are changing every day."

"I'll agree to that." Jack tried to see where they were going. "How can you see in the dark? Won't we trip over something?"

Ningal squeezed his hand. "There are no walls in here. Nothing to trip over."

"Where are we?"

"You will soon find out," she replied. "As our vibrations increase, our consciousness expands. Inside the fourth density, we integrate into the wholeness of life without losing our self-awareness. Our perception of the past, present and future become more entangled, more combined. Instead of time being linear, it becomes more fluid, similar to a pond's ripple. We begin to cross over the line and into multidimensional realities."

"Multidimensional realities?"

"Inside the higher densities, negativity is harder to maintain. If your heart is not pure, your vibration remains low."

"You told us that only those with a clean mind and spirit can enter Enlil's house. Does this have anything to do with it?"

"A little," Ningal said. "In order to rise into the higher frequencies, one's heart must be pure. Negative thoughts or desires cannot exist."

Ningal stopped walking. Jack's heart pounded and his mind raced. With no light to stimulate his eyes, it felt as if he were falling into a dark abyss, one he'd never get out of, one where he would be lost in forever.

"I can see and experience the first and second. However, I live in the third?" he asked.

"That is correct. Those in the higher frequencies can see and experience the lower ones."

Jack felt a slight tug. Ningal was pulling down on his arm. Dropping to his knees, Jack struggled to get comfortable. "Do not let go of my hand."

"I will not. Until you are ready."

"Tell me more about the other densities," he said.

"Certainly. In the fifth, we learn the true meaning of wisdom. Our awareness of the one becomes the whole. Our past becomes our future and our future becomes our past. We live and travel within time. We awaken and thus are the wise ones. We work with and guide those surviving in the lower densities."

"A shaman?"

"More of a spirit guide," she replied. "In the sixth and seventh densities, our physical bodies are left behind. We are consciousness in the purest of forms. Our minds become wisdom. Our histories fulfilled."

"What's the difference between the sixth and seventh?" he asked.

"In the seventh, we live in all the densities at once. We are multidimensional."

"During my youth as a hippie, we used to say that we were one with the universe." Jack laughed.

"The notion is similar. In the seventh, we are aware of everything and everyone. We connect at the subatomic level of life itself."

"Maybe that's why a negative person cannot go there," Jack said. "They would destroy it."

"Yes, they would." Ningal rubbed the back of his hand. "Are you ready, Jack?"

Jack sighed. *Am I ready? I have no idea.* "I guess so."

As her hand slipped away from his, Jack felt as if he were floating in a warm sea. Reaching out, he felt nothing but the warm air that surrounded him. He knew Ningal was close. He could sense her. However, he could not hear or see a thing. Then, sitting silently in the darkness, his mind flew everywhere at once. Voices and pictures clogged his hearing and vision. After a while, the confusion faded, and an eerie sensation surrounded him. As the warm turned to cold, his fears grew.

Sitting inside the emptiness, that one horrible night so many years ago became his reality. He was now standing at his old controls. The adrenaline rush at running his massive machine flowed once again through his veins. He hadn't felt this way since that terrible night.

As he pulled on the brakes, Jack screamed. Stuck between the levers and keeping him from applying full pressure was his middle finger. Metal on metal screeched as the massive iron wheels slid along the desolate tracks. Just a short distance ahead, a small car with the headlights blaring blocked his way. He could just make out the timid face of a small child. Jack stared at the passenger window, and the child was staring back at him.

"Lord Jesus!" Jack screamed. "Stop me, goddamn it. Stop me!"

Jack pulled on the brake, ignoring the pain that jolted from his finger and shot up his arm. Leaning back, he pulled even harder and prayed to a god he never met. But he lost his grip and smashed headfirst into the control panel. With the brake now released, the full force of the massive machine plowed through the small metal car as if punching through soft butter.

The emergency system kicked on and eventually the train slowed. Lifting himself off the floor, the terrified face of the young child refused to leave his mind. Jack jumped from the train, his legs protesting as they slammed against the solid ground. Rolling over several times, Jack struggled to breathe past the heavy weight in his chest.

Jack lifted himself onto his hands and knees and took several deep breaths. As his vision cleared, he looked toward the car. It lay sideways on the street. The front passenger wheel was menacingly lodged beneath the train. Waves of dread ran through Jack. He urged himself to run, the world whirling around him.

The woman was hunched over the steering wheel and covered in blood. She moved her hand slightly. Limping toward the mangled heap of smoldering metal, Jack touched the cracked window. The woman lifted her head and glanced up at Jack. Her bloody and tear-soaked face said it all. She mouthed the words, "My babies." Closing her eyes, she slumped over the steering wheel. The woman had died right in front of him, and all she was worried about were her two little boys.

Glancing into the back seat, Jack panicked. Half of the car was gone. *Where are the boys?* Grabbing the door handle, Jack pulled. The door refused to budget. Jack kept pulling.

"God help me!" Jack screamed. "You fucking son of a bitch, help me get these people out!"

As Jack screamed and pounded on the mangled car, several officers arrived. One pulled Jack away from the wreckage. The whole time, Jack kept yelling out for God to do something. To help him save the injured family. Upset and angry and about to lose his grip on what little reality he had left, Jack screamed. A paramedic gave him something to calm him down. An officer tried to talk to him, but Jack's garbled sentences didn't make any sense. They left Jack alone.

After sitting in the ambulance until his legs felt numb, Jack walked to the front of the train and circled around to the other side. Steam filled the night, making the accident scene look even more appalling like a scene in a horror movie. Only, in this scene, everything was real. His puny hands had just tried and convicted three young souls to death.

Walking through the trench filled with trash and leaves and water, each step felt as if he were lifting a ton. He stepped onto the road. The sight of an empty, bloody car seat ripped through his heart and tears filled his eyes. Leaning his head against what remained of the back of the car, Jack cried.

A different officer pulled Jack away. A wrecker wrapped chains under the torn vehicle. The worker kept glancing over at Jack. *Is he judging me? I didn't see the fucking car, okay? I didn't see them!*

Needing to get away, Jack took several steps down the dry, dusty road. Something small and red lying off to one side grabbed his attention. Picking it up, his stomach ripped apart. He ran to the side of the road, clutching the child's bloody tennis shoe, and lost the contents of his stomach. Each heave allowed a little of the evil festering deep inside to fade away. When the waves stopped, he stared at the small shoe. It just fit inside the palm of his hand.

"Dear God," Jack whispered. "What did I do? Why did you allow me to do this?"

Falling to road, Jack cuddled the small shoe against his chest and cried. As he rocked back and forth, a warm hand touched his shoulder.

"What did I do?" Jack cried out. "The shoe! Where's the shoe?" Jack franticly reached out. Swiping the ground with his hands, he screamed, "I can't lose the shoe!"

"Sir?" A soft young voice pulled him from his terror.

"Who's there?"

"Sir?" the young voice said again. "My name's Cayden."

Jack froze. There was no one with the name of Cayden in their group. Jack was sure of it.

"I can't see you," Jack said.

The area around Jack cooled. A soft hue now surrounded him. *That face*. The boy from the car had that same face. He remembered seeing it through the passenger's widow.

"Can you see me now?" Cayden asked.

"How old are you, boy?"

"Eight," Cayden replied.

"You were in that car that night?"

Cayden nodded. "That was really scary. But it didn't hurt."

Jack rose to his knees and glanced around. The young boy, with blondish-brown hair and large brown eyes, smiled at him. Behind the boy stood a woman with blonde hair. She held a little boy of about two in her arms. His dark hair and big blue eyes felt warm and inviting.

"That's my mom," Cayden said. "That's Henry. He's two."

Jack's tear fell as he reached out to the boy. "I'm so sorry."

"No sir," the woman said. "Please. Do not hurt anymore. Not for us."

Walking up to Jack, the woman knelt. Little Henry reached out and touched Jack's cheek. The little boy smiled. Jack smiled back.

"Would you like to hold Henry?" the woman asked. "My name's Liz, by the way."

"I'm so sorry." Jack cradled the little boy in his arms. "I honestly didn't see your car."

"You still do not understand." Placing her fingers over Jack's lips, the woman smiled. "It was all planned."

"What was planned?"

"We needed to experience a horrible accident before we could ascend," Liz said.

"What are you talking about?" Jack bounced Henry against his hip. Henry giggled.

"When you ascend from six to seventh, you must have experienced everything that is negative while in an earthly form. If not, then you cannot release all that is destructive. My children and I were already leaving the fourth density when your train hit our car."

"You knew you were going to get hit by a train?" Jack's eyes widened. "You deliberately parked your car on that track?"

Liz laughed. "Of course not. When you are in third density, you don't know the future. I was on my way to drop the boys off at my parents' house. The car stalled. When I saw the train, I tried to reach for Henry. He was so far away. I couldn't leave him alone. I told Cayden to get out, but he refused to go."

"I don't understand."

"I know you don't. We are sorry, Jack Lawrence. If we knew how much our deaths would have affected you, we would have stayed. We would not have died."

"What?" Jack shook his head. Henry laughed.

"We must experience in order to grow. You are growing within your nonphysical world right now. When we reach sixth density, we work hard to move up to the seventh. Our experiences are calculated. If something is missing, we must return and fulfill it. We had not yet experienced the fear that was required. The three of us wanted to experience our deaths together. If we had only known the effect that it had on you. Honestly, we would have chosen another way."

"Another way?"

"Maybe a house fire or a plane crash. I do not remember why we chose your train, Jack Lawrence. We apologize for ruining your life. We cannot ascend until we are forgiven by you."

"Forgiven?"

"Yes," Cayden said. "You have to say you forgive us for affecting your life so badly."

"My life?" Jack stared at the young woman. "That accident affected me, yes. But *I* ran into *you*. *My* carelessness is what caused the accident. You looked at me and said *my boys*. You were afraid for your boys."

"Of course, I was." Liz frowned. "I was in a mortal form. I had no memory of our plan to ascend together."

"You're still in mortal form." Jack touched her arm.

Liz took Henry from Jack's arms and stood back. Holding Cayden's hand, she smiled. "No Jack. This is our true form."

The air around Jack pulsated. A strong aroma of rain filled him with soft tranquility. As he watched, Liz, Cayden and Henry dissolved until there was nothing there but a soft, white glow.

"This is how you are now?"

"Yes, Jack Lawrence," Liz replied, her voice soft and angelic. "Do not cry for us. If it wasn't for you, we would not have ascended to where we are now. You helped us, Jack Lawrence, and we thank you. We love you very much. You are important to us. You are, and forever will be, a major part of our life force."

"I forgive you," Jack whispered. "I forgive you for affecting me so," Jack smiled at Cayden, "badly."

"Thank you, Jack Lawrence," Liz said. "Thank you."

As their light faded, Jack cried. He cried for the earthly children his massive train slaughtered all those years ago. He cried for the mother who begged him for help. He lifted his hand to wipe away his tears. Instead of his hand, a small tennis shoe touched his cheek. Smelling the small shoe, Jack's tears flowed.

"Do not cry for us, Jack Lawrence. Your love and forgiveness have allowed us to advance. Our frequencies are rising now. If you ever need anything, just call for us."

Jack breathed in deeply. His hands scanned the floor, searching for the small shoe. "Damn!"

"What is wrong?" Ningal asked.

"I lost the shoe."

"You have lost your shoes?"

"Not mine. The little boy's." A light hit his eyes. Slapping his hands to his face, he moaned. "Damn, that's bright."

"What's bright?" Elizabeth asked.

Jack looked around. He was standing near the large statue, again. "How long have I been gone?"

"Gone?" David asked.

"You didn't go anywhere," Worthington said.

"Are you okay, Jack?" Gerry asked.

"I went through that door with Ningal." Jack pointed across the room.

"What door?" Elizabeth asked.

"That door —" Jack froze. Instead of a large door, a stack of crates blocked the way. "Those were not there a moment ago."

"Jack," Ningal whispered. "Did you experience the fate of your boys?"

Jack nodded.

Ningal smiled. "Do not question a gift when given, Jack Lawrence."

Chapter Eighteen

Devon tapped on his knee as he watched. Mark stared at Carrie and Sumner. *Is Mark about to take revenge on the girls because we were captured by guys wearing bathrobes?* "You okay, buddy?" Devon asked Mark.

"Women!" Mark replied. "Nothing but trouble."

"I can relate to that," Devon said. "But we can't exactly blame everything on those two."

Devon's small group stood together. Colorful cloth draped the walls. Several tables with chairs filled the room. Devon wanted to know why they were not allowed to sit down. To his dismay, their guards didn't seem to speak English.

Everyone worried about something different. Mark wondered how far his head would roll after being chopped off at the neck. Carrie worried she'd never hold a baby in her arms. A baby that would eventually call her Mom. Sumner wanted the robed men to return so they could talk; she was titillated by the discovery of a living group of people who spoke the ancient Sumerian language. Anais thought about her parents and prayed they were okay. Scott rubbed his head. All he could think about was wanting to strangle his estranged wife. Dief wondered if he'd ever get his life back. Aaron kept glancing over at Anais. She was a goddess. The most beautiful woman he ever laid his eyes upon. If they died now, he'd never get the chance to really know her. Devon wanted to eat. His stomach growled and his dry mouth stuck to itself.

A woman dressed in green entered through one of the draped cloths. She carried a large pitcher over her right shoulder. Behind her, several more women entered carrying trays of food. One woman held plates. As they prepared the table, Devon's mouth watered.

"They're going to feed us?" Mark asked.

"Looks that way," Devon said.

"Last meal?" Mark whispered.

They watched as the women worked. Each maiden picked one person from Devon's group and escorted them to a chair. They filled a plate for them. Whatever they needed their supporter retrieved for them.

To Devon, no food ever tasted so good. The water was sweeter than honey.

"This is delicious," Sumner said, requesting more.

"Wonderful," Anais said.

Scott hummed his appreciation as he scooped another spoonful into his mouth.

"Thank you," Devon said to one of the women.

She bowed her head.

With the sun falling along the distant horizon, Loomsbury rested his head against the hard pillow.

"This is nice." Speaking to no one in particular, he studied the clouds as they passed overhead.

"Here." Bob's voice pulled him from his thoughts.

Loomsbury accepted the cold beer. "Thanks."

"So," Leonora said to Bob as she sat next to Loomsbury, "where are these big bugs of yours?"

"Just give it a few," Bob said. "Amy? Ready?"

"Everything's off and secured below," she hollered. "Getting the upper ones now."

"You're turning off the lights?" Leonora asked.

"We're closing the windows and doors too." Bob winked.

As she closed the door behind her, Amy glanced around. "I believe we're all set."

"The flies have nasty stingers," Bob said. "Please, do not provoke them."

"They'll fly right up to us," Amy said. "Just ignore them."

"Where are the resorts you talked about?" Loomsbury asked, sipping his beer.

"Over there." Bob pointed. "See the lights? That's one of 'em. The other one is a little farther on down. We're anchored right at the line. If I move a few miles to the east, the patrols will chase us away."

Setting one lone lantern on the railing, Amy clicked it on. She smiled at Leonora and Loomsbury as the back of the boat lit up.

"I'm dropping the net." Bob released a rope, and the net fell into place, protecting them from whatever would soon visit the small light.

After a while, the sun fell below the horizon, leaving only a blank canvas behind. As the islands faded into darkness, stars brightened one at a time. Dolphins jumped into the night's sky and splashed back into the abyss, their bellies slapping the surface.

Loomsbury took another drink. Tranquility and serenity entrapped him as he enjoyed the pleasant aroma from the island's flowers. Something large buzzed past the net. Sitting up, Loomsbury glanced around. All remained quiet. Taking another sip, he sat back. A loud buzzing headed straight for him. Something thudded against the deck.

"Get the swatters," Bob said to Amy. "These do not look happy tonight."

"What doesn't look happy?" Loomsbury asked.

"Look." Bob pointed at the small lantern.

Gray flying creatures attacked the light from all sides, their long, sharp stingers slashing at the small container. Several of the creatures noticed the humans and dive-bombed the net. As their bodies crashed into the nylon meshing, the small group jerked back. Leonora jumped up and ran for the glass door. A group of creatures soared after her together, hitting the net all at once.

"I think we should get inside," Bob whispered.

"I agree." Loomsbury pulled open the door and stepped through.

As Bob closed the door behind him, the mesh screen collapsed to the deck. Hundreds of flying gray creatures stormed the small boat.

"Are we safe in here?" Loomsbury asked.

"Not sure," Bob replied. "Never seem 'em like this before."

Breaking glass sent Loomsbury's heart into his throat. Glancing around, he sighed with relief. It was only the lantern hitting the back of the boat. With darkness all around them, the little creatures lit up as if carrying a hundred little lights. Sparkling, florescent greens, reds and blues surrounded their boat.

"They're actually quite beautiful." Loomsbury studied one of the creatures that had landed near a window. The little guy stared just as hard at Loomsbury. When Loomsbury smiled, it smiled. When Loomsbury raised his hand, the creature raised its hand. Loomsbury laughed, and the creature lit up like a Christmas tree.

"Wow!" Leonora stared out over the kitchen sink. "This is wild."

"Are they always this colorful?" Loomsbury asked.

"Not really," Bob replied. "I've never seen so many of 'em before. Nor have they ever been this hostile."

They nervously watched the acrobatic and colorful flying show throughout the evening. Loomsbury thought about the little boy, Everest, and now understood how he felt that terrible night when they tried to break through his window. *What do they want? Why are they being so hostile?*

"Wait a minute." Loomsbury glanced at Leonora.

"What?"

"Get into the shower. Turn on the water. I'll do the same. Amy, use as much air freshener as you can. If you don't have that, use something else that smells really strong. Hurry. Let us know if they leave."

Standing in the shower and using almost all of his shampoo, Loomsbury finally felt safe.

"It's okay to come out," Bob yelled through the cabin door. "They've left."

Drying off, Loomsbury sighed. He dressed in sweats and towel-dried his hair. Leonora met him topside.

"Wanna tell me what the shower was all about?" Bob asked.

"I don't know how I knew, I just did," Loomsbury replied.

"We dissected one of those creatures in our lab," Leonora said. "They probably were able to smell it, somehow."

"You've showered since then," Bob said.

Loomsbury nodded. "You're correct. I can't explain it. The creature had internal organs I've never seen before."

"Your assumptions must be correct," Amy said. "They went away."

"Interesting." Loomsbury frowned.

"So, what do we use so they don't attack us on the island?" Leonora asked.

"Good question." Loomsbury stared out the kitchen window. The upcoming expedition was fast becoming a lot more than he agreed to.

"Have you ever had to use one of these?" Elsie asked Dorothy.

"No. Have you?"

"Not really." Elsie turned the pistol over in her hand.

"Had training," Dorothy said. "Only remember the cleaning part though. One can never be too clean."

"That is true," Elsie replied. "I wonder when this was last washed."

"Don't know." Dorothy refilled her morning coffee. "I wonder how our friend is doing."

"Probably still sleeping." Elsie glanced over to the next balcony. "I don't see anyone moving around yet."

Dorothy smiled as Elsie walked into the bathroom and stilled when she heard running water. *She wouldn't, would she? Of course not. What a silly thought.* Taking another bite of toast, she added sugar to her coffee. She smiled again as Elsie sat back down.

"What yah doing in the bathroom, sister?" Dorothy asked.

"I thought I'd clean my pistol." Elsie dried the small object with a hand towel. "It was pretty dirty. Took some work to get the soap into these little crevasses."

Dorothy sighed.

"I'd like to study the Tablet of Destinies," Worthington said as they were leaving.

"Certainly," Ningal replied. "I'll have someone bring them to your room."

"You don't mind?" Worthington asked.

"You mean them no harm." Ningal winked at him. "No reason to worry."

After speaking to a caretaker about the Tablet of Destinies, Ningal headed back to the eatery. The others would be done with their meal by now. Stopping at the king's chamber, she waited her turn. When the king was alone, she approached, dropping to one knee and lowering her head.

Using the ancient Sumerian language, the king spoke. "Rise, my wife. Come sit and be with me."

"I wish to see your face," Ningal said. Placing her palms on his cheeks, she bent over and kissed his forehead.

"Your eyes give me pleasure," he whispered.

"And yours give to me as well."

"How are our visitors?"

"Comfortable," Ningal said. "I worry about the girl-child, Elizabeth."

"Talk to me."

"Her parents have moved on to the next density," Ningal explained. "She is alone in this world."

"We will talk later." The king winked.

Again, Ningal leaned forward and kissed the king. This time he raised his head so that their lips met. She smiled.

"Your eyes please me," she whispered.

As she walked the halls, Ningal paid attention to her citizens. *Are they happy? Are they content with their lives?* Maybe she'd ask their governors. Hold a special session to find out.

Two guards approached. In Sumerian, the man spoke. "They are ready."

Ningal nodded. Pulling the drape to one side, she stepped into the eatery. The small group, covered in sweat and dirt, looked defeated. Their spirits broken. Her heart warmed for these lost souls. She had to smile.

"*Silim.*" Sumner stood.

"*Silim.*" Ningal bowed her head.

"What do you want with us?" Devon asked. "If you even understand me."

"I understand," Ningal replied. "We want nothing of you."

"Why are we held hostage?" Mark asked.

"You entered the House of Enlil," Ningal replied. "We do not usually entertain unexpected visitors."

"You live here?" Mark asked.

Ningal nodded.

"We're trying to find our people," Devon said. "We believe they were brought here against their will."

"You are from the distant land known as America," Ningal said. "You're a long way from home."

"Yes," Devon said. "We are."

"What do you want with your missing people?" Ningal asked.

"To take them home," Sumner replied.

"You cannot take yourselves home," Ningal said. "How do you expect to rescue your people and guarantee their protection?"

"Now, this is the first smart thing I've heard in a very long time," Scott shouted out from across the table. "Give her a gold star!"

Ningal laughed.

"May we go?" Devon asked.

Ningal cocked her head to one side. "Where do you want to go?"

"I don't know," Devon replied. "But I *have* to save Jack Lawrence."

"You know Jack Lawrence?" Ningal asked.

"Not personally." Devon pulled out the little tennis shoe. "I have something I must give to him."

"You carry the shoe," Ningal said.

"How do you know about the shoe?" Devon asked.

Ningal smiled. "How do you carry the shoe?"

"It's so green here, sister," Elsie said as she watched the land soar past her window.

"Yes, it is green," Dorothy replied.

"Are they in front of us?"

"Yes, sister," Dorothy answered.

"Don't lose track of 'em." Elsie pulled two sodas from the cooler. "Would you like one?"

"No," Dorothy replied. "It'll just make me want to pee."

"Perhaps you are right." Elsie dropped the sodas back into the cooler. "Why did we bring 'em?"

"For later, dear sister."

"That truck doesn't look all that great," Elsie said.

"No, it doesn't."

"How far should we allow 'em to get?" Elsie asked.

"We'll let 'em get across the border," Dorothy said. "We're on Route 219 now. It won't be much longer."

"Canada is so green." Elise admired the landscape outside her window. "I don't see why we cannot stay here awhile."

"Maybe another time," Dorothy replied.

"Good morning." Loomsbury sat at the table.

"Morning." Amy placed a dish of scrambled eggs in front of him.

"What's on the agenda for today?" he asked.

"We're going to hike the island," Leonora replied.

"Hike?" Loomsbury repeated.

"Hike." Leonora patted him on the back. "There are hiking boots in your closet."

"I saw 'em but thought they were for someone else."

"You would." Leonora laughed and laced up her boots.

"We'll take a dinghy," Bob said. "I'll drop you off and pick you up when you call."

"Great." Loomsbury stared at his eggs.

"Eat," Amy said. "Your food's getting cold."

"Hike?" Loomsbury took a bite. "That means hills, and with hills" — he took another bite — "come the falls, and with the falls" — Loomsbury sipped his coffee — "come the broken bones."

"Is he okay?" Bob whispered to Leonora.

"They don't let him out much," she replied.

Bob nodded.

"Now that you have rested," Ningal said to Devon's small group the next morning, "I will escort you. Follow me."

"Thank you for the night's rest and shower," Devon said as they left the room.

"You are very welcome." Ningal waved for them to follow. "This way."

Devon tried to see into the other rooms as they walked down the pristine hallway, but he couldn't see anything. *Where are we going now? Maybe it's time to take off our heads. We've showered, filled our bellies and had time to reflect. Now would be the perfect time.*

Ningal pulled aside the drape and stepped through. Devon followed. His heart jumped as he stared at all the people. They looked happy and well cared for. So many were crowded into the small room. His eyes darted from side to side.

"Jack Lawrence!" Scott yelled before darting into the room.

Not waiting for an invitation, Devon followed him. He watched as Scott and an older man embraced, their smiles exposing everything. There was definitely a special bond between them. Pulling the small red shoe from his back pocket, Devon balanced it in his hand and approached the men. He wasn't sure if he should smile or frown.

Jack Lawrence's eyes grew wide, and his tears fell as he reached for the small shoe.

"Thank you," Jack whispered, kissing the object.

"I've been looking for you for a very long time. It's wonderful to finally meet you, Jack Lawrence." Devon reached out his hand.

Jack shook it. "And you are, sir?"

Devon pulled out his badge. "I'm from the FBI. The Agency assigned me to find the missing passengers from your train. How many are here with you?"

"A hundred and thirty-two," Jack replied.

"Over three hundred were on your train," Devon said. Realizing the impact of his statement, he felt terrible for saying anything.

"The others died either on transport or shortly after arrival. Sick, hurt. It was bad," Jack said.

"I'm sorry." Devon frowned. "I'm so very sorry."

Jack nodded.

As the groups talked, Ningal watched. It amazed her how similar her culture was to theirs, but how different their lives.

Loomsbury sprayed the trees and bushes with bug killer.

Leonora walked past him. "That won't help."

"It's better than nothing. There are little crawling *things* everywhere."

"Will you come on already?"

The natural path ended. Loomsbury and Leonora stared at the tree now blocking their way.

"Any suggestions?" Loomsbury asked.

"I don't think that can of yours will help with this." Shaking her head, Leonora pulled a machete from her backpack and waggled it at him. "I recommend you do the same."

"That wasn't hard," Elsie said as they left the custom station behind. "I wonder how they hid their goods."

"Recon said the passengers are enclosed inside wooden crates. The crates labeled as clothing."

"Not many will survive like that," Elise said.

"We're almost there."

As the car crossed over North Star Road, several black helicopters buzzed overhead. Elsie leaned out the window. Staring into the afternoon sun didn't help her oncoming migraine. "This is it, Dorothy."

"Get ready, sister."

"I am." Elsie pushed a small black button on the dashboard.

The back seat rose, exposing several automatic rifles. Grabbing a slender one, Elsie kissed it. "I just love this Centurion UC-9." Elsie stroked it as if it were a pet. "I know it's from the Israelis, but it's just so light and easy to use. The Agency is so cooperative."

"What do you mean?" Dorothy asked.

"They give us clean rifles. Not unlike my pistol. It always confuses me. So tiny and we're responsible for cleaning it ourselves. I don't like cleaning my pistol."

"Quit playing and get ready."

Two sheriff vehicles zoomed by.

"We're doing about eighty and those guys passed as if we were parked." Dorothy shook her head. "They should be ashamed of themselves."

"Naughty boys." Elsie wrapped several loads of extra ammo around her neck. "I have your stuff right here, sister."

"Thanks. Here we go." Dorothy glanced at the navigation screen. "It's just ahead."

With a sheriff car in front and one in the back, the truck carrying the victims slowed. Dorothy hit the accelerator as a farm came into view. Their black SUV sped down the road. When their speed reached a hundred, she slammed on the brakes and turned the wheel. The vehicle skidded down the road, sliding to a stop just a few feet in front of the huge diesel truck.

Before either deputy had a chance to get out of their cars, Elsie jumped onto the street and dropped to the ground, hugging her rifle to her chest. She rolled under the large truck. Now on her stomach, she scooted toward the back. Several boots jumped onto the blacktop. Elsie aimed and hit each one three times. Men fell to the ground, screaming. One pointed a rifle under the truck and shot.

Before he could hit his target, Dorothy ran up from the other side and opened fire. Her aim was accurate and deadly.

Elsie, already out from under the truck, shot into the cab, instantly killing the driver. Three black helicopters landed in the farmer's field. The wind whipped through Elsie's hair, spraying her face with rocks and dirt. Ignoring the pain, she climbed into the cab. Empty.

Dorothy kicked the men lying on the ground — dead. Tossing their rifles into the farmer's field, she kicked the closest one again just for good measure.

Twelve Agency men and women dressed in black stormed the massive double trailer. With ladders and chainsaws, they cut through the sides as if pulling paper off a wall. The first wooden crate that came off the truck reminded Dorothy of a makeshift coffin. Using her large hunting knife, she pried off the top. Blue jeans in plastic bags filled her view. Tossing the packages aside, she stared at the false bottom. Two Agency men lifted the thin wood. Between the high sides, a woman with a baby lay sleeping. Dorothy reached in and felt the baby's leg. Then she touched the mother's neck. First, she frowned. Then a tear ran down her cheek. Standing, she turned to the sheriff and screamed, "They're alive. Medic!"

Elsie ran up behind Dorothy and barked out orders. As jackets, shirts, pants and other clothing neatly packaged in clear bags scattered across the road, frantic hands searched for a pulse.

It took hours and a hundred ambulance trips to rescue every hostage. By the time the last victim was lifted into a waiting van, the evening stars were out and shining. Dorothy and Elsie sat in their black SUV and cried.

"Not one died, sister." Elsie wiped her eyes. "Why are we crying?"

"I don't know."

"Let's get some sleep." Elsie placed her rifle and ammo back into its hiding place.

"Yes, let's. And tomorrow, let's get that bastard."

Elsie smiled.

Chapter Nineteen

The helicopter landed on the roof of Inter Diagnostics located in the heart of New Jersey. At the same time, a different one landed on the roof of the Helios Corporation. The doors opened and agents in black jumped out. The first thing they destroyed were the communication towers. Next, they destroyed the external emergency generators. Blasting through the roof using precut string charges, the special agents entered and pulled the hard drives from every computer and server.

Agency scientists rescued any animal or human that was still alive. Once the living were safe, they confiscated the specimens and associated records. Within a few hours, all data had been extracted. Several large trucks pulled into the parking lots of Inter Diagnostics and Helios Corporation around two in the morning. Before the break of dawn, the buildings were empty.

While The Agency confiscated data and material from the two companies, the senior executives were arrested. Anyone with information were whisked away and secured within The Agency's vaults.

By 7 a.m., the parking lots of both companies began filling with employees ready to start the workday. They entered the buildings and froze. Nothing remained behind. Not so much as a pencil. The Agency staff had even vacuumed before leaving. At Helios Corporation, one young agent went so far as to leave a small note: *Cleaned by Agnes.*

After eating a breakfast of oatmeal, toast and coffee, Elsie and Dorothy left behind a hefty tip.

"Don't you think that twenty dollars was a little much?" Elsie asked.

"Oh, no."

"Well, I do," Elsie said as they walked down the hallway toward room 415. "Should we knock first? It's only polite to knock."

"If you'd like, sister."

Standing off to one side, Elsie knocked. The sound of bare feet hitting the tiled floor echoed into the hallway. Winking at her sister, Elise pulled out her small pistol.

"I do hope that is not the one you washed recently," Dorothy whispered.

"Of course it is. I wanted it clean for this occasion." Elsie knocked again.

The door opened only as far as the chain would allow. Before John Hershawl knew what was happening, the chain snapped and he was knocked to the floor. Elsie pounced while Dorothy shut and locked the door. With Elsie's gun pressed against his temple, John's eyes widened.

"I know who you two are," he yelled. "What the hell do you want from me? I have no money."

Elsie laughed. "Let me count, Mr. Hershawl. This assignment is paying us over six figures. Your measly couple hundred that's in your wallet does nothing to impress me."

"Then what do you want?" John tried to kick her off, but the woman held on firm with her legs. Her knees kept his arms pinned to his sides.

"We could cut off his private parts," Dorothy whispered.

"What the fuck?" John's eyes widened.

"I do not believe you'll be doing any of that anytime soon." Elsie laughed.

"You two are nuts!"

"Actually —" Dorothy smiled as she worked with a syringe. "We're the sane ones. It's you who's crazy."

"What are you talking about?"

"When I saw that lady asleep in that crate and holding her baby, something inside me just snapped." Dorothy used her fingers to mimic the sound.

"Seen any fairies lately, John Hershawl?" Elsie asked.

"The Agency knows everything." Dorothy slowly slid the needle into his pinned-down arm.

"What's that?"

"Something to help you relax," Elsie said. "For a very long time."

"What the —"

After a pause, Elsie stood and dusted off her skirt. "What a morning, dear sister."

"Yes, what a morning indeed." Dorothy placed the empty syringe into the special holder. Sliding it into her purse, she said, "Wouldn't want to get stuck now, would I?"

"Dropping that off in the mail on our way out?"

"In the lobby, yes." Dorothy nodded.

"Should we get him onto the bed?"

"I've got a better idea." Dorothy pulled out her cell phone. After tapping a few numbers, she calmly said, "Clean up in room 415; yes, thank you."

"I guess that takes care of that." Elsie opened the door and glanced out.

Down the hall, two men in gray jumpsuits with bright-red letters over the pockets that read *The Agency* stepped out of the elevator.

"That didn't take long," Elsie said.

"Never does, sister."

Without knocking or announcing himself, Nate Edwards charged into Colonel Oliver Rose's office. As the door banged against the doorstop, Bill Tarply stepped aside and scanned the front office. Men and women in uniform glared suspiciously back at them. *Will they shoot first and ask questions later?*

"Yes?" Rose stood. About a foot taller than Tarply, Rose met Nate eye to eye. The only difference between the two was that Nate didn't weigh as much.

Nate tossed his Agency badge onto Rose's desk. Not saying a word, he sat in a chair. With his hands shaking, Tarply closed the office door. Nate pulled a folder from his briefcase and slapped it down in front of Rose. Tarply sat next to Nate and smiled at the intimidating colonel.

"I see." Rose glanced through The Agency folder. "I instructed that I was to be informed prior to your arrival. I'm sorry I didn't personally meet you on the tarmac."

"Not interested in meeting you, Colonel," Nate said. "We need names and locations, and we need them now!"

Rose frowned.

"Wakey, wakey," a soft voice whispered into John Hershawl's ear. Too comfortable, he ignored it. When a sharp pinching pain jolted his arm, he jerked his head to one side, hitting the wall.

"Damn!" John slapped his free hand on his forehead.

"Ouch," Elsie said. "That's going to leave a mark."

John stared into the familiar faces; the same two old biddies that attacked him in his hotel room. "What do you want from me?" John glanced around. "Where am I?"

"You're safe." Dorothy smiled at John. "For now."

Taking the time to sit up, John noticed he was lying on a lower bunk. *But a bunk located where?* "Where am I?" he asked again.

"Below," Dorothy replied.

Growling, he stared around the barren room, trying to get his bearings. The room was empty except for the bunk and two chairs. Two chairs that now supported the two old biddies.

"You drugged me."

Smiling, Elsie nodded.

"You'll go to jail for this." He glared at her. "I'm a government official. Who are you?"

"Oh." Elsie frowned. "Where *are* our manners, sister? I honestly thought we introduced ourselves. I'm Elsie, and this is my older sister, Dorothy."

John rolled his eyes. "I know your names."

"Then why did you ask?" Dorothy laughed.

"What I meant ..." John rubbed his forehead. His head was pounding.

"That stuff can create such a nasty headache." Dorothy handed a plastic cup to John. "Here, drink some water. It'll help."

John gulped it down. "Why am I here?"

"Because," Dorothy answered.

"You're our guest," Elsie simpered.

"You've been hacking at that plant for over an hour and you've barely made a dent."

"Then you try," Leonora huffed. She sat next to Dr. Loomsbury and frowned.

"I'm wondering if it's real." Loomsbury stood and rubbed his hand along the base of the large tree. "Doesn't feel right."

"The vines don't feel right." Leonora wiped her face with her hands. "They grow back as soon as I cut 'em."

"If you were a laboratory that conducted secret genetic research, what better way to hide than to modify the plants surrounding you."

Leonora glanced around. All of the plants looked way too healthy. "I'm following you. Continue."

"A strong wall is one that cannot be destroyed." He placed his hands on his hips. "We have to climb over."

Leonora glanced up. "Up there? You fell off the boat, remember?"

"It's either up or around," Loomsbury said. "You pick."

"Around."

"I know where they are," Colonel Rose hissed. "I've kept an eye on 'em."

"The Agency is demanding to know why a rescue wasn't ordered," Nate said.

"It wasn't clear to do so," Rose replied. "They're safer where they are … for the moment."

"And where is that?" Nate asked.

"The ruins."

"They're in the desert without food or water?" Tarply asked sternly. "Not a good thing."

"A supply drop was ordered." Rose frowned. "I'm not that heartless."

Nate shook his head. "Too risky. We belayed that order. If they're surrounded and supplies are dropped, the trackers would find 'em."

"Damn," Rose said. "Their last communication requested supplies and reinforcement, and why are you asking me where they are if you already know?"

Nate shook his head. "We know where they are. What we want to know is who is Hershawl reporting to."

"Then their deaths are on you!" Rose stood. "Not me!"

Nate held out his hand. "Too dangerous to pick them up right now. John Hershawl, your friend, placed a kill order just before we picked him up."

"Picked him up?" Rose asked.

"He's in Agency custody," Tarply explained.

"Then why are you here?" Rose asked.

"We're here to either take you out" — Nate pulled out a small pistol with a silencer — "or retrieve information from you. The choice is yours. Who was Hershawl reporting to?"

Rose glared at the gun and frowned.

"This stuff's amazing." Sumner reached out to touch a golden instrument but stopped just a few inches away. "Where do I apply to become a caretaker?"

"I'll volunteer too." Anais held up her hand.

Ningal laughed. "We are born to be caretakers, not appointed. I wish I could allow you to touch. The natural oils from your skin, over time, destroys the artifacts."

Sumner smiled wistfully. "I'll wear gloves."

Again, Ningal laughed. "I'm sorry. Our caretakers are born without oil secretion glans in their hands. Unusual, I know. It's as if the gods created these people for just one purpose."

"I'll just look. It'll have to be enough." Sumner frowned. "No pictures either?"

"Bright light damages what we hold so dear," Ningal said. "And, if photos were to be released, others would come."

"We understand." Anais held Sumner's arm and glared at her. "Honestly, we do."

"Our king and gods thank you," Ningal said.

"How many people live here?" Anais asked.

"Our home expands outward in all directions," Ningal said. "Millions are here with us."

"Millions?" Sumner glanced at the others. "How do you feed 'em?"

"Would you like to visit our gardens?" Ningal asked.

Worthington, Gerry and David were quick to reply, "Yes!" Their voices echoed through the large cave.

"Why are we just sitting here?" John Hershawl asked.

"We're deciding on how to proceed," Elsie replied.

"Proceed?" John glared at the two old ladies.

Their graying hair, wrapped neatly in buns, gave them a grandmotherly appearance. Slight wrinkles outlining their eyes and lips hinted at their age, and both wore flowered dresses similar to what John remembered his grandmother wearing, but in his eyes, these two hoodlums were anything but grandmotherly. Glancing at the floor, John almost laughed. Both women wore something similar to combat boots — bulky, dark-green tie-ups that hugged their ankles.

"I don't know, sister," Elsie whispered.

"Would get us what we need," Dorothy replied.

Elsie closed her eyes.

"Now *that* might work," Dorothy whispered.

"What games are you playing?" John snapped. "I didn't hear her say anything for you to answer."

Elsie giggled. "It *would* be fun to watch, wouldn't it?"

"You are crazy as all hell!" John stood. Walking to the only door, he held back the urge to pounce on them, just as they did to him. He banged on the door instead. "Let me the fuck outta here!"

No one answered or opened the door.

"I do like *that* idea, sister," Dorothy said.

"What idea?" John asked.

"We're here for you to tell us who pays you," Elsie replied. "The call that came in was made from a disposable cell phone. It was discarded soon after."

"What call?" he asked.

"The one you received at the Botanical Gardens," Elsie said. "We recorded everything."

"It was a good number." John sat back down on the lower bunk. "How do you know?"

Dorothy pulled out her phone and punched in the number. "We're sorry," the voice said from the small speaker. "The number you've reached is no longer in service …"

"Need we say more?" Elsie asked.

"It's the same number he always used," John replied.

"Phones can be programed to show any number," Dorothy explained. "We extracted it for prints — wiped clean."

"Exactly." Elsie adjusted her skirt. "We need to know who you're working for. Who's paying you?"

"And if I refuse?"

"Elsie had a wonderful idea to help you decide," Dorothy said. "A wonderful idea."

"What's that?"

"Put you with hungry alligators. Did you know that when an alligator snaps —" Dorothy slapped her hands together. "It's over thirty-seven hundred pounds per square inch of pure bite. Three alligators should be a nice number to start with. Big, huge alligators."

"Hungry alligators," Elsie added.

"Alligators?" John laughed. "No police force in the world would allow such a thing."

"Correct, John Hershawl." Dorothy chuckled. "Fortunately for us, we do not work for a police force. Unfortunately for you, we work for The Agency."

"Which agency?" John laughed again.

"The Agency," Elsie replied.

"What department?"

"We're assigned to the Special Field Unit," Elsie said. "I'm agent 3-7-1-4." She winked at him.

John shook his head. "FBI? CIA? What agency?" John was no longer smiling.

"Neither," Dorothy replied. "We work for *The Agency*."

"The Agency," John repeated. "Never heard of it."

Elsie giggled. "Most haven't."

"May all be well with you." A very nice-looking man wearing only a loincloth with jewelry clinging to his chest sat next to Elizabeth. Long black hair fell down his back. "My friends and family call me Abum. You must be Elizabeth."

"Yes," she said. "I don't remember seeing you before."

"We have not officially met. Is it true you cannot find your parents?"

Tears filled her eyes with the mention of her mom and dad.

"I understand," he said. "Have you been completely truthful about your parents?"

Elizabeth shook her head.

"Would you like to share the truth with me?"

For a moment, Elizabeth stared into the shadows. "When I first woke up in that nasty cage, they were lying next to me." Tears ran down her face. "I thought they were just sleeping. But when I really looked at 'em, I knew. My mom must have hit her head on the floor. It was all bloody and her hair all matted. My dad's skin was cold and damp."

"They had already left this world by the time you woke up. It must hurt you in here." Abum touched Elizabeth's chest where her heart was beating. "To speak of such things only makes it hurt more. Do you have others? Others with your blood?"

"You mean relatives?" she asked. "My parents didn't have sisters or brothers. My grandparents died before I was born. I'm alone."

The man studied her. He emitted strong warmth, making her feel safe and secure — something she hadn't felt in a very long time.

"If you agree," Abum said, "you may stay here with Ningal and me. Live with us in our home. We would teach you our ways."

"Your home?"

Abum smiled. "If I tell you a secret, would you promise to not be afraid?"

Elizabeth stared into his kind eyes. His compassion felt sincere and inviting. She nodded.

"My true name is Nazi-Enlil. I am the king and ruler of this world. Ningal is my wife, my queen. We have three young boys. I would love to have a daughter. I would love you very much. Kindly agree to be part of our family and I promise you'll never want for anything."

Elizabeth sat quietly. Their gazes locked as if held by an unknown force. "I like your elephants. Your tigers are pretty cool."

"I could take you to them."

"I would like that very much." Elizabeth accepted King Nazi-Enlil's hand.

"Here's what I have." Rose pulled out several sheets from a locked drawer. He handed them to Nate. "A few people on that list might interest you."

Nate scanned down the names. "Don't recognize any."

"When I first met John Hershawl," Rose said, "my skinned crawled. Don't know what about him I didn't like."

"Everything." When the colonel gave him an odd glance, Nate added, "The man does that to people."

"He's part of a religious cult," Rose said. "Bought land just north of Ansted, West Virginia. Created a compound. Here's their pamphlet." Oliver pulled out a colorful brochure from the same locked drawer. "They adhere to something called Zoroastrianism."

"Never heard of it." Nate glanced at the brochure. Tarply leaned over to see.

"Looked it up myself," Rose said. "It's one of the world's oldest religions. Founded by a self-proclaimed prophet named Zoroaster. Lived in Iran about thirty-five thousand years ago."

"Says here there's only one true god," Tarply said. "Not too different from most beliefs."

"Instead of a Bible, they have something called Avestas," Rose said. "It's a collection of writings and laws."

"Our Bible is also a collection of various authors," Tarply said. "So far it sounds the same. This pamphlet states there's only one true god with the name of Ahura Mazda. And his evil opponent is Aura Mainyu. Sounds like God versus Satan to me."

"Yes, it does," Rose said. "That's why I wasn't too worried — at first."

"What do you mean by *at first?*" Nate asked.

"The picture of their god is a winged deity." Rose handed Nate a drawing. "They believe he's coming back."

"Christians believe Jesus is coming back," Tarply said. "So, what's the concern?"

"Do Christians believe that Jesus is coming back on a spaceship? Or that he lives on a planet that revolves around our sun every thirty-six thousand years?"

"That weird group —" Tarply tapped his chin. "What was their name? Heaven's Gate. Forty members committed suicide at the same time. I remember the blue blankets covering their bodies. They believed their souls would transport to a spaceship inside the tail of the Hale-Bopp. Now that was pretty farfetched."

Rose said, "That's why I'm concerned. Crazy people do crazy things when pushed into a corner. Right now, they're searching for people they believe carry the god-gene."

"The god-gene," Nate repeated. "You mean, in their blood?"

Rose nodded. "I'm not sure how they're searching for it, but they're serious."

"Do these leaders have jobs?" Nate asked.

Rose nodded. "The head guy is Frederick Urbat. Founder and CEO of Inter Diagnostics."

"What does Inter Diagnostics do?" Nate pulled out his notepad.

"Something to do with medical research." Rose, again, pulled something from the locked drawer. "Here's his resume."

Nate studied Frederick Urbat's credentials.

Tarply read them over, too. After turning the page, he gasped. "We'd better call this one in, Nate. He's chairman of the board at Helios."

"What's so special about Helios?" Nate asked.

"Oh, nothing," Tarply replied. "Unless you're tracking down the person who financed the killing of Kelly McGruffin."

"Who's Kelly McGruffin?" Rose asked.

"She painted the emblems on the train," Nate said. He held his cell to his ear. "Lewis, I believe we uncovered the name of the financier."

"He's also on the board of Bank Rakyat Indonesia," Tarply whispered. "Trail's starting to come full circle."

Chapter Twenty

"Here we are." Ningal pointed to the valley far below.

The group stood silently with their mouths gaping. Worthington stepped to the cliff's edge. A brightness from his right cast natural light into the deep fissure. Water fell down a rock wall into a huge, natural-looking lake. Large birds flew in and out of the light, casting shadows against the large trees.

"How did you do this?" Worthington asked.

"The light comes from the sun," Ningal explained. "We simply direct and magnify it."

"May we go down?" Gerry asked.

"Certainly," Ningal replied. "This way."

Stairs carved directly into the rock led down. A wooden railing kept them from falling many feet to the bottom. The slow descent allowed their eyes to explore the enormous cave. Fruit trees decorated the landscape. An area covered in purple grabbed Worthington's attention.

"What's growing over there?" he asked Ningal.

"Grapes," she replied.

"Amazing." Worthington chuckled.

"What's that over there?" Gerry pointed to an area colored in reds, yellows and lime greens.

"Tomatoes," Ningal said. "Our gardeners work within the varying temperature and plant accordingly. Some plants prefer warmth where others prefer coolness." Ningal smiled as she walked.

"The deep purple over there?" David asked.

"Eggplant. See the bright yellow and green in the field just beyond those fruit trees? They receive full sun." Ningal pointed to the far horizon. "That's maize."

"Maize?" Worthington repeated. "You mean corn?"

Ningal nodded. "We grow every vegetable we can in this cave. Pumpkins are along the far wall. Wheat is grown further back where there is more flat land. Although we must provide the artificial light."

"Absolutely amazing," Gerry whispered.

The cave was massive. The Empire State Building would be considered small if moved into this place. Thousands of Sumerian gardeners worked, tilling the soil, planting or harvesting the crops. Carved into the cave's floor, small streams carried the life-giving water.

"Our animals are in another cave," Ningal explained. "If set free, they'd destroy our crops."

"Amazing." Gerry repeated her words.

"Please," Ningal said, "walk through our gardens and enjoy."

With that statement, the small group took off in all directions.

"How much longer should we stay on this island?" Leonora gulped the last of her water.

"We've walked for hours and have not found a way in." Loomsbury dropped to his knees. "I'm exhausted."

As they rested, several animals ran across the path just a few feet in front of them.

"What was that?" Leonora asked.

Studying the creatures at a distance, Loomsbury laughed. "I can't believe it."

"What are they?"

"Macropodidae *Dendrolagus ursinus*," he replied.

"In English, please."

"Vogelkop, Tree Kangaroo," he explained. "I didn't know they grew that large."

"If they're going between the trees," Leonora whispered, "so can we."

On hands and knees, the two stared into the dark tunnel winding between the impenetrable trunks.

"I'll follow you." Loomsbury patted Leonora on the back.

"Do they bite?"

"They might," he said.

"Great."

As she crawled through the dense brush, Leonora's heart pounded. On hands and knees, how could she defend herself if she came face-to-face with one of those tree kangaroos? All she could think of were the ones from Australia. *I do hope they're not that big.*

Small rocks and sharp thorns dug into her skin. By the time they entered a small clearing, she was covered in blood. "That sucked." Leonora wiped her bloody hands against her pants.

"You're hurt?" Loomsbury asked.

"Not really. What's that over there?" A large field spread out just ahead. Near the middle, a tall building reaching to the sky stood proud and ominous, as if daring them to explore. No windows. Just a small metal door at each corner.

"I don't know," Loomsbury said. "But cameras are everywhere." He pushed Leonora back into the jungle. "We must not be seen."

"If we haven't already."

"We cannot get in this way." Loomsbury sat, pushing vines from his legs. "We'll have to think of another way."

As they rested and considered their options, several Jeeps sped past. Mud splattered them.

"Great," Leonora whispered. "Now I'm bloody and muddy."

"I'm going to set up a few cameras of my own," Loomsbury said. "Maybe ask for a hack into their cameras, too."

"Can we do that?"

"I can't. The Agency can." Loomsbury pulled out several small units from his backpack.

"You never told me we could do this kind of stuff."

Loomsbury winked. "Let me get these up and we'll head back."

"I'll help."

"See?" Elsie pointed at the large cages. "Alligators."

"This is one sick joke." John Hershawl's eyes were bigger than baseballs.

"The only joke I know is *what do you get when* —"

"Elsie!" Dorothy scolded. "This is *not* the time or the place."

Elsie pressed her pistol deeper into his back. John's hands shook. "So, John. You tell us who paid you, or you walk into that cage with the hungry alligators. Which will it be?"

John turned and glanced at the gun. He then glanced at the cages. Shaking his head, he frowned. "I'll talk. This crap isn't worth it. You'll have to guarantee my safety. Those nuts will kill me for talking."

Laughing again, Dorothy said, "We'll kill you for *not* talking."

Lewis stared at the photo of the wealthy investor and philanthropist Frederick Urbat. According to his website, the man would be turning eighty-four in a few weeks. He owned several large estates around the world, was married and had already raised six kids. Recently he married a much younger woman. Most of his wealth was tied up in something called the Civil Honesty Foundation. Urbat's grandparents had died in a Nazi concentration camp, which probably accounted for his eccentric behavior and anti-government beliefs.

"Anything interesting?" Allen Greghardt asked from across the room.

"According to this, Urbat's father hated government. He was the one that must have planted the ideals of socialism into Urbat's head. The Civil Honesty Foundation is working to eradicate communism. Somewhat of a noble cause. Then again, most socialistic countries usually turn into some form of dictatorship."

"Inter Diagnostics and Helios are major sponsors of his foundation, correct?"

"Correct. Urbat's the CEO of Inter Diagnostics, chairman of the board at Helios, and on the board of directors for Bank of Rakyat." Lewis chuckled. "The man's a major player. He also owns land in Ansted, West Virginia."

"How many acres?" Greghardt refilled his glass with bourbon.

Lewis sighed. "Several hundred in all. Bought up different listings off Route 60."

Greghardt walked to the flat screen that was almost as large as the wall. He always loved this office, especially during Super Bowl.

Lewis clicked on the remote. A large map displayed. "Turkey Creek Road is pretty established on the north side. So, Urbat bought all of this from Midland Trail to the town." Lewis ran his hand over the terrain. "Huge area. According to the locals, construction's been non-stop for months. Most of the work is accomplished during the night, according to our surveillance team."

"What's he building?" Frowning, Greghardt rubbed his chin.

"We need to order new satellite photos," Lewis said. "Get a closer look."

Worthington read over the amazing stone tablets again. "I wonder why they're called the Tablet of Destinies and not Tablets of Destiny. Afterall, there are two here and not one." The remarkable emerald-green tablets were huge. Larger than a twin-size bed. Filled with Sumerian hieroglyphs, the ancient slabs sent chills all through Worthington making him shiver.

"Both the tablet and the cylinder seal survived all these years," Gerry said, ignoring his musings. "Impressive. These must be originals."

"What do they say?" Worthington leaned in closer. "There are seals on them, too."

"The seals are made from a precious metal, such as iron or gold." Sumner's voice startled them. "The beginning of the first tablet states that Enlil is the supreme ruler of our universe."

"Word for word?" Worthington asked.

"Of course not," Sumner replied. "The Sumerian vocabulary and syntax do not allow for a word-to-word translation."

"Then what does it say?" Worthington asked.

Sumner sighed. "I must first explain that the Sumerians thought differently than we do." Sumner stepped closer to the tablets and grinned. "They lived with their gods. We only know of ours as a spiritual entity. If you walk and talk with a god, life is a little different."

"Okay," Gerry said, "go on."

"God Enlil was first assigned as king of this region. Iraq and Iran. He built large cities here. Enlil was a fair and wise man. But he also had a temper. Not as bad as his brother, Enki. When An, their father, left our solar system, he left the half-brothers in charge. Enlil and Enki."

"An?" Gerry repeated. "You mean the original Sumerian god and ruler?"

"An never ruled Earth," Sumner explained. "He only ruled his home world and his two sons."

"What does this tablet say?" Worthington asked again, only this time he waved his arms over the emerald-green stones.

"Since I must use our language to translate, I'll have to change things a little. Let me think." Sumner studied the ancient script. As she translated, she'd pause, ever so often, to consider her words. "It says, *Rise, my son, Enlil, and rule the land beneath and the skies above. The power I give ascends to no other. From here to where we see is for you to make the laws and control. From now until my return, all is yours and yours only. From your house, choose wisely.* In other words, stand up to my challenge, kid. As far as you can see from this world is yours to rule. Some interpret this to mean the whole universe."

"It's a decree then?" Gerry asked.

"Yes." Sumner pointed to the seal. "See this mark? It means that what's written on this tablet *is* the law. Ignoring it or disobeying just wasn't an option. The law said that Enlil's family would continue to rule until the father returned."

"What happened to Enlil?" Gerry asked.

"Enlil died during the great war," Ningal said from behind Sumner. "I did not know you could read our language."

"It's not easy to translate," Sumner replied. "It's easier to read the whole text and then relay the message."

"I agree," Ningal said.

"What war?" Worthington asked.

"All is written in our library." Ningal smiled at Sumner. "In our writings, we are told of a great war that almost destroyed our world."

Elizabeth walked up and stood next to Ningal. "During that war, our second moon was destroyed?"

Ningal nodded.

"Second moon?" Worthington asked.

"There is a lot of information that's contained in the Sumerian teachings," Sumner said.

"When was this war?" Worthington asked. "Who did you fight?"

"They didn't know who they were or where they came from," Elizabeth said. "They arrived in huge flying ships."

"Flying ships?" Worthington repeated. "You mean spaceships?"

Ningal nodded. "About a hundred Earth years after An left Enlil as king and ruler, large ships attacked our world. The writings are in our library." Ningal waved her hand toward the door. "Those who survived eventually moved into these caves. Enlil remained on the surface to aid in our escape. Several generations later when it was safe to walk on the surface again, our ancestors found Enlil's damaged ship. They also found his remains. Our ancestors had held hope that Enlil would one day return. That was never to be. Enlil died protecting his people. He led our enemies away from our caves."

"In other words," Worthington said, "Enlil sacrificed his life to save yours."

"Not mine, specifically," Ningal said. "But my ancestors, yes."

"And you never found out who attacked you?" Gerry asked.

Ningal shook her head.

"Fascinating," Gerry replied.

"Are *we* part Sumerian?" Worthington asked.

"We would have to run tests," Ningal said. "Over time, many gods from An's world returned and left behind their own legacy."

"All of the gods were not related to each other?" Gerry asked.

"An had two children, Enlil and Enki. He did have a nephew, but he died without a family."

"I've heard conspiracies about how the gods came here from a mysterious Planet X. How they created us as a slave race." Worthington laughed. "I never believed it."

"There is probably much about our history and theirs that we'll never know," Sumner said. "History's written by the victors. Not the losers."

"That is true. The strong will try to control the weak." Ningal nodded. "This is why our library is so extensive and protected. Not only do we have the original Sumerian cylinders, we also have writings from throughout this world's history."

"There was a library in Alexandra. It burnt down." Sumner's eyes closed as she tried to contain her excitement. "You wouldn't happen to have anything that would match what was destroyed?"

Ningal laughed. "Actually, we do."

"I have got to spend more time in the library," Worthington and Gerry said at the same time.

Sumner and Ningal laughed.

"Where did they go?" Rose asked.

"Satellite imagery showed them entering an area that resembled stairs," a young lieutenant answered.

"When recon returned, they reported finding no stairs." A captain spoke this time. "From the film, we thought they discovered an underground cave to escape the heat. When our troops arrived, they found only dirt."

"This is nuts." Rose stared out his window. Remembering the small pistol Nate had pointed at his face, he frowned.

"Why don't we just ring the doorbell?" Amy asked. "After all, they *are* a real company. And you *are* real agents. We'll dock and you walk off the boat and introduce yourselves."

"Would be a lot easier," Leonora said.

"A lot cleaner too." Amy laughed. "You're both a mess. Cut up and muddy."

"Every time I've tried to get close to their docks, the guys with the guns show up." Bob stood in the doorway and frowned. "It's a game now. How close can I get?"

Loomsbury pulled out his cell. "Connie? Dr. Loomsbury here ... I'm good and so is Leonora, thank you. Please set up a meeting with Inter Diagnostics. I'd like an audience ... Use the little creature as a cover. I have notes and photos with me ... Yes, I understand ... I'll print a few reports ... Thank you." He glanced up. "She'll let us know."

"I look too young to be an agent," Leonora said.

"If you're posing as my daughter, then why wouldn't I take you with me?" Loomsbury asked. "I take my daughter with me when I travel. Seems normal enough."

"Makes sense," Amy said. "Let's get your reports printed, get you two cleaned up and make you look official."

As Nate and Tarply walked around the ziggurat at Dur-Kurigalzu, Tarply counted shoe prints. "There are plenty here." Tarply was still counting.

"This is a tourist area," Nate said. "We need to find that entrance."

"That entrance? There's nothing here but sand. There is no entrance. Recon info is wrong."

"Satellite imagery shows the group descending." Nate stared at the map. "Over here, somewhere."

Several walls and doorways leading into demolished ruins beckoned them to enter. Neither took the bait. After walking around for a while in the hot sun, Tarply sat in the shade of a small tree, sipping his water.

"I don't see any entrances," Nate said, joining him.

"Nope," Tarply said. "Like I said, the imagery is wrong."

"It's never wrong." Nate shook his head. "They entered right here. Obviously, it's been blocked."

"Blocked? Who would do that? Who'd have the time?"

"Haven't got a clue," Nate replied. "I recommend we visit the ancient city of Nippur before we head back to Ur. We're missing something."

"Yes." Tarply chuckled bitterly. "We're missing a lot of people."

Sumner stepped up to Ningal and smiled. "Your library is something else." Sumner's head was still spinning from the excitement of reading the ancient manuscripts. "I could simply *live* in there forever."

"I'm glad you enjoy it," Ningal said.

"I do have one question."

Ningal nodded.

"On the library walls are carvings that interest me. Several resemble trees. There's one that's of a flower. We call that flower the fleur-de-lys. Why are those carvings there?"

Ningal smiled. "The tree represents the tree of life. We were taught that our gods created us, and that symbol represents our existence, their success. When our gods combined the heavenly world with the earthly world, our life began. The evolution of an endless circle."

"I don't understand."

"We are the product of our gods," Ningal said. "Their genetics mixed with ours; the combining of our DNA with theirs to create us. The tree of life symbolizes that change, that combination."

"The fleur-de-lys? How does that fit?" Sumner asked.

"You must mean the lily? It represents fertility." Ningal rubbed her stomach. "Or the harvest of our gods' work. After many trials and errors, the mixture was perfected. We were born."

"And the owl?"

"Wisdom," Ningal replied. "Once spliced with the gods' DNA, our souls materialized. With the gift of a soul came the acceptance of one's self right. Or the embodiment of the third density. The forever cycle starts and ends where the circle evolves."

"Jack explained a little about the densities to me. I would like to hear more about that."

"Certainly." Ningal smiled. "Curiosity is a good trait."

Sumner gathered her thoughts. "I'm sorry; I'm going off track. You sent for me, not the other way around."

"Yes," Ningal laughed. "The king wishes to lay his eyes upon you."

"Excuse me?"

"The king wishes a meeting," Ningal said.

"What do I have to do?"

"Follow me."

"Shouldn't I change first?"

"The king is not interested in your clothing, child," Ningal said. "He wishes to talk."

Sumner followed Ningal as she looped through the maze of corridors. When they reached a small room with several chairs and one table, Ningal stood off to the side. The barren walls and decorative tiles sent chills down Sumner's spine. *What does the king want with me?*

"This is the king's meeting room," Ningal said. "Where official business is discussed."

Several armed guards entered carrying large spears. Ningal kneeled, lowering her head. Sumner sat frozen, her fear growing as each second ticked by. Ningal didn't explain anything to her.

Should I bow my head or kneel on the floor next to Ningal? Will the guards rip my head off if I don't show great respect?

"Ningal, am I supposed to kneel too?" Sumner whispered. Ningal ignored her.

Walking solemnly behind the guards, a tall and handsome man with extremely long dark braids smiled. Approaching Sumner, he held up his right hand. "Please sit with me, Ms. Womack." Reaching down, the king pulled Ningal to her feet. "My wife." He kissed her forehead. "Please come and sit with me."

Sumner stared at Ningal. *Should I be angry or pleased? Why didn't Ningal tell me?*

"Ms. Womack," the king said. "My official title is King Nazi-Enlil. However, you may call me Abum."

"A bum. You wish for me to call you a bum? As in a homeless-type person?"

Ningal giggled. King Nazi-Enlil glanced between them. Obviously, he wasn't following their conversation, but then again, neither was Sumner.

"May I speak freely, my husband?"

King Nazi-Enlil nodded.

"*A bum* in English translates to an individual who refuses to work within his society. A person who lives off others."

King Nazi-Enlil's face remained calm.

"There is no word to translate this concept, Sumner. *Abum*, in our language, equates to a 'head of household.'" Ningal smiled.

Staring at the ceiling, a mortified Sumner whispered, "I literally just insulted the king. The true and only king on Earth. I just called him a bum."

Ningal giggled again and whispered something to the king in their native language. He chuckled. "No insult accepted," King Nazi-Enlil said.

"May I call you King Nazi instead? Calling you *a bum* doesn't feel right to me."

"Certainly," King Nazi-Enlil replied.

"So, King Nazi, what can I do for you?" Uncomfortable, Sumner glanced around. "Other than insult you, that is."

Chuckling again, the king replied, "It relates to young Elizabeth."

"Elizabeth?" Sumner's interest perked. She'd spoken to every survivor from the train, and Elizabeth's story broke her heart.

"My wife and I have three sons," he said, nodding at his wife. "I asked Elizabeth to stay with us."

"I see."

"We wish to adopt her," King Nazi-Enlil said. "She no longer has a family of her own. Here, Elizabeth would have the same rights and privileges as our boys. She would be loved and cared for as one of our own."

"We tested her blood," Ningal said. "She carries the lineage of Enlil."

"If she marries one of our citizens, her children will have a right to the throne." King Nazi-Enlil smiled.

"Amazing," Sumner replied. "Do I carry the gene?"

"We could test you, too," Ningal said.

Sumner nodded with enthusiasm and then, considering the issue of an adoption, shrugged. "When I finally have cell coverage, I'll contact The Agency. They will arrange for the adoption. I would like to talk to Elizabeth about this first. We must ensure she has no living relatives."

"Absolutely," Ningal replied.

"It is settled," King Nazi-Enlil said. "The king and queen will soon release the news. We are expecting a daughter."

Chapter Twenty-One

Several agents dressed in black SWAT gear stood in front of a house on Turkey Creek Road. The place, owned by Frederick Urbat, looked abandoned. About a mile down and inside a small clearing, other agents waited for their orders.

"Newberry?" a voice squeaked through the radio.

"Here," Newberry replied.

"We're stationed and ready to proceed," the voice relayed.

"Roger." Newberry clicked his radio to silent. He laughed, remembering how Devon had called him Steven at Your Service Sir.

With equipment strapped to their vests, the men looked ready for a war. Black helmets covered their ears and the backs of their heads. Wearing hoods and protective eye gear and carrying FN SCAR submachine guns, they looked fearsome. Not an inch of skin showed through their dark coverings. Adjusting the radio speaker to his mouth, Newberry pulled down his visor.

"Let's move," he ordered.

The men inched their way behind the abandoned house. A dirt road, recently cleared, led through the trees. Several men with infrared visors kept watch in the darkness. With each step, the men scanned the shadows for any signs of a hostile force. Only the sounds of a light wind and buzzing flies hit their ears. All remained ... too quiet. Newberry glanced over his shoulder. The darkness surrounding the path gave him concern. An evil presence bore down upon his shoulders. He could feel it. Almost touch it. His men were *his* responsibility, and he'd be damned if any died on his watch.

"Keep alert," he ordered as they continued up the narrow path wide enough for just one small vehicle at a time. "Sir," Newberry said into his radio. "See anything?"

"Nothing," the voice replied.

Two of Newberry's men ran ahead. After several minutes they returned, completely out of breath and very excited.

"You've got to see it for yourself." The agents gasped for air. "You've got to see it!"

Docking the boat, Bob nodded as an armed guard shouted out orders. Amy and Leonora watched patiently from below. When Bob shut the motor off, several armed men jumped on board.

"Don't anyone move," a guard ordered.

As the small group huddled together, the guards searched the boat. Satisfied that the four were alone, the guards stepped onto the dock.

"Who's Dr. Loomsbury?" one of the guards asked.

"I am." Loomsbury stepped forward. "This is my daughter, Leonora. And my *dear* friends Bob and Amy."

"You two follow me, and you —" He pointed at Bob and Amy. "Remain here with your boat."

Leonora hurried to match Loomsbury's stride. She grabbed his hand. He squeezed it a few times before smiling at her.

The massive building loomed high overhead. No windows. Just a double set of glass doors that led to a small lobby. Nothing spectacular or ostentatious, no trees or bushes anywhere near the building — just rough concrete and cameras everywhere.

Just before they reached the building, the doors opened. Two armed guards waved them inside, and the doors slammed shut behind them. Leonora gasped. Loomsbury had to chuckle.

A woman with her hair in a tight bun greeted them. "Good afternoon. My name is Siska Yudhoyono. I will be your escort."

"Nice to meet you. I'm Dr. Loomsbury, and this is my daughter, Leonora."

"Hi." Leonora stepped out from behind Loomsbury.

"She's a little shy," he said.

"Nice to meet you, Leonora. You can call me Siska, okay?"

"Okay," Leonora replied, still standing slightly behind Loomsbury.

"Follow me," Siska said. "I understand you found an odd creature you wish to discuss?"

"Correct." Loomsbury held out a photo.

She nodded. "It looks like one of ours. The question is, what was it doing in the United States?"

"South Dakota," Loomsbury said. "Whitewood, South Dakota."

"This little guy was a long way from home," she said.

"What are they?" Loomsbury asked.

"A mixture," she replied. "The United States, along with Great Britain and a couple of other major players, requested them."

"Who specifically from the United States?"

"Director of Military Affairs," she answered.

"John Hershawl?" Loomsbury asked.

"That is correct," Siska replied, still walking.

"Archeologists have been busy here." Tarply glanced around.

"Let's walk," Nate said.

As they hiked through what was left of the ancient city of Nippur, men with weapons ran toward them, blocking their path. Nate handed papers to an armed man. The guard said a few harsh words in their spoken language, and the other men with weapons stepped back.

"Is this where the Tower of Babel's supposed to be?" Tarply asked.

"Not sure."

The area, mostly rubble, looked like it had been destroyed with an atomic weapon. What was left of the brick structures dotted the landscape. On a hilltop a short distance away was a rectangular building that didn't look quite as old.

"That's not original," Tarply surmised.

"No, it is not," Nate agreed.

Men and women searching for ancient relics ignored the intruders. They dusted the bricks, registered their discoveries and took pictures. As Nate and Tarply walked by, the workers never once looked up.

"I know what they are looking for," Tarply said. "But what are *we* looking for?"

"Not sure," Nate replied. "Maybe a door of some kind."

"Talk, Mr. Hershawl." Elsie pointed her gun at his temple.

John sighed. "Heard of the Civil Honesty Foundation?"

Elsie and Dorothy shook their heads.

"Owned by Frederick Urbat," John said. "He's also CEO of Inter Diagnostics. The man's a fruitcake disguised as a person."

"Oh?" Elise raised an eyebrow. "A fruitcake you say?"

"Believes that the ancient gods are coming back. Said anyone who didn't have royal blood within their veins would die. That's why he's snatching people."

"What will they do when they find this royal blood?" Dorothy asked.

"Inject it into their veins?" John shrugged. "Don't really know."

"How much did they pay you?" Elsie asked.

"A few million," John replied. "Enough to retire."

"I see," Dorothy said.

The women looked at each other. Elsie spoke. "Which alligator do you want to take the first bite, John?"

"I told you what you wanted to know." John's eyes opened wider. "What more do you want from me?"

"All of it," Elsie said.

"And don't leave anything out," Dorothy added.

"What is that thing?" Newberry asked as he stepped into the large clearing.

"I told you," the agent said. "It's huge!"

An area, larger than several football fields, housed an enormous structure. A row of stairs led straight to the third level. The only way to the second floor was from the side stairs. Beyond the third level, the floors stacked one on top of the other like a step pyramid. At the very top sat something resembling a shrine.

"Take photos," Newberry ordered. As he jogged up the stairs, Newberry stopped several times to catch his breath. He stared up at the altar and his heart pounded. He pulled out his phone. He listened to the distant ring.

"Lewis here."

"Dr. Lewis, Agent Newberry. I'm climbing up a damn ziggurat, sir. That crazy bastard built a fucking ziggurat in West Virginia!"

"Is it as big as the real ones overseas?"

"I believe so," Newberry replied. "I'm not even halfway up the thing yet and I'm exhausted. Photos coming your way in a few. I need reinforcement. This thing is not good."

"On their way," Lewis said.

Newberry surveyed the landscape. He could see all the way to Virginia on the southeast side, Ohio to the north, and Kentucky to the west. After resting for a few minutes, he charged up the stairs. Finally making it to the first landing, Newberry stepped inside a small room. It was empty. Glancing over the side, he found steps that met together under his stairs. He didn't know if they dead ended or if a hidden room was somewhere inside.

Newberry continued up the stairs to the third landing. He didn't see any more stairs leading up. *How in the hell do I get to the top?* He had noticed that the side stairs turned sideways on the first landing. *Maybe that's the route I should take.* Hurrying down, he panted. His legs ached. This thing was more than a maze; it was a death trap. Newberry stood under a small arch holding the main stairs going up. Behind him was another set of stairs.

"Get your men up here," Newberry ordered. "I'm getting a bad feeling about this place."

Charging blindly up the stairs, Newberry's heart pounded. *Why would someone build such a structure?* Nothing made any sense. Newberry stepped into a small dark room and flipped on his helmet's light. Clinging to his rifle for some type of normality, he half expected an Egyptian god wearing a bird mask or something similar to jump from the shadows and challenge him. Instead, he found more stairs leading off in all directions. *Now which way?* Not wanting to stray too far from his reality, Newberry took the stairs leading north.

"Sir?" a voice stated through his earpiece. "We can't see you."

"I took the side stairs that lead north," Newberry said. "Hurry, I'll meet you at the top." A few steps ahead, a golden shrine sat ominously in the heart of the room. As his eyes fell upon the dead children scattered there, tears fell from his eyes. Newberry counted — *thirteen, fourteen, fifteen.*

"Jesus *fucking* H. Christ!" an agent yelled out as he entered the room from the east.

Standing in the entrance from the south and the west, two more agents stared at the carnage. Their wide eyes and open mouths gave away what they were feeling — disbelief.

"*Twenty-two, twenty-three.*" Newberry continued to count. If he didn't do something, he was going to lose it, and he couldn't afford to let go of what little sanity remained.

Thirty-four, thirty-five. Black Hawk helicopters hovered overhead. One at a time, they landed near the base of the mysterious ziggurat.

"*Thirty-six.*" Newberry fell to his knees. Lifting his head toward the heavens, he prayed. "Our Father which art in heaven, hallowed be thy name. Your kingdom come, your will be done, on earth as it is in heaven."

The other three agents also dropped to the floor. As they whispered their prayers, their tears fell.

"Give us this day our daily bread, and forgive us our debts, as we also have forgiven our debtors. And lead us not into temptation, but deliver us from evil …"

As Agency men closed in on the ziggurat, a man stood on a nearby mountaintop. From his vantage point, the agents resembled black roaches. Frederick Urbat silently watched through his binoculars as his sacred and most holy creation was tainted before his eyes. Urbat's anger swelled. He pulled a small device out of his pants pocket, cleared his mind and pushed a small red button.

From the middle of the ziggurat, a small spark ignited a small fuse — a fuse that ran through the maze of bricks and mortar and ended near forty tons of TNT. The explosion started out small. It vibrated through the structure from somewhere deep inside. Before Newberry could whisper the final word to his prayer — *amen* — the mountaintop in Ansted, West Virginia, soared into the air, carrying with it rock, dirt, trees and human body parts. For hundreds of miles, debris fell from a cloudless sky.

"Knock, knock." Sumner poked her head through the long, silky drapes.

"Sumner." Ningal placed the piece of cloth she'd been working on in her lap. "Is there something you need?"

"Yes." Sumner laughed. "I need you."

"Very well," Ningal said. "Please, come and sit with me."

Sumner sat across from the beautiful woman. "Ningal, when we last spoke, we talked about the carvings on the library walls."

Ningal nodded.

"I read up on your history. It's interesting how the gods created humans to work the gold mines."

"Your question?"

Sumner paused. "I'll just tell it like it is. When I first took this case, I found several drawings inside a train. The first was the fleur-de-lys or a lily. The second was of a tree of life. When I saw the third, an owl, there was a body. It was the artist."

"Terrible." Ningal lowered her gaze.

"The artist was young. A woman named Kelly McGruffin." Sumner handed Ningal a photo of the crime scene. Ningal gasped. "Kelly was only twenty-four." Ningal frowned. "Why would someone use those particular emblems? What would they signify? What do they mean?"

"Come with me." Ningal stood.

Ningal led Sumner through several hallways heading away from everyone else. Sumner didn't see anyone as they walked. Near the end, Ningal stood in front of a large oval door Sumner hadn't seen before.

"In here," Ningal said, "you may find the answers you seek."

Pushing open the door, Sumner gasped. "Oh my." It was as if she had just entered another world.

"This room holds the original equipment used to create humans," Ningal said. "We are familiar with some. A few elude us."

"That looks just like the tree of life that was painted inside the train." Sumner walked up to the tall structure. She reached out. Her very soul protested. Sumner shoved her hand back into her pocket. "What is this?"

"We are not sure," Ningal said. "All we know is that this instrument was somehow used to combine the DNA of our gods with the DNA of the indigenous creatures that once lived on this world."

"I've seen something like this before." Sumner stared at the odd instrument towering above her. A base of gold held it firmly to the floor. The center stem branched out into several limbs that bloomed into bulbs. It resembled a flowering tree. On closer examination, the bulbs were not round — more like miniature fleur-de-lys. "What's the name of this instrument?"

"Our gods called it a Tingis."

"Tingis," Sumner repeated, slowly. "Tingis. Life. No, tree. No, that's not right. More like, *a tree that gives life*."

"That is a good translation."

"I've seen this before. But in the renditions I've seen, men are standing next to it. In their hands are buckets or other instruments."

"Yes." Ningal nodded. "Do you mean something similar to what's on this table?"

Sumner climbed up a small stepladder in order to see on top. The furniture in this room was large — made for a giant. Sumner's heart pounded as she studied the strange-looking instruments.

"Why is this table so big? These instruments are huge, too."

"Our gods were big," Ningal replied. "The mighty men of old."

Sumner laughed. "Yes, yes. The men of renown. There were giants in those days. Genesis 6:4." Sumner shook her head. "What about the owl? You've said it symbolizes wisdom, but what else?"

"Vessels that held the human embryos." Ningal pointed across the room. Large ceramic vases with colorful designs lined the shelves.

Sumner gasped. "They look just like owls!"

Ningal nodded. "The wings are actually handles. The eyes are not eyes but what attaches them to the instrument that you call a tree."

Sumner's mind whirled. "Why would anyone paint these symbols on a train? A train where over three hundred people disappeared? How do I connect your medical instruments to the kidnapped passengers?" Sumner stared at the instruments.

"I do not know. These represent our beginning and our destruction. To some, they may be holy. To us, they are medical instruments. We do not worship or idolize these things."

There had to be a connection. *Why? Why?* "Ningal, does everyone on this planet carry the Sumerian gene?"

"No."

"Why not? If the Sumerian gods created us, we should all be the same, shouldn't we?" *Something is wrong. I'm missing something.*

"After the great war," Ningal said, "many humans were taken. Generations later, once the Earth had healed, they were returned. When we tested their genetic makeup, we found it was different from ours. We looked almost the same, but with DNA differences."

"Differences?"

"Yes," Ningal smiled. "The color of the skin was no longer dark but light. Hair was no longer red or black, but blonde or brown. Their eye color was brown, not green or blue like ours. Some had stronger facial structures, prominent jawlines or a slanting of the eyes."

"Your gods' DNA was removed from those that were returned?"

Ningal nodded.

"Why would someone do that?"

"We do not know," Ningal said. "Sumner take your time and look around. I just ask that you do not touch anything. We do not understand everything that is in this room. It would not be a good thing if you were to get hurt."

Looking at the actual instruments gave Sumner a deeper appreciation for the ancients' medicine. The carved images in the tablets gave the impression that the instruments were crude and barbaric. In reality, the instruments were more sophisticated than what were used today. The central device glowed in the light as if made from gold.

"Why gold?"

"Gold," Ningal said, "is a natural purifier. Bacteria cannot live on gold."

"I thought the gods used gold particles in the air for purification."

"Solid or dust," Ningal said. "Does not matter. Gold purifies."

"I've seen a snake associated with the tree of life." Sumner climbed down and walked around the odd tree-like instrument.

"A rod." Ningal picked up a metal staff that was leaning against the wall. "This activates the Tingis."

"This must be made from silver."

Ningal nodded and placed the rod back where she found it.

"Confusing." Sumner walked across the room, looking at everything. "How do I connect the dots, Ningal? Maybe they kidnapped to display their superiority."

"Maybe. But why?"

"To somehow connect it to the Sumerians. Reenacting what happened all those centuries ago. Does *anyone* know about you or your people? Does anyone up top know that you live down here?"

"Not that we are aware of," Ningal replied.

"Allen." Lewis stood at the large windows and watched as the spring rain watered the greenery below. "We need to bring in Frederick Urbat."

"That won't be easy." Greghardt filled his glass with a golden liquid.

"Don't see why."

"He has more money than God." Greghardt took a large gulp. "He's protected from all sides."

"Federal?"

"In just about every country." Greghardt shook his glass so the ice would mix his drink for him.

"What countries do not like him?"

"Russia and England, mostly. I'd place a bet on France."

"Rather odd, don't you think?"

"Not really." Greghardt sat on a sofa. "He's a socialist. Believes in a one-world government managed by the people. Although some countries claim to be such already, they're not. A true socialistic society would be managed purely by the people. Even in America we don't meet that criteria."

"What would you call us besides dysfunctional? Capitalists?"

"Yes." Greghardt chuckled. "I think of us as a democratic republic capitalist country."

"A mouthful, but accurate. If we cannot bring him in, what do you suggest?"

"That *we* go to him," Greghardt said. "The man has to come out once in a while."

"Dr. Lewis." Connie's voice crackled through his office.

"Something wrong?" Lewis asked.

"Sir!" Connie wailed.

"What's happened?" Lewis asked.

"There's been an explosion, sir."

"I wish to meet this Frederick Urbat." Elsie glared at John Hershawl.

"Can't happen," John replied.

"Then the alligators will have a nice dinner today," Dorothy said.

"Fuck the alligators!" John jumped to his feet. "At least it'd be a fast death. What Urbat would do to me would be worse."

"Now, this conversation *is* getting interesting." Elsie nodded.

"I agree," Dorothy said.

"Where in the hell are they?" Colonel Oliver Rose glared at the map. His men had them surrounded. No way could they have escaped. Pacing the room, he jumped when his phone rang.

"Rose here."

"Good afternoon, Oliver."

"Sir." The sound of the man's voice sent fear coursing through Rose. Sweat dripped from his temples.

"I have another delivery for you."

"Delivery. Yes sir."

"Instructions will follow."

Staring into the now silent phone, Rose's heart pounded. A silver frame with his daughter's huge smile and sparkling eyes confronted him. She recently accepted a position at Inter Diagnostics. Everything was fine until that one dreadful day, that one dreadful phone call. The same voice threatened to kill his daughter if he didn't cooperate. All he had to do was help deliver people to different destinations. Didn't sound difficult. Since that first call, however, Rose believed he had killed a thousand innocent civilians.

Now, more lives were on the line. All because his little girl wanted to live in another country and work for a major foundation. Listening to a phone ring from somewhere across the world, he knew he was signing his daughter's death certificate. *Will my wife forgive me? Can I forgive myself?*

"Dr. Lewis?" Rose stared at the map. "The name of the individual. The one who ordered the kidnappings — Frederick Urbat. And my baby girl will be next on his list."

Chapter Twenty-Two

"We've been all over this desert and we've found nothing," Tarply said.

"What do you suggest?" Nate asked.

"I'm not sure." Tarply rubbed the back of his neck. His skin, raw from the hot sun, screeched in protest at just a simple touch. Taking in a deeper breath, he stretched out his back and, with protesting hips, walked toward a small ruin. As his boots sank into the sand, he wondered if he'd ever see Sumner again. He rested his head against the ancient brick and prayed to a god that never answered, "Please help me find them. Please."

Feeling the heat sizzling deeper into his skin, he stared at the sandy bricks. Two dark shadows rested against the wall, not one. One wore a military helmet; the other was draped in a cloth. *A cloth? What the hell?*

Jerking around, he almost fell over. The sand sucked in his feet and refused to let go. Regaining his balance, Tarply stared into the face of an aging man. "Damn," Tarply yelped. "You scared the shit outta me."

The man tilted his head to one side and nodded. His white robe with red along the bottom brushed against the hot sands. His long white beard flowed down to his knees, as did the wrap covering his head.

"I'm not allowed to pray at this spot?"

The robed man nodded again. "You may pray as you feel the need."

Confusion raked through Tarply. *What in the world does this man want with me?* "Have I done something wrong?"

"No," the robed man replied. "I simply need you and your friend to follow me."

Protected by thick glass, Leonora stared at the strange flying creatures. Much larger than the one found at the train; they were about the same size as the ones that attacked them on the boat.

"Their wings are beautiful," Leonora whispered. As her fingers made contact with the window, several creatures slammed into the glass. Blood splattered everywhere.

"Oh my." Siska took several steps back and cuddled her clipboard in a tight embrace.

Men wearing white jackets darted into the room.

"What happened?" one of them asked.

"I do not know," Siska replied. "We were watching them fly when they suddenly aimed for the glass."

"This is most unusual," the man replied.

"The same thing happened on our boat the other night," Loomsbury said. The scientist turned to see who was talking. "I'm Dr. Loomsbury. From the states. Heard about your research. Wanted to see it for myself." Loomsbury held out his hand.

"I see." The man ignored the gesture of friendship. He turned back to the bloodstained glass. "I don't understand why this would happen."

"Maybe they can smell death," Leonora suggested.

"Excuse me?" The man stared at her.

"We —" Leonora frowned. "I mean, my father dissected one in his lab. I was there. Maybe the creatures know that we cut up one of their friends."

The man glared at the two strangers. "You dissected one of our creatures?"

Loomsbury glanced at Leonora before answering. "Yes."

"Why?" the man asked.

"Our government wanted to know what the creature was," Loomsbury said. "I had no other choice but to perform an autopsy."

"Not good," the man said.

"Why?" Loomsbury frowned.

"Because, their DNA will pass through protective gloves and into your skin. We'll need to run tests immediately for cross contamination."

Leonora played dumb. "What do you mean by cross contamination?"

"If their DNA passed into you ..." The man stared at Siska and then turned back to Leonora and Loomsbury. "This is not good. You don't understand. These creatures are programmed to destroy anyone or anything with the cross contamination."

"Warfare," Leonora whispered. "If you add the DNA to food or water or air, you can send these creatures in to kill. They'll attack and then leave."

The man nodded.

"Barbaric," Loomsbury said. "Does the United Nations know about these little bugs of yours?"

Frederick Urbat stood on a cliff overlooking the crystalline waters of the Mediterranean Sea. No waves today. Just a glistening, vast expanse of calming blue. Along the horizon, distant mountaintops hugged the shoreline. *How can the world look so calm but be so full of misfortune at the same time?* Taking another sip of his cool wine, he glanced at the ridgeline that cradled his exotic house. Rocks jutting out between the trees gave little assurance that his thirteen million dollars wouldn't slide down the mountainside to sink forever beneath the rolling waves. Although this little hideaway on the small island of Mallorca offered privacy, it never felt like home. Urbat preferred sprawling lawns and towering trees. A rocky cliff covered in rough greenery just wasn't his thing. Maybe a dip in the pool with his young wife would lift his spirits.

Admiring her from afar, he smiled. His eighty-fourth birthday was only a few weeks away. Brynlee, beautiful and smart, relied on him for everything. Although a recent graduate of Guilford College, she seemed more attuned to flowers and wildlife than reality. Brynlee studied poetry, medieval culture and, of all things, the history of agriculture. Some nights, he fell asleep listening to her stories of working on the college farm and picking grapes. Why he married a twenty-four-year-old child, he still couldn't explain. Was it the curves of her slender body that attracted him? The freshness of her anticipation for life? The innocence that radiated from her curiosity? Maybe it was just the splendor of her smile.

He felt a wave of guilt. Love? Yes, he loved her. He would do anything for her. She wanted a baby. Their baby. Would there be enough time? At his age, did he have the moral right to become a father again? His years left on this planet were no longer counted in decades. Maybe giving her a little part of himself to cherish after he left this place would be a good thing. She'd inherit a fortune when he died. Money would never be a problem. It was her immaturity that concerned him.

Walking into the open living area, he placed his wine on the counter. The plate-glass windows allowed the morning sun to bathe the room with the purest of natural light.

"What's wrong?" Brynlee stood at the open doors, her slender frame sparkling in the sun light.

In his eyes, she was a goddess. Someone he would protect with his life. *Have I already destroyed her?* "Nothing, my love." He embraced her as if she were a fragile porcelain doll. Kissing her shoulder, he rested his head against hers. "You are my life. My soul."

Brynlee laughed. "You are so silly. No, really." She pushed him away. "Something is wrong. I can tell."

"Everything is fine." He chuckled. "I must make a couple of calls, and then I will join you in the pool. Would you like that?"

"I would. Can you grab me a soda from the fridge? I don't want to drip on the floor."

"Certainly." Urbat watched her walk back to the pool. The way her hips naturally swayed as she moved always excited him. Picking up his cell phone, he dialed the number.

"Colonel Rose here."

The man was starting to get on his nerves. *Why does he always sound so normal, so average?* "Did you receive the instructions?"

"Yes sir," Rose replied.

"I want the delivery healthy and alive."

"Yes sir," Rose repeated.

"The dead do me no good."

Clicking off the phone, he tossed it onto the counter. Urbat pulled out a soda and rinsed it before taking it outside. He stepped into the warm water. Glancing up at the large statue of Enki that dominated the back of his house, he closed his eyes. Brynlee pulled the can from his grip and popped it open.

"Thanks, sweetheart." She kissed him on the cheek.

Pulling her in close, Urbat unhooked her top and tossed it aside. Her kiss tasted sweet and cool, the soda giving her a seductive flavor. Maybe it wasn't too late. Maybe the in vitro hadn't worked. Maybe right now was a good time to give her that baby she wanted, and not the one he feared.

Allie Rose glanced at the time and sighed. Another three hours before she'd shove everything into a drawer, lock the office and meet her friends for dinner. She loved working and living in Oslo, Norway. How she was lucky enough to land this assignment was something that eluded her.

"Hey, girl." Demi poked her head into the office. "Time for a break?"

"I'd love some coffee." Allie stood.

Walking to the breakroom, they gossiped about their coworkers as Allie kept an eye on the employees. Every day, Allie picked a different building in which to wait out their twenty-minute break. Today it was the science building. To Demi, the change in venue was just a way to get out of the office. But for Allie, it assisted with her assignment. Her assignment was a simple one. Show up every day and perform the duties as the financial executive of foreign relations for the Civil Honesty Foundation. The Agency placed her here about a year ago. Although she hated working with numbers, Allie didn't have to do any of it. The Agency completed her office work from a remote desktop. Allie just had to pretend.

When she told her father, Colonel Oliver Rose, about the job, he panicked. He didn't want his precious little girl moving to another country, which she didn't understand. He was never home anyway, so why should he care? Right this moment, he was assigned to a desert command overseas. It was her mother Allie worried about. But knowing that her little brother was still at home and her older brother was only a few hours away gave her a little comfort that her mother wasn't completely alone. To her surprise, though, her mother encouraged Allie to take the job.

"We didn't pay all that money for you to graduate college and stay home." Her mother always had an interesting way of getting her point across. "No, no, you go. Live your life. Explore."

Allie loved her mother with all her heart. She loved her father, too. He was just a bigger pain. She owed her father a phone call. Maybe tonight after dinner.

"What's the plan?" Demi asked, selecting her drink and filling the Styrofoam cup.

"Illegal Burger." Allie laughed. "It was my turn to pick and I'm hungry for a hamburger. It serves real American burgers."

Demi grinned.

"Let's take the long way home …" Allie put a top on her coffee. "… walk along the street."

"Fine with me."

Allie wanted to see who had signed into the register. Making friends with the guards had been her best idea so far. Entering through the main doors of the foundation, one of the guards flagged them down.

"Hey, Paul C," Allie said. "What's up?"

Paul C frowned. "Hilda's looking for you. You can use my phone."

"Thanks." Allie dialed the number. Hilda was her immediate supervisor at the foundation, and a major bitch. About a hundred pounds overweight and ten years older, the woman was a nightmare in heels. "You needed me, Hilda?"

"Yes," the frantic voice screeched into the phone. "Dr. Urbat will be here next week and needs a full briefing on the funding from the African distributors. I need you back here immediately."

"What for?" Allie replied. "I completed that report a couple of days ago. Just needs to be printed and bound."

"I must review it first," Hilda said.

"I placed it on your desk yesterday. I'll be back in a few and will give you another copy."

Hilda hung up before Allie could say another word.

"Are you in trouble?" Paul C asked.

"No, she panics every time Dr. Urbat comes to town. Don't know why."

"He owns this place," Demi added.

"He doesn't own it," Allie said. "A foundation is not owned by a private individual. Or it's not supposed to be."

Instead of walking past the fountains, they decided to head straight to their offices. Allie didn't fear Hilda, but Demi did. Sitting at her desk, Allie pulled out her cell phone. She typed in a short message to Lewis: *POC will be in town Wednesday, will send exact time when I receive it.*

"I need that report." Hilda stood in front of Allie with her hands on her hips.

"You really need to relax a little." Handing Hilda a colorful fifty-page report, Allie smiled. "It's complete. Let me know if you want to add anything. If I hear nothing from you, I'll send it to the printers Friday morning. Just as I always do."

Hilda nodded.

Following the robed man, Nate and Tarply exchanged glances. It was the weirdest thing either had experienced. One moment they were walking on top of the hot sand, and the next they were underground walking on a cool, hard surface.

"Do you remember any stairs?" Nate whispered.

Tarply shook his head.

"Do you know how we got down here?" Nate asked.

Again, Tarply shook his head.

"This is so odd," Nate said.

The long hallway abruptly ended in a large, brightly lit cave. What looked like train tracks led off in different directions. Individuals wearing loincloths managed each track.

"Where are we?" Nate asked.

"Way station," the robed man said. "Please, over here."

Standing next to a track, Tarply half expected a train to pull up. When a clear, oval-shaped pod glided to a silent stop, he blinked. The cylinder rested on a wooden cart with wheels that attached to the track. The top of the oval slid back, revealing a place to sit.

"Please." The robed man held out his hand.

Nate stepped up and into the small vehicle.

Tarply paused before getting in. "I don't see a motor."

The attendant smiled.

Taking the front seats, Tarply and Nate faced the back of the vessel. The robed man entered and took the seat opposite them. The opening slid shut encasing the three. Tarply yawned several times as pressure rose in his ears.

The cart rolled down the track toward an opening just large enough for their glass cylinder. The smooth rock walls shined as if lined with a mirror. The cart stopped before the opening.

Tarply stared at the old man, who didn't look at all nervous, as if this were a normal way to travel. "Where are you taking us?" Tarply asked.

Wordlessly, the man lifted his hand. The world around them disappeared, and only a web of haze filled the void. Although they were now traveling at an unrealistic speed, the only sensation Tarply felt was a little lightheadedness.

"We're moving," Tarply said.

"Fast," Nate replied.

"Doesn't feel like we're moving at all," Tarply said. "How is this happening?"

"Magnets," the old man replied.

Discerning their surroundings was impossible. They were traveling too fast. Before Tarply could ask another question, the outside world came back into view, and their small vessel filled with light. Back on another wooden cart, attendants helped them out.

"That was cool." Nate said, following the old man up the stairs.

"We need those in the states," Tarply said.

As they reached the platform, a woman with long black hair and a golden headdress greeted them. Smiling, she cocked her head to one side.

"My queen." The robed man bowed. "I have brought them as requested."

"Thank you." To the two confused-looking men, she said, "I am Ningal."

"Name's Nate Edwards and this is Bill Tarply." Nate held out his hand.

Ningal ignored the gesture. "This way."

"What's this all about?" Nate asked.

Ignoring his question, Ningal walked. "I will turn over our precious cargo if you agree to respect and care for them."

Ningal opened a large door and Nate let out a loud roar. "Devon, you major old fool!"

"Nate Edwards!" Devon yelled. "Damn if it isn't good to see your ugly face."

"Bill?" Sumner stared at Tarply.

"I've come to rescue you." Tarply grabbed hold of Sumner's hand.

"I don't need rescuing," she replied. "But thank you."

"What's going on?" Nate asked.

"Not really sure," Devon replied.

"How many are here?" Nate glanced around at all the happy-looking faces.

"Just a little under two hundred," Devon replied. "Come and sit, Nate. I'll tell you what I know."

The man stared at Loomsbury. "Your DNA has the signature … it will change. What those changes will be in a few years is hard to say."

"I see," Loomsbury said. "As long as I don't grow wings or glow in the dark, I'm sure I'll be just fine. When I return to the states, I'll make a full report. My government will not want those creatures running loose. What other interesting things are you working on?" The man continued to stare at Loomsbury. "If you're willing to share with us everything you are doing, we'll work with you. If you hide things from us, we will become one of your worst enemies."

"Perhaps you should speak to our director," the man said.

Leonora stared at her hands.

"What's wrong?" Loomsbury asked.

"Making sure I'm not changing into a fairy," Leonora replied.

Dorothy read over the orders before handing them to Elsie. Elsie glanced through the lines and laughed.

"What is it?" John Hershawl asked.

"You're not going to like this very much." Elsie handed John the paper.

"What the fuck is this shit?"

"Your sentencing," Elsie said.

"Sentencing for what?"

"All kinds of bad stuff," Dorothy said.

"At least you're not going to be eaten by alligators." Elsie laughed.

"I believe we're finished here, sister," Dorothy said.

"Yes, I believe you are correct." Elsie stood. "It's been nice knowing you, Mr. Hershawl. Honestly, it has."

"I agree." Dorothy opened the door and stepped out. "We wish you only the best."

John remained seated. He watched as the two old biddies walked out. He also watched as two armed guards entered. Shackling his feet and binding his arms, they escorted John into a waiting black SUV. John sat stunned and asked himself how he ended up here. *Who will explain everything to my wife and children? Will I ever see my family again?*

Wishing he were dead, but wanting to live, John Hershawl prayed to the Christian god he never met. It was worth a try.

Sumner showed Tarply around. One by one, she introduced him to the missing passengers. Jack was first, of course — Elizabeth second. Trying to comprehend everything, Tarply's head spun until he was too dizzy to stand, so Sumner showed him the gardens. As they sat under a peach tree, Tarply's world slowly calmed.

"This is wild." Tarply rested his back against the tree.

"I agree," Sumner said. "I wish I could stay here forever. There's so much to see. I guess there's never enough time."

"Just like visiting Disney World."

"I can't get Anais to leave the library. The archeologists refuse to leave Enlil's warehouse."

"It will be hard to get everyone to leave." Tarply picked up a peach and smelled it. Taking a bite, he hummed. "Mmm."

"Bill, why *are* you here?"

"I wanted to rescue you."

"Why?" Sumner stared into Tarply's eyes. His gaze looked sincere.

"There's something about you that intrigues me. I see your face everywhere. Before I fall asleep. When I wake up. I worry about you. Maybe that's wrong."

"No," Sumner said. "Not really. Kinda nice having someone care about me. Someone other than my mom."

"Honestly?"

Sumner nodded. "Bill, if we're going to date, can we take it slow? You may have thought a lot about me, but —"

"But once you started this case, I was gone."

"Poof," Sumner said. "Right out of my head. I did enjoy meeting you on my first day. You made it a good day."

Tarply smiled. "Dating, huh?"

"Unless you don't want to."

Tarply reached for Sumner's hand. "I want nothing less."

Colonel Rose stood near the tarmac, staring at the gigantic planes — Airbus A400M. These transports took off and landed on some of the roughest and shortest runways. He probably could have crammed everyone into one, but Rose decided these people had been through enough and needed a little space. Listening to the engines, tears stung his eyes. With his recent decisions, he probably condemned his daughter to death.

His phone vibrated inside his back pocket. Looking at the name, his heart froze. Allie was making her weekly phone call.

"Hey, baby." Heading inside and closing his office door, he sat at his desk. "How's Norway?"

"Great, Dad."

Her voice pulled him back in time to when she was a little girl. She was his life. "I'm glad to hear that."

"What's wrong?"

"Nothing." He never could keep a secret from her.

"I can tell."

"When are you flying home?" His heart pounded as his tears fell. "Maybe we could synchronize and be there together?"

"Not sure. Assignment's lasting longer than expected."

"Assignment?" *Does Urbat already know? Has she been set up? Impossible — I just notified Lewis.* The phone remained quiet. "Sweetheart? Did I lose you?"

Allie cursed her screw-up. The Agency had told her not to get comfortable in her assignment. It was too easy to slip up and say something stupid. Telling her father that she was on an assignment was careless. *How stupid can I be? Think, Allie, think.* Africa popped into her mind.

"I was given the African account," she said. "Couple of big donors. My first real assignment here. If this comes through, I might get a promotion."

"You going to Africa?"

"No, working it here." Thank goodness, he was buying her story.

"I'm proud of you."

"Thanks." Allie sighed.

Chapter Twenty-Three

"I'm going to turn into a fairy," Leonora said to Amy as they sat for dinner.

"I really doubt that," Amy replied.

"Everything'll be fine." Loomsbury touched the back of Leonora's hand. "We'll put our best geneticists on it."

"We need to be more careful." Leonora took a sip of water. "People are playing god with our DNA. No longer can we assume our regular safety precautions will work."

Loomsbury nodded.

"How about roasted chicken?" Amy placed the serving tray in the middle of the table.

"Looks delicious." Bob picked up a carving knife and fork. "Let's eat."

Leonora stared at the plate of steaming brown chicken covered in spices with little red potatoes.

Amy carried a bowl of broccoli to the table. Before sitting it down, she glanced over at Leonora and gasped. "You okay?"

Jumping from the table, Leonora ran to the side of the boat. With each heave, she cried out. Starting in the pit of her stomach, the ache radiated into her arms and legs. Wave after wave of pure agony glided along her nerves and into her muscles. As they contracted, she felt as if her bones would crack in two. Screaming, Leonora clung to the railing. "Dr. Loo!"

"I'm here." Loomsbury grabbed her shoulders.

"I can't breathe," Leonora whispered. Falling to her knees, she cradled her stomach with her arms. The pain was unbearable, swelling with each forceful surge.

Bob's eyes widened. "There's no hospital anywhere near us."

"The lab," Loomsbury blurted. "We need to go back to the lab."

"The guards will not allow us to get close," Bob said.

"We don't have a choice." Loomsbury stood. "Get us there now!"

"How many did we lose?" Greghardt asked.

"Sixty-three agents," Lewis replied. "From the photos Newberry sent, we counted thirty-six babies. There could have been more."

"What a sick bastard." Greghardt stared out the large windows. "Why babies? Why our agents?"

Lewis shook his head.

"Wednesday it is." Greghardt walked out of Lewis's office.

Soaring through the tubes, Sumner clung to Tarply's arm. Anais sat frozen in her seat; her face even whiter than normal. Aaron looked almost as pale. The clear vessel slowed, and Sumner took in a deep breath.

"Thank goodness," Sumner said.

"I concur," Anais added.

"It's a wild trip." Tarply helped Sumner out of the oval vessel.

"How did you enjoy your ride?" Ningal walked over to them.

"I didn't," Sumner said. "What did we just ride in?"

"Built by the ancients," Ningal said.

"Do they go all over?" Anais asked. "Even overseas?"

"Not anymore," Ningal said.

"Where are we now?" Aaron asked, glancing around the unfamiliar cave.

"Far away from our home," Ningal said. "Today it is called Kandovan. This way."

Ningal led the group up a flight of stairs carved into the cave wall. The stairs ended in a landing at the far side, which led to another set of stairs climbing upward. Sumner's legs ached. As the group reached an old metal door, Sumner leaned against the wall.

"That was some hike," Tarply said. "Why are you not tired, Ningal?"

Ningal glanced at the small group and smiled. Placing her hand against the rusting metal, the door faded away. Ningal waved her hand for them to follow and stepped into the darkness. Sumner poked her head in first. The cave was bathed in black — just an empty void. Before Sumner could say something, Ningal's hand reached out from the shadows and pulled her through the darkness and into the light.

Standing on what looked like a balcony, Sumner stared out at a small valley snuggled within rolling hills. Sumner blinked several times. The brown and tan cone-shaped mountains held a mystical appeal, as if she'd just stepped back in time several hundred years. She watched as Anais was pulled from the darkness. Using her hand to shield her eyes, Anais stepped onto the balcony. Tarply exited next, followed by Aaron.

"It's so brown." Anais came abreast of Sumner. "Where are we?"

"Iran," Sumner replied. "That's all I know. We're somewhere in Iran."

"Ningal." Anais turned toward the beautiful woman. "How far do your travel tubes actually go?"

Ningal smiled. "They suit *our* needs and that is all that matters. You are in the village of Kandovan, Iran. Your friends should be here soon. They will wait for you in the valley." Ningal pointed to an empty field in the distance.

"I will miss you," Anais said to Ningal. "May I hug you?"

Ningal pulled Anais into a close embrace. Resting her head against Ningal's shoulder, Anais sighed.

"I will miss all of you," Ningal whispered. Sumner hugged them both. Laughing, Aaron reached around from the other side. Tarply just watched.

"I will bring the others once your friends have arrived," Ningal explained. "If you would, go into the village. Find a man who calls himself Otanes. He will assist you. Others will be looking for you. Stay aware."

Sumner nodded.

"We will. Thank you," Anais said.

"You have money. Feed yourselves and use what is left to pay Otanes for his services. Also, give him this." Ningal held out her hand. A round pendant with a red center rested on her palm.

Sumner took the pendant. The reflecting sun seemed to energize the red crystal. Closing her hand around the small object, Sumner nodded.

"You must wear these while you are in the village." Ningal handed a green scarf to Sumner and a black one to Anais. "It is the law."

Again, Sumner nodded. Wrapping the scarf over her head and around her neck, she watched as Ningal walked into the darkness and disappeared. The darkness then faded into a light mist that floated away. Only a solid rock wall remained.

Sumner shook her head. "Now that was weird."

Anais laughed. "Let's explore the village."

Rose stared out the plane's window as they soared through the cloudless sky. The small troop looked more like an attack squadron than a rescue. Replaying his conversation with Allie, Rose couldn't help but feel that she was hiding something. Maybe she wasn't in Norway anymore. Maybe she would be safe after all. *No, that bastard will hunt her down.* As the flat desert changed into a rocky terrain, his fears grew.

"Sir, we'll be on location in fifteen," the voice said from inside Rose's helmet.

"Fine," Rose replied. Turning to his troop, he frowned. "Get ready."

An old brick path led down through the cone-shaped hills. Although still in good shape, the worn, aged surface made clear that many people had traveled this way before. Glancing up between the homes carved into the hillside, Sumner smiled.

"I'll bet this was a lava flow at one time," Anais said as they walked. "These people must be cliff dwellers. I've read about it. They carve their homes inside the volcanic rock."

"Handmade windows and doors," Aaron added. "Reminds me of *Lord of the Rings.*"

The pathway winded down between homes that bumped up next to each other. The aroma of cooking food made Sumner's stomach growl.

"Beautiful," Anais whispered.

"Quaint," Tarply added.

"I like it," Aaron said. "Look at the snow on those mountaintops."

"This is amazing," Sumner said. "But we need to stay focused. We need to find Otanes."

Quiet followed them as they descended the steep steps.

"How many steps have we climbed down?" Tarply asked.

"A billion," Aaron replied.

Sumner laughed and waved at a few children playing in a small courtyard. She nodded to an older woman hanging her laundry. Another woman smiled as she removed cooked flatbread off a hot grill.

Tarply tapped Sumner on her shoulder. "We've been hiking for over thirty minutes."

"Walking through this village won't be fast. I don't see any taxis," Sumner said wryly.

Anais spoke up. "I see shops on the street below."

"You mean we've made it to the bottom?" Aaron asked.

"Looks like it." Sumner stepped onto the stone pavement. "I see a shop with food and drinks."

Frederick Urbat stared at the slender stick. No question about it now — his wife was definitely with child. Urbat leaned over and kissed her cheek. Staring at his reflection in the bathroom mirror, he wanted to slap the old fool across the face. *What was I thinking?* In a best-case scenario, when his child celebrated his or her sixteenth birthday, he'd be turning a hundred years old. Way too old to properly raise a child. One thing was clear, though, this pregnancy changed everything.

Smiling, he whispered, "I must make a call."

"You're angry," she said.

With her tears threatening to fall, he shook his head. "Of course not. I love you. This is our baby. I just need to make a call."

Taking in a deep breath, she too smiled. "Good. I want to go shopping later."

"Of course." Urbat pulled out his cell. Scrolling through the names, his heart pounded. He counted the rings. Before he reached four, the voice answered.

"Yes?"

"I must speak with you in private." Urbat cleared his throat. "Today."

"Very well. Come now."

Loomsbury stared at the white walls surrounding Leonora's empty bed. When they arrived at the lab, they'd been immediately whisked inside, and Leonora had been whisked away from him just as quickly.

Everything that had happened played through his mind continuously. *How could I have been so stupid, so careless? Leonora's illness is my fault. What happened to her should be happening to me.*

"Doctor?"

Loomsbury wiped his eyes before turning around. "Siska. How is Leonora?"

"Ill. Very ill. Will you walk with me?"

As his heart broke for his critically ill assistant, he sighed. Nodding, he reluctantly followed the tall woman out of the room.

"Our fairies, as you call them" — she smiled at Loomsbury — "were created using RNA manipulation."

Loomsbury blinked a few times.

"Changing the codes within an RNA strand is much easier than working within DNA — double helix and all. At first, we used an RNA virus to effect the change. Unfortunately, the results were not as we'd hoped."

"Then what *did* you use?"

"Genome editing with —"

Loomsbury froze, grabbed his hair and held back a scream. Staring at the floor, he groaned, "cDNA."

"No." Siska frowned. "Not that easy. We used gRNA. Much more flexible."

"Because gRNA is synthetic," Loomsbury whispered, as if talking to himself. "It's manmade. It invades the genome the same way as an RNA virus, but without changing the overall cellular structure."

"Exactly."

"And this is why Leonora is so ill."

"We believe so," Siska said. "The original virus is still present in our little creatures. Something we were not aware of until now. When you dissected the specimen in your lab, the virus must have been released. Accidently, of course."

"Then it's airborne."

"We're afraid so," she said.

"Which means this virus could spread."

Siska nodded. "Our thoughts exactly."

"I need to call this in." Loomsbury pulled out his cell phone. "Leonora. Will she survive?"

"We're doing everything possible. She's receiving the antidote now."

"Antidote?"

"Whenever we create a virus, we also create an antidote, just in case."

"Just in case?" Loomsbury repeated. "Are you not the clever ones?" Loomsbury shook his head. "How ridiculously *kind* of you to think of such things while you're playing god!"

Refusing to look Loomsbury in the eyes, Siska frowned. "We need to give you the antidote, as well. A vaccine. As soon as possible."

"Bow down to the fire!"

Frederick Urbat stared at the man standing before him. Wearing only white and with his face partly covered by a rectangular cloth, the man reminded Urbat more of a surgeon than a religious mentor.

"Pay your respect to the flames!" the man ordered.

Urbat nodded. Stepping into the miniature temple, Urbat paused before falling to his knees. Staring up at the statue of Lamassu, the creature with a body of a winged bull and the head of a man, a tear fell. "Brynlee is pregnant." Urbat kept his gaze glued to the statue.

"We know," the man whispered. "'Tis good."

Walking out of the temple but still refusing to look at the man, Urbat asked, "I know the baby is part me and Brynlee, but what else is it?"

"The deity where you just knelt — what is it called?"

Urbat glanced into the fire temple at the animal crossbreed. The thought of his child having the body of a bull or the wings of a bird sent waves of dread all through him. As his body trembled, Urbat let out an unearthly wail.

"Our gods are returning." The man in white touched Urbat's shoulder. "They will surrender their control only to *your* child. Think of the possibilities. You are now the father of a deity. A god!"

As his tears fell, Urbat's mind whirled. Would his wife survive the birth of such a monster? "Does this make *me* a god?"

Thousands of lives stolen in search of an ancient bloodline, and not one sample showed any promise. Stepping back into the fire temple, Urbat watched the flames flicker. The shifting light cast an unnatural glow along the wall, reminding him of demons. Where was this Zoroastrian god he prayed to every night? *If it does exist, why doesn't it show itself?* Why were the demons allowed to rule this place he called home?

The readings taught him to be wise, fair and to practice good deeds. How could this man standing behind him call himself a spiritual leader? He ordered the killings of innocent people. It was as if the man thrived from the deaths. Murdering someone just for their blood was, in Urbat's mind, a mortal sin. No way could he consider slaughter a good deed; at best it was a necessary evil.

Slowly turning around, Urbat stared at the self-proclaimed prophet, whose wrinkled face, speckled with age, resembled more a monster than a man. Stepping closer to this evil creature, Urbat glared at him. From his waistband, Urbat pulled out a long silver knife and, without a second thought, shoved the cold metal into the man's abdomen. Taking a step back, Urbat watched the white outfit turn a dark red. As the man struggled to breathe, Urbat prayed to the only god he knew.

"Forgive me, my lord, for I cannot allow this abomination to continue. We are *not* doing good deeds. We are taking innocent lives and creating monsters. And one of them is *my* unborn child."

The dying man hugged his bleeding stomach. As the blood pooled, Urbat knelt. Pulling the knife from the man's belly, he used the man's robe to wipe it clean. When the prophet closed his eyes, Urbat entered the private bathroom. After washing his hands and knife, he locked the temple door behind him. His mind he kept blank. Heading to the airport and to his private plane, Urbat accepted what he had to do next.

Colonel Rose searched the hillside for any sign of the train's survivors. Nothing. As the helicopters descended from the heavens, the ping of bullets rang through his ears.

"Damn," he shouted into his headset. "Get us out of here!"

"That's gunfire!" Aaron shoved the small group up against a brick wall.

"I'll bet it's our ride," Anais said.

"This isn't good." Sumner glanced around the building. "We need to find Otanes." Sumner looked at Tarply. She felt his fear as if it were her own. Maybe it *was* her fear she was sensing. Needing to remain busy, she whispered, "I'll ask a shopkeeper."

Entering one of the smaller stores, Sumner politely pushed past folks picking out goods.

"Salam," she said to the shopkeeper in Persian.

"Salam," he replied. A good sign.

Continuing in Persian, Sumner asked, "I'm looking for a man who calls himself Otanes. Do you know of him?"

The shopkeeper glared at her before nodding. "I know *of* him."

"Can you tell me where I can find him?"

"He is of the ground people. He is not one of us."

"Ground people?" Sumner glanced around. Could this town be aware of the Sumerians living in the tunnels and caves?

The shopkeeper nodded.

"Can you tell me how to find him?"

Tilting his head, he grinned as his eyes darkened. "If you wait outside, I will have *him* find you."

Sumner paused. The man's expression looked evil and sent chills up her back. It was as if he knew of a dark secret that would soon fall upon her and her friends. Uncomfortable, she took several steps backward.

The shopkeeper turned and attended a customer. Paying for four bottles of water, Sumer left to join her friends. As she walked, she kept glancing over her shoulder.

"Well?" Aaron asked, accepting the cold drink.

"He said he'd have Otanes find us," Sumner said.

"I don't like the sound of that." Aaron took a sip. "I think we should leave."

"What about Otanes?" Anais asked.

"Let's go." Aaron grabbed Anais's arm. "We need to leave, now."

Hurrying down the busy street, Tarply glanced back at the shop. Several uniformed officers entered only to dart back out and scan the area. One of the guards went back inside.

"Looks like you were right," Tarply said to Aaron. "We need to hurry."

"I don't like this," Sumner said.

As they crossed an old rock bridge, a man dressed in a simple black robe blocked their path. Aaron took the lead while the others fell back.

"You are seeking Otanes?" the robed man asked in English.

"Yes," Aaron replied.

"Why do you seek Otanes?" the robed man asked.

"We were told to find him," Aaron said.

"Actually …" Sumner stepped in front of Arron. "Ningal told us to seek out a man who *calls* himself Otanes and to give him this." Sumner held out her hand. "That he would help us find our friends. Would that be you?"

The man nodded, taking possession of the small pendant.

"Is Otanes really your name?" Sumner asked.

"Yes," he replied. "But only to the ground people."

"Ground people?" Anais repeated.

Staring at Anais, the man's eyes widened. He bowed his head and whispered something into his hands, then raised his head. "Those who choose to live under us." The robed man pointed to the pathway.

The group glanced at each other.

"Will you help us?" Sumner asked.

"Follow me," the robed man replied.

The small group followed the man through the winding streets. Climbing up steep stairs and along narrow passageways, they eventually reached a courtyard. More stairs led up to more homes. But Otanes stopped. Pushing open an old wooden door, he entered.

"Please, this way," he said.

The home was small but comfortable. Colorful rugs covered the dirt floor. No furniture just pillows and blankets. From what Sumner could tell, there was another room off to one side and perhaps a hallway in the back.

"You may relieve yourselves here." Otanes pointed to a smaller room at the end of the hallway.

Anais peeked in. "Hey, there's a bathroom and bedroom back here. I'll go first."

"Have you eaten?" Otanes asked, still staring at Anais.

"A little," Sumner answered.

"When my wife returns, she will cook us a meal. Please sit. You are safe."

"How can you help us?" Aaron asked. "There are men with guns in the hills."

"You may stay, for now," Otanes said.

"We heard gunfire." Tarply stepped closer to Otanes.

Otanes nodded. "Your people tried to land in the fields. Men were hiding. I'm afraid your friends have left."

Sumner tapped on her cell phone. "Still no signal."

"How many in your group have remained behind?" Otanes asked.

"About two hundred," Aaron replied.

"It will be difficult to get them out alive," Otanes said.

Chapter Twenty-Four

Urbat stood in front of his mansion. *Do I have the strength to do what I need to do?* He wasn't sure. Opening the front door, he stepped in. He could see the pool through the house. Brynlee looked content as she floated in the crystal-clear water. Her beauty always amazed him. *Can I live without her?*

At the bar, he poured two glasses of soda. In one, he added four drops of a clear liquid. Colorless, tasteless, but deadly. Sipping on his soda, he sat by the pool and held up the other glass. Brynlee waved. His heart shattered into tiny useless pieces as he waited for her to join him. He loved her with all his life's essence. All that he was or ever could be resided in her.

"Hi." She sat next to him. "Thanks. I was just thinking about getting myself a drink."

She kissed Urbat before putting the deadly cocktail to her lips. A sharp ping echoed through the air, and the glass exploded in Brynlee's hand.

"Oh my." She jumped to her feet. Glancing down at her husband for answers, Brynlee screamed.

Urbat had dropped his soda onto his lap. His eyes were wide and unseeing as his chin drooped to his chest. Blood soaked through his white shirt, following the seams of the pocket, and pooled under his chair. He was dead. Brynlee's mind emptied of everything but fear, and she aimed for the house. Forgetting about the broken glass, her bare feet sucked in the sharp splinters. Pain shot up her legs and into her gut. She fell to the hard concrete, tears filling her eyes. Would someone shoot at her next?

A loud boom pulled Brynlee from her terror. The front door rattled and fell to the floor. Several men, wearing only black, charged into her home.

Crying, Brynlee tried to scoot away. Blood covered the bottoms of her feet, leaving a dark red trail.

"Ma'am," one of the men said. "Did you get any of that drink into your mouth?"

"What?" Brynlee asked, wiping her eyes.

"I need a medic over here," the man ordered. Kneeling next to her, he pulled off his helmet. "I'm sorry. I probably look pretty scary right now." He smiled at her.

"What's going on?" Brynlee cried as she talked.

A man carrying a medic's bag ran to her. As he tended to her cuts, other men carried Fredrick Urbat's body away.

"Who are you?" she asked, wiping her eyes again. "Who killed my husband?"

"Ma'am," the man replied. "We must treat your wounds." The man pulled out a syringe. "I will give you the antidote. You've cut yourself on the glass that contained the poison your husband was trying to give to you."

"What?"

"You're safe for now." He glanced around. "Somebody clean this shit up."

Brynlee watched as her husband's blood and the broken glass disappeared from their patio. Fear trembled through her small frame. What would she do now? *Who can I call?*

"We've notified your father," the man said. "He's on his way."

"My dad?" Gently touching her belly, she nodded. At least her baby was alive and safe. At least nothing would happen to her precious little one. With her feet bandaged and her patio cleaned, Brynlee sat in the shade sipping on a glass of water. Listening to the men talk filled her with dread. Especially when the man who had spoken to her earlier talked into his cell phone.

"Target hit. Mission successful."

It was a Wednesday.

"You two may see her now," Siska said to Amy and Bob.

Entering the small hospital-like room, Amy and Bob frowned. Loomsbury glanced up and nodded. Tubes ran from bottles directly into Leonora's arms and nose. A machine beeped in rhythm with her heart.

"How's she doing?" Amy asked, gently picking up Leonora's hand.

"Not sure," Loomsbury replied. "They're running tests. It's a virus they made."

"A virus?" Bob repeated.

"Yes," Loomsbury said. "I'm sure they'll want to vaccinate you just as they did me."

"Have you notified Lewis about this virus?" Bob asked.

Loomsbury nodded. "I also sent the genetic signature to my lab. Hospitals will need to be monitored. Don't need an epidemic."

Bob nodded.

"Has she been awake at all?" Amy asked.

Loomsbury shook his head. "I don't feel good about this."

Allie read over the message again before deleting it. *Why in the world is my father so concerned about me?*

Glancing around the office, all looked normal. All seemed quiet. But something didn't feel right. Perhaps the place was too quiet. Still no word from Hilda on the reports. *What is she waiting for?* If she wanted them ready in time for the meeting on Monday, Allie would need her approval in order to proceed with the printing. Maybe she should call her.

Glancing out the window, Allie saw Hilda and two armed men walking side by side across the campus. They were heading straight for her building. Allie felt a familiar pang in the pit of her stomach and ran different scenarios through her mind. Remembering her training and listening to her voice of caution, she stepped into a small closet. As she pulled the door shut, her heart pounded so loudly she wondered if others could hear it.

She froze as her office door banged against the wall. Praying silently, she held her breath.

"Not here," a man's voice said.

"She has to be here!" It was Hilda. "Check the hallways."

The woman sounded different. Sinister, almost evil. Allie held her breath.

"No sign of her," a man's voice said. "A lady outside said she hadn't seen her all morning."

"She couldn't have gone far." It was Hilda's wicked voice again. "Find her friend, Demi. She'll know where she is."

The office door banged shut, allowing Allie the freedom to breathe. Too afraid to move, her short life played through her mind. *Dad, I need you.* She pinched her nose so she wouldn't sneeze. The strong odor of mothballs made her a little dizzy.

"Allie?" a woman whispered.

Allie couldn't move.

"Allie? Where are you?"

A whisper could be from anybody. Allie tried to breathe silently, but soon a bright light hit her eyes.

"What are you doing in there?" With her hands planted firmly on her hips, Demi stared into the small closet. "Hilda's looking for you."

"Did you tell her where I was?"

Demi shook her head. "No, cuz I didn't know. Get outta there, would yah?"

"Something's wrong, Demi." Allie stepped out holding onto her friend's arm for support. "She had two men with her I've never seen before. They didn't look friendly."

"Hilda never looks friendly," Demi added. "But I think you're in real trouble this time."

"What did she say?" Allie grabbed her purse and keys. Shoving her cell phone into her bag, she stared at Demi.

"Just that she was looking for you. What's going on?"

"I don't know," Allie said. "I have to get out of here and fast."

"Why?"

"I think she's here to take me away," Allie said.

"I know this place can be a bitch to work for. But I doubt they're into killing people when they're not happy with the work."

"No," Allie whispered. "It's more than that. I can't tell you everything right now. Just help me get out of here."

"There are cameras everywhere. How can I get you out without somebody seeing?"

"Paul C," Allie replied. "Paul C will help. He always helps."

Oliver Rose watched from a nearby hilltop as his men combed through the trees and underbrush. He needed to land in a place where snipers couldn't hide. Here, on the barren hillside, he felt a little safer. Down there in the valley was a different story. His walkie-talkie hissed several times before he heard it.

"Rose."

"Sir," a crackling voice stated. "We found several snipers. They won't talk."

"Keep looking," Rose said. "I have another group coming. I'll have them search the town."

"Yes sir."

The walkie-talkie fell silent. Feeling the wind against his face, Rose glanced down at the dome-shaped homes looking more like boulders on a hillside than a place to live. *How could three hundred people hide in such a small area?* The homes didn't look big enough for a small family, let alone several hundred refugees. Thinking about his daughter, Allie, his stomach clenched. *Is she still alive?* He didn't know. His eyes scanned along the distant valley. Beyond that, snow-topped mountains rose daringly into the clear blue sky.

"Devon Arvol," Rose whispered into the wind, "where are you?"

As a hand waved from around the corner, Allie sighed with relief and stepped into the hallway. Paul C's firm grip immediately pushed her back into her office.

"Are you crazy?" he asked. "Put this on."

"Like they won't know it's me?" Allie stared at the odd items.

"Darn," Paul C said. "You're wearing a skirt."

"I have some jeans," Allie said.

"Put them on and this jacket. Push your hair into this cap. Hurry."

"What about the cameras?" Allie asked.

"I've got them temporarily off on this side of the campus." Paul C glanced out the door. "But that won't last long. Now hurry."

"You cannot move her." Siska's eyes widened. "She will die."

"You don't know that for certain," Loomsbury said.

"You can't move her," Siska ordered.

"I can't just sit here and do nothing."

"We're doing everything we can," Siska said.

"If she dies," Amy added, "your nasty little secret dies with her. If we take her and she lives, then your virus becomes known. You're just trying to save your own asses."

Siska glanced around the room with a blank expression.

"What is it?" Loomsbury asked.

"I didn't think about that," Siska whispered. "I'm sure it looks that way to you."

"Leonora comes with us," Bob said to Siska.

Siska shook her head. "Not a good idea. What I can do is have Dr. Loomsbury more involved."

"You'll give me access to your lab and the test results?"

Siska nodded. "It's the only way to ensure that our scientists are doing everything they can to save Leonora. Come with me."

"This is delicious." Anais wiped her hands on a cloth napkin. "Thank you."

The old woman smiled. The group sat on the floor with the food in the middle, and Sumner wondered how the elderly survived here. Her hips ached and her back spasmed like a Charley horse had just moved in. "I don't believe she speaks English." Sumner rubbed her waist.

"She does not," Otanes said.

"Can you tell her that the food is delicious?" Anais asked.

Meeting Anais's eyes, Otanes whispered to his wife. She smiled and nodded to Anais.

"Why us?" Sumner asked.

Tarply glanced up and frowned. "Why us what?"

"Ningal only sent us four to the surface." Sumner waved her arm. "Why not Devon or Mark? Why just us?"

Tarply stopped chewing, but Aaron chuckled.

"What?" Sumner asked.

"Because," Aaron replied. "You two speak the language." He pointed to Sumner and Anais. "You are the only ones. Tarply's an agent and I'm Special Forces. We're here to protect you. It's pretty clear to me."

"No," Sumner said. "It's more than that. I'm missing something."

"Missing what?" Tarply asked.

"Not sure," Sumner replied. "And whatever it is, it's driving me nuts."

Loomsbury's eyes darted around the enormous room. He couldn't believe what he was seeing. The walls, lined with the most advanced scientific instruments he'd ever seen, flooded his skinny frame with excitement. He had never imagined anything so wonderful. He thought The Agency was advanced, but even his massive laboratory didn't compare to all of this.

"Dr. Loomsbury." Siska closed the door behind them. "I'd like you to meet our top scientists, Dr. Chaudhary and Dr. Johar. Both are from India. Doctors," Siska said, "this is Dr. Loomsbury from America. He will be assisting you with Dr. Priddleton."

Loomsbury jerked his head so fast his neck cracked.

Siska smiled. "Yes, Dr. Loomsbury. We know Leonora is not your child."

"How did —"

"We have our ways," she said. "Just as you have yours."

"If you'd follow me," Dr. Johar murmured, "we'll share our findings with you."

"How do you know about the ground people?" Sumner asked Otanes.

The man stared at her for a moment before shaking his head and smiling. His eyes twinkled and gave Sumner her first clue. She laughed.

"What?" Tarply asked.

Sumner studied the old couple sitting on the floor. "You and your wife are Sumerians. That's why Anais and I were sent up here. We understand your culture. We speak your language. And, in your eyes, Anais is a goddess."

Otanes nodded.

"She is a goddess." Aaron winked at Anais. Anais frowned.

"How was Ningal able to reach you?" Anais asked. "She'd been with us the whole time."

Still grinning, Otanes pulled out a small device that was hidden under his cloak.

"A cell phone?" Anais asked.

Otanes shook his head. "Similar, but no."

"May I?" Sumner asked, holding out her hand.

Otanes nodded as he placed the small device in her palm. The little gadget was no larger than an old-fashioned flip phone. Golden in color but with a black band along the sides, it looked electronic. Sumner had never seen anything like it. The Sumerian inscriptions jumped out at her. Common words — *SA*, which meant "belonged," *ALU*, which meant "city." *How odd.* Then a few other symbols that were foreign to her.

"What is this?" she asked.

"It opens," Otanes replied.

Holding the golden device in her hand, Sumner tried to pull it apart. Nothing happened.

Otanes chuckled. "Tap the top twice."

Frowning, Sumner carefully touched the golden gadget — twice. The little device brightened as a small virtual screen flashed before her.

Leaning in close, Otanes said, "Ningal."

"Otanes." Ningal's ancient Sumerian dialect echoed through the room. Her head and shoulders appeared in 3-D. "You found our friends, I see."

"Ningal?" Sumner said.

Glancing at Sumner, Ningal smiled. "It is nice to see you, my friend."

"Hi, Ningal." Anais waved.

"Wow," Sumner said. "Your technology is way more advanced than ours."

Ningal nodded.

"I guess it's really none of our business." Sumner handed the device back to Otanes. "But why didn't you tell us?"

"There are many stories I cannot share," Ningal said. "Our desire centers on saving you and your friends. That is what is important. Please follow Otanes's directions. It is for your safety."

Crammed inside the trunk of Paul C's car, Allie struggled to breathe. The deadly exhaust surrounded her, choking her. Not wanting to cough too loudly, she took short little breaths. Every bump or jolt slammed her head against the metal frame. *Am I bleeding?* It was too dark to tell. Not wanting to cry, Allie filled her mind with pictures of her father. What was he doing? Was he thinking about her or her mom? And what was her mom doing now that she only had her little brother around? *Maybe I shouldn't have traveled so far from home. Maybe —*

Screeching tires pulled her from her thoughts and banged her head against the metal frame one final time. The trunk popped open and Allie stared up at two smiling faces.

"That sucked." Allie climbed out.

"Your head is bleeding." Demi reached out, pushing Allie's hair to one side.

"Here." Paul C pulled out a handkerchief. "Use this."

"Thanks." Allie wiped her forehead. "Where are we?"

"Huk Beach," Paul C said.

"The nude one?" Allie asked.

"It was all I could think of in such a hurry." Paul C grinned and hunched his shoulders.

Demi laughed. "Thank goodness it's too cold for anyone to be out here."

"I can't hide out here," Allie whispered. "There are only trees and sand and water. I'm miles from my flat."

"I wouldn't recommend going home right now." Paul C glanced at Demi. "I'm sure they're looking for you."

"Why *is* Hilda after you?" Demi asked.

"It's a long story." Allie stared at the bloody handkerchief. "Do I need stitches?"

Paul C shook his head. "Don't think so. But what did you do to piss her off?"

"I'd like to hear your story too," Demi said.

"Is the Hukodden open?" Allie asked.

"Should be," Paul C replied.

"Good. I can freshen up, and we can order something to eat." When Demi glared at her, Allie added, "I'll explain everything there."

Derick Vanderwerff stared at the bandages covering his stomach. *That stupid asshole almost killed me.* If the knife had hit only a few inches to his right, it would have sliced right through his liver. *What the fuck was the man thinking? Fucking idiot.*

"Ready?" asked Silvia, his wife of forty-some years.

Buttoning up his black shirt, he smiled at her. "Yes, dear. I'm ready."

"I still don't understand how you cut yourself like that. I know you're a klutz and all, but to fall directly onto your knife. From now on, only sandwiches for lunch. No more leftovers for you."

"Yes, sweetheart," Derick replied. "Absolutely."

Taking his wife by the arm, they walked out of hospital to the waiting car. As he sat in the back, his cell phone beeped.

"You should probably answer that." Silvia checked her makeup in a small mirror. "It might be important."

"Vanderwerff," he answered.

"Sir," a woman said. "I'm sorry to inform you that Frederick Urbat has died."

"How?"

"We're not exactly sure," she said.

Vanderwerff stared out the car's window. He couldn't think. Maybe it was the painkillers. Maybe it was just life.

"Sir?" the woman said.

"I'm here," he replied. "Contact the lawyers."

"Already have," she said. "Will be here within the hour. I also must report that Miss Allie Rose has vanished."

"Vanished?"

"We cannot locate her," she said.

"I know what *vanished* means." Rubbing his head, Vanderwerff closed his eyes. "Find her."

Before the voice could respond, he clicked off his phone.

"Everything okay, dear?" Silvia ran red lipstick across her aging lips.

"Yes," Vanderwerff muttered. "Nothing I cannot handle."

Chapter Twenty-Five

Loomsbury push himself away from the microscope and whispered a name. "Everest."

"Excuse me?" Dr. Chaudhary asked.

Loomsbury glanced at the doctor and frowned. "I need to make a call."

After explaining everything to Lewis, he prayed that The Agency would find the child in time. Loomsbury couldn't shake the image of the boy who first saw the fairies.

"Dr. Lewis, please do what you can." Loomsbury clicked off his phone. Staring at Dr. Chaudhary, he grinned without humor. "Your virus must be converted to a negative-sense. A purified RNA virus could counter the original virus particles."

"I'm following you, Doctor. If we purified *our* strand, which is positive and highly infectious, and then transcribe it into an RNA negative-sense, the result could prove promising." Dr. Chaudhary nodded, staring off at something only his eyes could see.

"We must hurry." Loomsbury stood. "RNA viruses have a high mutation rate. If we don't act now, our findings will become invalid."

Sumner stared through the small glass panes of the old door. *Why did Ningal send us to the surface and no one else? Why? Think, Sumner, think.* It must be something more than her knowing about the Sumerian culture.

"What is it?" Anais asked, standing behind her.

"Why us?" Sumner asked.

Anais shook her head. "I thought we determined that already."

Outside, a woman wearing ancient clothing stepped down the aging stairs. She paused. The odd clothing tickled a memory — the three goddesses that stood in The Agency's lobby. "Dike, Eunomia and Eirene," Sumner whispered.

"The goddesses," Anais said. "Justice, Order and Peace."

"The father, the son and the Holy Ghost," Tarply said.

"An, Enlil and Enki," Sumner whispered.

"The air, the dirt and the water," Anais said.

"The *fleur-de-lys*!" Sumner's eyes widened. "The three petals encircled by a band of rope. I get it now. That one symbol ties *everything* together. That's why we were sent here. Faith, wisdom and chivalry," Sumner murmured, deep in thought. "The tree of life and the owl. So, how do they fit?"

"The tree is life," Anais said, "and the owl represents wisdom, not evil and death as we first thought."

"But to some it does. War." Sumner stared into Anais's eyes. "That's what those symbols are trying to tell us! It's what Ningal's been saying all along and we didn't understand. A war. Whoever stole the passengers are preparing for a war."

"A war?" Anais asked. "A war with who?"

"Not who," Sumner said. "But what. I need to talk to Gerry. I believe Kelly was sending us a warning and that's why she painted and carved what she did inside the train. I honestly believe she was commissioned to paint the demon Pazuzu and went rogue. That's why they killed her. To shut her up."

"I cannot rescue them with just the military," Rose stated. "I need The Agency's support."

"It will need to look like a military operation," the voice said.

"Make it look like whatever you want!" Rose yelled. "Just get me some damn help out here."

Sumner held the golden device in the palm of her hand. As Gerry's 3-D face phased into view, she giggled. "This is pretty cool. I need to get *me* one."

"Nice to see you again, Dr. Miller," Anais said.

"Aside from giving you an opportunity to play with a new toy, what can I do for you?"

"We need a lesson in ancient history," Sumner said. "Can you explain the meaning of *three*? The father, the son and the Holy Ghost, or Dike, Eunomia and Eirene. I'm starting to see things in threes. How would that relate to everything we're finding out?"

Gerry smiled. "What a heavy question. Are you sure you're ready for the answer?"

Sumner and Anais nodded as Aaron and Tarply knelt behind them.

"Okay." Gerry took in a deep breath. "Place yourselves back to when the Sumerians walked on our planet. They were a young culture then. Similar to how we are today. Only a few thousand years old. We are just as naïve now as they were then."

Sumner nodded.

"For some reason, their gods left this world. Perhaps it was time for them to go. We're not sure of the whys."

"Will these gods come back?" Tarply asked.

"Maybe; we just don't know. The planet of the gods visits our inner solar system for only a short time. The window of opportunity to fly between our two worlds lasts only three or four months. From the ancient scripts, we do know that the gods left behind the Watchers."

"Fly? Are you referring to flying saucers?" Tarply asked. "Space travel?"

"Yes, I am," Gerry said. "Have you not heard of the vimanas?"

"Yes, it's Sanskrit for 'flying object,'" Anais said.

"The Watchers were good people at first. However, after many Earth years, a few turned bad," Gerry said. "The ancient cities became a dangerous place. Over time, the Sumerians left their cities behind in search of a better life. At that time, the Sumerians were known as 'the black-headed people.' Their land was called 'Place, Lords, Noble.' Or 'place of the noble lords.' Sumner, I believe that *this* is where the importance of *three* falls into place. When the Watchers ruled the cities, they treated the Sumerians as slaves."

"I can see why they would want to leave," Aaron said.

Gerry nodded. "When they left their homeland behind, they eventually met up with others who were also escaping harsh rulers. Three separate cultures eventually merged into one. One group were farmers — the Ubaidians. The second were herders — the Semitians. And the third were fishermen — the Sumerians. Together, these three cultures established the world's first democratic republic. Ruled by the people and for the people.

"They mourned the loss of the original gods, their grief creating an unbreakable bond. Farming, sheep and fish eventually came to symbolize the earth, the heavens and the waters."

"That doesn't really match," Aaron replied.

"Actually," Gerry said, "it does. Farming represents tilling of the ground — the earth. Fishing represents control over the waters. Sheep herding represents control over life, or the heavens."

"Baptism uses water," Anais said. "We bury our dead in the ground. And we worship a god in heaven."

"All three cultures," Gerry said, "worshiped only one god — An. Enlil and Enki, the sons, were the minor gods or the original rulers. The great wars destroyed much of our history. History that will forever be lost."

"And the owl or tree of life?" Sumner asked.

"We know that the tree of life is an actual medical instrument. Ningal shared them with us." Gerry laughed. "We're considered privileged since we now know the truth."

"And the owl?" Aaron asked.

"Wisdom. Knowing and accepting the truth is a wisdom," Sumner said. "And it too is a part of the machine, or whatever you called it."

"Sometimes knowing is worse than not knowing," Tarply said.

"We've seen the ancient containers used to create humans. They do resemble a sitting owl." Gerry chuckled. "How would you explain to a religious person that they were created inside a mason jar?"

"Still missing something," Sumner whispered.

"In Native American culture, the owl represents finding a higher self," Gerry said. "Accepting the realization of who or what you are is difficult for most. However, once a person accepts the knowledge, they can no longer be deceived. They can no longer be controlled."

"The truth shall set you free," Aaron whispered.

"Blood tests!" Carrie's voice echoed out through the small device.

"Carrie?" Sumner glanced over at Anais.

"Yes," Carrie said, her face replacing Gerry's. "A few days ago, Ningal tested *our* blood. We all wanted to know if we were somehow related to them."

"Are you?" Anais asked.

"Tell you that one later," Carrie said. "However, what if someone was looking for the ancient bloodline? They would want to run blood tests on everyone. Wouldn't they?"

"Kidnap people," Sumner said. "A lot of people."

"Morbid." Anais shook her head. "Someone snatched people just to test their blood?"

Sumner's mind whirled. Shaking her head, she added, "Then, if the results are negative, what do you do with them? You can't let them go. They'd report you to the authorities. So, you kill 'em."

"About half of us tested positive for the Sumerian gene," Carrie said. "The Agency has determined that Devon's train was the twentieth group to be kidnapped. That's why The Agency was called in. Over the last several years, thousands have disappeared. Our agents are intercepting a shipment from New Zealand right now. The Agency suspected Inter Diagnostic but couldn't connect the dots. Until now that is."

"Devon's group was on a train to attend a convention about the Sumerian culture," Anais said.

"Exactly." Carrie laughed. "Maybe these people were hoping that the desire to study Sumerian culture was because of some internal desire to go home. And maybe that strong desire was because they carried the ancient god gene."

"I've always felt lost," Sumner said. "As if something was missing in my life. A strong urge to go home, but when I'm home, I don't feel as if I'm truly home. My blood tested positive for the gene, too."

"But who?" Carrie asked. "Who's running the show?"

"We're stuck for now," Sumner said. "I still don't have cell coverage, and I think our ride was chased away."

"Sit tight," Carrie said. "The Agency will come. Just stay safe."

The car pulled up in front of the chateau in Montpellier, France. Derick Vanderwerff tapped his wife on the leg. He waited for the driver to open the door.

"Thank you, William." Derick nodded.

"Will that be all for today?" William asked.

"Yes."

Although he could have purchased any home he wanted, Derick enjoyed the quaint life in a smaller chateau. Built in 1871, the home was renovated only a few years ago. Cost him more to renovate than to buy. With seven bedrooms, three pools and wooded acres, the place gave him the privacy and privileged life he so desired and deserved. When he had an area cleared, they found a small chapel — the chapel where Urbat, the old fool, tried to kill him.

"Feeling okay, my love?" Silvia asked.

"I'm fine."

"Good," she said. "I'll see what the cook is preparing for dinner." As she walked away, he smiled. Did he love her? No, he did not. It was her old money that had attracted him. Did she know he didn't love her? Probably. *What a sad affair.*

Derick would be sixty-four next month, but he looked closer to eighty-four, having spent the majority of his life outside. Along with excessive sun, excessive drinking and partying probably contributed to his premature aging. But damn if life hadn't been everything he wanted. Buying decaying old homes for practically nothing, and then fixing and reselling them, started Derick on his way to becoming a billionaire. By the time he was in his thirties, he owned several hotels and huge estates across the world. Places only the rich visited. But it wasn't until he invested in oil that the big money came in.

Sitting on the softer cushion outside alleviated some of his pain. Holding his stomach, he moaned.

"Here." Silvia held out her hand. "Make you feel better."

Placing the pill on his tongue, he drank the water she offered. "Thank you."

"You should lie down. Would you like some help getting up the stairs?"

Derick shook his head. "I'll manage."

Colonel Rose sat in the helicopter on a ridgeline just outside of Kandovan, Iran. Returning to Ali Air Base without the missing passengers was just not an option. As the sun set behind the hills, he pulled out his phone. Maybe if he called Lewis again, he could persuade him to send more help. Allie crossed his mind. Finding her name in his phone, he clicked it. The phone rang several times before switching to her voice mail.

"It's Dad. Call when you get a chance. Nothing wrong, just touching base. Love you."

Even though it was a recording, it was great to hear her voice. Tapping the phone, he sighed. Should he call Lewis again? He'd already called several times. *How many times can a man grovel for help and still be considered a man?* Gathering his courage, Rose tapped on Lewis's name. Before the phone rang, his radio chirped. "Colonel Rose," he said.

"Colonel, this is Sergeant Major Hattery, sir."

"Yes, Sergeant Major."

"Sir, coming upon you now."

"What for?" Rose asked.

"Extraction."

"How many and what are you in?" Rose asked.

"Party consists of six Chinooks. Friends from the Reconnaissance Battalion brought three Longbows."

"Do you have the coordinates?" Rose asked.

"Sir, yes sir."

Six Chinook helicopters. Wow. They could carry a ton of people. And the Apache Longbow was a badass machine. No one would dare mess with them now. The loud *whoop-whoop* of the blades filled the air. Rose's chest vibrated as they skimmed across the sky.

"Damn that's a pretty sight," he yelled as they swooped in to clear the way.

"Gunfire?" Aaron jumped to his feet.

"What's going on?" Sumner ran to the front door.

Otanes blocked her way. "Not yet. She will come for you."

"Who will come for us?" Sumner asked.

"Please," Otanes said. "Wait."

The sound of gunfire echoed through the domed home, vibrating the floor as the massive machines glided overhead. Houses built inside cliffs didn't allow for much of a view.

"I've got to get out there," Sumner said.

Otanes shook his head. "Not yet." Otanes held out the odd device Sumner had given to him earlier from Ningal. He tapped on the top and the object lit.

"Hand this to the woman," he said. "Only those with the ancient bloodline may touch. This will bring the others to you. She will activate it at the river."

Sumner took the object from Otanes and frowned. Wanting to ask questions, she froze when a woman appeared at the front door.

"Now," the woman whispered. "Follow me."

Sumner darted past Otanes and handed the odd object to the woman. Cradling the object in her hand, she nodded and waved for them to follow. Anais ran outside with Aaron and Tarply close behind. Winding through the rocky homes in the dark wasn't easy. Several times, Sumner stumbled. The woman obviously knew where she was going. At the edge of the city, the valley sprawled before them, lit as if it were still day. Sumner counted three helicopters from where she stood.

"Please, this way," the woman said.

When they reached the river, the woman paused. It was then that Sumner noticed something inside the woman's ear. *An earphone?* Holding out the object that Sumner had handed her, the woman tapped on the top. The area lit even more. Before she could say anything, a man grabbed Sumner from behind. More men rushed toward them. Just as panic was about to set in, Sumner saw the red Agency emblem above their shirt pockets.

"Lord," she yelled out. "Can't you announce yourselves?"

"Ma'am, this way," one of the men ordered.

Running through the open field, Sumner felt like a moving target. Anais ran next to her with Aaron close behind. Sumner climbed into the nearest helicopter and was directed to a seat. Glancing around, she didn't see Tarply, Anais, or Aaron, although the bird was full of the missing passengers from the train. Her eyes landed on a very familiar face.

"Dr. Miller?" Sumner yelled. "How —?"

Gerry waved. The man next to Sumner tapped on her shoulder. He nodded before switching places with Gerry.

"It's good to see you." Gerry wrapped her arms around Sumner.

"Ditto." Sumner leaned into the hug. "How ..."

Gerry shook her head.

Before they could share their experiences, the loud roar of the engines drowned out their voices. Sumner felt the pull as the helicopter lifted. The sound of rattling guns filled the air. Resting her head in her lap, she covered her ears and counted. *One, two, three.* As the copter rose higher, her heart pounded faster. *Fourteen, fifteen, sixteen.*

Glancing down the aisle, Sumner watched as gunmen stood guard at the open door, their large weapons almost as big as they were. The night sky filled the backdrop. Not a star in sight. *Thirty-two, thirty-three, thirty-four.*

Feeling a hand on her shoulder, Sumner looked at Gerry, who was smiling. Sumner leaned into Gerry's warm embrace. Resting her head against Gerry's shoulder, Sumner cried.

"Have you lost your mind?" Demi asked, sipping her wine. "You expect us to believe you?"

Allie sighed. How could she explain who she really worked for without violating her oath?

"You work for your government?" Paul C glanced at the other tables.

"Why would you have two jobs?" Demi asked. "Isn't one enough?"

Paul C leaned in and winked. "Are you some kind of a spy, Miss Allie?"

Allie stared at her plate. Nothing was working out the way she wanted.

"Come home with me," Paul C said. "My wife won't mind. Then you can call someone to come get you."

"Someone to come get me," Allie whispered. She slapped the side of her head. "What a dumbass I am."

"Excuse me?" Demi glared at her.

Pulling out her cell, Allie scrolled through the names until she came to *Grandma*. Clicking on the seven-letter word, she waited.

"Extraction code," the stern voice said.

Taking in a deep breath, Allie cited the string of numbers and letters she memorized. "Delta, one-five, one-five, Tau, Tau, Heta, Heta, four."

"Agent Rose, we have your coordinates locked in," the voice said. "Extraction imminent."

Allie watched as a counter on her phone ticked away the seconds.

"What's that all about?" Demi asked.

"My phone's counting down five minutes," Allie said.

"Spooky." Paul C's eyes widened and a large grin lit his face.

"Ms. Rose?" a server asked, holding a phone with a very long cord.

"Yes." Allie stared at Paul C. For some odd reason, it was as if he understood what she was doing and why.

"You have a call, ma'am." The server placed the phone on the table and handed Allie the receiver.

"Allie Rose," she said.

"Come to the entrance," the male voice stated. "Immediately."

The phone died. Handing it back to the server, she smiled. With her friends staring at her, Allie stood.

"I have to use the lady's room," Allie said.

Walking around the tables, Allie glanced at the faces. Most were ignoring her. Stepping into the lobby, she paused. A man stepped up to her.

"Ready to go, dear?" he asked.

Without replying, Allie followed him outside. Descending the stairs, she prayed he was one of the good guys.

"Agent Rose," he whispered. "We must hurry."

The man opened a car door and pushed her inside. As they fled through the tree-lined streets, again she prayed he was from The Agency.

"I'm Agent Larsen," he said. "We're almost there."

As the car rolled to a stop near a small lagoon, Allie's heart pounded. At the dock, a man sitting in a motorboat waved. Allie's fears grew as she climbed into the small boat. The man aimed the small boat into the open waters. Passing the restaurant, Allie waved at her two friends who were still talking at the table. They didn't see her. *Will they miss me?*

The land dissolved into the foggy mist. She inhaled the fresh salty air. The horizon was nothing but water. The small boat slowed to a stop. *Is this guy going to toss me over?* A large ship slowed as it approached. A helicopter sat on its upper deck. It was the oddest-shaped ship she'd ever seen. The ship was long with wavy curves and arching windows. A rectangular door on the side gave them entry. Several men in uniform helped her out of the small boat.

"This way, Agent Rose," one of the men said.

Following the man through the large ship, Allie glanced down hallways and into the larger rooms. The place reminded her of a rich man's yacht. Women lounged by the pool sipping on drinks. Men stood at a bar engaged in heavy conversations. No one paid her any attention.

Following the steward up the stairs, she paused to look over the side. "Is this an Agency boat?"

"No," the man said.

"Then why are you here?" Allie held her breath. If this was one of Frederick Urbat's private vessels, she was in trouble.

"We're here to pick you up," he said. "This way."

On the top deck, a helicopter sat with the engines running. A steward helped her climb in. Nodding at the pilot, the steward closed the door and backed away. Allie smiled when the pilot winked at her. He handed her a helmet. As she tightened her straps, the pilot spoke. Allie listened through the earphones.

"Welcome, Agent Rose. I'll have you on board the USS *Carl Vinson* in no time."

"Am I allowed to breathe yet?"

The pilot laughed.

Epilogue

Lewis glanced at Greghardt. With the lights dimmed, it was difficult to read anyone's face. As always, Greghardt rubbed the back of his neck. It was going to be another long day.

"Good afternoon, Agents Arvol, Lumer, Womack and Ramsden." Lewis nodded to each as he mentioned their names. "It's nice to have you home safe and in good health."

Devon adjusted his weight from one hip to the other. Mark rested his chin on his hand.

"I read your reports," Lewis said. "I must say they're quite entertaining."

"It's the truth," Sumner said.

"I understand this is what *you* perceived." Lewis raised his hand before anyone could object. "But do you honestly expect us to believe there's an ancient race living under Iraq? People that no one has ever heard of? Inside large caves? Caves large enough to hold skyscrapers?"

Devon shifted in his chair again. Anais grinned and Sumner giggled. Mark frowned.

"Although" — Lewis glanced at Greghardt — "you did find the missing passengers. Took a while. But you rescued them. Many of 'em."

Devon stood. Greghardt and Lewis nodded.

"Sirs, this was quite an unusual case." Devon glanced at Mark. "Without much to go on. In my opinion, my team was quite successful."

"But to declare that the gods are to blame for what happened?" Greghardt said, who was also now standing.

Jumping to her feet, Sumner raised her hand. "We're not saying that the gods did anything personally. The crazies of the world will use any excuse to justify what they do. We only learned of Frederick Urbat after we returned. That was when we connected the dots."

"I had a lot of time to explore the relics," Anais said. "Unfortunately, I have nothing but my memories to justify our claims."

"Urbat was involved with another." Allie Rose walked into the room. "Sorry to intrude, Dr. Lewis. But Connie said you were in here and to join you."

"Please." Greghardt pointed to the table. "Do join us. This is Agent Rose."

"Thank you." Allie walked to the podium. "I worked with Frederick Urbat for a little over a year. The man wasn't *all* that evil. Most of what he did he was ordered to do. From what I've gathered and the documents I left with Connie to substantiate my statements, Urbat worked for an unknown individual that was searching for the true descendants of the ancient gods."

"The Sumerian gods?" Anais asked.

"Yes." Allie nodded. "According to the ancient texts, these gods are to return. And the time is ripe if one does the math. They should arrive any day now."

"Add in a crazy, unstable mind," Sumner said, "and there's trouble."

"Exactly," Allie added. "Those associated with this unknown individual believe that when the gods return, they'll be looking for their descendants. And if the original bloodline cannot be found, then those living on the Earth will be exterminated."

"This is why thousands of innocent people were kidnapped and killed?" Lewis asked.

Allie nodded. "Unfortunately."

"Have you located any of these descendants?" Greghardt asked.

"Funny you should ask," Mark whispered.

"Excuse me?" Greghardt said.

Sumner giggled. "They tested our blood. Many of us tested positive for being a direct descendant of the Sumerian people."

"Mark?" Lewis asked, grinning. "How did you test?"

"Positive," Sumner replied for Mark.

Greghardt laughed. "Do we have to pray to you now for our redemption?"

"Hogwash," Mark said. "I'm Jewish, not Sumerian."

"Hogwash or not," Lewis chuckled, "I must give a full report to the president. And I'm still not clear on how to address this case."

"Just say it was a crazy rich person who was afraid of a conspiracy theory," Sumner said.

"Do we have an active case to find Urbat's associates or the real reason behind the flying fairies?" Greghardt asked.

"It's my next assignment," Devon replied.

"Very well then." Lewis patted Allie on the shoulder. "Crazies it is."

"Religious crazies have plagued human civilizations for years," Anais added. "The Spanish Inquisitions, the Salem Witch Hunts. Must I go on?"

"No." Lewis smiled. "No need. I'll report it as religious crazies, and we're seeking others who may have been involved. Okay, team, good work and the case is hereby officially closed."

Sumner stood in front of the DC courthouse. The warm breeze was a comfort. As tourists hurried past, she nodded or smiled when someone noticed she wasn't moving. Glancing at her watch, she sighed. Time to go inside. Searching for the courtroom, she froze when she spotted a familiar face.

"Sumner!" Elizabeth shouted when their eyes met.

As Elizabeth hugged her, Sumner tried to breathe. "Hi, sweetheart."

"I'm so glad you came," Elizabeth said. "You're here for me, right?"

"Yes," Sumner replied. "I'm here for you."

As she hugged Elizabeth, Ningal and the king walked toward them.

"Sumner!" Ningal stole a hug. "How wonderful to see you again."

"What are you doing here?" Sumner whispered in awe.

"The adoption," King Nazi-Enlil said. "Is this not why you are here today?"

"Of course, I just didn't expect to see you in person. I honestly thought a lawyer would represent you, somehow ... um, you look odd in a suit." Sumner accepted a hug from King Nazi-Enlil. "And look at you, Ningal. Wearing a dress?"

"I know." Elizabeth giggled. "They do look uncomfortable in street clothes, don't they? Almost like real parents."

"But here ..." Sumner glanced around, "... in DC."

"Come, sit with us," Ningal said. "Here in the states, I am known as Nina and my husband is known as Eian."

"We own a home on Jenifer Street," Nazi-Enlil added.

"You have a house, here?" Sumner rubbed her eyes. They seemed to refuse to blink. "You live in a real house?"

King Nazi-Enlil laughed. "Yes and we come here often."

"Often?" Sumner repeated.

Ningal nodded. "Elizabeth will attend school here."

"School?" Sumner frowned.

Again, King Nazi-Enlil laughed. "All our children attend school here in the states."

"Here?" Sumner echoed, completely flabbergasted. "In DC?"

Loomsbury held Leonora's hand. No matter how hard he tried, he couldn't stop his tears from flowing. It felt so damn wonderful having her awake and feeling better. Her fever broke shortly after midnight. Once they cracked the virus's code, designing a cure was the easy part. On the other side of the bed and sitting on the couch, Bob and Amy leaned against each other sound asleep.

"I'm hungry," Leonora whispered, trying to sit up.

"They're bringing you something." Loomsbury adjusted her covers.

Gulping down water, she sighed. "I'm so thirsty."

"What do you remember?"

"Feeling like crap," she said. "Where's that food?"

"Should be here any minute. Any dreams?"

"Not really. Oh, here it comes now. Yum, looks like pancakes and sausage."

Loomsbury turned around. No one, just the wall. "It's not here yet."

"Siska's walking down the hallway right now," Leonora said, pointing at the wall.

"How could you possibly know that?"

"I can see her." Leonora smiled as Siska entered the room, carrying a tray of food. "Wonderful, gimme, gimme."

Loomsbury stared at Leonora. His mouth hung open. "You can see through walls now?"

"What?" Siska asked, her eyes wide.

"Huh?" Leonora said, with a mouth full of food.

"Mom!" Gerry yelled from the front door. "Anybody home?"

"Gerry?" Dropping the dishtowel, Karen ran to her daughter. Pulling her in close, she held back her tears. "Thank God. Thank God."

"I missed yah, Mom." Gerry cried as she hugged her mother.

Colonel Oliver Rose sat at his desk staring at his daughter's photo. Although he was ecstatic that he rescued every passenger that was still alive, his fear for his own child haunted him. He hadn't heard a word about her fate. How could he tell his wife and sons that Allie was gone? She was his baby, his little girl, his angel. As he thought about his options, a slight rap on his door pulled him from his thoughts.

"I said I didn't want to be disturbed." Rose kept his eyes on the photo. Another knock echoed through his office. "Damn. This better be important."

"It is," a soft voice replied.

Jumping to his feet, the frame with Allie's beautiful smile tumbled off his desk. Just before it hit the hard floor, a slender hand caught it.

"Shit," Rose yelled, pulling his little girl into a tight embrace. "Where have you been?"

"Working." Allie kissed her father. "What about you?"

"Working," he replied.

"Dad?" Arnold Worthington ran down the steps to the idling taxi. As his father climbed out, several tears fell. "Dad, where have you been?"

"Exploring," Samuel Worthington said. "I'd tell you all about it, but I doubt you'd believe me."

Arnold cried on his father's shoulder as two young girls ran from the house. Jumping onto Worthington's back, the small group fell to the grass and laughed.

"What's wrong?" Brynlee stared at the man wearing the white lab coat.

Working the small instrument, he smiled. "Nothing; everything is fine."

"Can I see?" she asked.

"I'll print you a picture in a minute," the technician said. "I'll be right back."

Walking down the hallway, the technician frowned. Entering his supervisor's office, he frowned even more.

"What is it?" the woman asked.

"Brynlee Urbat's here for her ultrasound."

"And?" the woman asked.

"I think you need to see this for yourself."

"See what?" she asked.

"A child with a body that almost looks like a cow or a horse. It has four legs and a tail."

"I'll call Dr. Lewis immediately."

"Finally," Devon whispered, dropping his bags next to the sofa. "Home."

"Yes!" Carrie plopped down on the couch and leaned into Devon's warm arms. "I'm tired."

"Me too."

Carrie laughed.

"What?"

"You're probably not tired for the same reason I am." Giggling, Carrie tilted her head.

"What's going on?"

Carrie kissed Devon on the cheek. "I'm pregnant."

Jack Lawrence stared at the large machine. With his pounding heart echoing through his ears, he clutched the small red shoe to his chest. The blood that once stained the white strings a deep red had faded, becoming unrecognizable. In many ways, his life was unrecognizable.

"Okay, Jack?" the man asked from behind.

The little boy who once wore the small shoe filled Jack's vision. Pushing the image from his mind, he answered, "I believe so."

"We're glad you're back," the man said.

"Thank you." Jack's eyes followed the smooth curve of his new train.

It didn't look anything like his previous ones. The blue and silver reflecting the morning sun blended together as if it were just one color. His first train was dark blue with a bright-red front that resembled a face. A humorous face with a large nose that doubled as a headlight. His second train, silver and red with blue and white stripes, always reminded him of a child's toy. It was this toy train that killed that young family all those years ago.

They assigned him the big black train next. Something about it always bothered him. He honestly believed it was haunted. Sometimes he thought he saw people who weren't really there. Then, one night while operating that ghostly train, he woke up in a chicken-wire cage not knowing if he was alive or dead. Many times thereafter, Jack believed he'd landed himself in hell as punishment for killing that little boy.

"Everything okay, Jack?"

"Yes, yes."

Jack climbed the small ladder and opened the door. Stepping into the compartment, he glanced around. Small computer screens filled the area once housed by large, round dials. The levers were much smaller, too. The seats looked comfortable. Sunlight flowing through the larger windows filled the compartment. Nothing felt familiar.

"I'm here to show you how to operate it," the man said from the small door. "It's not hard, once you get the hang of it."

"Thank you." Jack ran his hand over the back of the chair. Glancing around, he frowned.

"Jack?" The young man held out his hand. "Here."

"What's that?"

"You might need this." Reaching above Jack's head, the man placed a self-adhesive hook against the ceiling. "Let me see that shoe of yours."

Handing it to the man, chills ran up Jack's spine.

"Hang it here, Jack Lawrence." The man held the shoe gently by the strings as if it deserved the utmost respect. Placing the shoe onto the hook, he stood back. "There, it's perfect."

"Thank you," Jack said.

"Why do you keep it?"

"Why?"

The man nodded.

"Have you ever killed anyone?"

"Can't say that I have."

"I can." Jack bowed his head. "I killed three a long time ago. One was just a child, a baby. Then, only recently because I wasn't diligent enough, over a hundred died."

"You can't be blamed for that."

"Yes," Jack said. "I can. I've already judged myself for what happened."

"Sounds like you've condemned yourself, too."

"Maybe I have," Jack said.

The young man stepped to the door. "I'll leave you alone for a while. Get familiar with the controls. I'll be back."

"Thank you. Will this be my train?"

"Yes, Jack. This train is assigned to you." The young man closed the door.

Pulling a felt-tipped pen from his pocket, Jack leaned against the large window and carefully moved the tip over the slick glass. A tree sprang to life. Then, Jack traced the outline of a fleur-de-lys. Sitting back, he sighed before glancing up at the shoe.

Bowing his head, Jack whispered, "My God. I know I haven't been a perfect man. I have faults. I'm sorry for everything that displeases you. I'm begging for forgiveness." Sitting in the silence, Jack looked around the compartment. All remained still and quiet. As he contemplated his future, a light rap reached his ears.

"It's open," Jack yelled. The door opened and closed. "Back already?"

"Sir? Are you Mr. Lawrence?"

"Yes, how can I help you?"

"Sir, this is rather an odd situation," a young woman replied. Turning around, Jack smiled. A pretty woman in her early twenties smiled back at him. "My name's Ashley Warren."

"Nice to meet you, Ms. Warren. How can I help you?"

"You look different than what I imaged."

Lowering his eyes, Jack frowned. "Do I know you?"

"No sir. I came to say that you're forgiven."

"Forgiven for what?" Jack's mind churned. Was this a relative of one of the deceased passengers?

"Sir, I'm not really sure what that means. It's a message."

"A message? From who?"

"When I was a baby, my mom left me with my father while she ran an errand."

Jack's heart exploded. She did resemble the mother he'd met in the other dimension. The mother who said that he needed to forgive them.

"That night, your train hit the car my mom and two brothers were in."

"That night still haunts me," Jack whispered. "No matter what I do, I cannot forget."

"I'm not here to pass judgement."

"Then what do you want? I'm sorry for what happened."

"I had a dream," she said. "My brother told me about a shoe my father hid in the attic. He told me to give it to you. So, here." Ashley held out her hand. In it was a tiny red tennis shoe. The exact match to the one that hung above Jack's head.

Reaching out and taking the small shoe, Jack's tears fell.

"He told me to give it to you. In fact, he demanded that I tell you to stop punishing yourself."

"I'm not sure I can do that."

"Mr. Lawrence." Ashley reached over and touched Jack's shoulder. "I was just a baby when the accident happened. I never knew my mom or brothers. A person can't miss what they've never had. Growing up it was just me and my dad. Because of that one terrible night, my father became the most caring and attentive father that ever lived. With the settlement, I was able to attend the best schools. My life has been great. You see, Mr. Lawrence, your tragedy became my destiny."

"The Tablet of Destinies," Jack whispered.

"The what?"

Jack laughed. "According to an ancient ruler, our destiny becomes our judgement. Our judgement becomes our destiny. A circle that surrounds us, repeating over and over. Three hundred and sixty steps. Each one taking us a little closer to the truth."

"What an interesting concept."

"Please sit." Jack pointed to the other seat. "I'd like to tell you more, and how I met your mother and two brothers."

Confused and frightened men, women and children climbed down the stairs and stood next to a massive, empty hangar. Men with automatic rifles glared at them from a few feet away, their evil eyes more frightening than their weapons. Huddled together, the strangers cautiously eyed each other. No one knew what to say or do. The hot desert sun baked them from above. With no water or shelter, all they could do was stand there, helpless. Several dusty buses skidded to a stop, the windows so dirty it was impossible to see inside.

"Inside, now!" A man pointing his weapon directly into the crowd shouted out. "Move!"

As the frightened group stepped into the dirty buses, two men in business suits hid inside the shadows of the hangar. One took a long drag from his pipe, wallowing in the flavor. The pilot and copilot walked over to the men but remained in the sunlight.

"How many?" the pipe smoker asked.

"A hundred and four," the pilot replied.

"I'll call it in," the other man said. "Mr. Vanderwerff doesn't like to be kept waiting."

Lynn Yvonne Moon is an award-winning, bestselling author whose many accolades include the prestigious *Dante Rossetti Award* and the *Independent Publisher Book Award*. She is a two-time winner of the *Moonbeam Children's Book Award* and is a five-star recipient of Reader's Favorite. Lynn resides in Virginia Beach, Virginia with her family.

In

The

Defendant's

Chair

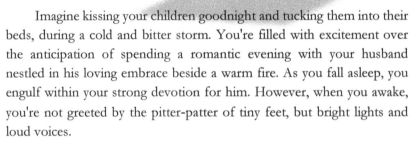

ISBN 978-1-953278-00-5 SB

ISBN 978-1-953278-01-2 Eb

Imagine kissing your children goodnight and tucking them into their beds, during a cold and bitter storm. You're filled with excitement over the anticipation of spending a romantic evening with your husband nestled in his loving embrace beside a warm fire. As you fall asleep, you engulf within your strong devotion for him. However, when you awake, you're not greeted by the pitter-patter of tiny feet, but bright lights and loud voices.

You're confused, dizzy and sick. You reach for the television remote to turn down the noise, only to reach into the hard reality of a cold table. You realize where you are—in a courtroom. You scream for your husband of six years to protect you, and the only response is the yelling of strange voices about the comatose baby killer who is suddenly awake and talking.

This is the nightmare and reality of Early Sutton. Early's eyes focus on a young man sitting next to her who has excitement and horror written all over his face. A judge is banging her gavel and demanding order. With no memory other than making love to her husband, Early's devastated to learn that her family was brutally murdered over three months ago.

Deep inside, Early knows that they are alive—somewhere.

Available at Barnes and Noble and Amazon

Don't miss these other Agency novels by Lynn Yvonne Moon

Publisher: AuthorHouse (October 4, 2004)
Language: English
ISBN-13: 978-1418473549
Product Dimensions: 6 x 0.9 x 9 inches
Binding: Hardback/Softback/Ebook

The Agency
When Souls Collide

Publisher: AuthorHouse (July 8, 2005)
Language: English
ISBN-13: 978-1420859218
Product Dimensions: 6 x 0.9 x 9 inches
Binding: Hardback/Softback/Ebook

The Agency
What Rings True

Publisher: AuthorHouse (April 11, 2007)
Language: English
ISBN-13: 978-1434302748
Product Dimensions: 6 x 0.9 x 9 inches
Binding: Hardback/Softback/Ebook

The Agency
Dysfunctional Bloodline

CPSIA information can be obtained
at www.ICGtesting.com
Printed in the USA
BVHW071248080321
601990BV00008B/568